Also by Dorothy Hearst

THE WOLF CHRONICLES

Secrets of the Wolves

Promise of the Wolves

THE WOLF CHRONICLES

SPIRIT
OF THE
WOLVES

WITHDRAWN

DOROTHY HEARST

SIMON & SCHUSTER

NEW YORK   LONDON   TORONTO   SYDNEY   NEW DELHI

Simon & Schuster
1230 Avenue of the Americas
New York, NY 10020

First Simon & Schuster hardcover edition December 2014

SIMON & SCHUSTER and colophon are registered trademarks of Simon & Schuster, Inc.

For information about special discounts for bulk purchases, please contact Simon & Schuster Special Sales at 1-866-506-1949 or business@simonandschuster.com.

The Simon & Schuster Speakers Bureau can bring authors to your live event. For more information or to book an event, contact the Simon & Schuster Speakers Bureau at 1-866-248-3049 or visit our website at www.simonspeakers.com.

Jacket photographs: full moon © Mmphotos/Getty Images; wolf © Eric Isselee/Shutterstock

Manufactured in the United States of America

10 9 8 7 6 5 4 3 2 1

Library of Congress Cataloging-in-Publication Data
    Hearst, Dorothy, 1966–
    Spirit of the wolves : a novel / Dorothy Hearst.—First Simon & Schuster hardcover edition.
        pages cm.—(The wolf chronicles ; bk. three)
    1. Wolves—Fiction. 2. Prehistoric peoples—Fiction. I. Title.
    PS3608.E27S44 2014
    813'.6—dc23
                                                                    2014001440

ISBN 978-1-4165-7002-8
ISBN 978-1-4165-7023-3 (ebook)

Dedicated to my sweet, stubborn Emmi, and to wolves, dogs,
and all who strive to make a world worthy of them

SPIRIT
OF THE
WOLVES

1

I crouched at the edge of Fallen Tree Gathering Place, a freshly caught rabbit warm and limp in my jaws, my haunches trembling. The Swift River wolves were preparing for a morning hunt, touching noses and speaking quietly to one another. Dawn light filtered through the branches of two tall oaks that stood guard at the clearing's edge, dappling the Fallen Spruce that divided my pack's largest gathering place.

No, not my pack. I was no longer a Swift River wolf and Fallen Tree was no longer my home. It was the place where I had learned what it was to be wolf, to run the hunt and howl the song of the pack, but I no longer knew if I was welcome there. I had chosen my task over my family, and my former packmates were as likely to chase me away as they were to greet me. I was tempted to turn tail and run, but in the last hours I'd seen a packmate murdered, survived a fight with a human who had sliced open my haunch, and climbed painfully out of a pit I'd thought inescapable. I wouldn't turn coward now and forsake the wolves who'd raised me. I had just one chance to get them to listen to me, and if I could not, they would die.

A soft grunt drew my attention to a patch of moss just outside the gathering place and to the human girl asleep upon it. TaLi, whom I loved as much as I would my own pup. Her legs were drawn up to her chin, and she shivered under the preyskin clothing the humans wore to keep warm. When I was four moons old, I had pulled her from the hungry waters of the Swift River, saving her life and breaking one of the most sacred rules of wolfkind. Our legends—and the unforgiving Greatwolves who ruled over us—forbade the wolves of the Wide Valley from having any contact with the humans, and I should have left TaLi to die. I could not do so, for the moment I first looked into her dark eyes and smelled her smoky scent, I knew I could never leave her.

A dark gray wolf sat guard next to the girl, his ears pricked and his silvery eyes alert. Ázzuen was my best friend and the smartest wolf I knew. He was also the wolf I trusted most in the world. TaLi would be as safe with him as with me.

The girl stirred, and her long dark headfur fell away from her face, revealing the jagged cut on her forehead. At the sight of the wound, a sudden fierce anger rose up in me. TaLi was mine to protect, but I hadn't been able to stop the human male DavRian from hurting her when he injured me. He had wanted TaLi for his mate, and when she'd refused him, he'd gone crazy. He'd killed my packmate Trevegg and TaLi's grandmother, and wounded me. I stifled my growl. I would get TaLi to safety, but I couldn't let my birthpack die to do so.

Lowering my ears and tail as I would to greet wolves I

didn't know, I turned back to the gathering place and walked slowly across the mossy ground. I set the rabbit down and whuffled to announce my presence. Minn, a thin, weasel-faced wolf, saw me first. He was a year older than I and had never liked me, which didn't bother me much; I'd never liked him either. Werrna, Swift River's warrior secondwolf, saw me next. Ruuqo and Rissa, the pack's leaderwolves, followed her gaze. Ruuqo frowned, but Rissa opened her mouth in a wide grin. Her scent of spruce and oak brought with it memories of my first hunt, of running through the territories with my pack, and of warm milk and a safe den.

"Kaala!" she said, eyeing the rabbit. "You don't have to bring gifts to Swift River. You're always welcome here." She lowered her white-furred head in greeting. "Have you decided to stay with us after all?" The hope I heard in her voice made my throat tighten. She wanted me to stay with the pack. I could not do so.

"I came to tell you something," I said.

"We already know about Trevegg," Ruuqo growled. "And the old woman."

"Something else," I said. I wanted to meet Rissa's gaze to let her know how important my message was, but a wolf not yet a year old couldn't just stare into the eyes of her leader-wolf. I looked over her left shoulder instead. "You have to come with me outside the valley."

Because outside the valley was where we needed to be, and quickly. When I defied my pack and the Greatwolves to be with TaLi, I discovered that our legends were lies, and learned the true Promise of the Wide Valley wolves: we were to be guardians of the humans and to watch over them for all time. For, left on their own, the humans thought of them-selves as different from all other creatures and would destroy the very forests they depended upon to survive. It was up to us to prevent this. In the time before time, a wolf named Indru had promised the Ancients that we would convince the humans to accept us into their packs and thus embrace the world around them. The Greatwolves had lied because they wanted to keep power over the humans for themselves.

When I discovered their deception, responsibility for the Promise fell to me. I had failed and if I could not succeed soon, the Greatwolves would kill me and all those I loved. If the humans didn't do so first.

"Why would we leave our home?" Ruuqo's dark-rimmed eyes narrowed as he glowered down at me. He could still make me feel like I was a smallpup when he looked at me that way. I took a breath and then another.

I had one last chance to keep peace between wolves and humans. Ruuqo had chased my mother from the valley when I was just out of the den. Less than a moon ago, my mother had sent a wolf to me with a message: I was to meet her out-side the valley, at a rock as large as a hill, and I must do so for the sake of all wolfkind. I was not to tell Ruuqo or Rissa. The only reason I could think of that she would send such a mes-sage was because she had the answer to the Promise. Until I had that answer, the Swift River wolves were not safe.

"DavRian's blaming us for killing the old woman," I said to Ruuqo. "He's telling the other humans that all wolves are vicious, and that they have to get rid of us before we slaughter them. They didn't believe TaLi when she told them it was a lie. They're coming for us."

Ruuqo growled and Rissa looked stunned. I don't know what I expected. Perhaps that they would have a plan for how to get out of the valley, or that they would tell me what to do, but all of them just looked at me as if I should have the answer. As if I were the adult and they the youngwolves.

"The Greatwolves will protect us from the humans," Rissa said at last. "They said they would."

Milsindra, the Greatwolf who most wanted me dead, had told her that. It was one of her many lies.

"They won't," I said. "If the humans start murdering wolves, the Greatwolves will say we've failed in the Promise and they'll kill us. They want to kill every wolf who shares my blood." Rissa was my mother's sister, and every wolf in Swift River was related to me.

"They said we would be safe," Rissa insisted. "And they told us you could leave the valley unharmed."

"They're lying. Like they always do. You're in danger."

"We can protect ourselves," Ruuqo said. "We'll fight the humans if they come for us, Promise or no. If they can even find us with their weak noses and useless ears." He snickered. "We're staying."

"You shouldn't go either." Werrna glared down at me. "Rissa will have pups in a little over a moon, and we'll need help feeding them."

It was even more reason to leave. Pups would make them that much more vulnerable.

I tried once more. "The Greatwolves won't help you. They'll kill you."

Ruuqo picked up the rabbit in his mouth and carried it away.

One by one, the others turned away from me. Minn began to dig a hole next to the small hill the pack used as a lookout. Rissa and Ruuqo spoke quietly to one another. Only Werrna continued to watch me reproachfully. A few moments later, Ruuqo barked sharply and all four of them darted from the clearing and to the hunt. I backed away and out of the gathering place, the taste of failure once again bitter on my tongue.

Ázzuen was waiting for me by the moss patch, still guarding the sleeping TaLi. When he saw me, he stood, stretched out his long back, and trotted to me. He had shed his winter fur, and his lighter spring pelt showed a lean wolf, almost fully grown.

He touched his nose to my face. His scent of juniper and Swift River wolf eased the tense muscles between my eyes.

"They won't come?"

"No. They think the Greatwolves will protect them."

He cocked his head to one side. "Most wolves won't listen to the truth if they don't like what they hear," he said.

"They'll die if they stay."

"Not if we get to your mother in time," he said. "She'll tell us what we need to do to keep the Promise and they'll be fine. We can leave the valley now, find Neesa, and get back before the humans or Greatwolves do anything."

He looked toward the eastern mountains at the valley's edge, his tail wagging. "We can do it," he said. Ázzuen's human, BreLan, had left the valley almost half a moon before and Ázzuen longed for him.

Every wolf in the valley knew how clever Ázzuen was. If he thought we had a chance, we just might.

My chest ached at the thought that I could be with my mother in a few days' time. I hadn't seen her since I was a newborn pup, and I missed her so much that every time I thought of her I had to hold back a whimper.

Ázzuen started to say something else, then his eyes widened and he woofed a warning. I caught the scent of spruce and mud and fur and whirled to meet the gaze of the one wolf in the valley I least wanted to see.

Milsindra stalked forward on long legs, her muscles rippling under light brown fur. Dark flecks colored her pale eyes and malice darkened her disposition. She smelled of Greatwolf—a deeper, meatier scent than that of an ordinary wolf—and of spruce. Her scent was marred by an undercurrent of bitterness that I thought must come from her malevolent nature. Like all Greatwolves, she was half again as large as an ordinary wolf. I started to shake, and my mouth went dry. Milsindra believed that I was a danger to wolfkind. She was also in a battle for the leadership of the Wide Valley Greatwolves, and my taking on the Promise was one of the things in her way.

She stood over TaLi, her teeth—twice as long as mine—almost touching the girl's face, her breath ruffling TaLi's headfur. I held my own breath, hoping that TaLi wouldn't awaken to see the jaws of a Greatwolf over her. A moment later, Milsindra's mate, Kivdru, a shaggy, dark-furred Greatwolf, strode into the grove, knocked Ázzuen onto his back, and stood atop him. Ázzuen scrabbled under Kivdru until the Greatwolf dug his huge paws deep into Ázzuen's belly. Ázzuen went still.

Milsindra smiled, her teeth sharp, her eyes cold, and her

message clear. She and Kivdru could kill those I loved best and there was nothing I could do about it.

I raised my chin to her.

"You promised we could leave the valley safely," I said, my heart pounding so hard I could hardly hear my own voice. "You told Ruuqo and Rissa you wouldn't hurt us if we left."

"And yet you have not gone," Milsindra purred. "You came back here. Your problem, Kaala, is that you cannot decide which pack you belong to, wolf or human. It is one of the things that makes you so dangerous. It is what makes you the drelshik."

Drelshik. It meant cursed wolf. Our legends told of a wolf born to destroy wolfkind. Such a wolf, the legends said, would be of mixed blood, would bear the mark of the crescent moon, and would treat humans as if they were wolf. My mother had mated with a wolf outside the valley and I had a moon-mark of pale fur on my chest. When I found TaLi and led some of my packmates into an alliance with the humans, many wolves came to believe I was this drelshik.

"Or the drelshan," Ázzuen gasped from beneath Kivdru's paws. The legends also said a mixed-blood wolf, the drelshan, would come to save wolfkind. Half of the Greatwolf council believed I was the drelshik, half the drelshan.

"You will keep your muzzle shut unless I tell you otherwise," Kivdru growled. He lowered his head and took Ázzuen's neck in his jaws.

I hurled myself at Kivdru, hoping the force of my leap would tumble him off Ázzuen. I would have had more luck toppling an oak tree. Kivdru swung his huge head into my side and knocked me to the ground. I landed hard on my wounded haunch, and yelped in pain. At least Kivdru's teeth were no longer at Ázzuen's throat.

TaLi came awake then, roused by the fight. She looked up at Milsindra and gasped, then scooted backward so that her back rested against a tree stump. She held her stone blade out toward the huge wolf, gripping it in both hands. She was one of the few humans who knew of the Greatwolves and of their role in the lives of wolves. If she was afraid of Milsindra and Kivdru, she didn't show it.

"Are you all right, Silvermoon?" It was her name for me, because of the moon mark on my chest.

The humans could not comprehend our speech, or the language of any of the other creatures of the woods, but sometimes I could make TaLi understand me in other ways. I whuffed softly at her to let her know I wasn't hurt. She loosened her hold on the stone, got to her feet, and bowed unsteadily to Milsindra and Kivdru. She had grown so rapidly in the past few moons that her long legs and arms made her awkward.

"Greetings, Lordwolves," she said formally.

Milsindra whuffed a laugh and took a step toward the girl. Then she looked over her shoulder at me and opened her jaws.

"If you hurt any of us, the Greatwolf council will find out," I said desperately. "They said we could go. Zorindru is still leader of the Greatwolves." Zorindru was an ancient Greatwolf who believed that I was the savior, not the destroyer of wolfkind, and had sworn to help us with the Promise.

Milsindra turned away from TaLi. Three long, stalking

strides brought her face-to-face with me. She kept walking forward, forcing me back into the trunk of an aspen. I heard Ázzuen growl. When my rump hit the tree's rough bark,
Milsindra bent her head to mine.

"You are disrespectful as well as dangerous, youngwolf. I
told you that your involvement with the humans would bring
death. You should have stayed away and left things to wiser
wolves." She pulled her lips back still more. "Though, perhaps
it was for the best. Now I can convince the council that that
old fool is too age-addled to lead."

"What fool is that, Milsindra?"

The voice was cool, almost friendly. Milsindra startled and
swung her head toward the ancient Greatwolf who sat calmly
at the edge of the clearing. Zorindru returned her gaze
through half-lidded eyes.

Two other Greatwolves settled on either side of the oldwolf,
their ears pricked and their haunches tensed as they guarded
him. They dipped their heads to me. Jandru and Frandra were
the Greatwolves who watched over the Swift River pack, and
they had helped me more often than they had harmed me. They
also supported Zorindru's rule of the Greatwolves.

Milsindra shoved me hard with her shoulder as she turned
to step forward and address Zorindru. Her voice was calm, but
her flanks quivered. Zorindru was her leaderwolf, even if she
did defy him.

"You were wrong, Zorindru," she said. "A wolf is dead at
the spear of a human, and it's this drelshik's fault." She jutted
her chin at me. "We need to get rid of her and all who share
her tainted, human-loving blood."

Zorindru stood. He had ruled the Greatwolves since long

before any wolf I knew was born. He was so gaunt that his spine showed through his ragged fur and he seemed much frailer than I remembered.

He stared at Kivdru, who still stood atop Ázzuen. Kivdru glared back. Zorindru held the younger wolf's gaze so long, I was ready to howl to break the silence. Then the oldwolf lifted his lip. His teeth were worn down, and I wondered if he could still even hunt for himself, but his snarl held enough power to make Kivdru lower his ears and step off Ázzuen, who scrambled to his feet, coughing.

Milsindra stalked over to Zorindru, her haunches still shaking. She was half a head taller than he was, and her muscles showed as clearly through her sleek fur as his bones showed through his. Still, she seemed to fear the ancient wolf. When she spoke, there was entreaty in her voice.

"The humans killed the oldwolf, for no reason at all," she said. "It's only a matter of time before they start hunting wolves throughout the land. Humans and wolves always fight. It's happened over and over."

It was the greatest challenge to fulfilling the Promise. Wolves had to stay with humans to keep them from feeling separate from the world around them, but every time wolves and humans came together, they fought. I was supposed to change that.

"We told the drelshik that she, her pack, and her humans could live if she was able to keep peace between humans and wolves," Milsindra said. "She hasn't done so. The only solution is to get rid of the humans and the wolves who run with them."

"You told us we had three moons," Ázzuen interrupted. "It's only been one moon since we started."

Kivdru leapt for him again, then staggered back as a large, black-feathered shape dropped from above and slammed into him. The raven spread his wings wide as he landed in front of Ázzuen and stared beadily at Kivdru.

Tlitoo was a young raven, but his head still came up to Ázzuen's chin and his wings were nearly as wide as a wolf is long. That, plus a thick beak and sharp talons, made him a formidable fighter. He had been my friend since I was a small-pup and a staunch ally against the Greatwolves. He was also the Nejakilakin, the raven who could move between the worlds of life and death. He could bring me with him, and could also take me into the minds of others. But I was the only one who knew that.

I took advantage of the distraction he'd caused to check on TaLi. The girl was standing on her tree stump, watching us carefully, her stone blade still clutched in her hand. She was safe, for now.

Tlitoo eyed Kivdru and spread his wings.

"Gruntwolves think they rule,
But sometimes must be humbled.
Ravens help with that."

Ravens often spoke in this strange way. I usually found it annoying, but when I saw Kivdru's frustrated expression, I wanted to lick Tlitoo from beak to tail. For some reason I'd never understood, the Greatwolves were wary of ravens. Kivdru stepped back.

"The youngwolf is correct," Zorindru said, inclining his head toward Ázzuen. "There is not yet war between the wolves and humans here." His tawny eyes met mine. "How do you plan to make sure it stays that way, Kaala?"

"I'm going to find my mother—" I began.

Milsindra interrupted. "Your mother who broke the rules of the Wide Valley by whelping you!" She glowered down at me, deliberately turning her back on Zorindru as anger seemed to overcome her fear of him. "This oldwolf and the fools who follow him believe that she has the answer to why wolves and humans cannot live side by side, and that her answer will allow us to fulfill the Promise. They believe that she will give this information only to you, her daughter, the drelshik. I think that humans will fight with us no matter what we do, and that you will only help them destroy us. The council, however, overruled me. They said you may leave the valley to find her."

Zorindru coughed softly.

"It would appear that you are once again dissatisfied with my leadership, Milsindra, and the decisions the council makes under it," the ancient Greatwolf said. "Do you wish to challenge me?"

Milsindra swung her head to regard him for a long moment, then looked away, lowering her tail. Zorindru lifted his.

"We will give her until Even Night to do so, Zorindru, that's all," Milsindra said.

There were two Even Nights every year, when day was as long as night. The next one was less than a moon away.

Milsindra raised her tail. "If she does not bring us an answer by then, we—and those who follow us—will take the Greatwolf council from you. We will kill the humans and the wolves who consort with them." She dipped her head to Kiv-

dru, and the two Greatwolves loped out of the clearing. Frandra and Jandru chased after them.

My legs gave out from under me. Now that Milsindra was
gone, I could admit to myself how terrified I'd been. Zorindru
lowered his nose to mine.

"Milsindra is under control for now, but not for long," he
said. "She is convinced that the only way to save wolfkind is
to stop you. There are many on the council who are tempted
to follow her, and I will not live forever. Find your mother,
Kaala, and do so quickly. I can help fend off the humans—and
Milsindra and Kivdru—until Even Night. After that, I can
make no guarantees." He dipped his head to me, and slipped
into the woods.

I released a long, relieved breath. TaLi exhaled at the same
moment. She jumped down from her stump and ran to me.
She threw her scrawny arms around my neck, and hugged me
hard enough to make me grunt.

Tlitoo gurgled impatiently. "Wolflet," he quorked, "if you
get into trouble every time I leave you, we will get nothing
done. I cannot watch you as if you are newly fledged." He regarded me with beady eyes, the ruff of feathers around his
neck puffed up in annoyance. He spread his wings, revealing a
white crescent of feathers on the underside of one of them.
"You should not have returned to your old pack. You are not
of them anymore."

"She had to try," Ázzuen said.

Tlitoo regarded him for a moment, then darted forward,
grabbed Ázzuen's ear, and yanked. When Ázzuen yelped and

stumbled away, Tlitoo dove for his nose. He was about to attack Ázzuen's tail when a pale gray wolf trotted into the clearing.

Marra was Ázzuen's littermate, a tall, fleet wolf who could outrun any prey in the valley. Her light gray fur was damp and muddy. A human boy ran up to stand beside her. He carried two of the preyskin bundles the humans called packs, one in his arms and one on his back, as well as two of the walking sticks some humans liked to use. His preyskin leg coverings were as damp as Marra's fur. The two of them must have come from the river. The boy was breathing hard. He fell to his knees and began to wheeze. Marra liked nothing more than to run, and the slow pace of humans—even of the human she loved as much as I loved TaLi—frustrated her.

"Are they coming?" she asked.

"They are too cowardly," Tlitoo answered. "They will hide here like mice in a burrow."

TaLi grabbed one of the packs MikLan had brought. Like us, TaLi had to leave the valley. Her grandmother had been training the girl to take over her role as krianan, or spiritual leader, of their village. The krianans were tasked with keeping the other humans in balance with the natural world, but many humans in the Wide Valley no longer listened to them. TaLi's grandmother had made TaLi promise to reach the krianans outside the valley to tell them what was happening here. BreLan, the boy both TaLi and Ázzuen loved, was already there, waiting for her. Before I could get to my mother, I was determined to see TaLi safely there. I licked her hand, and tasted sweat and dirt.

"Now can we go, wolflet?" Tlitoo quorked. "We do not have time to dawdle."

I couldn't argue with that. We had less than a moon to find my mother and return to the Wide Valley with a way to fulfill the Promise. I tried not to think of what might happen to Rissa and the rest of Swift River in our absence. I couldn't help them by staying in the Wide Valley.

I took a deep breath. I was only ten moons old. For most of my life, older wolves had made decisions and led the way. That time was past. TaLi shifted her pack on her shoulders. Ázzuen and Marra watched me expectantly.

I yipped once, and led my packmates from the aspen grove. We had no time to waste.

2

As we neared the banks of the river that marked the edge of Swift River lands, Ázzuen, Marra, and I kept the humans between us. The riverbank was exposed and a good place for an ambush. But the only one waiting for us there was a friend, a tall, broad-chested wolf with fur the color of summer grass.

"So Ruuqo and Rissa wouldn't come?" Pell didn't bother to hide his disdain. He was larger than the wolves of Swift River and well-muscled. At nearly three years old, he was supposed to be the next leaderwolf of the Stone Peak pack, a rival to Swift River. Instead, he had chosen to come with us, though he had no fondness for humans. Marra said it was because he wanted me for his mate. I thought he just craved adventure, as many youngwolves did. I was glad to have such a strong wolf with us on our journey.

"No," I said. "They think the Greatwolves will protect them."

I told Pell and Marra what had happened with Milsindra in the aspen grove. I was afraid that Pell would say something contemptuous about my birthpack. He'd always thought them weak. Instead, he licked the top of my head and nipped me lightly on the ear.

"You already knew that Milsindra wanted to kill you, Kaala," he said. "We just have to get to your mother quickly."

Marra yipped in agreement and splashed into the river. Ázzuen and Pell charged in after her and began to paddle across. MikLan waded in until he was up to his chest, then swam.

I looked at TaLi in concern. She couldn't swim. She had grown taller since I'd found her clinging to a rock in the rain-swollen river and she'd crossed the river many times since. Still, it made me nervous every time she did so. She was tired and injured, weaker than I'd seen her in a long time. The river was as wide across as thirty wolves standing nose to tail, and fast-moving after the end of winter rains. I wished I was strong enough to carry her across.

"I'll be fine, Silvermoon," she said.

She stepped onto a rock in the river and then leapt to another. I swam as close to her as I could. To my relief, Ázzuen, who had reached the far side of the river, waded back in so that he was standing at the spot right before it got too deep for a wolf of his size to do so. The water pulled at his chest, but he kept his footing. I remembered him as a smallpup, struggling the first time we crossed the river. He had been the weakest wolf in the Swift River pack. Now he stood as strong and steady as the most dominant youngwolf.

When Pell saw Ázzuen standing in the river, he looked at

me and then splashed in, too. TaLi was more than halfway across.

"I don't need your help," Ázzuen said to him.

Pell ignored him. He was taller than Ázzuen and could wade a full wolflength farther into the river. Ázzuen, trying to follow him, lost his footing and fell into the water.

TaLi, watching them, fell, too, just before she reached a rock two leaps away from the riverbank. She splashed face-first into the water and, for a terrifying moment, disappeared. Ázzuen, Pell, and I all lunged for her. Right as Ázzuen and Pell reached her, she sat up in what I could now see was a shallow part of the river. Unable to halt their momentum, Pell and Ázzuen crashed into her and she almost went under again. She shoved both of them away, struggled to her feet, and staggered toward the riverbank. Ázzuen took the preyskin clothing the humans called a *tunic* in his jaws and tried to pull her to shore. She fell once more. Crawling on her hands and knees, she reached the riverbank just as Ázzuen and I did.

"Please don't help me across the river again," she said to Ázzuen and Pell, wringing out the dried preyskins she wore as clothing. She was beginning to smell like wet deer.

I pressed against TaLi to try to warm her, only to realize that my fur was as wet as her clothing.

Adjusting her pack on her back, TaLi glared at all of us and stomped into the woods.

It was darkfall when we reached the low hills that abutted the eastern mountains at the valley's edge. While the humans built a small fire and laid out preyskins to sleep on, I ranged up the nearest hill. It would take the humans at least half the next day to climb it, and I wanted to see what awaited us. Áz-zuen, Marra, and Pell explored other paths, looking for the best way up the hill. I soon found a trail that rose gently enough to make for easy walking. Faded scents of humans and the more recent aroma of deer told me who had used the path before us. The human scent was old enough that it didn't concern me. Satisfied, I trotted back to our humans.

They had allowed their fire to go out. I was glad. Smoke in the night would have made it easier for anyone—human or wolf—to track us. MikLan was curled up around both packs as if guarding them. I looked for TaLi next to him. She wasn't there.

I lowered my nose to track her, following her trail away from the embers of the humans' fire to a birch grove nearby. Her scent was there, along with one I knew all too well.

Churned earth and human footprints scrambled one upon the other beneath my paws. One of TaLi's foot-coverings, her *boots*, as the humans called them, lay crumpled in the dirt. The human male DavRian's scent of sweat and dream-sage was all over it. My lips pulled back from my teeth in a snarl as I barked sharply three times to call my pack-mates.

DavRian had taken her. She was gone.

⊡

I couldn't believe I'd been so careless. I shouldn't have left her unguarded. DavRian had stolen her once before, after striking her so hard she'd fallen unconscious. He was violent and dangerous and TaLi was alone with him. Panic weakened my legs.

TaLi had blunt teeth and weak jaws and was almost as helpless as a pup. I forced myself to move on unsteady legs. I'd sooner place my own throat in Milsindra's jaws than leave TaLi with DavRian.

Deep in the birch forest, I heard a shout and then a scuffle. I ran toward the sound.

DavRian had left a trail like a rampaging elkryn and I easily followed the broken branches and trampled earth he'd left behind. In a small clearing among the birches and spruce, I caught up with him, then slowed so I could approach unseen.

DavRian knelt, gripping TaLi and clamping his hand over her mouth. I crouched down, forcing myself to control my fury at DavRian and my fear for TaLi and trying to think of the best attack. Then something in DavRian's expression caught my attention. I expected to see anger or hatred in his face, but he looked down at TaLi with tenderness. DavRian had wanted TaLi enough to leave his own village to try to win her. He had been devastated when she'd chosen BreLan over him. I knew that a wolf without a pack could act strangely, could feel so alone in the world that he did foolish things, and DavRian was a lonely human. He was whispering something to TaLi, and it looked like he was telling her his deepest secrets. For a moment, I pitied him. I had been rejected by my pack when I was a smallpup and knew what it was like to be shunned by those I wanted most to care about me. Then I saw the bruises and cuts on TaLi's face and the fear and fury in her eyes, and I snarled. DavRian was alone because he was malicious and weak, not the other way around. I watched him, trying to decide how to free TaLi from his grasp.

He had set his sharpstick within grabbing distance. It was

made of alder wood, and looked like a long, thin branch. Unlike an ordinary branch, it was almost completely straight and smooth. On the end of it was one of the stone blades that the humans could make as sharp as any fang. The humans called them *spears* and they were among their favorite hunting and fighting tools. At his waist DavRian had another blade, this one fastened to a smaller piece of wood. He must have thought I was foolish enough to run after him without making sure it was safe to do so. He'd told other humans over and over that we wolves were lesser creatures and that we were savage and stupid. It was my good luck that he actually believed it.

Ázzuen padded up behind me. He touched his nose to my face. His familiar scent of Swift River Pack, moist earth, and juniper calmed me. I found myself wanting to return his touch by curling up beside him and letting our breath mingle in sleep. I shook myself, wondering how I could think of resting while TaLi was in trouble.

"You know it's a trap?" he whispered.

I dipped my head in acknowledgment.

"Like we hunted the aurochs," he said, then circled around so he was crouching on the other side of the two humans, hidden by thick grouse bushes. DavRian was shifting uneasily from knee to knee, turning his head sharply back and forth as he waited for me. Ázzuen and I didn't even have to look at each other. When we had killed an auroch—a huge, evil-tempered beast—just a few days before, we had brought it down by angering it and then pouncing. Considering DavRian's disposition, Ázzuen must have figured it should work just as well with him.

Ázzuen rustled the leaves of the bush where he hid. DavRian stood and, still clutching TaLi, whirled toward the sound. I stalked up behind the human and took the edge of his tunic in my teeth and pulled. He squealed like a forest pig and spun back around. TaLi stomped hard on his foot and drove her elbow into his stomach just as Ázzuen darted from his hiding place to jump at DavRian. DavRian released TaLi and dropped his sharpstick. TaLi fell to her hands and knees, snatched up DavRian's sharpstick, and darted into the woods. Ázzuen butted DavRian once more and I slammed into the back of his legs, toppling him to the ground.

Ázzuen bolted into the woods after TaLi, but I stood over DavRian. My anger drew my lips back from my teeth and made my fur stand up along my spine. Saliva dripped onto his chest. He had killed TaLi's grandmother and would have killed me and all of my packmates. He'd hurt TaLi. And I knew he'd come after us; he'd try to steal TaLi from me again.

Never kill a human unprovoked. It was one of the most important parts of the Promise. If wolves killed humans, then the humans would attack us more often than they already did, so we never harmed them unless it was in defense of our lives. Some creatures break promises as easily as a raven snaps a twig. We do not, for trust is everything in a wolf pack.

I stepped away from DavRian.

"Silvermoon!" TaLi called. "Come on!"

I snarled one more time at DavRian and ran to find TaLi. I caught up with her as she loped, with Ázzuen at her side, through the woods and back toward the humans' resting spot. When we reached MikLan, I fetched TaLi's foot-covering for her.

MikLan scrambled to his feet.

"What happened?" he demanded.

"DavRian found us," TaLi answered, taking the boot from me. I expected her to be frightened, but she just sounded determined. I nosed her hand, wondering if she was all right. She smiled down at me, her eyes fierce in the moonlight.

"I knew he would," she said, "so I let him take me." She balanced on one foot and pulled on the boot. "When he asked where we were going, I lied. I told him we were going to the Rellin village in the southern hills."

It was a smart thing to do, and brave, but I hated it when TaLi took risks. I pawed her leg.

She grinned. "By the time he figures out that's not where I went, he won't be able to follow our trail." MikLan frowned at her. He was worried, too.

"I do know what I'm doing," she said to us. I had protected TaLi since the first day I met her, and I couldn't help but think of her as a pup. But when I looked at the firm set of her jaw, I knew I could no more keep her from facing danger than I could keep Ázzuen or Marra from hunting vicious prey.

She squatted next to the preyskin she had slept upon and began gathering the humans' belongings into their packs.

"Let's move camp," she said.

I sat next to her as she worked, looking out beyond the clearing and listening for the sound of DavRian's footsteps, guarding her as best I could against the darkness of the night.

3

The humans found a new sleeping place an hour's walk away, between three tall rocks that would both shelter them from the rising wind and hide them from DavRian. I was glad, not for the first time, that humans had such weak noses. He wouldn't be able to find us by scent.

With the wind came the beginnings of a rainstorm. MikLan took a large rolled-up elkskin from his pack and TaLi took one from hers. The humans had found a way to keep the skins from decaying and to make them as supple and strong as if they were still on a living beast. They unrolled the skins, then shoved their walking sticks into holes they dug in the soft dirt. Ázzuen watched, his ears pricked in interest. The humans and their tools held an endless fascination for him. TaLi and MikLan used their clever hands to secure the skins to the walking sticks, then tied the two together with strips of dried deerskin woven with reeds to form a small shelter. Ázzuen sniffed along the bottom of it. Tlitoo followed behind him, quorking deep in his throat. When the humans turned away, he pecked hard at the bottom of one of the walking sticks so that the skins fell down around Ázzuen. Tlitoo cackled.

"Stop that!" MikLan said. He scowled at Ázzuen, pushing the skins away. The rain had flattened the boy's headfur, making him look smaller than usual. There was no way for Ázzuen to tell MikLan that it was the raven who had made the shelter collapse. Tlitoo chuckled, pleased with himself, and strode a few paces away.

"If you could talk to your humans, you could tell them what happened," he said. "It is too bad you never learned." TaLi's grandmother was the only human I'd ever met who could understand us.

Ázzuen snapped at the raven. Tlitoo leapt just out of reach, quorking happily.

The humans shoved the walking sticks back into the ground and crawled into their clever shelter. The skins repelled the rain, and, though I was impatient to leave the valley, I was also exhausted, and the humans' cozy den tempted me.

Pell jumped up onto one of the rocks. I couldn't help but notice the strong muscles moving under his wet fur.

"I'll keep watch, Kaala," he said. "You need to rest." He'd chosen a rock as far from the human shelter as he could get. Pell didn't trust humans, and he'd once told me he had no desire to hunt with them. As we'd walked, I'd caught him watching MikLan suspiciously more than once, and he startled easily when he was around them.

Ázzuen claimed another rock and Marra the third. I wanted to keep watch with them, but it had been two frenzied, panicked days of running and fighting for my life since I'd had a good rest. My eyes were closing as I stood.

MikLan sat cross-legged at the shelter's entrance, his spear across his lap, his face serious. He was younger than TaLi. It was hard to trust him to watch over us, but he wanted to take on adult responsibilities, just like I did, and I admired him for it. As I stumbled toward the shelter, he smiled at me. MikLan had always been easy with us, even more so than TaLi. From the first time we met him, he had treated us just as he would his own kind. Marra thought that it was because he was still fully a child. I hoped he wouldn't lose that easy trust now that he was leaving childhood behind.

I left my packmates on guard and crept into the shelter. TaLi was already asleep, and I settled down next to her. I listened to her even breathing and waited for sleep to come. But as tired as I was, my eyes would not stay closed. I wriggled closer to TaLi. I needed rest, but there was something I needed more.

"Tlitoo!" I whispered. He didn't answer. I called again, a little louder. I was about to call a third time, when he stalked into the shelter.

"I am not an owl, wolf. I am not a bat. I have been up too much of this night already."

"I want to see what she's dreaming," I said.

He clacked his beak in annoyance. I lowered my ears.

"All right, wolflet," he grumbled. "If you look at me like a hungry pup, I have no choice. But next time you are most in need of a nap, I will wake you up."

Still grumbling, he pushed in between me and the sleep-

ing girl. I had told no one, not even Ázzuen, what Tlitoo and I
could do together. I didn't want my friends to know how different I really was.

Tlitoo and I had gone into the minds of Greatwolf and ordinary wolf alike, but it was entering TaLi's thoughts that
most fascinated me. I wanted more than anything to be able
to talk to her. When Tlitoo took me into TaLi's mind, I felt as
close to her as to another wolf, and I craved that closeness
now.

Tlitoo quorked softly and lay against me, so that he was
touching both me and the girl. He needed contact with both
of us to make the journey.

I readied myself for the lack of sound and smell that always accompanied me into the mind of another, and for the
sudden feeling of falling that still made me gasp. I couldn't
prepare for the confusion and dizziness that followed me into
TaLi's mind. Entering into the thoughts of another wolf was
less jolting. The strangeness of the way humans saw their
world—through vibrant colors and soft edges—was especially
disorienting.

I waited until my nausea receded, then sank into TaLi's
thoughts.

I saw the old woman's face and cringed away, remembering how I'd helped cause her death. Then I took a deep
breath. If this day in the old woman's shelter was important
enough for TaLi to dream of it, I could have the courage to see
it. I allowed myself to relax into her thoughts.

TaLi knew that her grandmother would not be with her much longer. The old woman had told her that her lungs had weakened, that
she would not live out another winter, and that TaLi would have to
be ready to take over as krianan.

"You have the wolves," NiaLi said. "You are the first to run
with them in many years. That will help you." TaLi looked over her
shoulder. A young wolf slept heavily against the mud-rock wall of
the shelter, snoring a little and moving her paws in her sleep.

TaLi walked over to the wolf and sat beside her.

"I can't talk to her," TaLi said. "Not the way you do." She had
spoken to the animals when she was little. She'd talked to rabbits
and ravens who told her she smelled bad, and even to rock lions.
She had understood the giant wolves her grandmother had taken
her to see when she still stumbled on her feet like a colt. But now
she could not. Often she thought she saw meaning in Silvermoon's
eyes, but she could never be sure.

"You will have to find another way," NiaLi said.

TaLi lay down next to the wolf and inhaled the rich forest smell
of her. When she was four, her grandmother had begun training her
to become the next krianan for the village, and from then on she
had been alone. So many of the village did not want the krianans
telling them what to do and what they must and must not hunt.
They laughed when TaLi told them they were just as much a part of
the forests as the animals they hunted and the plants they ate, and
they had shunned her. She'd felt as if she no longer had a family.

Until the day she had fallen in the river.

She had struggled for life, but part of her had wondered what
would happen if she let herself float down the river and over the
distant falls. When the wolf splashed into the water and swam to-

ward her, she thought it must be coming to kill her, for she'd been told since she could walk that wolves lived to kill humans. But the wolf bobbed near her and TaLi grabbed its fur. It swam with her to shore, saving her life.

Then it stood over her, panting, and she could see huge teeth. She waited for it to kill her then, but it did not. It helped her home.

She rested her back against the warmth of the wolf and looked up at her grandmother.

"They might not let me be krianan," she said.

"I know, child," her grandmother said. "If they do not, you must leave the valley. You are a krianan whether they accept you as one or not. You must find the krianans who live in the forest surrounding the village of Kaar. They know that we must be part of the natural world. They know that if those like DavRian prevail we are all lost, and they are fighting for our cause. You must go to them and help them. You and your wolves."

TaLi stared at the old woman. It was enough that she was supposed to convince her own village to keep the natural way. She couldn't possibly do so among strangers.

"You must," the old woman said, as if she could read TaLi's thoughts. "What happens in Kaar will influence what happens throughout much of the land. They are a village larger than any you have ever seen, and they are deciding whether to go the way of the krianans or the way of those who believe that humankind must rule all other creatures. I am too old to make the journey and I trust no one else. It must be you."

"What if the wolves won't come with me?"

"It is their task, too." The old woman's voice grew sharp. "You have not been listening. The wolves and the krianans share this task. Your wolves are discovering it, they have told me so. If you

can't find a way to talk to them, you will have to find other ways to keep your tasks aligned."

The old woman struggled to her feet and limped toward TaLi.

"You have the strength to do whatever you choose. You and your wolves. It is your duty, and I know you can do it."

"I will," TaLi whispered.

The old woman looked down at the girl and the wolf, and an expression so complex passed over her face that TaLi could not cutch exactly what it was.

"Her name is Kaala, you know," NiaLi said, smiling down at the snoring wolf. "And her friends are Ázzuen and Marra. You are all lucky to have found one another." She rose slowly and returned to her seat by the fire, wincing as she sat and pulled her furs around her.

TaLi buried her face in the wolf's thick fur. "I love you, Silvermoon. Kaala." She whispered the words she had never said aloud to anyone, not even BreLan. "I can do this if you help me."

Each beat of the wolf's strong heart, each steady breath it took, relaxed her and at the same time gave her strength. She didn't know when she fell asleep, but when she awoke the wolf was gone and her face was wet and sticky. She smiled. Silvermoon—Kaala—always licked her when she left. TaLi stood, kissed her sleeping grandmother on the cheek, and slipped out into the cool morning air.

▣

"Wake up, wolflet," Tlitoo rasped. "Daylight comes."

I blinked up into Tlitoo's beady gaze and forced myself the rest of the way awake. Going into the mind of another creature always made me tired, but I wanted to howl with exhilaration. I had learned something important from my journey into TaLi's memory: our tasks were one and the same.

I should have known as much, for the krianans were responsible for keeping other humans in touch with the Balance. The Balance was what kept the world whole. Every creature strove to live, and to have as much food and territory as it possibly could. But if one creature grew too strong or took too much, the Balance would collapse and many creatures would die. The humans upset the Balance, which is why the Promise came to be. The human krianans reminded their people of their place in the world.

I remembered that day in NiaLi's shelter. I'd arrived weary from a failed hunt and had paid no attention to what the old woman said to the girl. Now that I had, it made my heart race. I already knew that both wolves and krianans were sworn to keep the humans in touch with the natural world, and I knew that TaLi had to leave the valley. Now I knew that her task and mine were the same and that the krianans she was looking for might be able to help us achieve it.

I also saw something TaLi had not. She had not understood the expression on the old woman's face, but I did. The humans relied so much on their words that they were not as skilled at reading expressions as we were, even among their own kind. The old woman's face when she looked at us was full of fear and worry. But there was more. There was hope. The old woman was not naive. If she had hope, then so did I.

I licked TaLi's face until she awoke. She wiped her face with the back of her hand.

"That's disgusting, Silvermoon," she said. "Grandmother said your name is Kaala."

I licked her again, from chin to forehead. Then I stood and went to the opening of the shelter to let TaLi know it was time to go. When she blinked sleepily at me, I leaned toward her, tongue out.

"All right!" She held up her hands in front of her face. "I'm awake."

She got to her feet and pushed her way out of the preyskin shelter. MikLan had fallen asleep, but my packmates were still on guard. I followed TaLi as she disappeared behind a rock. The scent of slightly bitter spruce made my nose twitch.

"You don't have to watch me, Kaala," she said as she squatted behind the rock. Yes, I did. I couldn't lose track of her again.

Leaves crackled behind me and I turned, expecting to see Ázzuen or Marra. Instead I saw a flash of gray fur disappearing through the bush.

"Did you see that?" Ázzuen asked, his eyes wide as he leapt down from his watch spot above me.

I lowered my nose to the ground, following the scent of spruce, dry and sharp with a bitter undertone.

Ázzuen was the one who found the paw print, clearly defined in the mud. Just one, but so distinct I couldn't believe it hadn't been left deliberately. I placed my own paw next to it. It was half the size.

"Greatwolf," Ázzuen said.

Not just any Greatwolf, I realized, burying my nose in the print. It was Milsindra. She hadn't even tried to hide her scent as the Greatwolves could. She was following us and she wanted me to know it.

The fur on my back prickled. I didn't know what Milsindra was up to, but I knew her well enough to know that it wouldn't be good. She'd been forced to let me leave the valley, but I knew she thought that doing so was a mistake. And I knew, as certainly as I knew the moon would rise, that she would do anything she could to make me fail.

4

I stood atop the mountain pass that would lead us from the Wide Valley and looked back at what had been my home. I could see the long, snaking path of the Swift River and the outline of Wolf Killer Hill, but everything else looked small and unfamiliar in the afternoon light, as if the Wide Valley were already a strange place to me. Ázzuen looked back, too, but Marra and Pell gazed only forward. Tlitoo spiraled overhead, dipping and soaring on the updrafts. Another raven flew beside him. I recognized Jlela, a female raven who often flew with him.

Next to us, TaLi and MikLan gasped for breath. Humans, even young ones, moved more slowly than we did. Though I had not caught Milsindra's scent again, I kept imagining that I could feel her hot breath on my back, and Even Night was not much more than three-quarters of a moon away. We'd kept the humans moving quickly, tugging on their preyskin clothing when they slowed and nudging them with cold noses when they rested too long. Still, it had taken us a full day and half of another to reach the high pass that would lead us to the lands beyond the valley.

I'd thought the Wide Valley was vast. Now I could see how small it really was. The land before us, grasslands mixed with forest, stretched so far that I couldn't see the end of it. Large hills covered with dry, scrubby grass rose to our right, and to our left stood a forest of pines, cypress, and spruce. My stomach rumbled. That much land would hold enough prey for ten packs. It had been a long time since I'd eaten my fill.

Just beyond a copse of cypress stood a rock the size of a hill. It had to be the place where I was to meet my mother, but the vastness of the land disoriented me, and I couldn't judge how far away the rock was. I didn't even know if she'd be there yet. It was still over a moon until I was supposed to meet her and she was hiding from Greatwolves. Yet my breath caught. For the first time since I was a smallpup, it seemed possible that I might really see my mother again. I remembered the scent of her milk, and the warmth of her belly, and most of all the sense of feeling safe and protected.

When you are grown and accepted into the pack, you must come find me, she had told me before Ruuqo chased her away, and I had never forgotten it. I couldn't believe that in as little as a day I could be with her.

TaLi's hoarse voice shook me from my thoughts. "We have to find a place where two fallen pines cross over one another at a stream," she said to MikLan. Both she and the boy were swaying on their feet as they gazed across the grasslands. Dark clouds drifted over the plains, promising more rain.

TaLi clutched a piece of deerskin. She looked at it and

then toward the lake. "We go as far as that rock, then follow the map to the Crossed Pines."

Humans were limited to using their eyes to find places they'd never been. Their *map*, I guessed, was another clever way they'd found to compensate for their weak senses.

We made our way down the mountain and to a small hill below. The rain found us then. It had taken the humans hours to walk down the mountain, and it was nearing dark. It was time for them to rest.

They set up their shelter beside a large boulder. I had hunted many times in the rain and run across Swift River lands in a thunderstorm, but I preferred being dry. Ázzuen, Marra, and I crowded into the shelter. Pell, still suspicious of the humans, waited outside in the rain. TaLi and MikLan took firemeat out of one of their sacks. I knew I should let them save their food, but I was so hungry that I couldn't help whining a little. Firemeat was even better than ordinary food. It was rich and chewy, tasting of the smoke of the humans' fires, and a mouthful of it was as satisfying as twice as much ordinary meat. Ázzuen and Marra were no better than I was. They watched the humans and their food unblinkingly. TaLi smiled and gave me a chunk of her firemeat and handed some to Ázzuen. MikLan did the same for Marra. Guiltily, I gulped down my share.

"We'll have to get more food soon," TaLi said, as she watched their supplies go down our throats.

That, at least, was something we could help with. The two young humans talked for a while, then lay down to sleep, curled up on a preyskin they had spread upon the ground. We waited until they were deep within their dreams, then

Ázzuen, Marra, and I crawled from the shelter. The rain had stopped, leaving behind a night lit by a sliver of moon.

When Pell saw us, he bent his forelegs and lifted his rump high.

"I'm hungry," he said.

We had been running—eating what bits of food we could find and bolting what scraps the humans could spare for us—ever since we'd left Fallen Tree three nights before. A hunt was just what we all needed. I looked back to where the humans were sleeping.

"We can't leave them alone," I said.

"We will watch your humans." Tlitoo bobbed in front of the shelter. Jlela perched atop it. "And we have found their Crossed Pines. They are just beyond the place where the spruce trees give way to pine."

"You can't watch the humans. You have to sleep," I said. Ravens, like humans, slept during the night.

"We will wake if anything comes near," Jlela said, settling her wings and hunching her head down between them.

"It is very hard to sneak up on a raven," Tlitoo added, "and neither the Grumpwolf nor the human male are near." Grumpwolf was one of his many names for the Greatwolves. When I still hesitated, he spat a berry at my head.

> "The fur-brained wolflet
> Thinks it knows more than ravens.
> That will not end well."

I couldn't help laughing. I dipped my head to the ravens.

"Let's find some prey," I said to my packmates.

Marra yipped in excitement and took the lead. She had an excellent nose, which was especially important in unknown lands. We would have to not only find prey but also stay alert in case we crossed into any wolf territories. In the Wide Valley, we knew where every pack's domain began and ended. Here we would need to be careful.

Marra snuffled her nose low to the ground, then lifted it in the air.

"Prey!" she woofed, her tail wagging. "Nothing I recognize, but definitely prey."

She stepped aside, and without thinking about it, I took the lead. I realized I was acting like a leaderwolf, and looked back at the others, embarrassed. Ázzuen crouched low just to my left, his nose twitching, while Pell and Marra stood a little behind me, waiting for me to decide what to do next. My heart filled with the exhilaration of leading a hunt. I gave a deep, low bark like Ruuqo did at the beginning of a chase.

I took a step down the hill and managed to get my paws tangled in tree roots and slip in the mud. I splayed my legs to catch myself before I tumbled down the hill but landed hard on my chest. I got to my feet, mud sticky on my chest and face.

Marra raced past me.

"Wait!" I said. I wanted to make sure there were no other wolves around to claim the prey. But Marra didn't worry about things like that. By the time Ázzuen and I reached her, she was atop a small hill, looking down at a meadow where a herd of what looked like some kind of elk grazed in the cool, clear night. Pell followed more slowly, checking behind us for threats. It was something I should have thought to do.

I looked more closely at the prey. They looked something like elk and a bit like snow deer. Their legs were long and gangly and their bodies lighter than most of the prey in the valley.

My mouth moistened.

Several of them looked up at us before we had even begun to move toward them; they were wary prey, used to confronting hunters. We had just begun to sneak down the hill on our bellies when Pell whoofed a warning.

Five wolves ran across the plain, scattering the prey and heading straight toward us. We must have been easy to see, even in the faint moonlight. I had been stupid, standing there so exposed. Even from a distance, I could see the wolves' teeth bared in snarls.

We stood to meet them, and I found myself once again slightly ahead of the others. I tried desperately to remember how Ruuqo and Rissa would greet a pack of wolves in hostile territory, but nothing came to me. I tried to decide if I should be threatening or welcoming. Then I realized that the best thing to do *would* have been to run. I was still deciding how to react to them when they reached us, tails stiff, ears laid back in anger.

"Are you stealing our prey?" the female in the lead asked. Her proud gait and the way the other wolves deferred to her made it clear that she was the pack's leaderwolf. I would have expected a wolf in her prime, someone Ruuqo's age. This wolf was younger than Pell. The rest of her packmates were either wolves in their second year, like her, or our age.

"We didn't realize it was your territory," I found myself saying. My tongue was dry, but my voice came out confident and calm. "We won't take what isn't ours, and we'll leave your lands if you give us permission to pass through." I'd heard

Ruuqo and Rissa speak this way, but it had never occurred to me that I could.

The five wolves stood growling at us, teeth bared, fur raised along their spines. The leaderwolf didn't reply. I waited for them to attack. We'd trespassed into their territory and were standing within hunting distance of their prey. It would be within their rights to try to kill us. They were all young and strong, and they outnumbered us. Ázzuen, Marra, and Pell stepped closer to me.

"Why do you smell like humans?" one of the wolves asked, still growling. He had dark fur and a bare patch behind his left ear where a jagged wound was healing. I prepared to fight. If they tried to follow our scent to TaLi and MikLan, I would stop them.

"They came from the Wide Valley," the wolf in the lead said. "They all smell like humans there." Her pale gray pelt seemed to shimmer in the faint moonlight. Her tail jutted out behind her and she held herself ready to fight.

"What happened to your leg?" she asked me.

I hesitated, not wanting to admit weakness.

"A human cut her," Pell said, his voice deep and arrogant. It was the tone he used when he was trying to intimidate. He took two steps forward, limping a little. The rain always made his leg hurt. He'd injured it fighting maddened elkryn four moons before. "She fought with him and he sliced her with his sharpstick."

"Did you kill it?" the dark-furred male asked.

"No," I said, "but I bit him." It was DavRian who had wounded me, when he tried to kill me, but I didn't want to tell them any more than I had to.

The five wolves confronting us seemed to relax a little, and the light-coated leaderwolf lowered her tail.

"I'm Lallna, of the Sentinel pack," she said, her mouth softening into a smile, "and this is Sallin," she said, poking the dark-furred male with her nose. Behind me, Marra snorted. It did seem like a stupid name for a wolf pack. What did the five of them think they were sentinels of?

"You're a wandering pack, then?" the young leaderwolf asked. She either didn't notice Marra's ridicule or was ignoring it.

"A what?"

"A wandering pack. You don't have your own territory."

I thought about that. Swift River was no longer our home.

"No," I said. "I mean yes. We don't have a territory."

"Are you trying to find one here, or do you plan to keep journeying?"

"Who's your secondwolf?" the male standing next to her—the one she'd called Sallin—asked abruptly.

My secondwolf? I thought. The Sentinel wolves all looked at me. They thought I was a leaderwolf and that the others followed me. Sallin's eyes flicked from Marra to Pell and back to me again. If they knew we weren't a real pack, that I wasn't a leaderwolf, they might challenge us to a fight. They weren't as large as Stone Peaks and didn't look any stronger than we were, but we couldn't risk any injuries. And we couldn't let them past us to find our humans.

"We're still working that out," I answered.

"You're a new pack, then," Lallna said, as if that explained a great deal to her. She leaned close to me. "I would choose the willow-smelling male," she said, "even though he's lame. I don't think you should have a female second. If you have a male second, he can also be your mate." She looked Pell over once more and smirked.

"So why did you fight a human?" Sallin asked. The wound on his head was bleeding, but it didn't seem to bother him.

The more I talked to the Sentinel wolves, the more determined I was to keep them from knowing about our humans.

Lallna, Sallin, and their packmates stared at me, waiting for me to say more. Marra came to my rescue.

"You're called the Sentinel pack?" she asked. Her tone was polite but any wolf who knew her would know she was holding back laughter at their pack name. I glared at her and she lowered her eyes. Not in submission to me, but to keep from laughing.

"Yes," Lallna said. "Sentinel holds all the lands from the spruce grove to beyond the Hill Rock."

I held back a grunt of disbelief. I'd never heard of any one pack holding that much land.

"How many wolves are in Sentinel?" Ázzuen asked. The fur between his eyes wrinkled as it did when he was thinking hard. It hadn't occurred to me that the pack might be larger than the five wolves before us.

"I can't tell you that," Lallna growled.

Ázzuen took a step forward. "What are you sentinels of?" he persisted, his nose twitching as if he was on the scent of prey.

Lallna lifted her lip at him. "You'll find out soon enough. We're supposed to bring any wolves that come through the Wide Valley to our gathering place. You can go on your way if our leaderwolves say so."

My backfur rose. We couldn't abandon our humans. Even
if the Sentinels' leaderwolves let us go on our way, I wouldn't
leave TaLi and MikLan protected only by ravens. I looked at
Marra. She was the best of us at pack dynamics, and I hoped
she would find a way to talk the Sentinel youngwolves into
letting us go. But it was Pell who answered, at his most arrogant.

"Why would we go with you?" Pell looked down his muzzle at Lallna. "We're not part of your pack and we'll pass
through your lands as we choose. We won't be ordered about
by a bunch of curl-tails."

A curl-tail was the lowest ranking wolf in the pack and
the last to feed. It was an insult, and the Sentinel youngwolves responded to it. Before I could even snarl at Pell,
Lallna launched herself at me.

By the time I tensed my muscles to react, she was on me.
Out of the corner of my eye, I could see the other four Sentinel wolves leaping at my packmates. Sallin and a tawny-furred
male dove for Pell, who grinned as he crouched to respond.
The two remaining wolves attacked Ázzuen and Marra. My
heart pounded so hard I was certain Lallna could hear my
fear. Some wolves enjoyed fighting. I did not. My chest was so
tight I could barely breathe.

Lallna hit me hard, trying to knock me over with the force
of her leap. My first impulse was to resist her, to stand strong
and meet power with power. Then I remembered Torell's
fighting lessons. He was Pell's father and leaderwolf, and he
had taught me to use cleverness as well as strength in a fight. I
let the momentum of Lallna's jump knock me over, but continued to roll so that she tumbled past me. Before she could

get up, I threw myself on top of her. She snapped her teeth in my face, startling me, and heaved me into the air. I fell onto my side.

Muscle and sinew moved under her fur as she landed on my chest, pressing down with her full weight. She wasn't that large a wolf and I hadn't expected her to be so strong. The hard landing had knocked the wind from my lungs, but I managed to curl away from her and get partway to my feet before she tackled me again. We scrambled on the ground, each of us trying to pin the other. Her legs trembled with what I thought for a moment was fear as strong as my own, but then I realized it was excitement. She grinned and I knew she was enjoying the fight.

I arched my back, twisted my hips, and snapped my head forward, slamming Lallna to the ground. Before she could get up, I dug my forepaws into her belly and bared my teeth to bite her, hard.

I saw Pell throw the tawny male halfway down the hill, then flip Sallin onto his back, stand astride him, and take the smaller wolf's neck very gently in his jaws. He didn't bite down but just kept his teeth around Sallin's neck as Sallin averted his gaze and tried to lick Pell's muzzle. I remembered, then, what Ruuqo had told us about dominance fights when we were pups: they were to determine which wolves would be submissive and which would be dominant. Only a weak, scheming wolf would hurt another wolf more than necessary. It was Pell's gentle treatment of Sallin that made me gain control of myself. Pell had challenged the Sentinel youngwolves when he refused to go with them. No one had yet drawn blood, and if I did so, I would change a battle for control to a

fight to the death. I looked at the others. Both Marra and Ázzuen were struggling but holding their own.

My inattention allowed Lallna to throw me off her belly,
but she didn't attack again. She narrowed her eyes at me and
woofed softly to her packmates. The wolves fighting Ázzuen
and Marra got to their feet, and Pell stepped off of Sallin. The
fifth wolf scrambled back up the hill.

Lallna kept watching me. It was only when Ázzuen
bumped my hip that I realized that Lallna was waiting for me
to speak. They still thought I was a leaderwolf.

We had won the fight and so gained the right to make the
next move, but the Sentinels were strong wolves. They could
follow us back to the humans, or attack us again, or bring
more wolves to fight us. We couldn't escape them, but we
could gain some time.

"We'll come meet your leaderwolves," I said, "but we have
something to do first."

"What do you have to do?" Lallna asked.

"Meet someone," Ázzuen said before I could answer.

If I hadn't been afraid to turn away from Lallna, I would
have snarled at him for thinking I was stupid enough to tell
the Sentinels that we were looking for humans.

Lallna regarded us with her cool gaze.

"We'll let you escort us to your pack," Marra offered.
Lallna looked at me for confirmation.

"Yes," I said, understanding what Marra had figured out
already: if Lallna brought trespassing wolves to her pack, she
would gain status with her leaderwolves.

"We could've won if it weren't for the willow-smelling

male," Lallna said, "but you fight well." She jutted her chin in challenge. "If you let us escort you to our pack, you can go."

"You won't follow us," Pell ordered. I was grateful to him. I hadn't thought of that. "And you will give us until two nights from now." I would never have had the courage to be so aggressive.

"One night and half a day," Lallna countered. Pell looked at me and dipped his head slightly.

"Yes," I said. "We'll meet you back here."

Without another word, the five Sentinel wolves turned tail and dashed down the hill, kicking up mud behind them.

5

The humans were awake and waiting for us when we returned to them near dawn. They took down their shelter and tied up their packs, then set out some firemeat and tartberries for their morning meal. Again, I couldn't help staring at them as they ate. We still hadn't been able to hunt. Again, they fed us from their supplies. There were wolves who said that the humans were so different from us that we could never fully trust them, but TaLi and MikLan fed us just as packmates would, with no hesitation. I knew wolves who were not so generous. Ázzuen, Marra, and I devoured what they gave us. Pell stood off to the side, refusing the humans' food. He smelled of voles he must have caught on our way back to the humans, but a few voles weren't enough to keep a wolf healthy. If he was anything like the wolves of Swift River, he'd be irritable and difficult to deal with if he didn't eat.

"Would you just take some?" I said, annoyed. "If I'd wanted a pup along I would have brought one."

He snarled at me. "I hunt my own prey."

"We need every wolf strong," Marra said, "and you're our best fighter."

He looked at her and then at the humans. He licked Marra on the top of her head and stared at MikLan. Again, the boy seemed to understand us better than other humans did. He dug into his pack and held out some firemeat on the flat of his hand. Pell kept staring at him until the boy dropped the meat on the ground and stepped away. Pell gobbled it.

"Thank you for sharing your prey," Pell said formally. MikLan swallowed a few times and then lifted his pack onto his shoulders. TaLi hefted her own pack. It was more important than ever to hurry them along. I was certain that Milsindra was close by, and even if the Sentinel wolves honored their word and gave us a night and a day to come to them, we had no time to waste. To my relief, the humans set off at a brisk pace across the plain.

Getting them to follow us to the Crossed Pines was not so easy. Humans could be as stubborn as ravens, and they kept looking at their map, then at their surroundings, and then walking away from the quickest route to the woods where Tlitoo had told us the pines were. Ordinarily, I would have let them go the long way, but if Milsindra was stalking us, I needed to get TaLi to safety as soon as possible. And the sooner the humans reached the human village, the sooner I could find my mother. When TaLi stopped at a tree with a strangely bent branch and frowned at the hide again, I grabbed it from her hand.

"Silvermoon!" In her annoyance, TaLi used her old name for me. "Bring it back!" She stopped, planted her feet, and put her hands to her hips.

I trotted over to her, just close enough so it looked like she might be able to grab the hide. Both she and MikLan lunged for it. I dodged away. They lunged again and I dodged again. Marra and Ázzuen ran between their legs and bumped their hips, making them stumble. I let them chase me and almost catch me several times. Then I began to run, slowly enough that they could keep up, in the direction of Crossed Pines. They followed.

NiaLi was wrong. We communicated just fine when we needed to.

The humans were angry and tired by the time we reached the stream two hours later. I waited for them to stop gasping, then walked up one of the two fallen pines that crossed over one another. I set down the hide and panted at TaLi. She had clambered halfway up one of the fallen trees when she stopped and really looked at where I was sitting.

"Two pines crossed over one another at a stream," she said to herself. I looked around, expecting to see humans at any moment.

"This next part isn't on the map," TaLi said to MikLan. She went about two hundred wolflengths into the woods, turned to the left, and walked for five minutes. Then she stopped near a trickle of a stream.

"This should be it," she whispered.

Pell knocked me in the shoulder. "I'll explore the territory around here," he said. I was going to protest, then smelled his unease. He had put up with our humans to help us, and I liked him all the more for it. I wouldn't insist he stay to meet a packful of strange humans.

At first I couldn't figure out where the humans would be,

although I could smell them close by. I looked for the large mud-and-rock structures and burning fires that made up Ta-Li's village back in the Wide Valley. Then I remembered Nia-Li's shelter, how it had seemed to grow from the forest, so much so that other humans often walked by it without noticing it. When I looked more carefully, I saw signs of humans: a flat place where they would build their fires, and mounds of stone and dirt that seemed to grow naturally from the earth but that had to be shelters.

An old male human crawled from one of the mounds.

"Welcome," he croaked, "we've been waiting for you." The man addressed me as well as TaLi. He wore a longfang tooth attached to a bit of alderwood on a preyskin strip around his neck, just like the one NiaLi had given to TaLi when the girl accepted the role of krianan. I realized that he must be a krianan, too. We had found their village.

Just then, a young male dashed from behind one of the smaller mounds.

"BreLan!" TaLi yelped. That was why the old man knew who she was. TaLi's mate-to-be must have told him about us. TaLi threw off her pack and galloped to BreLan.

Ázzuen got to him first. BreLan was his human, and he loved the boy as much as I loved TaLi. When he was still two wolflengths away from BreLan, he launched himself. The young human was tall and well muscled, but the force of Ázzuen's leap knocked him on his rump. Ázzuen licked his face over and over again, his tail whipping so hard it kept hitting TaLi, who was trying to get to BreLan, too. Other humans began to gather, quietly emerging from shelters and from behind trees as if they were wolf rather than human.

BreLan returned Ázzuen's greeting, thumping his ribs so hard that Ázzuen coughed. BreLan shoved Ázzuen away, stood, and lifted TaLi off her feet. He swung her around several times before setting her down. He held her so close I didn't know how she could breathe. I walked over to them and pawed BreLan's leg.

"Hello, Silvermoon!" he said.

Then he saw MikLan standing next to Marra.

He grinned at him, releasing TaLi. Then he looked MikLan up and down. "You've grown," he accused.

MikLan walked shyly to his brother. He thumped the blunt end of his spear on the ground in formal greeting. BreLan pulled him close. "Thank you for bringing TaLi safely," BreLan said.

MikLan smiled up at him. "I have to go back soon," he said. "I promised the other krianans in the valley I'd tell them what's happening here."

BreLan's face grew serious as he stepped away from his brother. "You'll have a lot to tell them. There's more going on here than even NiaLi knew. I don't know if she would've sent TaLi if she had known."

BreLan pulled TaLi close again, wrapping one arm around her while his other hand rested on Ázzuen's back.

"How is NiaLi?" he asked. "She wasn't strong enough to come?"

"DavRian killed her," TaLi said, beginning to cry. "He killed her and blamed it on the wolves."

BreLan looked down at her.

"She's dead?" He rubbed his eyes. He had loved the old woman, too.

TaLi nodded. She pulled his head down to hers and told him what had happened since he'd left the valley. His face grew grimmer and grimmer.

"I never would have left if I'd known DavRian was so dangerous," he whispered. "And it won't help things here." He started to say more, but a female human came forward.

"You've had a long journey," she said. "Would you like something to eat?"

At the word *eat* I looked up. Ázzuen's stomach growled. Marra yipped, and the woman laughed.

They brought us more food than I had ever been given by a human. It was older elk meat and not cooked in the fire. I had grown used to the humans' firemeat, but the rich elk was so good, I gulped it down and then ate more. Ázzuen and Marra ate as voraciously as I did, and Tlitoo darted in to grab scraps. I licked my muzzle to get the last of the meat from my face.

"They were hungry," TaLi said, apologetically, and I realized how quickly we had bolted the food.

The faint scent of wolf blew through the pines. It wasn't Lallna or the other Sentinels, but it was familiar. The wolf was too far away to cause us trouble, but something about it tugged at me. Something made me desperate to follow it.

TaLi was safely delivered to the humans and gazing up at BreLan. I could leave her for a little while. The strange wolf scent pulled me as strongly as my love for TaLi did. I nosed Ázzuen's cheek. "Watch over TaLi for me," I said, and began to slip as unobtrusively as I could out of the little village.

"Come back here, youngwolf," an imperious voice rang out. I stopped, one forepaw raised. Ordinarily I would have kept going, so strong was the pull of the scent, but the leader-wolf authority in the voice made me pause. And I couldn't fig-ure out where it was coming from. It seemed to come from the sky. My paw still raised, I looked over my shoulder.

Perched like a raven in a pine tree above the fire pit was the old human male who had first greeted us. Tlitoo flew to land beside the old man on a sturdy branch, cocking his head back and forth and quorking curiously at him. I'd seen TaLi and the other young humans clamber about in the trees—it was one of the things I envied about their long limbs and nimble hands—but never one so old. The old humans I had seen were less agile.

The old man slid down so that he was hanging from his arms and his feet touched a lower branch. He then hung from that branch and dropped to the ground, landing next to TaLi as gracefully as if he really did have wings.

"I am so sorry to hear of your grandmother's death," he said to TaLi, placing a gnarled hand on her head. "I knew NiaLi when she was a young woman, and she has done more for us than any other krianans I know. She told me that you were the one who would take her place when she was gone."

"I'll try," TaLi said softly.

"Can you speak to your wolves?" the old man asked, his voice sharp in spite of his smile.

"No," TaLi said, ashamed. "I could when I was little, but then I forgot. Silvermoon, I mean Kaala, and I were trying to learn Oldspeak, but then Grandmother died." Oldspeak was the ancient language all creatures once spoke. I knew more about it than TaLi did, but not enough.

The old man's cheerful expression faltered just a bit. "So I am the last one," he said so softly I wasn't sure the other humans could hear him. He raised his voice. "NiaLi was able to speak to them and we hoped you would as well. Did you try to learn, wolf?" he asked me.

Startled to be addressed, I answered without thinking. "Yes," I said. "But we didn't have time."

"And we don't have time now," he said. His eyes crinkled at my surprise. "I can understand you, even if your girl cannot. You and TaLi will have to find another way to communicate with each other." He gripped TaLi's arm in one hand and MikLan's in the other. He nodded to us. "Come with me now, all of you. We have little time and much to do. We have a plan in place, and will need your cooperation as soon as possible. I have friends that you must meet." He turned and strode away, dragging TaLi and MikLan with him.

The wolfscent blew past me again, and my heart began to pound as I realized why I knew it.

It was my mother's scent.

I tried to catch Ázzuen's eye, or Marra's, but they were following behind the humans, and they wouldn't recognize the scent even if they were paying attention to it. They had only met my mother once, on the day she had been chased from the Wide Valley. They had not suckled at her belly nor slept against her warm fur. They would smell only a wolf passing too far away to be a threat. They followed the humans into one of the mounds.

I was rooted where I stood. The scent blew past me again, a bit closer this time, and with it came memories of warm milk, the soft dirt of the den, and safety. I remembered her giving me my name and defying Ruuqo when he killed my littermates. As the humans and my packmates crawled into the shelter, I bolted into the woods.

□

I ran full pelt through thick trees and thicker underbrush, following the scent until I reached the open plain. Tlitoo flew low, just over my head. It was nearly high sun, and the Hill Rock seemed to shimmer in the late morning light. My mother's scent came from just beyond it. I ran faster.

"Wolflet, wait!" Tlitoo said. "You do not know what awaits you."

I didn't care what awaited me, except that it was my mother. After all this time, I was within wolflengths of her.

I galloped across the grass and back into the woods, following the scent until I reached a stream. Across it stood a smallish, light gray wolf. She looked up sharply, her nose twitching.

I would have known her anywhere.

I had no words. I just ran to her, stumbling like a small-pup through the stream. I had waited for her for so long. I had wished for her for so long. The one thing I wanted more than anything in the world was to find her. A puplike whimper of happiness escaped my throat.

For just a moment, I thought I saw a flash of joy and welcome in her gaze. Her ears, for an instant, lifted in pleasure.

Then, when I was three wolflengths from her, something changed. She pulled back her lips as far as they could go and flattened her ears. The fur along her back rose, making her look bigger than she was, and a deep, throbbing growl burst forth from her.

Stunned, I tried to skid to a halt but I was running so quickly that I tumbled into her instead. Her scent overwhelmed me, the scent of the den, the scent of the one time in my life I had felt safe. She threw me to the ground and pinned me hard. Then she took my neck in her jaws and bit down, hard enough to hurt.

"You aren't supposed to be here," she snarled. "Go and don't come back." She stepped off me and I staggered to my feet, my legs so weak they could barely take my weight. When I didn't move, she snapped at my face again and again, growling until I stumbled away.

A confusion of scents rose from her. I smelled anger and frustration, but also terror. I couldn't imagine what about me could frighten her. I took a few steps and then looked back at her.

"Go!" she growled.

I couldn't find anything to say. I couldn't think of anything to do. I could only stumble back in the direction I'd come, my mother's ferocious growl sounding in my ears.

6

When I was just three days out of the den, Ruuqo whispered to me that I would not survive to adulthood. A wolf without mother or father, he said, had no true pack. I'd lowered my eyes and said nothing, as any pup would, but I'd told myself he was wrong, and that just because he had exiled my mother didn't mean I didn't have one. Every time I caught the scent of dusk sage on the wind or saw a slight wolf with pale fur, I thought of her. I knew that someday I would meet her and she would place her head over my neck and pull me to her and tell me she was proud of me. I would feel whole again. I'd never been more wrong about anything.

I ran blindly, ignoring the scents and sounds around me. I started to wheeze, as if my lungs were filled with dirt, and I couldn't stop. Tlitoo screeched something above me, but I couldn't make out the words.

"Kaala!" Pell's voice sounded as if it came to me through a windstorm. I'd run right past him without noticing. I stopped

and tried to tell him what happened, but I could only blink up at him. "What's wrong?" He buried his nose in the fur on my back.

"You smell like Neesa!" he said. "You found her?"

"I found her." My voice sounded dead. We were in a stand of pine and juniper that smelled like home. Ázzuen and Marra pushed through the juniper bushes. They caught sight of my expression and looked from me to Pell and then back again.

"She found Neesa," Pell told them.

"Is she all right?" Ázzuen asked.

"She's fine." Anger overtook my hurt and shock. She had left me to fend for myself in the Wide Valley. She had let my littermates be killed and then told me to risk everything to find her. I closed my eyes and gathered my breath, trying to find a reason for what she'd done. I told my packmates what had happened, hoping that they would have some explanation for her behavior.

"She growled at me," I said, holding back a whimper. "She bit me and chased me away."

"Neesa always was unstable," Pell said. "She went to the humans and bred with a wolf outside the valley. She bore pups of mixed blood." He stopped suddenly. I was one of those mixed-blood pups, and if she was unstable, that meant I could only be worse. He averted his eyes.

Tlitoo glared at him. "Oafwolf," he quorked.

"She attacked you, Kaala," Pell insisted. "Her own pup. What kind of wolf would do that?" His eyes, when he lifted them to mine, were gentle. "When my father wanted to kill a wolf in our pack, he would invite that wolf to a meeting somewhere without the rest of the pack and then attack.

Maybe Neesa was doing that. Or maybe she's just crazy." He pawed the dirt. "We should go back home. I don't think Neesa has anything to offer us but trouble."

I was saying the same thing to myself, but I didn't want to hear it from another wolf. I snarled at him.

"There has to be a reason, Kaala." Ázzuen had been so quiet that his voice startled me. "She wanted you."

"How do you know?" I demanded, still snarling. He lowered his ears.

He had no answer. Because there wasn't one. The image of her snarling face would not leave me. I'd left my home and led my packmates into danger because she had called to me, because she was supposed to tell me what I needed to do to keep the Promise. It was all for nothing. The Greatwolves would kill my packmates, and our humans, and the Swift River pack.

And my mother didn't want me.

I tipped my head back and opened my jaws and allowed all my misery and sorrow to rise up from my heart and escape through my throat. I howled of loneliness and failure and my despair.

"Quiet, Kaala!" Pell swung his head back and forth to look around the copse. Marra spun around to look deeper into the woods. Ázzuen took three steps toward me and then stopped, flattening his ears.

"What are you *doing*, wolf?" Tlitoo demanded.

I cringed. I'd just announced our location to every wolf in Sentinel lands.

"We should get out of here," Marra said, shifting from paw to paw, ready to run.

I was shaking so hard I couldn't take a deep enough breath to talk, much less run away. It was as if the howl had drained me of every drop of energy I had. My legs weakened and I sank to the earth. I didn't care if Milsindra found me and killed me.

"Get up, Kaala," Ázzuen said. He grabbed me by the scruff and tried to drag me to my paws. He wasn't strong enough.

Tlitoo pecked me on the rump. "You are boring when you mope, wolf. I would not have come with you if I had known you would curl up and whimper again."

Back in the Wide Valley, I had been haunted by a great sorrow that came over me whenever I thought of my lost mother. I would be hunting, or running with my packmates, and find myself whimpering, unable to go on. Since she had called to me, I had almost forgotten about it. I'd imagined, again and again, how my mother would greet me when I found her. I'd dreamed of her welcoming me as pack. Now my despair threatened to return.

Tlitoo pecked me harder. "Will you let your packmates die because you wish to sulk?" he quorked.

Ázzuen, Pell, and Marra were watching me anxiously. I knew better than to tell them to go without me.

I pulled myself together and staggered to my paws. Pell bolted from the copse. I stumbled after him, Ázzuen and Marra at my side. Tlitoo flew just beneath the branches of the dense trees. As soon as we began to move, I felt a little better, the rhythm of a forest run steadying me. If we were lucky, I thought, no wolves nearby would care enough about a wandering pack to track us.

We weren't lucky. Lallna and the other young Sentinels

caught up with us ten minutes later, just as the trees thinned and we reached the edge of a grassy plain. There were more of them this time. Eight to our four. They surrounded us, their stances aggressive, their teeth bared.

"What's the matter with you?" Lallna demanded, showing her fangs. "You promised not to let anyone else know you're here!"

Then she fell silent and stared at my chest. The stream had washed the mud away, exposing the moon mark on my fur.

"You're the drelwolf," she whispered.

I didn't know what she meant. I'd been called drelshik and drelshan, but no one had called me "drelwolf" before.

"If we'd known that, we wouldn't have let you go," Sallin growled. The cut on his head was bleeding into his eye and I found myself staring at it, wondering why no one cleaned it for him.

Lallna sat, bent back her head, and howled.

"I found the drelwolf!" she bayed. "At the edge of the plump horse plain!" It was a hunting cry.

One by one, the other Sentinel wolves joined her in her howl. I'd always loved the sound of the howls that called wolves together, especially the summons to a hunt. It was different when I was the one being hunted.

"Time to run, wolves," Tlitoo quorked from a low branch above us. He dropped down and landed on Lallna's back.

Pell slammed into two of the Sentinel youngwolves, knocking them over and clearing a path for us. We bolted out of the woods and onto the plain.

Pell loped across the grass and toward the spruce wood on

the far side of it, his long stride carrying him across the grass. I lowered my head and followed. If we could make it across, we might be able to lose the Sentinel youngwolves in the woods, or at least take advantage of the terrain to outfight them.

Then I heard Ázzuen yelp behind me. I lifted my head and saw wolves pelting toward us from different directions. My throat went dry.

More and more wolves emerged from the woods behind us and in front of us. We ran faster, veering away from the approaching wolves, angling toward open plain. More wolves appeared. Singly and in groups of three and four, they charged onto the grass as Lallna and the other youngwolves came up behind us.

There was no hope for escape. We stopped and stood rump to rump in a circle, waiting for what was to come, facing the wolves who ran at us from all directions. I couldn't tell whether the trembling in my haunches was my own or my packmates'. Ázzuen's breath was harsh and labored and Marra coughed in fear. Pell lowered his head and rumbled a challenge. Tlitoo streaked into the woods in front of us and then back again, shrieking obscenities at the approaching wolves.

"They'll kill us," Marra wheezed. And I knew with sudden, sure intensity that I didn't want to die. Even though my mother had chased me. Even though I was failing in the Promise and might be the wolf destined to destroy wolfkind. I felt a surge of hunger that had nothing to do with my full belly. Strength returned to my legs and I tried to think of something to say to the approaching wolves—if they let us speak before they attacked.

They didn't attack. They began to herd us, as we might herd elk, to the far side of the plain. As silent as prowling rock lions, they closed in on us, giving us no choice but to run in the direction they took us. Tlitoo dipped and dove at the wolves, grabbing tufts of fur and probably bits of skin, but they ignored him. They ran so quickly, it was all I could do to keep up. I could hear Ázzuen gasping beside me. Even Marra was panting.

They drove us at their unrelenting pace until we reached a small pond. I tried to lap up some water to ease my parched throat, but the wolves growled and snapped at us, forcing us to go on.

A few minutes beyond the pond, we crested a low hill. Below us stretched the dense line of pines that marked the forest's edge. The wolves around us picked up their pace and I was sure I would stumble and be trampled. At last they slowed as we reached a thick grove of birch, pine, and spruce. The trees stood close together, and I expected that we would wend through them to get to a clearing of some sort. Instead we stopped beneath a single oak surrounded by smaller trees. I smelled still more wolves. The wolves guarding us spread out among the trees, and for the first time, I had a clear view of my surroundings.

I looked up to see Greatwolves everywhere. Standing on rocks and sitting upright on the ground, they watched us. I didn't know that there were so many of them in the world. A familiar bitter spruce scent wafted toward me. Some of the wolves who had brought us there pushed Ázzuen, Marra, and Pell to one side, leaving me to stand alone. Then they crouched low in deference to the Greatwolves. As I dropped to my belly, I heard a contemptuous laugh, a sound I knew almost as well as TaLi's voice or Ázzuen's howl. I hoped I had mistaken the sound, but knew I wouldn't be so lucky. I lifted my head to gaze into the cold, scornful eyes of the Greatwolf Milsindra.

The Sentinel pack was led by Greatwolves, and Milsindra was one of them.

7

In the time I had known her, Milsindra had lied about the duty of wolfkind and the Promise, had tried to kill me, and had killed a packmate I loved. She had done everything she could to sabotage our efforts to live peacefully with the humans. Now she had tricked me into leaving the valley and delivered me to a packful of Greatwolves.

"You pups are so easy to manipulate," she whispered to me. "Did you really think I would just let you destroy us?"

She lowered her head to a large dark-coated Greatwolf male. He had a patch of pale fur between his eyes and the bearing of a leaderwolf.

"This is the one, Navdru," she smirked. "The drelshik. I told you I'd bring her to you."

"We're the ones who brought her," Lallna grumbled from just behind me, but she kept her voice a whisper. It was as much defiance as she was willing to show Greatwolves.

The Greatwolf that Milsindra had called Navdru strode

toward me, flanked by a light gray female as dominant as he was. There was nowhere to run. Milsindra had trapped us neatly. I'd have thought that if I ever found myself surrounded by Greatwolves planning to kill me, I would be frozen in terror. Instead, I felt my legs straighten under me as I stood. Tlitoo rasped challenge from an oak branch just above me. My lips peeled back and a growl rose in my throat. I wouldn't just lie there to be killed.

Navdru moved forward in the Greatwolves' long, stalking stride until he was just a wolflength from me.

"I am Navdru," he rumbled, ignoring my lack of respect, "leaderwolf of the Sentinel Pack. This is my mate, Yildra"—he nodded to the pale Greatwolf on his right—"and this is Hidden Grove Gathering Place." He looked at me as if I were somehow a disappointment, then sighed and dipped his head in greeting. "You took long enough to get here."

I fell silent in mid-growl and stared at him like a stunned deer. He wasn't going to kill me, at least not yet, and he had been waiting for me to come. I swayed, my mind understanding that I wasn't in immediate danger, but my body was still tensed to fight. I couldn't gather the words to return his greeting.

Milsindra growled in fury.

Navdru's teeth showed between his lips in the barest of smiles. "Youngwolves are not the only ones easy to manipulate, Milsindra. Your hunger for power makes you foolish. I needed you to allow her to leave the Wide Valley without a fight."

I found my voice. "I'm just here to see my mother," I whispered. My mother, who didn't want me and who wouldn't help me with the Promise. "My packmates and I will leave your territory if you let us go." I didn't know what I'd do after that. I just wanted to retrieve our humans and get someplace safe.

Navdru looked down his long muzzle at me.

"You will not go anywhere," he said. "You are Kaala, late of the Swift River pack of the Wide Valley, born of mixed blood when your mother, Neesa, bred outside the valley in defiance of our laws. You have brought with you your packmates, Ázzuen and Marra, as well as Pell, heir to the leadership of the Stone Peak pack, who has chosen to follow you rather than accept his birthright. When you were a smallpup, you saved the human girl TaLi, and hunted with the humans, also in defiance of wolf law. In doing so, you and your packmates became the first wolves in generations to live peacefully with humans without either fighting with them or giving up the wildness of the wolf. Which means you are, most likely, the drelwolf, the wolf of legend, and our last chance."

He knew TaLi's name. That was the first thought that came to me. He knew who she was. That meant he could find her and he could kill her. I wanted to ask him how he knew so much about us and why, and what he intended to do with us. I wanted to ask him if he was going to hurt TaLi.

"What does drelwolf mean? I know drelshan and drelshik, but not drelwolf." I sounded so calm, as if I were discussing the next hunt or a new den site.

"No one has told you." Navdru frowned. He lifted a lip to Milsindra, who averted her gaze. "We believe that the drelshan, the savior wolf, and the drelshik, the destroyer, are one and the same, and that what she does or does not do will determine the fate of wolfkind. We believe you may be that wolf. It is why we considered killing you when you saved the human pup. Your mother, and the Greatwolf Zorindru of the Wide Valley, convinced us to give you a chance. When some of us saw you stop the battle between wolves and humans four moons ago, we believed we had made the right choice." He frowned again. "The drelwolf is supposed to be a wolf of great power." He looked me over from nose to tail. "You are young, yet."

"She has already caused destruction and the death of a packmate!" Milsindra said. She strode up to Navdru. "She could mean the end of all wolfkind."

Navdru growled. "This is not the Wide Valley, Milsindra, and you do not rule here."

"She does not rule in the Wide Valley, either," Tlitoo quorked from his branch.

Milsindra gave Navdru a long, measuring look and lowered one ear. I remembered her giving in just as easily to Zorindru back in the Wide Valley. I realized, then, that she was frightened of Navdru just as she'd been of Zorindru, but was standing up to him because she believed in what she was doing. She was convinced that only Greatwolves had the strength to control humans and that if we smallwolves tried, disaster would follow. She really thought my existence threatened wolfkind.

"My offer stands," Navdru said to her. "If the youngwolf fails, leadership of the Wide Valley is yours, and we will have no more to do with the humans. For now, however, you will not disrupt my pack."

Milsindra lowered the other ear. She started to speak, but behind her another wolf growled a warning. I heard running pawsteps.

A moment later, Neesa bolted into the clearing and hurled herself at Navdru. He was so much bigger than she was that she didn't even make him stagger. She fell to the ground, got to her paws, and leapt again.

"Get out of here, Kaala!" she gasped. "Why didn't you escape when you could?"

I could only stare at her, baffled. I'd thought she hated me. Now she'd trespassed into a Greatwolf gathering place to find me.

Navdru swung his great head, knocking my mother across the copse and into the trunk of a pine. She fell, her legs splayed on the hard ground. I yelped, and before I knew what I was doing, I was standing in front of her. She had chased me away. She had told me to leave my home and then rejected me, but she was my mother and I wouldn't let Navdru kill her. Ázzuen, Pell, and Marra burst through the line of Greatwolves guarding them and scrambled to my side. Pell bore a fresh wound on his neck. I heard a croaking above me and darted a glance up to see that Tlitoo had flown to a branch of the pine we now stood beneath.

"You should have run when I told you to, Kaala," Neesa gasped, struggling to her paws. "They mean to use you like the humans use their tools."

Navdru strode forward, his backfur raised, his teeth bared. "You should not have told her to run, Neesa. It was a betrayal of the Sentinel pack."

"You lied to me," she retorted, as if a wolf half again her size were not glowering down at her. She lowered her head to whisper to me. "I came out of hiding because they promised you could come to me unharmed. They told me they needed you. But they didn't say you would be in danger. I tried to warn you before you left the valley but I was too late. I would never have called you in the first place if I'd known. You're the only pup I have left."

I could only stare at her. I knew I could be killed at any moment by the Greatwolves surrounding me, but all I could think of was that my mother hadn't chased me away because she didn't want me. She'd been trying to save my life.

"We're all in danger, Neesa, you know that," Navdru snapped.

He lowered his head and swung it back and forth, looking from Neesa to me, and then to Ázzuen, Pell, and Marra, anger rising off him like mist. Then he sighed, settled the fur along his back, and closed his eyes. Ruuqo did that, too, when he was trying to control his temper. When the Greatwolf leader-wolf opened his eyes, he seemed to be speaking to himself as much as to us.

"I should have remembered the reckless courage of the Wide Valley wolves," Navdru said. "It is, I suppose, the reason you have all survived." He turned his gaze to me. "I need you to listen to me, youngwolf. Stop snarling at me and listen."

"The drelwolf," someone whispered. "No other wolf would stand against Greatwolves."

"I heard she is not a true wolf," another Greatwolf murmured. "That she is part human."

"Leave us!" Navdru ordered, glaring around the clearing. "I cannot speak to the youngwolves with all of you panting at the backs of our necks."

One by one, Greatwolf and smallwolf alike began to leave the copse. About ten Greatwolves stayed, including Yildra and

Milsindra. At the very edge of the woods, Lallna paused, looking back at Navdru, her face pinched in anxiety. He followed
my gaze and watched her for a moment, then trotted across
the copse. He took her muzzle in his jaws.

"You have done well, youngwolf," he said. "Thank you for
bringing the drelwolf to us."

Lallna lowered her ears to Navdru, but her tail wagged.
Her status in the pack would almost certainly rise consider-
ably. When Navdru released her, she grinned at me and
bounded into the woods.

The copse was almost silent. I could hear Tlitoo's low
quorking and the heavy breathing of my mother and my
packmates. I tried to loosen the muscles in my chest.

"I cannot fault a mother for wishing to protect her pup,"
Navdru said, inclining his head to Neesa. "As for you, youngwolves, I admire your willingness to fight for yourselves." He
nodded to me and my packmates. His manner had changed
and he spoke to me kindly but firmly, with the assurance of a
leaderwolf addressing a member of his pack.

"I did not begin well. We have been waiting a long time
for the drelwolf." He softened his muzzle. "We waited for you
because if we cannot fulfill the Promise now, we may have no
other chance." He let that sink in. "There is a human village
twenty minutes' lope from here, and what happens there may
very well determine whether we succeed or fail."

His mate, Yildra, spoke for the first time, her voice deep
and rumbling. "The humans of Kaar are making a choice between two ways of being, youngwolves. Some think that humans are one creature among many. Others believe that
humans are different, that the Ancients have given them the

task of ruling every creature, every forest, every plain. They believe that the larger their village grows, the more power they have. And they have taken over many villages as proof."

"It was starting to be that way at home, too," I said. The humans were so arrogant. A wolf feels responsible for her territory. She must ensure that prey is not hunted so much that entire herds flee, and has the right to fight any wolves who try to invade the pack's territory. But she does not stray beyond the confines of her own land, and if she does, she does so with deference to the wolves who guard that territory. To think oneself the leaderwolf of all creatures seemed like the ravings of a mad wolf.

"The decisions are being made everywhere humans live," Navdru said. "But Kaar holds great influence. It's the most powerful village for as far as any wolf has run or raven has flown. As goes Kaar, so will go the other humans. And if the humans choose to be rulers of all creatures, we will lose our chance to sway them, for they will see no wisdom outside their own thoughts and beliefs. They will see other creatures only as either enemies or tools."

"Which is why you should not have run away like a skittering mouse, youngwolf." The harsh, rasping voice came from above. The old human krianan, RalZun, was perched on the pine branch next to Tlitoo. A rustling drew my gaze to the higher branches of the trees, where several more ravens stood, warbling softly.

RalZun jumped down and gave Navdru a jerky bow. The Greatwolf dipped his head to the old human. The human krianans and the Greatwolves of the Wide Valley had once worked together toward the Promise. The ones in Sentinel lands evidently still did.

"I would have brought her to you, Navdru, but she ran off." He glared at me. "You are no longer a pup, free to be concerned only with herself," he snapped.

I lifted my lip to him. He wasn't my leaderwolf.

"The humans at the big village like wolves, don't they?" Ázzuen blurted, his ears twitching. "It makes sense, Kaala." His silvery eyes met mine. "TaLi's village wanted to use us to steal territory from other villages. That's why we're here, isn't it?" he challenged Navdru.

Navdru looked disconcerted.

"They like wolves," he confirmed. "Or, rather, they like what we can do for them. Wolves have lived with them before, helping them hunt and protecting their lands. It is one of the reasons they have grown so strong."

"They see us as tools," Yildra said, "and if they find us to be useful enough tools, they will do a great deal to keep us. Once they have welcomed us—welcomed you—as pack, we can help them understand that they are creatures of the wild like we are, and that they are no different from the world around them."

"But we will not allow any wolf to go to them unless we can be assured that the humans will not stray farther from the Balance as a result," Navdru rumbled.

"How is Kaala supposed to do that?" Pell rumbled back. Marra growled softly.

It was RalZun who answered, looking pleased with himself. "I have told the leaders of Kaar that wolves will only come back to the village if a krianan brings them. They are choosing a new krianan at their Spring Festival on Even Night."

"They care about Even Night?" Ázzuen asked. It intrigued me, too, that the humans sometimes marked time the same way we did.

RalZun dipped his head. "It is how they celebrate the beginning of spring and autumn. They used to understand that they shared traditions with other creatures. Now they imagine that only they have such ceremonies. There are those among them who believe that the krianan's role is to lead humans away from the natural world, to set them as far apart from other beasts as possible." He waved his arms at Navdru and Yildra. "That is why my friends here will allow you to go to the human village to try one more time." Then the old man grinned. "If the humans wish to have you wolves help them in their hunts and in guarding their homes, they must choose the krianan I recommend, and thus follow the old ways."

"TaLi," I said. "You want TaLi to be their krianan. You told NiaLi to send her here without saying why." I didn't like that he was putting TaLi in danger.

"I called her to her duty as you are called to yours."

I growled at him. He was as manipulative as a Greatwolf.

Navdru poked me in the chest with his nose. I coughed.

"Do you accept this duty, youngwolf?" he demanded.

I'd thought that once I found my mother, she would tell me what to do, and I could go home and let grown wolves take responsibility for what came next. Now a pack of Greatwolves who had tried for generations to control the humans wanted me to do what they could not.

Ázzuen whuffed to me. I met his eyes. They were warm with encouragement.

"Yes, I accept," I said to Navdru. It wasn't as if I had a choice. The alternative was to be killed, along with those I loved.

"Good," the Sentinel leader said. "But, listen to me. You must not be submissive to the humans. Have you been so with your human girl? Ever? Even to keep her from becoming angry?"

"No," I answered. "We're equals."

"And did that cause trouble?" Yildra asked. "Did the humans react badly to you when you were not docile?"

I thought of DavRian thrusting his spear into my haunch, of NiaLi lying dead in her shelter. I looked at Milsindra out of the corner of my eye. She would contradict me, but my pack-mates would support me, and it would be our word against hers.

"No," I lied, "they didn't." Instead of challenging me, Milsindra whuffled a laugh and lay down, her face resting in her paws. I wondered what she was up to.

"You must not submit to them here, youngwolf. If you are their curl-tails, you will have failed. Do you understand?"

"Yes," I said, though I wasn't sure I did. No one had been able to explain to me why it was so bad to be submissive to the humans, other than that it made us less than wolf. I looked up into Navdru's tawny eyes. "What happens if we fail?"

"You know what happens," he answered. "You and those of your blood must be killed."

Milsindra rumbled in agreement. Pell growled, and Ázzuen and Marra echoed him. I looked away. It was no different from the threat Milsindra had made.

"I am not the sort of wolf to kill those weaker than I," Navdru said, sounding ashamed, "but we have no choice." To my astonishment, he seemed to be asking me for forgiveness.

"It is to protect wolfkind that we must be so harsh," he said. "If you cannot find a way to control the humans, we will leave these lands and go somewhere the humans cannot find us. Thus we will keep wolfkind safe, along with the wildness that is our legacy. That may be enough to stop the humans. There are those among us who believe that without our help, the humans will breed too quickly and starve themselves to death, or fall victim to other creatures of the wild, who despise them. Others among us believe it is too late and that the humans are already too strong. That is why we are giving you a chance to try one last time to change them. If you succeed, we will find a way to reward you."

"What about the wolves back in the Wide Valley?" Marra asked. I could feel her trembling next to me. I looked at her out of the corner of my eye and saw that it was fury, not fear, that made her shake.

"If you succeed, we will not harm them. What happens between them and the humans is up to them."

I was getting angry, too. I was tired of being manipulated by wolf and human krianan alike. But I kept my face still. Navdru seemed to approve of what he saw in me, for he gave me a small smile. Then his face grew serious again.

"You have until Even Night, youngwolf." He looked over his shoulder to RalZun, who had leapt up on a tall rock.

"Take them to Kaar," he said. He whuffed to the wolves around him and loped into the woods.

One by one, the other Sentinels began to follow. My mother started toward me. Yildra nipped her on the shoulder. "You'll stay with us, Neesa," she said. "This is the pup's task, not yours."

My mother's legs stiffened with defiance. Then she dipped her head to the Greatwolf. "Find me if you need me, Kaala," she said. "I am not permitted near the humans, but the Sentinels cannot stop me from giving you advice." She ran forward, licked the top of my head, and darted after the other wolves.

Milsindra was the last to leave. "I'll be waiting for you when you fail, Kaala." She lifted her lip in a snarl, then bounded away.

RalZun clouted me on the head. He ignored Pell and Ázzuen, who growled at him.

"I have told the humans you are here. They are curious and wish to hunt with you. If you prove yourselves in the hunt, they might allow you into the village. Just a few of you at first. They will meet us for the hunt tomorrow at dawn. If you run away again, I will feed you to the first rock bear I find."

With that, he stalked into the woods. Weary from fear, anger, and the enormity of my task, I could think of nothing else to do but follow.

8

Some hunts fail and some succeed. Every wolf knows that. This hunt, however, could not fail. We had twenty days to influence the humans of Kaar, twenty days and nights to get TaLi, whom they did not know, accepted as their krianan. We could make no mistakes.

On a grassy, dawn-lit plain replete with elk and rich with their musky scent, a gathering of at least twenty humans stood watching us. RalZun led TaLi, BreLan, and MikLan across the plain to join them. We four wolves flopped down on our bellies where the trees met the plain to assess the humans as well as the elk we were to hunt. The humans clutched their spears and the antler-bone sticks they used so that they could throw the spears long distances. They smelled of anticipation and the eagerness of the hunt, but not of the fear or suspicion I was accustomed to in humans who didn't know us well. The elk shifted their gaze nervously from the humans to us and then back again.

I should have been worried, but as I watched the humans preparing for their hunt and inhaled the enticing scent of uneasy prey, I was hopeful. We had hunted with our humans many times. It was something I knew we could do well.

The humans were murmuring to one another, and I was struck, not for the first time, by their odd appearance. No other creatures stood always on their hind legs, and when I'd first seen the humans, I'd wondered that they could balance without tipping over. I'd come to understand that their two-legged stance allowed them to use their tools with their clever hands, but it still disturbed me. Bears reared up on their hind legs to threaten, as did some prey. When I first met the humans I'd thought they were always challenging us.

They also had much less fur than we did. It grew on their heads, on the adult males' faces, and in patches on their bodies. I found myself staring at one male in particular who had absolutely no fur at all on his head. He caught me watching him and glared at me with a sudden, fierce hatred. Then his features smoothed out and he looked as mild as a sleeping oldwolf.

The wind carried a strong gust of elk scent to us. Blood rushed so quickly to my head that I grew dizzy and my haunches began to twitch. My body warmed. As the call to hunt pounded in my blood, I wished I could leave the humans behind and hunt with my packmates, to chase the prey until it could run no more and bring it down with sharp teeth and strong jaws. I could almost taste the elk flesh on my tongue. I shook myself hard. This was not just any hunt; it was our chance to begin winning over the humans. If we succeeded, they would give us the chance to prove our worth—

and TaLi's. If we did not, we would have failed before we'd begun and the Sentinels would kill us. Suddenly I was as nervous as a pup chasing her very first prey.

I heard a familiar whoosh of wings. Tlitoo alighted above us on a low spruce branch. The ravens were excellent hunting partners, distracting prey and keeping watch for danger as we ran the ground below.

"You'll help us?" I asked before I saw that he wasn't alone. Jlela was perched next to him, preening Tlitoo's wing feathers.

He ran his beak through her head feathers before answering.

"I will not," he said. "The humans are interested in what wolves can do for them, not ravens."

I glared up to tell Tlitoo that the humans would never notice a raven or two helping us, but he avoided my gaze. He twined his neck around Jlela's, and they were warbling softly to each other. Jlela ran her beak from Tlitoo's head down to his tail feathers.

"I don't think they'll be much help right now," Pell said, a laugh in his voice. But when I looked at him there was a strange intensity in his gaze. "It's spring, after all."

Marra snorted. Both ravens glared down at us.

"Babywolves," Jlela grumbled. She disentangled her neck from Tlitoo's and took off for a higher branch.

Tlitoo puffed up the feathers around his neck and croaked irritably. I thought he might spit a twig at us, but he just spread his wings, wide and strong, and flew up to rejoin Jlela.

A human voice sounded across the plain.

"Begin the hunt!"

The call came from a tall female. The furless-headed male

stood on one side of her, RalZun on the other. TaLi gestured to us. We walked slowly across the plain, keeping our bodies relaxed until we reached the humans. We all lowered our ears politely and sat.

"They're smaller than I remember," the tall female said without returning our greeting. I ignored her rudeness. She probably didn't know any better.

"That's HesMi," TaLi whispered to us in a voice too soft for humans to hear. "She leads Kaar's council of elders this season." The female looked strong and smelled of power. "And the bald one is IniMin." She nodded toward the furless-headed male who had glared at me. "He's the one who doesn't want wolves around."

I was relieved to see that Kaar didn't believe the nonsense that females couldn't lead, or hunt, as some of the humans in the Wide Valley did. The dominant human called HesMi watched us curiously. The furless IniMin wore a pleasant expression, but if he'd been a wolf, his backfur would have been raised. Humans didn't seem to understand that their scents revealed as much about them as their words, and this human smelled of malice.

I leaned against TaLi as Marra huffed in anticipation. Ázzuen yipped softly and licked the top of my head. I turned to share the excitement of the hunt with Pell, but he was watching me and Ázzuen with narrowed eyes.

BreLan bent down to whisper in TaLi's ear.

"Tell the wolves which elk to hunt," BreLan said. "Show HesMi that the wolves will do what you tell them to do."

I couldn't let her do that. Not if we were to prove to the

Sentinels that we were the humans' equals. Navdru had probably sent someone to watch us.

I sat down, then looked away from TaLi, as I had when I'd once refused to swim across the river without her back in the Wide Valley.

And she understood me. As clearly as if I had spoken to her. Watching me carefully, she whispered to BreLan.

"No. We want HesMi to see what the wolves can do on their own." I stood and panted a smile at her and then licked her hand. She smiled back at me and spoke to HesMi and IniMin.

"The wolves can pick out the best animals to hunt. It's one of the ways they help us." She stood tall, more like a grown human than I'd ever seen her.

"Fine," HesMi said, and several humans whispered to one another. I looked behind me to see if any of them were going to argue, but they just watched us, intrigued. RalZun had said that many of them had lived in Kaar when wolves still hunted with the villagers there.

A strong smell of spruce wafted across the plain, even though there were no spruce trees nearby. I sneezed.

"Find a good one, Kaala," TaLi said. I licked her hand and set out onto the plain. My packmates followed.

I took a deep breath. I needed to find prey we could catch quickly. We would need to work with the humans to bring down the prey, without submitting to them, getting them injured, or making them uncomfortable. It would take all of our skill and strength to do so.

"What first, Kaala?" Pell said. He had led almost as many

hunts as a leaderwolf and didn't seem at all concerned about this one. I smiled back, opening my mouth to taste the rich scent of elk.

"Find the easiest prey you can," I said. If I had been trying to impress a wolf pack, I might have hunted the most challenging beast I could find. For the humans, I would bring down prey as quickly as I could. I heard my voice grow strong. "Marra and Pell, you start chasing them. See if any tire quickly. Ázzuen, you run among them and see if you can smell any weak ones."

All three dipped their heads to me and darted to the elk.

I waited, resisting the urge to run to the hunt like an eager pup, and watched as Marra and Pell bolted a group of elk. All of them were healthy and fast. Pell put on an extra burst of speed, outrunning Marra for a moment, splitting the elk into the faster and the slower. It was a beautiful move, done so smoothly that the elk didn't notice that my packmates had divided their herd. Marra swerved to join him and they split the slower group of elk once more. Pell's long legs followed one upon the other, the muscles in his haunches stretching and contracting.

Ázzuen barked.

He had been running low to the ground next to the group of elk that had run off when Pell and Marra had first split the herd. The elk he'd found looked healthy and ran well, but he stuck to her side.

"This one has bloodflies!" he yipped to me. Ruuqo and Rissa had taught us about the parasites that invaded prey's lungs, and had shown us how to recognize their scent in the carcass of a dead horse. A prey infested with bloodflies could still eat and could sprint short distances, but tired quickly and had slower reactions.

I stood, torn. Pell and Marra would find a slower elk, and it would be weary by the time they did so. But the elk they chased all seemed alert and strong. Ázzuen's might not be so. And it was fatter than the others—prey the humans would appreciate more.

I woofed to Marra and Pell, alerting them to Ázzuen's choice. They barely broke stride to look at me, follow my gaze to Ázzuen, and then turn to run toward him and his elk. I caught TaLi's eye and stared at Ázzuen and his prey. She understood me.

"That one!" she said to HesMi. "With the black forehead and the white patch on its back!" I hadn't seen anything different about the elk's back but I'd noticed that the humans relied on visual clues to tell each other things. Ázzuen thought that they saw more colors than we did. They certainly needed something to compensate for their weak noses and ears.

Hoots and shouts filled the air as long, lanky young humans led the charge. Marra and Ázzuen drove the elk to them. In a flurry of thrown spears, the elk went down. It screamed and kicked as more humans converged on it, spears raised. Before the dying beast's legs stopped moving, Marra pelted toward several of the elk she and Pell had been chasing earlier. MikLan took off after her, and several humans followed the boy. The humans couldn't keep pace with Marra, but when she drove two elk toward them, their sharpsticks flew once more. Humans and wolves moved with the ease of a pack that had hunted together for years. One of the elk fell, three spears in its flesh. The other shied away. Right into Pell's jaws. He leapt on it, with a swift graceful jump, biting into its haunch. My heart caught when it kicked out at him, and I ran to his aid just as TaLi pulled back her arm and let her spear fly from the throwing stick. The tool made it possible for even a relatively small human like TaLi to throw a spear far and fast.

The beast staggered and fell just as I reached it. I dodged hooves and rolled away from the wounded prey. It kicked twice more and then was still. When I got to my paws, I saw humans surrounding the fallen elk.

TaLi ran to me, whooping. She stumbled and landed on her rump. I stood over her and licked her all over, aware of the humans celebrating all around us. The scent of joy and triumph arose from wolf and human alike. We had killed three elk with the humans before the sun had climbed halfway up the sky.

I scanned the plain as the elk fled, and a flash of movement drew my attention to the trees bordering the plain. Milsindra stood watching us. That was why I had smelled spruce before. I didn't know whether the Sentinels had sent her or she had come on her own, but I had no problem with her seeing our success. She bared her teeth in her unpleasant smile and stalked off into the woods. I waited until she was gone, then snarled at the place where she had been.

The scent of fresh meat taunted me from across the plain. I restrained myself from running to one of the elk to tear into its rich flesh, and was pleased to see Pell, Ázzuen, and Marra doing the same. Most of the humans, including their leader, HesMi, were celebrating our successful hunt. TaLi and RalZun made their way across the plain to stand next to the human leader, and the old man beamed at me. Then I caught the sour smell of anger. IniMin was not celebrating. He stood apart from HesMi and the others. When he turned his head to meet my gaze, I saw the small shift in his face, a tightening of the muscles around his mouth and eyes, a slight thinning of his lips. His forehead stretched so that his ears moved a little farther back on his furless head. He was furious, and none of the humans seemed to realize it. There was no way I could warn TaLi with our clumsy way of communicating. RalZun whispered something to the girl. She glanced at IniMin and narrowed her eyes.

"The wolves get their share." I almost didn't recognize the strong, authoritative voice as TaLi's. There was nothing of the uncertain human child I'd known in the Wide Valley. She was looking toward one of the dead elk, her hands clenched into tight fists.

That was when I saw that Pell and Marra had stopped waiting and had torn into the beast. A few of the humans were moving forward in protest, but stopped when TaLi spoke. HesMi nodded to them, and they backed off. Ázzuen bolted to join the others at the prey and, after one last anxious look at HesMi, I did, too. Soon I was lying next to the beast and biting into its belly. For a few moments I knew nothing but rich meat, warm flesh, and the glorious feeling of food in my stomach. Ázzuen was on one side of me, Pell on the other, as we fed. It was Marra who pulled away first.

"We should stop," she said thickly. "Leave good greslin for the humans." Greslin was the best, richest part of a prey. Marra had eaten so fast she was gasping.

I managed to drag myself away from the elk. Ázzuen and Pell did the same. Most of the humans were bent over the other carcasses. But six of them, including IniMin, were making their way toward us, determined expressions on their faces.

"Let them have it," I said.

"Are you sure?" Pell asked, flicking a glance to where Milsindra had stood. He'd seen her, too.

"I'm sure." It was one thing to avoid being submissive, but there was no reason to purposely challenge the humans. A wolf who fought every time she saw another wolf wasn't strong. She was foolish. I had learned that in the Wide Valley. The balance of a pack was kept by standing up for oneself, but also by thinking of the good of packmates. I wanted the humans to see us as packmates, not rivals.

We stepped away from the carcass. TaLi scrambled after the six approaching humans. HesMi followed behind, keeping pace easily with her long legs. The humans swarmed around the carcass. As they cut into what was left of the elk, I watched TaLi. She crinkled her eyes at me.

"Kaala," she said, "will you bring me the rib bone?" She pointed to a smallish bone to my right. I picked it up and dragged it over to her. Even a small elk bone wasn't light. When I brought it to her, she smiled up at HesMi.

HesMi smiled back. IniMin stepped away from the carcass and stomped over to us, frowning.

"Get me that bit of meat there, wolf," he ordered. I looked up at him, sat, and yawned. He shoved his foot into my ribs, not kicking me but trying to push me toward the carcass. I lay down.

TaLi crouched down beside me and buried her face in my fur. She was laughing. She lifted her head, her face composed. "Kaala, would you bring me the piece of meat by the rock?"

I got to my paws and raced to the small bit of meat. When I brought it back to TaLi, she put it in the sack that HesMi carried. The human leader grunted and walked away. TaLi crouched, wrapped her arms around me, and rested her cheek on my head.

"We did it, Kaala," she whispered. I leaned against her, my chest warming.

"It's only the beginning," I said, twisting around to lick her face. I thought I saw a flicker of understanding in her eyes before she hugged me hard and stood to race after HesMi. It felt like there was nothing we couldn't do together.

A grunt of effort came from my left. Pell was pulling a chunk of the elk's rib cage into the woods. He struggled to haul it over a small rise at the edge of the plain. Ázzuen was listening intently to HesMi and TaLi. He would tell me anything important they said. I trotted to the edge of the plain to help Pell. Together we dragged the rib bones into the woods.

He'd gathered a large pile of meat in the shade of the pine trees. Tlitoo and Jlela stood atop it, picking at bits of flesh and skin. I helped Pell drag the rib bones to the pile.

"That should keep the Sentinels happy," I said. The Sentinels hadn't asked us to bring them meat, but it certainly couldn't hurt to do so. And it would prove that we weren't just doing what the humans told us to.

A patch of sun streamed in through the trees. I stood in it, reveling in the warmth on my back. I stretched, working out the kinks in my spine and the tightness in my shoulders. Pell smiled at me. We had done well. Tlitoo and Jlela perched in a pine tree, watching us intently.

"The humans don't seem to mind our hunting with them

as equals," Pell said. He was still grinning at me, his mouth wide and his tongue peeking out from between his teeth.

"There's still a long way to go," I warned. It wasn't like Pell to be so overeager. "It's just one hunt."

"If anyone can do it, you can, Kaala," he said. His face softened. "You're extraordinary. I've known you could be a leaderwolf since you were a pup running through the territories with no idea what you were doing. I knew it when I first saw you spying on us at Wolf Killer Hill. You'll be a strong leaderwolf someday. And I want to be there when you are."

I blinked at him. I opened my mouth to answer. Nothing came out.

"It's late in the season, but we still have time to make pups," he said, moving closer to stand next to me in the patch of sun. "Torell wanted me to mate last year, but there wasn't any wolf I wanted. I'm glad I waited."

As I started to protest, he pressed up against me. I knew Pell liked me. I knew it was one of the reasons he left the valley. I wasn't sure how I felt about him and I didn't have time to figure it out now. He would make a good mate for someone—someday. I looked up at Tlitoo, hoping that he would do something, say something, to stop Pell. He and Jlela were watching us curiously. Jlela warbled softly and ran her beak through the ruff of feathers around Tlitoo's neck. They would be no help.

Pell placed his head over my neck and pulled me close to him like I had seen Ruuqo do to Rissa many times. My blood rushed to my head, as it did before a hunt, but I was never so light-headed before hunting. My belly grew warm and my legs weakened. I staggered, but before I could fall, Pell pressed more closely against me so that I was aware of nothing other than his soft fur and warm skin and the beating of his heart.

I stumbled away from him, breathing hard.

"I can't," I gasped. "I'm not old enough to have pups." Wolves did not mate until their second year.

"You are," he said quickly as if he had anticipated my argument. "Some wolves mate in their first year."

I tried to remember what Rissa had told us about having pups. I'd been too busy trying to survive and fulfill the Promise to pay attention.

Pell's warm body drew me. I thought only the humans could pull me to them with such force. I took two steps toward Pell and it took all my strength to stop there. I shook myself hard.

"We don't have time!" I said, starting to get angry. If we failed with the Kaar village, it could mean disaster for wolfkind. TaLi could die. We all could die. Did Pell even care about our task?

"That's why we should be together now," he said. "None of us might live until next year."

"Then why would we have pups?" I argued, my logic reasserting itself. Pell whuffed in frustration. I sat down hard, tucking my tail underneath me and placing my front paws as close to my rear ones as I could. Pell looked at me, confused.

"I thought you liked me, Kaala. That's why I came with you."

"I *do* like you," I said. "But I thought you came to help with the Promise." I stared at him, not sure what to do next. I did like him.

"Kaala," he said, "this may be our best chance." He moved toward me again. My breath started coming faster and faster.

Pell stopped suddenly, then snarled as a scuffling came from the bushes to my right. I jumped to my feet as two wolves tumbled into the clearing.

Pell pinned one of them under his forepaws and growled at the other, who immediately rolled over onto her back.

"What are you doing here?" Pell snarled. "Who sent you?"

"We came to find Kaala," said the wolf he had pinned. My head cleared enough to recognize both wolves. They were Prannan and Amma of the Vole Eater pack back home. They had light gray fur and were small like all Vole Eaters, who got their name because they rarely hunted large prey. Prannan and Amma had offered me their support with the humans in the Wide Valley.

"Leave them alone," I said sharply to Pell. "Let him up."

Pell lowered his ears, looking like a scolded pup rather than a wolf in his prime, and stepped away.

Prannan got to his paws. He dipped his head politely to Pell, but it was to me he came, ears and tail low. He greeted me with a deferential lick to my muzzle. The female Vole Eater, Amma, did the same.

"Why are you here?" I asked, alarmed. "Did the humans kill your pack? Or the Greatwolves?" I couldn't think of any other reason the Vole Eater youngwolves would have ventured so far from home.

"We came to find you, Kaala," Prannan said again.

"I'm Amma," the female said. She was standing next to Pell, her face tight with anxiety as if she thought I might hurt her. I was struck once again at how small the Vole Eaters were.

She was my age, but standing next to Pell she looked like a pup no more than five moons old.

"I remember you," I said. Her face softened.

"May I greet you?" she asked.

"Of course," I said. She bolted forward and licked my muzzle, then stood staring at me. I couldn't figure out what she wanted. Then I remembered how Rissa and Ruuqo greeted us when we'd been away for a long time, when we were still small, and I took Amma's muzzle gently in my mouth. I could feel her whole body relax when I did so. Only then did she and Prannan greet Pell. He watched them, his expression a mix of annoyance and amusement.

Both youngwolves looked expectantly at me. I didn't know what they wanted.

"Vole Eater is safe?" I asked again.

"They're fine," Prannan answered.

"Why did you leave, then?" I asked him. "Now you don't have a pack." I couldn't imagine anyone leaving the safety of a pack if they didn't have to.

"Kaala," Pell said softly.

Prannan blinked up at me, his tail falling down between his legs. Then he looked away.

"I understand if you don't want us in your pack. We aren't very strong. But we'll help you hunt and help you with the humans, and then you can decide if you want us."

"My pack?" I said. They thought we were a real pack, just as Lallna had. They had left their home to join me. I needed to tell them they were wrong and get them back to the Wide Valley. I couldn't guarantee their safety. And I didn't need any more responsibilities.

"Wolflet," Tlitoo said, winging down to land next to me. "It does not matter if you are a pack leader or not. They need one. And you do not know what the future holds or what wolves you may need. They are in no more danger here than in their home."

I snapped my teeth at him, getting only a mouthful of air as he flew away. Then I looked back at Prannan and Amma. They were both trying to avert their gaze, but kept sneaking hopeful looks at me. I remembered the way Rissa had welcomed me into the pack when I was a smallpup. The way she and Trevegg had accepted me and taught me the way of wolf when Ruuqo spurned me.

"You can stay with us," I said.

Their ears shot up and they pelted at me so quickly and enthusiastically that they knocked me over. I got back to my paws. "You'll need to stay away from the humans for now," I said.

"We know," Amma said. "The raven man doesn't want too many wolves with them at once and you are supposed to go slowly and carefully and not frighten them." She stopped when she ran out of breath.

I stared at her, wondering how long they had been following us. Then I laughed. "Raven man" was a good name for RalZun.

Ázzuen dashed into the clearing then, panting. He looked at Pell and frowned. Pell was staring at me. I caught his amber-eyed gaze and for a moment couldn't look away.

I looked guiltily at Ázzuen but he just opened his mouth in a smile.

"Hello, Prannan. Hello, Amma." The Vole Eater wolves

wagged their tails at him. Ázzuen greeted each of them with a gentle nip to their muzzles, then poked me in the ribs.

"Your girl is looking for you," he said. "Their leader wants us to come to the village!"

It was exactly what we'd hoped for. The humans wanted us to come to their home, which meant we had the chance to win them over. I felt a smile pull at my muzzle. It had taken us less than a day to get them to ask us into their territory.

I looked back at Pell. He was watching me as if he was preparing for another hunt.

He touched his nose to my face. "I'll take some meat to the Sentinels." He smiled down at Amma and Prannan. "You can come with me partway if you like."

They yipped in agreement, and when he took some elk meat in his jaws and trotted into the woods, they followed. I took a couple of steps after him.

"Come on, Kaala," Ázzuen said, exasperated. "What are we waiting for?"

I looked over my shoulder into his bright, eager eyes and my desire to follow Pell melted away.

We could win the humans. I knew we could. I woofed to Ázzuen and took off toward the human village.

9

It was like no human dwelling I'd ever seen.

At the center of the village was a clearing. This was true of most human gathering places, but this one was so huge that every wolf I'd ever met could lie nose to tail across it and not reach from one end to the other. It seemed more the size of a hunting plain than a gathering place, and it felt so open and exposed that I cringed as if some great bird might swoop down upon me. I hadn't felt that way since I was a pup, small enough to fear owls in the night.

Deerskins and elk hides were stacked in piles taller than two standing wolves, and large structures rose twice the height of an ordinary human shelter. They had stone bases, like the ones in TaLi's home, but the tops were made of weavings of branches and hides. There were huge piles of the carved stones and sharpened bones that the humans used to make their hunting, cutting, and scraping tools, and all around us rose the scents of more humans than I would have believed there were in the entire world.

RalZun led Ázzuen and me through the smaller outer clearings that surrounded the largest central one. He had insisted that only the two of us accompany him, fearing that more wolves would overwhelm the humans. They didn't seem overwhelmed to me. As we walked through the village, they gathered around us. They made no threatening moves and they all kept at least a full wolflength away, but I couldn't help but feel I was being stalked. I walked as closely as I could to Ázzuen. Tlitoo kept pace with us, flying low at first, then landing to walk beside us.

RalZun held out an arm to stop us six wolflengths from where a group of humans stood atop a flat rock. The human leader, HesMi, and the sour IniMin were among them. All of them stared at us. Among wolves, such an aggressive gaze would be a challenge, but humans didn't understand our ways.

"Wait here until I call to you," RalZun ordered, stalking toward the rock.

A cluster of small humans ran in front of us. There were at least eight of them, all younger than MikLan. A group of even smaller ones galloped behind them, shrieking in high-pitched voices that hurt my ears. I noticed that one child ran apart from the others and that whenever he tried to join the larger group, one or another of the children would push him away.

"How will they hunt enough prey to feed so many young?" Ázzuen whispered, his eyes darting around the clearing, where still more humans were gathering. "How will they find enough plants to eat? They feed from the forest as much as any deer."

"They think they can control every bit of forest," Tlitoo quorked. "They wish to replace trees with the plants they eat. And they plan to kill any creatures that compete with them for prey."

That kind of thinking went against the very heart of the Balance. We killed foxes and hyenas that tried to steal from us, but we wouldn't seek them out to kill them because they might take our prey someday. A wolf who did so would be considered insane and sent away from the pack.

Humans, like wolves, had lived most of their existence following the prey they hunted. They ate as many plants as prey, and moved from place to place to find food. Until recently. By the time I was born, the humans stayed longer in one place and built larger villages, destroying the land around them and taking more than their fair share of prey. But I had seen nothing like this.

RalZun flapped his arms at us, which I took to mean he wanted us to come to him. Humans had gathered in front of us by then, but they parted as we walked toward RalZun and the humans atop the rock. I was grateful for that; it allowed me to breathe. When I saw TaLi and BreLan beside the old man, I forgot myself and dashed to the girl, stopping only when TaLi crouched down to me. Ázzuen was right behind me, running to greet BreLan. I froze, then, thinking the humans might be upset that we had charged across their territory, but I heard a laugh and looked up to see HesMi smiling down at me.

"They're quite friendly," she said to TaLi. I wagged my tail. HesMi spoke to RalZun.

"They followed the girl from the Spruce Valley?" she asked.

"They did," RalZun said.

The humans on the rock began murmuring to one another. They spoke so quickly that I could pick out words but not hear exactly what they were saying. The woman called HesMi held up both arms and they fell silent. When she spoke, her words had the feel of ritual.

"We have agreed that we will choose who will be trained to be our next krianan at the Spring Festival." Her voice filled the clearing. "RalZun has brought us TaLi, granddaughter of NiaLi, who served us so well." She held out a hand to TaLi. "You believe that we should continue with the old ways?" she asked the girl.

NiaLi had once told us that TaLi would need the approval of village elders to become krianan. This was her chance. She took the woman's hand and climbed upon the rock. Standing tall, she addressed the gathered humans.

"Like my grandmother before me and her mother before her, and all of their ancestors before them, I believe that we must share the world around us with other creatures. While we must protect and feed ourselves and fight for what is ours, we cannot kill every animal who hunts that which we hunt, nor destroy the forests around us in our attempts to gain more land. I believe, as my grandmother did, that it is the role of the krianan to ensure that we do not give into our pride, that we do not destroy what surrounds us or take too much or kill too often." The words were familiar. They were the ones TaLi's grandmother had spoken so many moons ago, when I had first learned of the krianans and their role in human lives. TaLi and I had spied on the old woman when she spoke with the Greatwolves of the Wide Valley.

TaLi lifted her voice. "We must learn from the creatures who share our lands, and keep the Balance, so that we and those who come after us can live in harmony with the world." She nodded to HesMi and jumped down off the rock. RalZun watched her, pleased.

IniMin stepped forward. Tlitoo thrummed a warning.

"Be careful of that one, wolf. He will pretend to be friendly, but he will scheme like a hyena at your kill. The krianans who live in the forest stay away from the village because he has made the elders suspicious of them."

IniMin smiled at the assembled humans. *If I didn't know better, I would have thought him friendly.* "We live in a dangerous world," he began. "There are beasts that live only to kill us, and those who will steal the very food we and our children need to survive. The only way we can survive is to control the wildness around us. More than that, it is our sacred duty to do so." His voice rose. "We used to be one beast among many, running wild and no better than these brutish wolves who stand before us." *I had to stop myself from snarling at that.* "We are not like those beasts anymore. We have been chosen from among all others to lead. It is our duty to tame that which is wild and to remove the dangers from the lands around us. Why else would we be the only creatures in the world to stand tall, to use tools, and to build homes? Why are we the only creatures able to speak, and think, and plan?"

"The wolves think!" TaLi said. "They talk. We just don't understand them."

A few of the humans laughed at her. HesMi frowned at the girl. "You've had your chance to speak," she said. TaLi looked rebellious, but stayed silent. DavRian had said something similar about humans and their tools back in the Wide Valley. It unnerved me to hear the same belief here.

"I've finished," IniMin said. "And I admire young TaLi's passion." He, too, stepped down from the rock, an insincere smile stretching his face.

He was so condescending, I wanted to bite him. And I couldn't believe that he thought that humans were supposed to control every beast in the land. He sounded like a Great-wolf!

HesMi nodded to TaLi.

"I met NiaLi when I was not much older than you. You look like her, and you have her grace. I am pleased to welcome you as RalZun's candidate for krianan."

"Thank you," TaLi said formally. "I would be honored to serve as your krianan."

The human leader spoke more sharply to IniMin. "Do you know when your brother's son will arrive?" she demanded.

"No," he said respectfully. "I know that he is on his way."

"He's a good candidate, IniMin, but we won't wait forever."

"I don't expect you to." He smiled. "In the meantime, I look forward to seeing how useful these wolves really are."

"IniMin's nephew is his candidate for krianan," HesMi said to TaLi. "He now lives in another village, but has spent many winters in Kaar, as did his father before him."

A soft scrabbling drew my attention to the tartberry bushes at the far edge of the clearing. A wolf was lying flat on its belly, so that just its head and forepaws were visible as it peered into the village. It was much too small to be Milsindra or even Lallna, and at first I thought that Prannan or Amma had snuck into the village. Then I looked more closely. There was something wrong with the little wolf. Its head was too round and its muzzle too short. I tried to make eye contact with it to warn it away. Kaar was my territory now, and no strange wolf should trespass.

RalZun pulled on my ear. I yelped.

"Were you paying attention?"

"Yes."

He glowered at me. Prannan's name for him was apt. He was every bit as bossy as a raven.

Ázzuen pushed between me and the old human. "HesMi said that IniMin has to get his candidate here in three days, and then they'll decide by their Spring Festival on Even Night who their next krianan will be," he said.

I felt a surge of confidence. TaLi's challenger wasn't here yet. We had hunted with the humans, and HesMi liked TaLi. For the first time since we had left the valley, I believed we could succeed. We had a long way to go in a short time, but we had done well so far. Ignoring RalZun's irritated huffing, I nosed Ázzuen's muzzle and trotted toward TaLi.

"Let's go," I said, looking back at Ázzuen. We had work to do.

10

For the rest of that day and through the night, Ázzuen and I stayed at the edges of the human homesite, letting the humans grow accustomed to us. The next morning, we dared to slink close to their fires. None of them seemed to mind. Marra then joined us in the village, and when her presence didn't make the humans nervous, Pell arrived, too, though he refused to come any closer than the very edge of the largest clearing. I waited for our next task, but the humans seemed in no hurry to have us prove ourselves. I bit back my impatience. Though Even Night was near, I didn't want to frighten the humans by pushing them too hard. Finally, when our second day with the humans was half over, TaLi and MikLan came to find us. When Pell saw them, he slipped back into the woods.

"We've been invited to swim with some of the younger villagers," TaLi said excitedly. "They want you to come, too. They said that hunting with you was the most fun they've had in moons!"

I panted a smile at her. Young humans always took to us more quickly than their elders. If we could get them to like us as much as TaLi, BreLan, and MikLan did, they could influence the others. TaLi galloped from the village. Ázzuen, Marra, and I followed.

🔲

The young humans cavorted in a stream a five-minute lope from Kaar. It was shallow enough that I didn't have to worry about TaLi. The humans were all about the same age as TaLi and BreLan—near or just past adulthood—and they had the energy and sense of fun of youngwolves. My tail began to wag as our humans waded in to join them. A moment later, we splashed in, too. The water was cool and tasted of minnows. I could smell Pell's willow and wind sage scent nearby and wondered if he was hiding in the bushes watching us.

The males wrestled like youngwolves seeking dominance, dunking one another under the water and splashing the females. TaLi, giggling, splashed them back. When one of them tossed an armful of water on me, I charged him, knocking him onto his rump. The other humans whooped in laughter as the male I'd knocked over tried to dunk me. I let him chase me around, stumbling in the knee-deep water. When I smelled him getting frustrated, I allowed him to catch me and push me over. He grinned and rubbed the fur between my ears. My chest warmed as it did when I lay side by side with TaLi.

I waded out of the stream to find Marra and Ázzuen soaking wet and being chased by a group of young humans. The humans all had huge smiles on their faces. I shook the water from my fur and lay down next to TaLi, basking in the afternoon sun.

"Can your wolves hunt anything besides elk?" a male asked TaLi, stretching out beside her.

"They can hunt everything," she said. "We've hunted elkryn, horses, and aurochs with them."

The other human grunted. Then a slow grin spread across his face.

"Do you have rock bears in the Spruce Valley?"

"Yes," BreLan said.

"Grass lions?" the young human asked.

"Of course," TaLi said, beginning to sound annoyed.

The young human's grin widened. "Are you and your wolves afraid of them?"

When our humans just glared at him, the young human got to his feet.

"Come on," he said.

TaLi and BreLan stood, and Ázzuen and I got to our paws. We all knew a dare when we heard one. MikLan was fast asleep, Marra at his side. She raised her head and yawned, then set her head on MikLan's chest and began to snore.

I followed the humans from the stream, wondering what we were getting ourselves into.

⊡

The humans stopped in a copse of rough-trunked trees and dense bushes. I watched as they clustered together like a herd of prey, hiding under the cover of the thick brush. A pungent, meaty scent wafted from just beyond the trees. I knew I'd smelled it before, but couldn't place it.

Whispering now, the humans pushed through the brush. Sharp thorns scratched their skin where they wore no preyskins and I pitied them their lack of fur. I wondered if the humans had long ago lost their fur and then learned to make clothing, or the other way around. I was so focused on my thoughts that it wasn't until we were at the very edge of the plain that I saw them: an elk carcass, stripped almost bare, and three longfangs guarding it. I swallowed a yip of fear.

I'd never seen a live longfang before, and had only picked up their scent after they were long, long gone from a place. Now that I was closer to them, I understood how the scent of these living beasts became the strong taste of the fang TaLi wore around her neck as the symbol of her role as krianan.

The longfangs were more than twice the size of a grown wolf and had flat, light-colored fur that reminded me more of the pelt of prey than that of a hunter. Even from a distance, I could see the long, curved fangs that gave them their name. With these fangs, they could spear prey through the neck, sometimes causing it to bleed to death, sometimes crushing the air from its throat. A single longfang could take down an elkryn or an auroch. We never, ever competed with them for prey. Hyenas did, once the prey was dead, but they weren't good at hunting on their own and, as much as I hated to admit it, they were better at stealing prey than we were.

The humans were murmuring with fear and excitement.

"HesMi won't let us fight them if they come after our kills," a girl said, "even though we could win if we wanted to."

I heard a chortle from above. Tlitoo peered down from a high branch.

"What would happen if one of your wolves fought one?" asked the male who had dunked me.

"I don't want to find out," TaLi said.

I looked from her to the other humans. Human groups were ruled by dominance just like any wolf pack, and with courage came status.

I turned my back to the humans and watched the long-fangs. The three adults hunched over the carcass. The cubs, as they called their young, tugged at a piece of hide that still had thick strips of meat hanging from it. Each cub was trying to eat it, but whenever one got close to doing so, the other would snatch it away.

"I want that hide," I said to Ázzuen. If I could steal it, I would impress the young humans. I expected Ázzuen to tell me it wasn't safe, but mischief lit his eyes and his mouth opened in a grin.

"Let's get it, then," he said.

Two adult longfangs chased the third away from the car-cass. She tried once to go back to it and they rushed at her, growling fiercely. One of them reared up on its haunches and swiped at her. The two cubs darted to her side.

The cubs were thin and lanky and about two-thirds the size of the adults. Longfangs grew more slowly than wolves did. It took them two years to reach adult size, which meant that the cubs were about our age, but only as mature as a pup four months out of the den. The longfang who had to be their mother looked down at them and then back at the dead elk.

Slowly, she crawled on her belly toward the carcass where the other two longfangs continued to feed.

There was still quite a bit of meat on the bones. The cubs mewed and, though I didn't speak their language, I knew it was a cry of hunger. Their mother tried to sneak in to get some of the carcass and the feeding longfangs growled at her. She backed off again. She lay down on her belly, staring at the other longfangs and the meat they guarded. The cubs watched her for a moment, then began their battle for the hide again. Ázzuen's breathing quickened. He was watching the cubs as intently as the mother longfang was watching the carcass, and the tip of his tail twitched as it did before a hunt.

The cubs were energetic in spite of their hunger. They were bigger than we were, and, unlike prey, they had sharp fangs and teeth. It was too risky to just run out and grab the hide from them. I snuck a look at Ázzuen out of the corner of my eye, ashamed that I had to ask his advice yet again. If I wanted to be a leaderwolf, I should've been able to come up with my own ideas.

Ázzuen bent close to me to whisper in my ear. A slight crackling of the undergrowth was all the warning we had before a black shape darted from the bushes and a sharp beak grabbed Ázzuen's tail.

Ázzuen yelped and the longfangs looked up from the plain. Tlitoo chuckled deep in his throat and stared at our noses. I covered mine protectively with my paws and saw that Ázzuen had done the same.

I snarled at Tlitoo. He chuckled again.

"You are so fearsome you will scare the beetles, wolf,

with that snarl. I am here to help you. I will distract them and you will grab the hide. It will be fun. You have been too dour of late.

> *"Dark times need more play*
> *And gloomy wolves are boring.*
> *Thus the ravens come.*

"Make them think you are playing," he quorked. "That you are doing nothing. Then steal."

"I could have told you that," Ázzuen said.

"But you did not, wolf."

"Because you bit me before I could!" Ázzuen protested, his voice rising. The longfang cubs looked in our direction.

"You should not be so loud, wolflet," Tlitoo quorked, and flew to a rock in the middle of the plain. He set his beady gaze on the longfangs and began making low, growling noises, sounding exactly like a wolf. I hadn't known he could do that. Every longfang on the plain, even the two at the carcass, were now looking at him.

Tlitoo was annoying, but he was right. A little trickery was in order. And Ázzuen was better at it than I was.

"You lead," I said to him. He looked at me, a gleam of pleasure in his eyes. Then he licked the top of my head. Warmth rushed through me, and I had to blink to clear my vision as Ázzuen crawled forward on his belly. I noticed the smooth play of muscles under his fur. When he was younger, his lankiness made him awkward. Now it gave him a fluid grace as he slid through the grass, as sinewy as a lizard. He looked over his shoulder at me and I realized I was staring at him like an idiot. Flattening myself as low as I could, I followed him.

Ázzuen stayed on his belly until we were well onto the grass, then stood and began to trot around the perimeter of the plain. I followed.

"Silvermoon!" TaLi gasped behind me. "Kaala! Get back here."

She started to follow, but BreLan held her back. The other humans whispered excitedly.

The mother longfang saw us immediately and lifted her head to stare, her gaze so piercing that I was tempted to stop in my tracks. But Ázzuen kept moving, so I did, too. We ran as if we were just exploring the plain, and the longfang went back to gazing at the carcass. As long as she didn't see us as a threat, she would leave us be.

Both of the cubs now seemed more intent on winning their game than on actually getting any of the meat. They were snarling at each other and tussling over the hide, growling fiercely as if they were fighting in earnest, but I saw how their thin, vine-like tails whipped in circles. My own tail began to wave.

We trotted a few paces closer to the cubs. Intent on their game, they didn't notice us. We dropped down on our bellies once again and began to creep forward, very slowly. When we got close enough that a quick run would bring us to them, Ázzuen whispered to me, "Go around to the other side and get their attention."

I touched my nose to his muzzle. It seemed unfair to take advantage of their immaturity, but Tlitoo was right. It was fun. We weren't going to hurt them.

I got behind the cubs and gave a soft whuff. Both cubs looked up, and one dropped his end of the hide. Ázzuen darted forward and grabbed it. The cub still holding on pulled with enough force to tear the hide from Ázzuen's mouth. Ázzuen growled fiercely at her and she jumped back, pulling the hide with her and tumbling into her brother. I growled, too, and the cubs flattened their ears and snarled at me. Ázzuen trotted away, then circled back behind the cubs while they were watching me. I ran in, butting the rump of the empty-mouthed cub with my head. He yowled and swiped at me, and I stumbled backward. I had forgotten about their sharp, deadly claws. I smelled the cub's fear, and bent my forelegs and raised my rump to show him I was playing. He watched me closely and retracted his claws.

"Ours," he growled. But it was a playful growl. He said something I couldn't understand to his sister, who still held the hide in her jaws. The two of them took off across the plain—right into Ázzuen. I pounced on them from behind.

We scuffled and rolled in the dirt and, for a moment, it was like playing with Ázzuen and Marra and our humans. The cubs were stronger than we were, but clumsier. I twisted under and around them, avoiding swats from their large paws. I scrambled to my feet and whuffed encouragement at the cub closest to me.

Then a mountain of muscle and fur hit me from behind. The mother longfang pinned me with one great paw. Ázzuen threw himself at her and she knocked him aside with her head. The two cubs immediately began wrestling with him, keeping him from getting to me. The longfang opened her great jaws and bent her head down to my exposed throat.

She had golden eyes that held a sad, weary expression. I couldn't look at them long, not with those fangs so close to my face.

"Pups," she grumbled, her voice low and raspy. "Stupid little pups. Go back to your pack. We have no time for games." She pressed her paw down on my chest and extended her long claws. I lowered my ears to her and she grunted and retracted her claws. I lay there for a moment, caught in her amber gaze. There was a sorrow I had not seen since my pack learned that Yllin, one of Swift River's youngwolves, had been killed by Greatwolves. "Go, pup," she said, stepping off me. "Play somewhere else."

She snarled something at her own young. When they looked up at her, I heaved myself up, grabbed the hide in my jaws, and ran. Ázzuen darted under the longfang mother's belly, making her stumble. We raced back to the woods.

TaLi and MikLan were running toward us, spears raised. When they saw we were safe, they skidded to a halt. Pell bolted past them. The expression of fear on his face made me stumble and trip over the hide, and Ázzuen crashed into me from behind. We scrambled to our paws and ran. Only when Pell, TaLi, and MikLan had all reached the safety of the woods did I look back at the longfangs.

The mother, her head lowered between her shoulders, led her pups in the other direction, away from us and from where the other longfangs had dragged the carcass. There was such heaviness in her tread that I began to feel a little sorry that we had stolen from her.

"Are you all right?" Pell demanded, sniffing me all over.

Ázzuen pushed between us. "We're both fine. Thanks for asking."

TaLi sank to her knees and threw her arms around me.

"Don't ever do that again, Kaala," she said.

"You either," BreLan said to Ázzuen. His voice was so stern I looked up. I hadn't realized how worried for us our humans would be.

I gave the hide to TaLi, nudging her toward the other young humans. She tossed it to a young male, who snatched it out of the air, grinned at me, and took off at a run toward the village, whooping and waving the hide above his head.

The other humans bolted after him. Pell, after checking me over anxiously one more time, slipped back into the woods to follow at a distance. Ázzuen and I ran with our humans most of the way back to Kaar, but as we neared the village, I grew impatient with their slow pace.

I nipped Ázzuen on the ear.

"Race you back to the village."

He yipped and took off running. We tore through the woods, jumping over the bushes and fallen branches, the late-afternoon sun warming our fur. Tlitoo dipped and arced above us, screeching encouragement. I felt like I could fly up to join him. We had spent two days with the humans, and they already admired us and treated us as pack. It was as if we were meant to be with them. If I hadn't been out of breath, I would have howled in triumph.

Ázzuen and I pelted into Kaar, side by side, and stopped, panting. There was a scent in the village that was familiar, a scent that made my throat close in fear.

A group of humans clustered together, their attention on a stocky male standing in their midst. I saw IniMin first, with his back to us, a young female at his side. HesMi looked at the newcomer, her arms crossed over her chest. I sneezed twice, expelling the new human's scent. My nose had known who it was before my eyes did.

DavRian turned and met my gaze with a cold stare. He pointed at me.

"That's the one," he said. "That's the wolf that killed the old woman."

11

I wasn't the one who'd killed her. It was DavRian who had murdered NiaLi, slicing her throat with his spear. He'd carried TaLi to her village and told the humans there that I'd killed the old woman. When I tried to rescue TaLi, he aimed his spear at my heart and lunged. I dodged just in time, deflecting his spear into my haunch.

I didn't kill her, but her death was at least partly my fault. I'd angered DavRian and had not thought of the risk to the old woman. Remembering her crumpled body, I began to back away in shame. What if I really did bring only death to those I loved?

"We called her 'Bloody Moon,' in the Spruce Valley," DavRian said, pointing his spear at me. "Because of the mark on her chest and because she stalked us."

I stopped and looked down at my chest. My fur was stained with blood from the hide we'd stolen from the long-fang cubs. Tlitoo landed next to me.

"Be careful, wolf. There is something here we have not been told."

"Will they attack now?" a human male asked, staring at my open mouth. I was out of breath from our dash to the village and couldn't stop panting. My tongue hung out and all of my teeth showed. Ázzuen, too, was panting hard, his sharp teeth exposed.

I waited for the humans to pull out their sharpsticks and hurl them at us. I almost bolted. But I knew that if I ran away, I would lose the ground I'd gained in the last two days. I looked from HesMi to DavRian, trying to figure out what to do. Then Ázzuen closed his mouth, rolled onto his back, and waved his legs in the air. A human laughed. I forced my own mouth closed, my ribs heaving with the effort to control my panting. I felt the tension around us ease.

TaLi and BreLan burst into the village, arms linked, laughing and gasping for air. TaLi stopped when she saw DavRian. BreLan did not. He hurled himself at the other human, knocking him flat to the ground. I reached TaLi with one leap, and stood between her and DavRian. Ázzuen scrambled to his feet and placed himself in front of me.

"Guard TaLi's left side!" I said. DavRian could easily slip by me to grab her.

Ázzuen planted his paws more firmly. It was me he was protecting, not TaLi. He lowered his head and glowered at DavRian.

BreLan slammed DavRian's head to the ground. "I'll kill you," he bellowed. "By the Ancients, I will."

Within two breaths, he'd used his strong legs to pin DavRian's arms to his sides, his hands around DavRian's neck. It took three large humans to pull him off.

"Let me go!" BreLan shouted. "He's a murderer. He killed NiaLi and almost killed TaLi." His voice broke. "He almost killed her because he wanted her and couldn't have her."

Murmurs rose from the humans around us. DavRian staggered to his feet, choking.

"He's a liar," DavRian gasped. "The girl entranced him." His voice was ragged. "All the wolf-krianans of the Spruce Valley can do it."

Several humans laughed. It was a ridiculous thing to say.

"It's true," DavRian said, a sulky tone entering his voice. "Yours probably do it, too."

"It is something I have heard as well." I squinted to see where the voice came from. It was IniMin. He set down a small sack he was carrying. "It is one of the reasons we need to break away from the old ways, and bring a new kind of krianan to guide us. We need to control the wildness around us, not welcome it into our homes."

He smiled his insincere smile at TaLi. "It appears that you know my brother's son, DavRian," he said.

"He's your brother's son?" TaLi asked. "The one you were waiting for?"

A growl rumbled in my chest. DavRian was the young man IniMin had mentioned. And thus his candidate for krianan. He was as far from what a krianan should be than any human I'd ever met.

"Quiet, wolf," Tlitoo warned. "This is not a good time to growl at humans."

"The Rian village of the Spruce Valley was started by those who left Kaar to find new lands," HesMi told TaLi. "There are villages related to us in every land we know of." She spoke

with pride. Navdru had said that Kaar's influence went beyond the village itself. I hadn't imagined it spread as far as the
Wide Valley.

A human female spoke. "If DavRian says that the wolves
killed NiaLi, we shouldn't have them here."

"He's lying about NiaLi," BreLan said, catching his breath.
"He killed her himself and blamed the wolves." Ázzuen
swayed on his paws, clearly wanting to go to his human.

"Why would he do that?" HesMi asked, a frown wrinkling
her forehead, her strong arms crossed over her chest.

"He's mad." The calm, steady voice came from behind me.
I whipped my head around to see TaLi, her face still, her
stance confident. She had pulled the longfang tooth—the
symbol of her role as krianan—from her tunic so that it hung
visible on her chest.

"He makes up stories about enthrallers and fierce wolves.
He killed my grandmother and hurt me." She pulled back her
hair to show the healing wound where DavRian had struck
her when he'd killed NiaLi. "The leaders of all the villages
wanted him dead, so he wouldn't hurt anyone else, but his father wouldn't allow it."

DavRian blinked at her stupidly. The last part was a lie
and a good one. No one in Kaar could know which human
was speaking the truth.

"She's right," BreLan said.

"Were you there when the old woman died?" IniMin
asked him. "Did you see it happen?"

"No," BreLan admitted. "TaLi told me."

HesMi's frown deepened. DavRian seized on her uncertainty. "He wasn't there. He believes anything she tells him."

IniMin cleared his throat. "This is why I have tried to convince you to keep the wolves away from us. They are unpredictable and dangerous. They can go from friend to enemy in an instant and kill us as we sleep. It is the nature of the wild and we must guard against it."

RalZun strode into the village, stopping at my side. I snarled up at him.

"You should have told us that DavRian was IniMin's nephew," I snapped.

"You should have told me that you let him follow you!" he rasped back.

He stalked to HesMi.

"IniMin speaks nonsense," the old man said. "No one can be enchanted by a wolf. He's a fool to think so. The wolves helped us before and they can help us now."

"They swam with us at the stream without hurting us." That was the young male who had dunked me.

"And they gave us this," another male said, holding up the hide we had taken from the cubs. They said nothing about the longfangs. I was certain that they were not supposed to go anywhere near them.

"I like them," a young female said.

"They're dangerous," DavRian countered, "no matter how friendly they seem."

All around us, humans rumbled and whispered and shouted. They were like a group of ravens before they mobbed something.

"Wolflets," Tlitoo whispered, "if you let them argue, they will talk themselves so far into fear they will not be able to find their way out. Show them."

"Show them what?"

"Show who the dangerous one really is," he said, nodding to a small sack at IniMin's feet.

I caught his meaning and grinned at him, then started to trot through the crowd.

"Where are you going?" Ázzuen whispered.

"To provoke IniMin," I answered.

The other humans fell silent as I padded toward IniMin. He leaned back when I drew near him, but did not step away. Without bothering to meet his gaze, I took the sack at his feet and held it in my mouth. Then I looked up at him.

Had he been a rational human, he would have just let me take the pouch, but he reminded me of DavRian, who could never bear to look foolish. IniMin didn't disappoint me. He kicked out at me and shoved the blunt end of his sharpstick at me. I dodged it easily, trotted to HesMi, and dropped the sack at her feet. She chuckled.

"You would have deserved it if she'd bitten you, IniMin," she said. I licked her wrist. She rested her hand on my back and I heard the slowing of her heart, a sound I'd come to associate with humans when they stroked us.

"She likes having her ears scratched," RalZun said.

"I remember," HesMi said. She rubbed the fur between my ears gently. I leaned against her.

"These wolves don't behave like killers," she said, "and DavRian hasn't spent enough time with us for me to know whether to trust him more than NiaLi's granddaughter." She stroked my back. "I accept DavRian as your candidate, Ini-Min," she said, "but I don't want to hear any more about enchantments. As for whether or not they are dangerous, we can keep an eye on a few wolves until the festival. They're easy enough to kill if needed."

She strode across the clearing and ducked into one of the shelters. DavRian and IniMin watched her go, then crouched down to whisper together while the other humans dispersed around the village. When the humans holding BreLan released him, he staggered to TaLi and RalZun. Ázzuen and I ran to join them.

TaLi released a long breath.

"Now what?" she asked RalZun.

"Now prove to them that you're the best candidate. Your wolves have impressed HesMi, as have you."

He sounded sure of himself, but I was worried about what DavRian might do. I hadn't counted on his interference. I'd never imagined that he would be TaLi's competition for krianan. As TaLi, BreLan, and RalZun spoke quietly to one another, and Ázzuen paced beside them, I worried. I'd failed so many times before. I couldn't bear to do so again. I needed help.

My mother had told me to find her if I needed her. I'd hoped that it would be more than two days before I did so, but I had no idea what to do about DavRian. As soon as the late afternoon light faded, I went in search of her. I picked up her scent at the stream where I'd first found her, and followed it to a shady grove of cypress. She was napping lightly in the cooling air.

"I can't do it," I said, the moment she awoke. "DavRian is here, and he's telling the humans we'll kill them. A lot of them believe him. There's no way I can prove he's lying before Even Night. I need more time."

"You can't have more time, Kaala, you know that. The Sentinels won't allow it."

"Then some older wolf should do it. You should do it. I can't."

She got to her feet. "You lost the right to give up when you refused to leave your human girl. If you were going to run away with your tail between your legs, you should have stayed with Ruuqo and Rissa and left the humans alone."

I had expected at least some sympathy or advice. She sighed when she saw my hurt expression and nosed my cheek. She trotted off in the direction of Kaar. "Come with me."

I was so angry that she had scolded me that I almost stayed where I was. Instead, ears and tail low, I followed her.

▣

I had never seen any place so beautiful.

The moonlight illuminated lush grass that smelled of recent prey. Tall pine trees and thick juniper reminded me of home, and a stream burbled nearby, promising fresh, clear water. The stretch of land before us was a mix of hunting plains and dense woods and I couldn't help but smile as I looked down on it.

My mother and I lay on a small hill overlooking the good land, breathing in its rich scents.

"I wanted to show you this, Kaala," she said, "so that you know what you fight for. Navdru told me that this land is yours if you succeed with the humans. It's close enough to the human village that you can spend as much time as you need to with your girl and the other humans, and still take care of your pack."

"My pack," I said. "My own pack?" Navdru had said he'd find a way to reward me.

She dipped her head. "Hiiln and I thought we would raise a pack here. But he is gone and I won't have pups with another."

Hiiln was Ruuqo's brother, and he was supposed to have been Rissa's mate and the leader of Swift River. When he'd refused to stay away from the humans, he'd been chased from the valley, and Ruuqo and Rissa took over Swift River. I didn't know that he and Neesa had been mates.

"He died?" I asked. She'd said he was gone.

"He was killed," she answered.

"I'm sorry," I said, and she inclined her head to me.

My own head buzzed. Hiiln had been drawn to the humans and he was Neesa's mate. He had to have been my father. I ached to ask Neesa, but I didn't have the nerve.

"I thought I'd go back to the Wide Valley after Even Night," I said.

"You might be able to for a little while," she said, "but if you succeed, the humans will still need to be watched over."

And if I don't, I thought, there won't be a pack to go back to.

My mother looked down at me. "What did you think would happen after TaLi became their krianan? You would have to stay nearby."

I hadn't thought that far ahead. I felt a pang of sorrow at the thought of not returning to the Wide Valley. Then I looked again at the good land before me. I wanted it. I wanted it as much as I wanted to be at TaLi's side.

I thought about Pell's offer. He wanted to have pups with

me and he had, I knew now, left the Wide Valley not to fulfill the Promise, but to be with me. Yet when I envisioned myself with pups and a pack in the beautiful land before me, it wasn't Pell's face I saw at my side.

As if my thoughts had summoned him, Ázzuen crept up beside us.

"You weren't there when I came back," he reproved, then greeted Neesa.

Neesa returned his greeting. "I remember you now," she said to him. "You're Rissa's smallest pup. You hadn't been given a name when I left. Ruuqo and Rissa were certain you'd die before winter."

If a pack believed a pup was too weak to survive, they would not name him. Everyone expected Ázzuen to die before he was old enough to hunt.

"What happened?" Neesa asked him. "How did you live?"

"Kaala helped me," Ázzuen said.

We had helped each other, fighting together against the bigger pups.

My mother looked from Ázzuen to me and back again, a small smile on her face.

"Then I hope you will continue to do so," she said. "The Sentinels will no longer let me be with the humans, Kaala. It has to be you. But I will give you what guidance I can." She smiled again at Ázzuen. "And you are not alone in your task."

⊡

We left my mother and returned to Kaar.

"I have some ideas about how we can make DavRian look like the fool he is," Ázzuen said as we trotted into the village.

"He's not as smart as IniMin. He hates us and he's still in love with TaLi. He lets his emotions affect him too much. He'll make mistakes." He panted a grin. "We can help him make big ones."

"We should just concentrate on making ourselves valuable to the humans," I said. "We have to show them that choosing TaLi as krianan is their best choice."

Ázzuen looked at me like I was the most naive pup he'd ever met. "DavRian will be looking for ways to make us fail. You know he will. You're too trusting, Kaala. You're honest and so you expect others to be, too. It's why you trusted the Greatwolves so often back home."

"I'm not." But I'd been fooled more than I liked to admit. I didn't acknowledge the other reason I wanted to avoid a battle with DavRian: I was still afraid of him. I walked to a small fire pit and lay down next to it. Ázzuen stretched out next to me. My eyes grew heavy. I tried to keep them open.

"We should sleep." Ázzuen yawned. "We need to rest for the next hunt."

I wanted to protest but could only yawn back at him. I heard TaLi's footsteps and looked up as she settled beside me. "We can do it, Kaala," she said. "We can show them that their lives are better with wolves here." Her voice faltered. "RalZun will help me."

I twisted my neck around to lick her face. I wished I could tell her that I would do whatever I could to help her. She fell asleep with one long arm slung over me. I listened to her even breathing. Failing in Kaar would mean failing TaLi, and that's something I would never do.

12

A cold nose in my ear woke me. I opened my eyes to find Ázzuen standing impatiently over me.

"Is it time for another hunt?" I mumbled, trying to blink away sleep. The sun was just rising, and the air was cool and moist. I yawned.

"Wake up, Kaala," he said. "I have an idea."

Of course he did. Ázzuen probably got ideas in his sleep.

He galloped across the huge clearing. I got to my paws and stretched. TaLi rolled to a sitting position and watched sleepily as I followed Ázzuen. Marra slept next to MikLan by the warmth of a fire.

I stopped when I saw a group of human young staring at me, all smaller than TaLi was when I first pulled her from the river.

They watched me intently, and I wondered if they were afraid. I relaxed my face into the soft, welcoming expression Rissa greeted us with when we were smallpups. Humans

126

trusted us more easily when they met us when they were young, and it wouldn't hurt to have as many friends as possible in the village.

I walked toward them very slowly, then lay down so that I would be as unthreatening as possible.

The children began to chatter excitedly. Several came forward to me. A bold female reached out a hand to stroke my fur. I licked her hand. The next thing I knew, I was surrounded by laughing, smilling human young, all of them gently stroking my fur.

"TaLi said there are more wolves that will come help us," the bold girl said. "She said she'll teach me to hunt with them."

"She told me they sleep next to her," a thin male said, looking directly in my eyes. A wolf would consider such a look a challenge. I would have to remember to tell any other wolves who came to Kaar that humans did such things without malice.

"I'm going to bring one into my shelter," a soft voice said, and I saw myself looking into the eyes of a dark-furred, soft-skinned boy whose head would come up to my nose if I were standing. I licked his face and he giggled.

Then I heard a harsh grunt and saw a boy standing apart from the others, his eyes downcast. It was the child who had been running alone the first day I was in Kaar, excluded by the others. I stood.

"That's JaliMin," the skinny male said, sneering. "He won't talk to you. He can't even think." But the child stared at me in fascination. I found myself growing angry with the sneering male. Ázzuen had been the smallest pup in Rissa's litter. When her other pups had harried him and kept him from her milk, I had fought for him. Now I felt the same urge to defend the quiet boy.

I stood, slipped past grasping hands, and made my way to the shunned child. He smiled when he saw me and held out a hand. I licked it.

A sharp whistle cut through the village and the rest of the children scattered. As I watched them go, RalZun strode toward me, his lips pursed. Ázzuen trotted at his heels.

"He was like all the other children until just before he was old enough to walk," RalZun said, looking at the boy. "Then he was attacked by a rhino that charged through the village. The rhino killed his older brother, and JaliMin stopped talking, stopped responding to anyone. No one knows why. Some think he must have fallen and injured his brain. Others say he was so frightened, he lost the ability to speak. He's HesMi's only grandchild now. It's her great sadness that her grandson will never serve on the council of elders."

He squatted down next to us. Ázzuen licked my cheek.

"I told RalZun we want to teach the humans to hunt salmon," he said. "The way we did in the Wide Valley."

We hadn't hunted salmon in the Wide Valley, but Ázzuen clearly wanted RalZun to think we had. Probably so the old man wouldn't insist on following us to make sure we knew what we were doing. I grinned at Ázzuen. I was tired of RalZun treating us like incompetent pups, too.

"We do fish the river," RalZun said, "but if you can help us do so, it's another way to show the elders you can help us." He frowned at TaLi.

"Go with them and see if it is worthwhile. Can you do that?"

"Yes," TaLi said, with impatience of her own.

"We've hunted together for moons," I added.

"I know you have, youngsters," RalZun said. "But do not be so sure of yourselves that you are careless. You are all young to be trusted with the tasks we are burdening you with. But there's no help for that." He peered at TaLi through narrowed eyes. "Try not to let HesMi see how much you despise DavRian. It won't help things."

TaLi grinned at the old man. "I'm used to pretending I don't think people are stupid. Come on, wolves!" she said cheerfully. She galloped into the woods. Ázzuen followed her.

I stopped, feeling that I was being watched. When I turned, I saw the silent human child, JaliMin. I darted over to him and touched my nose to his cheek. His eyes widened and then he laughed. I licked his face, then followed TaLi and Ázzuen.

As we approached the river, I smelled a familiar, pungent piney-earthy scent. I expected Ázzuen to stop, but he went straight toward the smell.

"Ázzuen," I said, "don't you smell the rock bears?"

"Of course I do." He grinned. "That's how you find the salmon. You follow the bears. I've done it before."

When? I wondered. I thought I knew everything Ázzuen did.

He slowed when we neared the river, and the scent of bear intensified. I wasn't sure I wanted TaLi so close to a bear, even though they usually didn't attack unless we tried to fight them or steal from them. Which seemed to be exactly what Ázzuen intended. I stopped, and blocked TaLi's path with my body.

Ázzuen poked me with his muzzle. "I'm not stupid enough to fight bears for prey, Kaala." He whuffed softly. Jlela dropped down from a limb directly above us, almost landing on my head.

"They are leaving, wolves," she quorked. "We will warn you if they return."

I would have asked her to go after them to find out where they were going, but ravens come and go as they please.

Ázzuen trotted toward the river. Since I was a pup, I had hunted with Tlitoo to find prey. I didn't know when Ázzuen had started hunting with Jlela's help.

"Are you waiting until you are an oldwolf?" Jlela quorked. TaLi pushed impatiently at me, and I followed cautiously after Ázzuen.

We emerged at a narrow, fast-moving stretch of river. It was a place where the riverbed dropped sharply several times, so that the water danced downstream along rocks and tree limbs. Two bears were on the far side of the river, shambling away from the rushing water. Tlitoo and Jlela hopped from tree branch to tree branch behind them.

"Hurry up!" Ázzuen yipped.

TaLi watched the bears leave, her spear clutched tightly in her hands. When they were out of sight, she relaxed and crouched down on her haunches on the riverbank.

Competing for prey is all about balance. A wolf who challenges a bear or rock lion directly will end up dead or too wounded to hunt. But a wolf who waits too long to go after another hunter's prey will starve to death. Salmon is good greslin. The problem is catching enough of them. We usually missed so many more than we caught that it wasn't worth our time.

Ázzuen leapt onto a rock in the river and looked at the rushing water, then back at us. He stood, swaying a little, the spray of water making his fur cling to his body. I watched him, wondering what he had in mind.

"I've found two ways to hunt the salmon," he said. "One works in the shallows, one in rushing water like this. We can take the humans to the shallows if your girl wants to." He didn't look at me as he spoke. He held perfectly still, as I'd seen water birds stand. Then he thrust his head into the water and came out with a writhing salmon.

He waded back to the riverbed and dropped the salmon at my feet. I pinned it under my paws. Ázzuen returned to his rock and, after several long moments, plucked another salmon from the river. This time, when he brought it back and set it on the riverbank, TaLi darted from the woods and smashed the salmon's head with a rock.

"There'll be more in a minute," Ázzuen said. "They move in groups."

He nosed the salmon I held down and looked up at me.

"You first," I said. "You caught it."

He bit the salmon in half, swallowing a huge piece of it. I tore into what was left. As we devoured the fish, TaLi sat on the bank, weaving together river reeds. From time to time she looked anxiously across the river. She didn't have to worry. We would warn her if any bears came back.

Then, as the wind changed, I caught the scent of bitter
spruce. Milsindra was somewhere nearby. I ran along the bank
to find her, but the scent had disappeared. Uneasily, I returned to Ázzuen.

The next time he waded into the river, I went with him,
standing by his side on the flat rock.

"When did you learn to do this?" I asked him, watching
the silvery fish swim by.

"Back in the Wide Valley," he said. "When you were with
your girl. I watched the bears, and I thought if bears could do
it, we certainly could."

I saw a fish glide by and thrust my head into the river
after it, but I came up empty jawed. I hadn't stuck my head
far enough into the water. Ázzuen snatched another from
the river and hurled it to TaLi, who crushed its head and set
it by the other one. I growled in frustration. A huge salmon
swam right by my feet. I lunged at it, missing it completely
and falling face-first into the water. I struggled to my feet to
see Ázzuen grinning around a salmon that writhed in his
mouth.

We caught four more. That is, Ázzuen caught three and I
caught one. TaLi finished weaving the reeds into a large gourd
shape the humans called a *basket* for our catch.

Ázzuen and I stood on the opposite side of the river,
watching her.

"That was smart," I said to him, licking his cheek. His fur
tasted of river and salmon.

"I have other ideas," Ázzuen said, his face solemn. When
he was a smallpup, his serious expression made him look like
a little oldwolf in a pup's body. Now it suited him.

"I'm sure you do." I grinned at him and gave him a sturdy shoulder slam.

He bent his leg so he didn't stagger, then placed his head over my neck. His warm breath tickled the fur on my muzzle.

I startled away from him. I didn't know what I'd do if he asked me to have pups like Pell had. His bright gaze met mine and the fur between his eyes wrinkled. Then he shook himself and stepped away from me. He lifted his nose to the air and whuffed a warning.

Milsindra's scent was back, and very close. Tlitoo landed next to us on the riverbank and krawked a warning.

TaLi was still crouched over her basket. A shadow appeared over her as Milsindra emerged from the bushes behind the girl. TaLi, intent on arranging the fish in her basket, didn't see the Greatwolf. Milsindra looked straight at me and opened her great jaws just behind the girl's fragile neck.

As I splashed into the river, Ázzuen at my side, Milsindra barked a laugh at us. TaLi spun around just as Navdru and Yildra, the Sentinel leaderwolves, emerged behind Milsindra.

By the time we reached the riverbank, TaLi had hefted the basket to her shoulder and turned to face the Greatwolves. Yildra and Navdru stared, fascinated by the girl. The Greatwolves never showed themselves to ordinary humans, but TaLi was a krianan, and one of the few humans they could greet. Ázzuen and I ran to TaLi's side.

Navdru lifted a twitching nose to the basket resting upon the girl's shoulder and began to sniff at the fish. TaLi, keeping her eye on the huge wolf, set down her basket and pulled out a large fish.

"This is for you," she said to Navdru.

He shifted uneasily from paw to paw. For all he was leaderwolf of Sentinel and a Greatwolf, it seemed he didn't know what to make of the human girl. He looked to me.

"It's all right," I found myself telling the Greatwolf, "you can take it."

He hesitated a moment longer, and Yildra huffed in amusement.

"Well, if you don't want it, I do." She snatched up the salmon and swallowed it in three huge gulps.

"You learned to catch so many salmon in the Wide Valley?" she asked me, licking her chops.

"We learned it from the humans there." Ázzuen lied so convincingly that even I almost believed him for a moment.

"You'll have to show us how you do it," Navdru said, then rumbled to Milsindra, "I don't see a problem with their hunting fish together. The human girl is not dominant to them, and if they learn things from the humans, so much the better."

"Yes, Leaderwolf," Milsindra said. Her lip lifted in a condescending snarl and her voice was so full of arrogance, that I couldn't believe Navdru didn't challenge her. He just narrowed his eyes and dipped his head, and he and Yildra bounded into the woods. Milsindra stayed behind.

I lifted my chin to her. She had brought them to try to make us look bad and had failed. She met my raised muzzle with her own. Ázzuen growled. Next to him, TaLi raised her sharpstick. Milsindra ignored them both.

"I can find her anytime, Kaala. I can find her anyplace and snap her neck in two or shove her off a cliff."

"The Sentinels will kill you if you do," I responded, but my voice shook.

"Only if they can tell what I did. Humans get injured and die all the time."

"Why do you care what happens here?" Ázzuen said. "You can go back to the Wide Valley and rule there."

"The Wide Valley is nothing," Milsindra growled. She swung her head to Ázzuen, who stood steadily, averting his gaze only the slightest bit. "If wolves stay with humans, they *will* lose everything that makes them wolf. They will become the humans' curl-tails, and I will not let that happen." She turned back to me. "You will make a mistake, and when you do, I'll be sure the Sentinels know."

She cocked her head and grinned. "You have friends coming." She bent down, snatched a salmon from TaLi's basket, and bounded into the woods.

I heard humans tramping through the bush.

"Do you see that?" It was DavRian. I'd know his sweat and dream-sage scent anywhere. "That can't be an ordinary wolf. And those paw prints are as big as a bear's."

A growl rose in my throat. "Milsindra led them here on purpose," I said to Ázzuen. The Greatwolves usually took great pains to hide their presence from humans. "She wants them to find out about the Greatwolves."

DavRian pushed through the long, sinewy branches of a willow and stepped onto the riverbank. A frowning HesMi followed. When she saw us sitting on the bank with TaLi, her frown deepened.

"Did you bring me all the way out here for this?" She waved her long arm at us. We sat, trying to look harmless.

DavRian shook his head. "There are giant wolves about, HesMi. I've seen them. They just hide when they see us."

One of Milsindra's paw prints was just to the left of TaLi's foot. The girl shifted so her own foot covered it, then rubbed at the mud until Milsindra's print was indistinguishable from ours.

"I've never seen them," TaLi lied. "Some wolves are larger than others, of course." She shrugged.

"And some humans are more easily frightened than others." BreLan hopped from the woods to a tall boulder, and jumped from the boulder to stand next to TaLi on the riverbank.

DavRian's face darkened and I thought he would leap at BreLan. Instead he looked down into TaLi's basket. "Five fish," he sneered, for that was all that was left after Yildra and Milsindra had eaten theirs. He smirked. "That will feed a few families for a night." It would do more than that. From what I knew of how humans ate, the five salmon would feed several families for several nights. But that wouldn't go far in a village as large as Kaar.

TaLi narrowed her eyes at DavRian. "We can get more, DavRian. The wolves will help us."

DavRian smiled down at her. "I'm sure you can. And it's good to be careful. If the wolves can't help with dangerous hunts, it's best to go after things like fish."

Anger came between one breath and the next. Milsindra's threats and DavRian's insults burned in me.

"Do you think the humans steal from longfangs?" I asked Ázzuen.

He grinned at me.

"It is not needed, wolves." Tlitoo paced between us. "It is a risk you do not need to take."

I leapt over him then, walked up to DavRian, and stared

into his eyes, which always made humans like him nervous. Then I walked a few steps, twisting my head around to look at him.

"I will get the others," Tlitoo grumbled, and took flight.

"What does it want?" DavRian asked nervously, looking down at me.

"She wants us to follow her," BreLan answered, smirking.

It took the humans twice as long to get to the longfang plain as it would have taken us, and it was past high sun when we reached it. The longfangs had killed another grass elk. Again, the mother longfang and her cubs stood far back from the kill while two others tore at the carcass. This time, though, the three of them had a large piece of elk shoulder of their own and the cubs were eating hungrily, scattering smaller bits of meat around them. I had heard that longfangs, unlike cave lions and grass lions, hunted in packs. I wondered how the mother and her cubs had fallen out of favor.

"We're leaving," HesMi said when she saw the longfangs. I kept forgetting that the humans couldn't smell threats from a distance. I thought they'd followed us knowing what was on the plain.

"The wolves know what they're doing," TaLi said. The fear in her voice was so well disguised that I was sure none of the humans could detect it. I leaned against her, offering her my strength. DavRian looked at her and then at HesMi. HesMi shrugged and crouched down, holding her sharpstick. DavRian had no choice but to stay or look a coward.

BreLan grinned at the Kaar leader. "You didn't listen to me

when I told you about what the wolves can do for us," he said. "Now watch."

For long moments, all the humans *could* do was watch. The longfangs were guarding their meal so closely we didn't dare go near.

Then the mother longfang left her cubs and began to shuffle on her belly toward the rest of the carcass. The other longfangs looked up and snarled at her, but she kept moving toward them, pawswidth by pawswidth. We wouldn't have much time.

I dipped my head to Ázzuen.

We pelted across the grass. Ázzuen wasn't as fast as Marra, but he was agile and could turn quickly. He came up behind one of the cubs and nipped it on the rump. Both cubs whirled at him, snarling and growling.

"Ours!" one said. He had dark-tipped ears and a longer muzzle than his sister.

I ran at him, butting him in the side with my head. His ribs were hard and sharp, close to the surface. They must be growing quickly to have so little flesh on them, I thought.

The cub Ázzuen had nipped whirled to me, her eyes frantic. Ázzuen and I ran two quick circles around both cubs. Then Ázzuen grabbed one of the small pieces of meat and bolted.

"Ours," the black-eared cub said again, and both cubs took off after Ázzuen, leaving the rest of the meat unguarded. Then Marra streaked onto the plain. Tlitoo had indeed found her. She dashed to the cubs, tripping them up. She moved so quickly that they couldn't respond fast enough to right themselves before she tripped them again.

I snatched up the larger piece of meat just as Ázzuen tossed his smaller piece of elk into the grass. The cubs followed, pouncing on the bit of meat as it fell. By then, Marra and I had made it more than halfway back to the humans with the larger piece of elk.

I knew that sound. I knew it from when I was not yet out

Gasping, I plunked the meat down by the humans. The cubs were running toward us, but TaLi, BreLan, and HesMi all stepped forward and raised their sharpsticks. The cubs stopped, staring at the weapons. Ázzuen helped me pull the elk into the woods.

HesMi grinned. TaLi watched the human leader, a gleam of triumph in her eye.

"Can they do this again?" HesMi asked.

"Yes," BreLan said. "Whenever we want them to." Ázzuen growled softly at him, and BreLan laughed. "Or whenever they want *us* to."

HesMi looked from BreLan to Ázzuen, confused, then laughed as well, as if just getting a joke. She picked up the meat and strode off toward the village. DavRian hissed like an angry raven and looked at me with such malice, I took a step back. Then he stalked after HesMi.

That was when I heard the desperate mewling sound. I looked at Ázzuen, wondering if he was hurt, but he was looking out toward the plain. It was the longfang cubs, crying to their mother, who had returned empty-jawed from the carcass, a freely bleeding wound across her side. They watched us, and their whimpering grew louder.

I knew that sound. I knew it from when I was not yet out

of the den. It was the sound of hunger and desperation. I looked again at the cubs, remembered the sharp ribs of the one I had tackled. Even from the edge of the woods, I could see the panic and despair in their mother's eyes. They were starving. And we had taken their food from them.

I didn't know why I cared. They were not wolf. They weren't pack. But when I followed the humans into the woods, my tail fell between my legs and my ears folded flat with shame.

13

After the humans returned to Kaar, Ázzuen and I found a shady clearing amid elm trees and sage bushes and sank down in a soft patch of cool dirt. Marra had gone in search of MikLan, leaving the two of us to relax in the evening air. Within a few breaths, Ázzuen was snoring. I rolled onto my side and then onto my belly, but I was too restless to join him in sleep. I was pleased, both with our salmon hunt and with HesMi's reaction on the longfang plain, but Even Night was less than seventeen days away, and it would take more than a few hunts and prey thefts to win the humans. I shifted restlessly.

"You are fretting again, wolflet." I hadn't seen Tlitoo land on the branch above me. He dropped down with an inelegant thump and stalked toward me. The glint in his eye made me very nervous. He pushed in between me and Ázzuen.

"What are you doing?"

"You need to remember that not everything is duty and strife."

"I don't think everything's duty and strife," I protested. "You ravens are the ones who yelled at me for not taking on the task." They hadn't actually yelled at me. They had clouted me with their wings and threatened me with sharp beaks and called me a coward when, back in the Wide Valley, I had been hesitant to take on so daunting a task.

"And you must complete it, wolflet. It is what the Neja and the Moonwolf—the drelwolf—must do together." He cocked his head to the left and then to the right, and the look in his eyes was as gentle as I'd ever seen it. "But you must remember why."

Before I could stop him, he placed his back against Ázzuen and his chest against me. I felt the sensation of falling. The aromas of mud and wolf and elm faded to nothingness.

⊡

Flank by flank they ran, chasing the fear-blinded deer. Ázzuen scented the hunt-thrill rising from Kaala and heard the rapid beat of her heart. Each time her paws hit the earth, his slapped down beside them, each time she drew breath, his own breath . . .

⊡

I yanked myself from Ázzuen's thoughts.

"No," I gasped to Tlitoo, "it isn't right." I couldn't ask Ta-Li's permission to go inside her mind, because she didn't understand me, but it was wrong to invade Ázzuen's thoughts without asking. I had gone into his mind once before and still felt ashamed.

Tlitoo regarded me curiously. "I had forgotten you could do that, wolf. I did not remember that you could make us leave."

I glared at him.

"Very well, wolf," he quorked. "I will not take you there if you do not wish to go. I just wanted you to see that there are days to come that will be good."

He settled next to me. Then he gave a startled croak and I was falling again, more quickly this time. Scent and sound flew from me. This time, though, they were replaced with a deep and painful chill.

"I did not mean to bring us here, wolf," he quorked.

We were surrounded by what appeared to be the tall rocks of the Stone Circle of the Wide Valley. That plus the terrible cold told me where we were. The Inejalun was a place between the worlds. Tlitoo and I had been there before. He could not always find the place and sometimes it came to us unbidden. From there we had met the Greatwolf Indru, who, in the time before time, spoke to the Ancients to save wolf-kind, and from there we had spoken to my ancestress Lydda, who had kept the Promise before me. I couldn't stay there. The Inejalun was not safe for any living creature except for Tlitoo. If I stayed too long, the Inejalun would steal the warmth, and the life, from my body.

"Get me out of here," I said through a muzzle that was quickly freezing.

"What do you think I am trying to do, wolf?" Tlitoo rasped, annoyed.

We both saw something move across the Stone Circle at the same time. The shadow of a huge wolf fell upon the rocks, but there was no wolf to cast it. The Shadow Wolf turned his huge head, and I knew he was looking at me. *We failed and we gave up,* I thought I heard him say. *We hid in a cave and forfeited the Promise and would not admit our shame. It is time to make amends. You are the one who will help us.*

My chest grew cold.

"Go," the Shadow Wolf said aloud. "You must not die here. I will find a way to come to you. I have been waiting for you to find me. There are things I must tell you. Go."

Then, as if someone had grabbed me by the scruff and hurled me across the Stone Circle, I awoke, back in the clearing next to Ázzuen.

I gasped. Exhaustion overwhelmed me. Every time I went to the Inejalun, I was as tired as if I had run for three days straight without sleeping. That was another danger of the place. The longer I stayed, the worse it was. This time I had been there only a few moments.

"I'm sorry, wolflet." Tlitoo peered down at me. "I do not yet know all of the ways of the Inejalun. It has its own will." His head sank down between his wings. "Are you all right?"

"Yes," I said, my eyes drooping. "I just need to rest." That was all I was able to say before my eyes closed and I fell into a deep sleep.

I awoke to the sounds of human and wolf laughter and opened my eyes to the bright light of high sun. Marra and MikLan were wrestling in the dirt, tumbling over each other. Marra stood atop MikLan's chest, grabbed his spear, and pelted across the clearing. MikLan followed and snatched it back. Marra chased after him, letting him stay ahead of her. They were having so much fun that my own tail began to wave. Next to me, Ázzuen yipped at them.

"You slept for almost a full day, Kaala!" he said. "I was going to drag you into the river if you hadn't woken up soon!"

I wished he had. I was so thirsty I could've swallowed an entire lake. I found a puddle of stagnant water and lapped it up. I'd lost a day. I tried to figure out how much time we had until Even Night, but my head ached from going to the Inejalun. I looked for Tlitoo. The branches above me were empty.

MikLan lowered the stick just enough for Marra to grab it in her teeth. She pulled it from his grasp. Then it was his turn to chase her. She was faster than he was, of course, but she let him get just close enough to her that he almost caught her. Then she darted away. MikLan whooped at her as Ázzuen and I barked in encouragement. It felt so good, just for a moment, not to be worried about DavRian or Kaar or the fate of wolf-kind.

MikLan snatched the stick and pulled. Marra dug her paws into the dirt. The boy tried to drag her forward, and Marra stood on her hind legs and pushed her front paws into his chest, toppling him. Shouting with laughter, he shoved her back, and the two of them rolled over each other again and again in the dirt.

They were making so much noise that I didn't hear the other humans approaching. Three of them, led by DavRian, ran into the clearing, spears raised. I leapt to my feet and whoofed a warning to Marra.

"Get it away from him!" DavRian yelled, running toward

Marra. He slammed the point of his sharpstick down fast. She dodged out of the way.

"She's not hurting me!" MikLan shouted.

The humans were too agitated to hear him. They had decided that Marra was a threat and were advancing on her, spears raised. MikLan put himself between Marra and DavRian, who shoved him away. The boy fell into the dirt.

"Go!" MikLan shouted to Marra. She sneezed in protest and pawed at him. MikLan shoved her with his leg. "They won't hurt me," he said, his voice frantic as DavRian lunged again for Marra.

Marra dodged. She looked at MikLan and then at me.

"What are you waiting for?" I said. "MikLan will get hurt trying to protect you!"

She bolted into the woods. Ázzuen and I followed her. We found her just a wolflength from the clearing, watching the humans from behind the cover of a laurel bush.

"They won't hurt him," I said. She ignored me. She continued to watch the humans, her haunches tensed to leap.

DavRian had slung an arm over MikLan's shoulders. "You think the wolves are your friends but they aren't," he was saying. He ruffled MikLan's hair. The younger boy tried to pull away and DavRian's grip tightened around his shoulders. To the other humans it might have looked like DavRian was being friendly. I knew better.

"Do you really want to be with those false krianans?" He said the word as if it were something disgusting. "I'm taking some of Kaar's hunters to the Far Plain to hunt some aurochs I found on the way from the valley. Come with us."

MikLan just glared up at him and tried to pull away again, then seemed to think the better of it. He looked toward the bush we hid behind as if he could actually see Marra there. Maybe he could. She was quivering so violently, the bushes trembled.

"I'm going back to Kaar," he said, trying once more to pull away from DavRian.

"We should all go back," one of DavRian's companions said. "Tell them about that wolf attacking him."

DavRian smiled. The three humans surrounded MikLan and hustled him from the clearing.

Marra lunged. Ázzuen and I tackled her. I lay across her shoulders, Ázzuen across her rump.

"They won't hurt him," I said again. "DavRian's not that stupid."

"I shouldn't have left him," she said.

"You had to," I said, though I knew how she felt. I would have hated to leave TaLi alone with DavRian. I twisted to touch my nose to her face and felt her relax beneath me. Ázzuen and I stood, letting her up. Instead of following the humans back to Kaar, as I expected her to, she looked down at the dirt between her paws.

"What is it?" I asked. It wasn't like Marra to hesitate to speak.

She shifted from paw to paw, and when she lifted her head to meet my gaze, there was a challenge in her eyes.

"MikLan wants to go back to the valley to tell the krianans there what's happening here," she said.

A hollow spot opened in my chest. He had said as much when we'd first brought TaLi to RalZun. It hadn't bothered me then. Now, with such a huge task before us, I needed all the help I could get. And I knew what she wasn't saying.

"You want to go with him."

"It's not safe for him to go alone"—she looked down again—"and I don't want to be away from him so long."

It was something we'd never talked about. The love between human and wolf was so strong that being apart from them was as painful as a spear through the chest. When I was away from TaLi for too long, I felt as if part of myself was missing. It sometimes made me wonder if I was truly loyal to my pack.

I wanted so much to ask Marra to stay. I couldn't imagine winning Kaar over without her. Yet I knew I couldn't. Not only would it be unfair to ask her to be apart from MikLan, but I knew she was right. The trip back could be hazardous. I would never let TaLi travel back to the valley alone. That was the thing about loving a human. They always seemed to walk into danger and it was our duty to protect them.

Besides, if the humans thought Marra was dangerous, it was no longer safe for her in Kaar.

"Yes," I said. "You should go."

She lowered her ears just a little. "I'll come back," she offered, "once MikLan is safe."

I looked at my paws. "Tell the pack what's going on here. I was going to ask Jlela to, but they'll trust you more than a raven. Come back and tell us what they say. Tell us if they're all right."

She swung her head back and forth a few times, and licked my cheek. Then she shook herself and trotted toward the village.

I worried all the way back to Kaar. The humans didn't trust DavRian, but there had been other humans with him when he saw MikLan and Marra playing. He would tell the others that Marra had been hurting MikLan, and his friends would support him.

"Will you wait outside the village for now?" I asked Marra as we neared the human dwellings.

"As long as I can see MikLan," she answered. She settled down among the thick spruce trees as I walked into the large clearing. MikLan crouched with TaLi and BreLan, speaking urgently to them. Marra didn't take her gaze from her human. I hid behind shelters and stacks of preyskins so the other humans wouldn't see me. DavRian and his friends stood with HesMi, and I listened as they told their lies. I grew more and more nervous as they talked.

Ázzuen slammed his shoulder into mine. I hadn't heard him slip up next to me. "You knew it wouldn't be easy, Kaala." He looked across the clearing. "We're smarter than DavRian. We just have to find a way to show HesMi that we're the ones she should trust."

It wouldn't be easy to convince the human leader to trust a wolf over one of her own kind. I could only hope Ázzuen would come up with one of his clever ideas in time.

Marra and MikLan left for the Wide Valley before darkfall. Ázzuen, Pell, and I followed them as far as the edge of the pine and cypress woods, then watched them walk at the slow human pace across the grassland. I knew it was right for them to go. MikLan needed to take word back to the Wide Valley krianans, and Marra would be safe from any further harm Dav-Rian's accusations might cause. She could also help Rissa and Ruuqo with the new pups when they came. And she had promised to come back if I needed her. The ravens could find her quickly, and she was fast enough to make it from Swift River lands to Kaar in a day or so, but it wasn't the same as having her with us. It wasn't the same as having my pack with me.

They looked so small leaving us, vulnerable to Great-wolves, humans, and whatever dangers these strange lands held. Marra's fleetness would do her no good when she had to protect a slow-moving human. My concern must have been obvious, because Pell leaned down and touched his nose to my face.

"I'll go with them as far as the hills," he said.

Pell was our best fighter, and large enough to look intimidating. They would be much safer with him.

"Thank you," I said.

He rested his head on my neck, and the rush of warmth and excitement I'd felt after the elk hunt threatened to engulf me. I stiffened.

Pell stepped away, looking confused. He stared at me for a long, uncomfortable moment, then shook himself and loped after Marra and MikLan. Ázzuen and I watched them until they climbed a low hill and disappeared over the other side. Then we headed back to Kaar.

We slunk into the village, making sure no one panicked when they saw us. TaLi and BreLan were sitting next to an herb-scented den and we made our way to them. DavRian's lies had made the other humans wary. Several humans looked up suspiciously when we came in and a few picked up sharp-sticks.

We had almost reached our humans when I heard a child's boisterous laughter. My tail wagged before I could tell where the sound was coming from. I heard the slap of human footsteps and the whuffling of a wolf at play.

JaliMin, the speechless, fear-wounded human child, was running in circles around Prannan, who was lying on his back waving his paws in the air while several adult humans watched. JaliMin's eyes were bright and his smile wide. When Prannan stopped waving his legs, JaliMin stopped, too, and stomped one of his feet.

"Play!" he said imperiously, pointing a bit of antler bone at Prannan. Prannan rolled onto his belly and then onto his back again and wriggled as if he had an itch. The boy ran a few more circles around Prannan, then flopped down next to him.

Prannan stood and ran to the edge of a fire pit and picked up a cooked root that was cooling by the fireside. He ran back to JaliMin and dropped the root at his feet. The boy picked it up and took a bite, grinning hugely. I watched the surrounding humans carefully, concerned that they might be afraid Prannan would attack, but some were looking on with smiles, some with looks of astonishment. The fear I'd first sensed in the village was rapidly fading.

"He hasn't laughed since his brother PavMin died," a half-grown male said. "He hasn't said a word in more than twelve moons!"

"I didn't think he could." That was HesMi. I remembered

that RalZun had said that PavMin and JaliMin were her grand-sons. Her voice sounded strange, harsh and choked.

Prannan ran to her, his face crumpled in concern, looking so much like a puppy I wanted to call out to him to be careful. JaliMin stomped over to me.

"Play with me, wolf," he ordered clearly, dropping the piece of antler at my paws. I looked over at the humans watching me. I licked the boy on the ear, grabbed up the ant-ler bone he had dropped, and ran with it. He chased me and, after a few circuits of the fire pit, I let him catch me. He pushed me in the ribs and I pretended to fall over. I dropped the bone and the boy snatched it up. He ran, shrieking with laughter, into one of the shelters. TaLi and I used to play that way, before she had taken on so much responsibility and be-come so serious.

HesMi walked slowly over to me, Prannan trotting at her heels.

"Thank you, wolves," she said. "I never thought to hear his laughter again." She spoke as if she knew we could under-stand her.

Prannan panted up at her. His teeth showed as he grinned. Often humans found that intimidating. But she smiled down at him.

"There is more to you than the hunt, isn't there?" She reached down and stroked Prannan between the ears. He rolled over onto his back. Vole Eater wolves were always sub-missive. HesMi looked at me expectantly. As the leader of the council of elders, she would have much more influence than IniMin or DavRian would. I flopped onto the ground, rolled onto my back, and offered her my belly. She laughed and bent down to stroke my belly fur. Prannan yipped happily. HesMi smiled at both of us before walking away. We had completely won her over.

I got to my paws, looking after her in satisfaction. I saw IniMin watching me and lifted my lip to him. Then I smelled bitter spruce. I turned around, dreading what I would see. Milsindra was standing just at the edge of Kaar, staring at me with contempt, the youngwolf Lallna at her side. They had seen me offering my belly to the humans. I started toward them, ready to explain, but they turned and bolted into the woods.

14

I waited just beyond the village, my tail wrapped around my legs in an attempt to look confident, but my heart raced and I found it difficult to breathe. Ázzuen hid behind a tartberry bush to my left. I'd wanted him to stay in the village to strengthen our new bonds with HesMi and the other humans, but he'd refused to let me wait alone. It wouldn't take the Sentinels long to send someone after us. They had made it clear that we were not to be submissive to the humans, and I had no doubt that Milsindra had told them what she'd seen. I was afraid it would be Navdru or Yildra who came for me. When Neesa approached through the dusk, I drooped with relief.

I dipped my head to Ázzuen, who backed out of the bush and back toward Kaar.

I spoke before Neesa could.

"We had to make them comfortable," I said, talking as quickly as I could. "Otherwise they'd be afraid of us. We can change them once they trust us. We can worry about whether

the humans want to be dominant to us then. If DavRian convinces them we're dangerous, none of it will matter."

She waited until I ran out of breath. "Come with me, Kaala," she said. "There's something you need to see." She nipped me lightly on the muzzle and turned to lope toward the distant hills.

I followed. In spite of my concern over the Sentinels' reaction to my submission to HesMi, I savored my mother's closeness. I'd lost count of the number of times I'd dreamed of running beside her. I half closed my eyes and pretended that we were on our way to a hunt and that this was the first night of many when I would run at her side. But we were not on our way to a hunt, and I knew there would be trouble. I kept sneaking looks at her to find her watching me.

"What's Navdru going to do?" I finally asked.

"I don't know," she said, slowing to a walk, "but there is something I want to show you before he finds us. You need to know that there is reason behind their rules. You're not going to stop doing something just because someone tells you to," she said. "You're like your father that way."

"My father?" I asked quickly. I knew that Hiiln had been a reckless wolf. But she said no more about my father.

"So I will show you what can happen when wolves are submissive to the humans. You're not the first one to think of it, Kaala, of being with the humans. Far from it. It's something we've tried many times. And every time it fails. And sometimes it fails in disastrous ways."

"Everyone says that but no one will say why," I said.

In answer, she began to run again. We loped through a birch forest and then through a wood of pine and spruce. When my paws were aching and my throat was dry from thirst, she stopped.

"We're here," she said.

We stood on a small hill overlooking a rocky plain. My mother settled on her haunches and I did the same. I could smell, just barely, unfamiliar wolf upwind. I hadn't been able to until we were on the hill, and my mother had positioned us so that we were downwind of the wolves, which meant they wouldn't be able to smell us. When entering another wolf's territory, it's good manners to let them scent you coming. That meant that Neesa must have had a reason for not announcing our presence.

When she crawled forward on her belly, I followed as quietly as I could.

The yips and barks of pups reached us across the plain, though it was too early in the season for there to be pups out of den. Then I saw them. The wolf pack was resting in the moonlight, and a few of them were playing a game of chase. My first thought was that it was a pack of youngwolves like me, but then I looked more closely. There was something odd about them. Their heads were rounded like newborn pups', some had limp ears, and their muzzles were shorter than that of any wolf I'd ever seen. They looked like the little wolf who had been spying on us when we first reached Kaar.

"Are they sick?" I asked.

"In a way," Neesa answered. "This is what happens when wolves are submissive to humans for too long. After many generations, they begin to look like this. After the lives of twenty wolves have passed, they change even more and look and behave always like pups. They forget the reason behind our involvement with humans." She placed her head in her paws. "The Sentinels kill them if they find them with humans."

"Why?" I couldn't see how these not-quite-wolves could

be a threat. They seemed to be so joyful in their play. "Why would they kill wolves who aren't after their territory?"

"The little wolves want the humans for themselves. And they are not wolf. They are our death. If we allow such streck-wolves to be with the humans, the Promise will be forgotten. The humans like such wolves because they don't challenge their sense of power. They like them so much better than they do us, that they kill us and let only these streckwolves live. That is the end of wolfkind and the Promise."

"Streck" was what we called the most contemptible kinds of prey, the ones that wouldn't even fight for life. A streck was weak and cowardly, and to call a wolf streck was an insult worthy of a fight.

Neesa began walking again, back toward Kaar. The night was half over when she trotted up a low hill covered with scrub grass. She looked down the hill at what I thought at first was a huge hunting plain. Then I looked more carefully. What I saw was no hunting plain.

Before us stretched a withered, broken landscape. It re-minded me of Oldwoods, a burned-out hunting ground in the Wide Valley, but this place was so vast, I couldn't see the end of it. There were some scraggly plants, but not enough of them for a meal for more than a few elk or horses. There was also almost no small prey—the mice and voles and squirrels that thrived even where large prey could not. There were rem-nants of human shelters, their mud walls crumbled to dirt but parts of their stone bases still standing. As far as I could see, there was starkness, a devastation like none I'd ever seen.

"What happened here?" I whispered, afraid my voice would disturb the ghosts of the place.

"The humans happened," my mother answered, "and wolves who would not heed the Promise. These are the Barrens. They are the result of wolves becoming less than wolf."

Which still explained nothing. I lowered my nose to sniff the earth, then ventured out into the dead place. The ground held the long-faded scent of humans and their fires. Overlaying it all was the scent of old death. I returned to the rise, where my mother awaited me.

She spoke before I'd finished settling onto my haunches.

"This is one of the places where, many years ago, we tried to get humans to remember that they are part of the world around them," she said. "Wolves like you, who were drawn to humans, befriended the humans who lived here, and it seemed that the humans would accept them as pack. But then the humans began to drive away or kill any wolves who wouldn't submit to them. They wanted a pack of curl-tails."

Most packs had at least one curl-tail, or submissive wolf, but a packful of them made no sense. There would be no leaders, no fighters.

Neesa continued. "They kept only the most docile wolves, and then only the meekest of their pups. These wolves eventually became streckwolves. In changing wolves so, rather than welcoming the wildness of wolf as we intended, the humans took the wildness from the wolf."

From the very first time I saw the humans, I'd been told that when we were with them, we risked becoming less than wolf. No one would tell me why it was so important. "Why does it matter?" I asked.

Neesa shifted on her haunches. "There are things that make us uniquely wolf," she said. "Among them, our skill in the hunt, our sharp teeth and strong jaws, our loyalty to pack, and our willingness to fight when needed. Each creature has such qualities. The rock bears have their claws and their stubbornness; the aurochs, sharp horns and fierce dispositions. But, most important of all, each creature has the instinct to follow its own will. That's what makes up the Balance: each creature is uniquely itself and yet part of everything around it. This is the wild. If the humans accept only wolves that are willing to forsake their will, then the humans are not becoming part of the natural world; they are changing the nature of the world. This makes them feel even more different. They see the world around them as one of their tools, something to be used up. And they create Barrens."

"That's what happened here?"

"It is," Neesa confirmed. "The humans used their curl-tails to become the strongest village in the land. The village grew larger until the prey was gone and the land destroyed. They burned what was left so that no others could use it. They created the Barrens. Then they left it. The Sentinels ordered all streckwolves to leave the humans. A few agreed and were spared. The rest refused. The Sentinels killed them so that such a thing would never happen again."

"But it did," I said, beginning to understand. The streckwolves, in being submissive, had given up their will and forsaken the wild. "In Kaar."

"It wasn't allowed to happen," she answered. "Streckwolves were never allowed near humans again. When the Sentinels tried again to change the humans, they sent ordinary wolves like us to Kaar, but they began to submit to the humans. They started to change like the wolves before them. Then they stood with humans against wolves in a battle over prey. Yildra and

Navdru demanded that they be destroyed by any wolf who found them." Her voice shook. "Hiiln protected some of them. He said they were needed. So the Sentinels killed him, too." She was silent for a moment. I'd known two wolves who had lost their mates. I still didn't know what to say to her. I wanted so much to ask if Hiiln was my father, but Neesa looked too sad. I couldn't do it. She shook herself. "With Hiiln's help, some of the tainted wolves from Kaar escaped. They found a pack of streckwolves who had been hiding nearby, breeding among themselves from the time of the Barrens. The wolves you saw are their descendants. They are closer to real wolves than those in the Barrens, but are strecks nonetheless. That is why you must not be submissive to the humans, Kaala. Because the Promise would fail. And because you would die for it."

"Why don't the Sentinels kill all of the streckwolves?" I asked. They were ruthless enough to be willing to kill my whole pack. "The ones you showed me could still go back to the humans."

"It would go against the Balance to do so. Even Greatwolves will not kill off an entire group of creatures just because they might be a threat. As ruthless as they are, they are not so mad as that. But any streckwolves who go near humans are killed."

"I can handle the humans," I began, but Neesa was no longer paying attention. She stood and whirled to look back down the hill.

"Run, Kaala! Get out of here. Now!"

I saw them then, four Greatwolves running across the plain with the determined lope of wolves on a hunt. Two ravens soared and dipped above. Tlitoo and Jlela reached us as we turned to dart down the hill.

"The Grumpwolf told them you are the humans' curl-tails," Tlitoo quorked. "She told them you were the humans' curl-tails in the Wide Valley, too. I do not know why she says this now and not before."

"They would not have believed it before," Jlela rasped. She caught an updraft and hovered ahead of us. "Now that it has happened here, they do. They say you are a streckwolf and a menace."

I didn't have the breath to answer. I lowered my head and ran. Neesa stayed by my side. The Greatwolves gained ground, running with a grim, relentless gait. I saw a line of trees in front of me. Greatwolves were faster than ordinary wolves, but not as agile. If I could make it to the trees, I might have a chance. Tlitoo and Jlela soared back to the approaching Greatwolves and flew in their faces, but the Greatwolves snapped at them and kept running.

We were less than ten wolflengths from the trees when they caught up with us. Milsindra leapt and knocked me over. I tumbled over my paws, yelping in pain as rocks dug into my flesh. I rolled three times and came to a stop. She had hit me so hard I couldn't get any breath in my lungs. Neesa, who had run on ahead, pelted back to me.

Navdru and Yildra were there. The fourth wolf was Kivdru, Milsindra's mate. I hadn't known he'd left the Wide Valley with her.

"Stand away from her," Navdru said to Neesa. "She allowed wolves to become the humans' curl-tails. That is not permitted. We will decide later, Neesa, if we'll spare you."

"You don't have to decide," Neesa said. "If you kill her, you kill me, too."

"That would be for the best," Kivdru growled, "since you're the cause of all this. Kill both of them."

"Or try," a voice warbled. More ravens than I could count had gathered above us, hovering in the updraft. I didn't know which one had spoken. I had never seen so many ravens awake at night. Yildra and Navdru looked at them uneasily.

"The ravens can't guard them forever," Milsindra snapped.

"But we can always find Grumpwolves," Tlitoo croaked.

My mother sat calmly in front of me. Her breathing had slowed and she looked as confident as if she were merely hunting mice.

"Would you kill the wolf who travels with the Nejakila-kin?" she asked.

I gaped at her. I had no idea she knew Tlitoo's other name. I'd told no one. Not even Ázzuen. Navdru reacted as if some-one had set fire to his tail. He darted forward and snapped his teeth at Neesa. "There is no Nejakilakin. It is a story."

"Just because you do not know things does not mean they do not exist," Tlitoo warbled.

"How the Ancients laughed
Making wolves with larger heads
And yet smaller brains."

A rain of twigs dropped down around the Greatwolves. I couldn't help but laugh at Navdru's befuddled expression as he looked up at the ravens. Once I started, I couldn't stop. My life was in danger and there was nothing I could do about it, and I couldn't stop a hoarse laugh from choking out of me. Navdru snarled and hurled himself at me, pinning me under huge paws.

"You claim to be the Nejakilakin to mock us?" He lowered his open jaws to my throat. All I saw was teeth.

"Show them, Kaala." My mother's voice was desperate now and seemed to come from far away.

I couldn't do anything but look up at Navdru. The next thing I saw was feathers as Tlitoo landed on my belly, squeezing between me and the Greatwolf. He shoved his head up against Navdru's chest.

I welcomed the familiar falling sensation. All scent and sound faded. I had been in a Greatwolf mind once before. Like the humans, they saw the world differently than we did and I had to fight against the dizziness and nausea that threatened to overcome me as I sank into the strange mind of the Greatwolf.

□

Navdru was the largest pup in the litter and so he was the one who was to lead the Sentinel pack. But he would never be allowed to do so if he couldn't hunt. And he could not, for he feared prey. He was terrified of their hooves and horns and the way they looked at him with contempt. He was almost a year old and had not made a kill on his own. If any other wolves knew, they would not only force him from the pack, they would kill him. The Great-wolves did not abide the weak. If he could not catch something now, he would not return to his pack. He would leave and live or die as he could.

He had watched his packmates hunt and had watched the longfangs hunt and even watched the smallwolves. But it made no sense to him. How could they not be afraid?

He circled the herd of horses. They, at least, did not have sharp, curved horns to gore him. But they stampeded and they stomped.

He retreated. Ravens descended on the plain, poking his rump and pulling his ears, driving him back to the horses. Every time he

backed away from the herd, one of them would smack him with its
wings or peck at his eyes until he was back among the prey.

An old raven with raggedy feathers landed on his back.

"I will tell you something, wolf," he said. "All are afraid. It is
not fear that is bad, but giving in to it. We will help you with the
first one, then you are on your own."

"Why?" Navdru was suspicious. "Why would you help me?"

"Because we will have need of you when you are grown. If we
help you, do you promise to do your part for us when we request it?"

He would do anything to remain with his pack.

"I will," he said.

More ravens came. They drove a horse toward him, and he
smelled, then, that it was sick, and when he snarled at it, it stum-
bled. The ravens flew above it, harrying it, scraping at its eyes with
their sharp talons. Without thinking, he jumped and sank his teeth
into the horse's neck. His sharpest side tooth punctured its throat.
He held the thrashing beast until it was still. The taste of blood
washed away his fear. He knew the scent, now, of the kind of prey
that could be killed. And he knew, for the first time, that he could
do it. He looked up to thank the ravens, but they were gone.

＃

A howl sounded and I was yanked from Navdru's thoughts.
Scent and sound returned in a rush. For just a moment, I
thought I saw the old raven from Navdru's memory standing
before me, glaring like Tlitoo did when he was angry with me.
I knew who he was. Hzralzu, the ancient raven who had lived
in the time of Indru. I had met him in the Inejalun once before. Then he was gone and I was staring into Navdru's
stunned gaze.

"You were afraid to hunt," I whispered. "And the ravens helped you kill a horse."

"I've told no one that," he said, his voice shaking.

"And you made a promise." That was Jlela, standing next to us, her beak level with Navdru's chest. "Now is the time to keep it."

Navdru stepped away from me. I staggered to my feet.

"We have been waiting a long time for the Nejakilakin," he whispered. "We have waited for longer than I have been alive. The Nejakilakin who can see into other minds and find the way to fulfill the Promise." The awe in his gaze made my skin itch.

He was shaking when he addressed his packmates. "I keep my promises," he said. "We will give the youngwolf another chance."

Milsindra's low, throbbing growl shook the earth beneath my paws. In spite of my fear of the Greatwolves, her frustration filled me with fierce pleasure. Navdru snarled at her.

"Do you have something you wish to say to me, Wide Valley wolf?"

Milsindra's rumbling deepened, and I thought she would challenge Navdru. I hoped she would, and that he would kill her. But she just looked at her mate and dipped her head. "We are guests here," she said. "We will abide by your wishes. But I do not think it is wise to let this wolf live. She caused death in the Wide Valley and will cause it here."

"Why didn't you tell us the youngwolf and raven were the Nejakilakin?" Navdru demanded. That was the third time he'd called me, not just Tlitoo, the Nejakilakin.

"I didn't know." Milsindra was watching me, now, as if I were prey she wished to hunt. It wasn't her usual arrogant, spiteful expression. She wanted something from me.

She murmured something I couldn't hear to Kivdru. Her mate whuffed in return, then glared at me in a way that chilled me.

"Tell me, Kaala," Milsindra asked, "are you and the raven able to go to another place? A cold place between the worlds?"

Tlitoo flew at her, shrieking.

"That is not for you to know!" he shrilled. "It does not belong to you anymore!"

Jlela joined him, harrying the Greatwolf until she turned tail and fled. Three other ravens swooped down on Kivdru. The two Greatwolves sprinted into the woods, ravens flying behind them to make sure they didn't return.

Yildra watched, amused. "The Wide Valley Greatwolves need to learn some manners," she said when she saw me watching her. "I am perfectly happy to have ravens teach them." She frowned at my mother. "What about you, Neesa? Why didn't you tell us your pup was the Nejakilakin?"

"I didn't know until tonight," my mother answered, slinking respectfully past the Greatwolves to stand beside me. "I suspected, but I wasn't certain."

I wanted to ask her how she knew. I couldn't think of anything I'd done in the past hours that would make her realize what Tlitoo and I could do. But I wouldn't ask in front of the Greatwolves.

"You showed her the streckwolves?" Yildra asked my mother.

"I did," Neesa answered.

"I would rather she had not seen them," Yildra said. "I would have preferred she did not know such wolves existed, lest she follow their example. She is not to speak to them, Neesa!"

Navdru interrupted her. He looked shaken.

"Our legends say that drelwolf will destroy or save wolf-kind. The legends also say that the wolf who is one-half of the Nejakilakin can forever change the path of wolfkind. I do not know what to make of a wolf—a pup—that may be both. Part of me thinks that we should kill her now, before she can disrupt everything we have worked for." He looked down at me, his expression a mix of fascination and fear. "But I cannot kill the wolf that might save us. Not yet."

"I agree," Yildra said. She seemed less spooked by me than Navdru was. But then again, I hadn't moved through her mind as if it were merely part of the forests we lived in. "We will allow you to continue with the humans, Kaala, but if you are submissive again, or if the humans are changed in a way that is not good for us, we will kill you, Nejakilakin or not."

"And those of your blood," Navdru said, as if I needed reminding. "I am not convinced that you are truly committed to our cause. A wolf like you is just as likely to have her own plans. A wolf like you is as likely to befriend streckwolves as to defend against them. If we decide you are a danger to us, we will not let your bloodline continue." He shook himself as if he had just emerged from a river. "Even Night is fifteen nights away, youngwolf. You'd best act quickly."

Yildra looked down at my mother standing determinedly at my side. "And you are not to help her, Neesa. We need to know that she is truly on our side. Return to Hidden Grove by moonset."

My mother lowered her ears to them, and the Greatwolves stalked away.

15

Navdru and Yildra broke into a trot and then a run. Tlitoo, returning from chasing away Milsindra and Kivdru, winged toward us. I looked up at my mother. She was still keeping secrets from me.

"How did you know what Tlitoo and I can do?" I asked her.

"Because of something a wolf I met once told me."

Tlitoo alighted next to me, his feathers damp in the night air. He would be irritable after being awake in the night once again. I knew I should be grateful that he'd saved me from the Sentinel wolves, but I kept wondering when and how he would take out his displeasure on me.

"Why did Navdru keep saying I was the Nejakilakin?" I asked him. "The Nejakilakin is a raven."

"No, wolflet, it is a raven and wolf together, willing to trust each other and risk everything. It is why it has been so long since there has been a Neja."

"One wolf, one raven

No longer separate souls.

Two will change the path."

He shook out his wings and bowed to Neesa. "We are the Neja," he acknowledged. It didn't seem to bother him that Neesa knew. It still bothered me.

"What wolf told you?" I asked Neesa.

My mother's smile turned shy. "If you will allow me, Kaala?" She lay down. "There is something I would like to show you, now that I know you and your friend are the Nejakilakin. The wolf I mentioned. And more."

I had spent most of my life yearning for my mother. There was so much lost time I could never get back, so many lessons I never learned from her. How could I not take the opportunity to see inside her mind? We had so many moons of time to make up.

I lay down next to her. Before I was properly settled, Tlitoo wedged himself between us. One moment I was inhaling my mother's aroma, and the next, all scent was gone and I felt as if I was falling. I wanted to sleep next to my mother and feel her steady breathing while still seeing her thoughts, but I could not have both. Reluctantly, I released my hold on the present and allowed myself to fall.

It was not the first time Neesa had stolen away from the valley, but it was the first time she'd gone alone.

She and her sister, Rissa, had first snuck away when they were not much more than pups. The Warm Hill pack hunted the nimble sheep that climbed the foothills of the High Mountains guarding the valley's edge. While the adults of the pack napped, the two bored youngwolves would slip away to explore. It was Rissa, always bolder, always more adventurous, who had first suggested seeing what was beyond the mountains. Rissa succeeded at everything she tried. She was a graceful hunter and turned the noses of all the male wolves they came across, even before they were a year old. Neesa needed to find a place she belonged, far from the pack that fondly saw her as less than Rissa. On this day, Rissa had followed the leaderwolves to learn how to mark the edges of the territory, and Neesa was left on her own.

She stood at the top of the pass and looked down at the expanse before her. It was so much bigger than the Wide Valley that there must surely be a place where she could find her own way.

She loped down the hill, feeling her muscles stretch in the cool morning air. She sensed rather than heard another wolf running behind her. She stopped when she reached the flatland and faced the approaching wolf.

Hiiln of the Swift River pack grinned at her. Swift River was one of the strongest packs in the valley, and everyone knew that Hiiln was their next leader, with his brother Ruuqo as his secondwolf. She and Rissa hunted with the two of them, and Hiiln wanted Rissa for his mate. He'd never paid attention to Neesa before. She whuffed a shy greeting.

"I didn't know anyone else ventured outside the valley," he said. She thought she detected admiration in his voice.

"I haven't gone far," she admitted.

"Want to come with me to explore those caves?" he said.

If Rissa had asked, she would have said no, that it was too dan-

gerous, but she didn't want the young Swift River wolf to think her a coward. They ran along the narrow valley between the mountain and the hills, and then up a craggy hill to the openings in the rock.

"Pick one," Hiiln said.

She almost chose the closest one so that they could be in and out more quickly, but something drew her to another cave, higher up on the hill. She climbed nimbly up the rocks and Hiiln laughed.

"Your pack must be half rock sheep!" he said, and she smiled shyly at him. They reached the entrance of the cave and Hiiln bent down to whisper to her, his breath tickling her ears. She held perfectly still, trying to breathe.

"Does Rissa ever come here with you?"

Her racing heart seemed almost to stop, and bitterness seeped onto her tongue. "Yes," she said.

Heedless of any risk, she pushed past Hiiln into the cave.

She had thought the cave would be empty. If it had smelled of another creature, she would not have entered so boldly. The shadow of a wolf directly in front of her stopped her cold, but she still smelled nothing. Hiiln, following behind her, collided with her rump. He whuffed in annoyance, then followed her gaze.

"I thought you would get here sooner," a wolf rumbled. His voice was old, but his shadow on the cave wall moved with the suppleness of youth. Neesa couldn't help but bend her knees in obeisance to the Greatwolf, even though what she should have done was run. She noted, through her fear, that the Greatwolf was not trying to threaten them, as those in the valley so often did. That was also when she realized that there was no solid wolf casting the shadow that spoke to her.

She spared a quick look for the rest of the cave and saw the bones. Piles and piles of them. They smelled of wolf but were too large to be those of an ordinary wolf. Greatwolf bones. Many wolves' worth of them.

"What happened here?" she asked.

Hiiln nudged her, a warning to be cautious, but her curiosity always got the better of her sense.

"This is where we came," the Greatwolf said, "when we failed, when we were too ashamed to go on. Long before any wolf you know was born."

"I think we should leave, Neesa." Hiiln began to back away.

"Do not go," the wolf said, but it was Neesa, not Hiiln, he addressed. "You have come this far to find your task, do not quit now."

"What task?" Neesa asked, mystified.

"Have the ravens not found you?"

The ravens bothered Neesa all the time, asking her to follow them, but she had always ignored them. When she didn't answer, the old Greatwolf grimaced.

"The Warm Hill pack has allowed its bloodlines to weaken."

Neesa snarled at the insult. The Shadow Wolf smiled at her anger.

"Have you not found yourself drawn to the humans?"

"I have," Neesa was startled into saying. She thought that no one knew. For, when she and Rissa were not sneaking off to see the outside of the valley, they were watching the humans. Rissa wanted to take Hiiln to see them.

"Why do you want to know?" Hiiln asked.

"It is the way wolves and humans are supposed to be," the Shadow Wolf said.

Neesa's throat went dry. It was her darkest secret, that she felt drawn to the strange, patch-furred, two-legged creatures.

"My leaderwolves said it was unnatural and that we should stay away."

"That is our doing," the shadow Greatwolf said, regret softening his voice. Then, from his shadow face, glowing green eyes met hers, and she felt her legs give way. She hadn't meant to do it, but she found herself lying flat on the cold ground of the cave. Hiiln, lying prone next to her, gave a soft whimper.

"I will not keep you long, steadfast young wolf," the shadow said to Hiiln. "And you will play your part in this." He whuffed in amusement. "You have a weakness for the females of the Warm Hill pack, as the Swift River wolves often do. You are not obligated as young Neesa is, but I have a feeling you are not the type to run from a challenge. I will not keep either of you here long. But you must learn of what has happened here and why your task is important."

Neesa felt as alert as she did before a hunt. When the Shadow Wolf spoke again, it was as if his words settled into her mind like rain into welcoming earth.

"All creatures once were one," the Shadow Wolf said. "In the time before time, there was only Earth, Moon, Sun, and Grandmother Sky. Together, these Ancients made up the Balance. But after many years, the Ancients grew lonely and tired of one another, and they began to squabble. So, one night when Moon had turned her face away and Sun was conversing with Sky, Earth made Creature to keep her company. At first, Moon, Sun, and Sky were furious and thought to destroy Creature. Yet Creature entranced them. For the first time in as long as they could remember, the Ancients ceased their squabbles and watched Creature play. For the first time, the Ancients had found something to diminish their loneliness.

"But when Creature reached adolescence, it grew fractious and unmanageable. It wanted more than its share of Earth, and wanted to possess Moon, Sun, and Sky. The Ancients had come to love

Creature so much that they could not destroy it. Instead, they split it into a thousand pieces, which split and split again until the world was filled with creatures.

"And yet each of these pieces was so lonely that the Ancients feared that each part of what had been Creature would waste away."

The Shadow Wolf moved toward Neesa and lowered his cold shadow nose to her warm muzzle.

"A lonely creature is a dangerous creature," he said, *"and so the Ancients ensured that every creature would know it was a part of every other one, and part of the Balance. And for many years the creatures of the world were able to keep the Balance. Until one day a wolf and a pack of humans met at the edge of a great desert. The humans were dying of hunger, and the wolf taught them his own secrets so that the humans could live. Wolves and humans became the closest of friends."*

Neesa grunted. She knew the story of Indru, as every wolf did.

The Shadow Wolf continued. *"But, like the Ancients, they quarreled and then they fought, killing and wounding. For in every creature there is the battle between the need for love and the selfishness of the will. The humans were so wounded by the wolves' betrayal that they pulled away from all other creatures. They began to destroy everything around them, using the new skills they had learned from the wolves. The Ancients decided that they must wipe out these creatures, lest they destroy all others."*

"And the wolf Indru begged for the life of wolf and humankind," Neesa said, remembering her legends. *"And the Ancients allowed it."*

"And the wolves promised to watch over the humans," Hiiln added.

"The Greatwolves did," Neesa said, bowing down to the shadow before her.

"And we failed," the shadow Greatwolf said. "We were meant to watch from afar, to keep the wild while your kind guided the humans. But we were jealous and took what was not ours. Then we gave up and hid away. We came to this cave and chose to forget the Promise. But the smallwolves did not. Some of you could never stay far from the humans, and that is what can save us. It is up to your kind."

He stopped speaking. Neesa stared at him, uncertain of what he wanted of her.

"You want her to take on your task?" Hiiln's voice held a snarl.

"It is the last thing I want," the Shadow Wolf snapped. "There is no other choice. The smallwolves must succeed where we failed. Or the human aspects of Creature will destroy themselves, wolf-kind, and many others. It is in your blood, Neesa of Warm Hill. Your sister will seek the life of the pack. You can succeed if you trust the ravens and do not resist the humans. Or, if you will not, if you cannot, find me the wolf who will, a wolf who travels with raven and can enter the world of spirits. You must, or wolfkind will fail."

Neesa found that she could rise to her paws. She bolted from the cave, Hiiln close on her tail. She didn't stop until she reached the gentle foothills of the Wide Valley.

⊡

Scents of wolf and dirt and pine flooded my nose as I rolled away from Tlitoo and Neesa. My mother was wide awake and watching me.

"I was too much of a coward, Kaala," she said. "Rissa and I took Hiiln to see the humans. He was as drawn to them as you are and was exiled for it. I stayed in the Wide Valley and chose a safe life with my pack. The ravens came to me and I refused them. Then I began to have dreams of whelping pups that would save wolfkind and wanted to try again. I left the valley and found Hiiln, and we began to work together to fulfill the Promise."

She had tried again by having pups. By having me. If she had taken on the Promise like the Shadow Wolf had told her to, I would not have had to leave my home and my pack. I wouldn't trade my time with TaLi for an easier life, and if my mother had accepted the Shadow Wolf's challenge, I might never have been born, yet I couldn't help but feel resentful. She had left me on my own to deal with the consequences of her choices.

An angry howl resounded in the trees. I realized that the Greatwolf Yildra had been howling over and over again.

"Will you be in trouble with the Greatwolves?" It was past dawn.

"I will"—Neesa smiled—"but it was worth it." She lowered her muzzle to mine. "You saw the wolf made of shadows?"

"Yes," I said. The Shadow Wolf had to be the same one I'd met in the Inejalun. He had said he would find a way to communicate with me.

Yildra's howl echoed again off the distant hills, calling to my mother.

"You have to go," I said, wishing I could have more time with her.

Approaching pawsteps made us both look toward the woods. Lallna trotted toward us, her muzzle in the air. The youngwolf looked as arrogant as she had when she'd first challenged our entry into Sentinel lands. She reached us and gave Neesa a barely civil greeting, then grinned at me.

"I'm to watch over you"—she smirked—"to make sure you and your packmates aren't submissive to the humans again. If you are, Yildra and Navdru will let us kill you." She seemed pleased at the prospect.

"I wouldn't be so happy about that," Neesa said to the younger wolf. "If Kaala doesn't succeed, we all die."

I heard the rumble of distant thunder, though the night was clear.

"So you say." Lallna twitched a lip. It wasn't enough to be a snarl and thus a challenge, nor was it a proper response to an older, more dominant wolf. "Navdru and Yildra made all the smallwolves except for us and Kaala's pack leave so they wouldn't be tainted by her. I think we should leave the humans to the mercy of the wild. But it's not my choice."

"No, it isn't," Neesa said. "Remember that."

She licked my muzzle, then ducked her head under Lallna's belly, lifting her up and tossing her to the side. She whuffed a laugh and trotted toward Sentinel lands.

Lallna got to her paws, scowling. "Let's go," she said, stalking away from me and then breaking into a run. The thunder grew closer, and I ran faster, hoping to make it back to the village shelters before the rain began. But I had already spent the night loping through the territories and trailed behind Lallna. I wasn't too worried about her watching us. Ázzuen, Pell, and I could keep her out of our way as much as we needed to.

Then the rumble of thunder made the ground beneath our paws tremble. I froze as I realized it was not thunder I'd heard. Lallna stopped and shifted from side to side, ears lifted, looking more like hunted than hunter. I caught up to her and stood still, listening. The ground beneath our paws shook harder. Lallna whipped her head toward the sound and her eyes widened in fear.

"Killer prey!" she barked, and took off running.

I followed her gaze and saw a huge beast bearing down on us. Chasing it was the Greatwolf Milsindra. And, for just a moment, I couldn't breathe.

⊡

Most prey has some way to protect itself. Some are just fast, making any hunt an exhausting chase. Others, like the thorn rat, have spiny bodies difficult to chew, making it challenging to get to the good, soft meat within. Some, like horses, have hard hooves and vile dispositions. The elkryn and their smaller elk cousins have both sharp hooves and large antlers that can knock a wolf to the ground with broken ribs and no way to escape trampling. Then there are beasts like the auroch, which have hard hooves, large powerful bodies, and sharp horns capable of goring a wolf to death in an instant.

The beast running at us was such a creature. It was as tall as the auroch but much, much broader, and I guessed it to be twice as heavy. The first time I saw an auroch, I was certain that I'd die trying to hunt it. We'd killed it, though, and barely escaped unharmed. This beast was even more terrifying.

It had two sharp horns. The one on its forehead was almost as long as a wolf's head and muzzle, and the one on its snout was even longer. Its lower lip protruded sullenly and its body was covered in thick, coarse fur, longer than I had ever seen on prey.

And it was fast. It had lowered its head and was running blindly from Milsindra, straight at me.

I bolted after Lallna. I should have known better than to think Milsindra would just go away. If she couldn't get the Sentinels to kill me, she would do it herself. No one could blame her if I were to be trampled by prey. I looked over my shoulder. I was outrunning the beast. A smirk stretched my muzzle. Milsindra had underestimated me again. I put my head down and ran faster.

When I neared Kaar, I altered my path so the beast would not find its way to the humans. Lallna, still at least ten wolf-lengths ahead of me, did not. She headed straight to the village. I would have growled at her if I'd had the breath to do so. I slowed so that she could get farther ahead of me, then turned sharply and ran back toward the beast so it would come for me, not Lallna. I was sure Milsindra would drive the creature after me—I was the one she wanted dead—but instead, she sent it after Lallna and toward Kaar.

That's when I realized what the beast was. TaLi had told me what the rhino that had killed JaliMin's brother looked like. She'd said the creature hunted humans. I caught Milsindra's satisfied expression as she drove it after Lallna and toward the human village. She saw me watching her, snarled, and left off chasing the beast. Then she bolted into the woods.

The rhino kept running toward the village. Now I chased after it. I saw Lallna crash into the section of woods near Kaar, and the rhino followed. I knew I couldn't get there before it did, but I ran anyway. By the time I reached the woods, I couldn't see either Lallna or the rhino. I heard terrified screams, angry shouts, and a fierce unearthly bellowing from the edge of the Kaar.

The village was in chaos when I reached it. Bits of wood

and stone were strewn on the ground and smoking specks
from the fire pits drifted down onto the humans' shelters,
sparking small fires that the humans beat out with preyskins.
Lallna cowered next to the herb den as a pack of humans
chased the rhino from the village. I couldn't see Ázzuen or
Pell. I found TaLi in the crowd, and ran to her. BreLan stood
next to her, holding her arm.

I buried my head in TaLi's preyskin tunic. Ázzuen's familiar juniper scent told me he had come to stand beside me.

DavRian staggered over to us.

"The wolves brought it!" he gasped, pointing a shaking
finger at us. He was limping, though I could smell he was not
injured. "They led a rhino into the village."

HesMi was standing over the still form of a female. I
panted hard, trying to catch my breath. If they thought we
were responsible for the death of a human, they would kill us.
The woman moved, though, and got weakly to her feet. Her
leg was bleeding. Two humans led her away, limping.

I looked up at TaLi, wondering why she wasn't defending
us. Her face was thoughtful. HesMi glared at her.

"It was chasing a wolf." DavRian waved an arm at Lallna,
who was still crouched by the herb den, staring around the
human village, her chest heaving and her eyes still wide
with fear.

"You said it came here before," TaLi said reasonably. "The
wolves are not the problem. But they can be the solution."

I looked up at her. She couldn't mean what I thought
she did.

HesMi looked her over. "You think your wolves can help
us kill it? We've tried before. I've lost three hunters to it."

"You won't lose any with me and the wolves," she said with such certainty that I began to believe her myself.

I expected HesMi to argue with her, or ask her to prove herself. But she just gave TaLi a long, measuring look and dipped her head sharply. She must have really wanted the rhino dead.

"Be ready by tomorrow morning." She stalked after the wounded female.

BreLan gripped TaLi's other arm.

"It's too dangerous. I won't let you."

TaLi pulled away and glared at him, arms crossed and chin raised. BreLan took both her shoulders gently, then, and spoke to her as I had once heard TaLi speak to a crying child. Ázzuen crouched at their feet, looking from one to the other.

"You can't help the krianans if you get yourself killed," BreLan said. "You have to be careful."

"There isn't time," she responded. "Careful will have us on the edges of the Spring Festival watching as DavRian becomes the new krianan. He's convinced half the young men that I'm addle-witted and weak and that the wolves are dangerous."

"DavRian has been talking to the young males," Ázzuen whispered to me. "He calls you 'Bloody Moon' and keeps telling them that Marra was attacking MikLan. Some of them believe his lies. What happened with Neesa?"

"Later," I said, looking around. I saw neither RalZun nor IniMin, but I could smell them both nearby. Tlitoo flew across the clearing to land next to us. He immediately began pulling at one of the elkskin ties that held BreLan's foot-coverings in place.

"I have to prove myself quickly. Now." TaLi ducked away from BreLan's grasp. "It's like home. Half the people in the village are starting to believe that their females are less important than their males. If I don't show them I'm as strong as they are, they'll dismiss me as weak."

"It's a ridiculous risk," he said.

"You take risks all the time," she countered. "You have to trust me, BreLan. You can't keep protecting me. Not if I'm going to be the village krianan. You wouldn't have tried to stop NiaLi."

I saw the answer in his eyes: he hadn't been in love with NiaLi.

"I'll need all of you, Kaala," she said. Her voice trembled the slightest bit. I licked her hand. Then she strode off toward the large clearing at the center of the village. BreLan took a step and tripped over his raven-loosened foot-covering. Tlitoo gurgled happily and hopped to my side. "It will be a good hunt," he said. "It will be good to kill a rhino for the humans."

It was an easy thing for him to say. He could hide in the trees. My legs trembled at the thought of facing the huge, horned beast. But if we didn't hunt it, DavRian and IniMin could say we were more a threat to the village than a help, and Milsindra would tell the Sentinels we were not committed enough to their cause. *"I'll need all of you,"* TaLi had said, and I could still taste her salty skin on my tongue. I would rather be gored by a hundred rhinos than disappoint her. I forced my legs to stop shaking, butted Tlitoo with my head, and nipped Ázzuen's muzzle. We had prey to hunt.

16

At dawn the next morning, TaLi strode purposefully across Kaar's central clearing to greet HesMi and Ral-Zun. I kept as close to her side as I could without tripping her. She whispered to me as we walked.

"Ever since a rhino killed JaliMin's brother, HesMi has hated them. She says they charge humans on purpose." HesMi had lost a grandchild to the rhino. I could understand why she would despise them.

Ázzuen loped up beside me and looked up at TaLi. "Does she know what she's doing?" he asked. I had no answer for him. TaLi was smart, and she was brave, but she was still only a partly grown girl. A rhino could trample her to death easily.

HesMi and RalZun stood with a large group of humans around one of the larger fire pits. I saw reluctance and ridicule in some faces, excitement in some, and fear in most of them.

"It's a good test of what the wolves can do for us," HesMi said as if ending an argument, then turned to loom over TaLi.

"Do not endanger any of my hunters unnecessarily." She glowered.

"I would never risk the lives of those who follow me to the hunt," TaLi said formally.

HesMi picked up a hollowed-out auroch horn that she wore on a strap across her chest, and blew into it. A sound like the lowing of a wounded elkryn resonated through the village.

"The hunt has been called," she said. "See to it that you do right by it."

TaLi dipped her head to the human leader. Then she clutched my backfur tightly and pulled me as she turned away. I looked up to see her jaw clenched and her lips tight with anxiety now that the others could no longer see her.

"Get Pell," I said to Tlitoo. He had to have returned from the hills by now. Tlitoo flipped his wings back, considering. "Please," I added.

"He does not like the humans, wolf. I am not sure it is a good idea to have him here."

I growled, wondering why nothing could ever be easy. When Ruuqo and Rissa told someone to do something, they did it. Though perhaps not with ravens.

"I'll go!" Prannan said. I hadn't heard him come up behind me. "I'll find him for you!" He raced off into the woods, his tail whipping with excitement.

Too soon for my liking, we left the village in search of the rhino. Its path wasn't hard to follow. It had crashed through the bush like a Greatwolf. I'd never known any one creature to make so much noise or cause such destruction. Sage bushes, junipers, and saplings lay trampled in its path.

RalZun and HesMi walked side by side at the front of the

line of humans. IniMin and DavRian were a step behind them, even though the hunt was TaLi's. She and I walked quietly in the center of the pack of humans. A rustling from above told me the ravens were nearby. Many of the humans were laughing and poking each other, which seemed like odd behavior as we prepared to hunt such vicious prey.

"I'll bet you run screaming back to the village when you see it," one male said to another.

"I think you'll wet yourself when it looks at you," the taunted male replied.

"I'll bet my spear draws the first blood," a girl near TaLi's age said.

"There won't be a rhino to hunt if you all don't shut up," HesMi said, looking over her shoulder, but she smiled when she said it. Ázzuen whuffed softly next to me, then darted forward in front of the three young humans who had been arguing. He lowered his elbows and lifted his rump in an invitation to play. The humans laughed and one of the males poked a walking stick gently at Ázzuen. He seized it in his teeth and then let it go as he trotted back to me. The humans laughed again. I stared at Ázzuen.

"What was that?"

"It's like our hunt ceremony." He licked a splinter from his muzzle. Before a hunt, we often played as a way of preparing to risk our lives for each other, and to come together as a pack instead of as individuals.

The humans quieted as the woods thinned. I expected them to lead us to an open plain, like most hunting grounds, but they stopped before the woods opened up. There, rooting among the vines and bushes at the edge of the woods, was the rhino.

It looked even bigger close up.

"There used to be more of them," RalZun rasped to me, leaning on his spear. "When it was colder here, years ago. Most of the ones that are left live north in the cooler regions."

"Like the mammoths," Pell said, stepping up quietly beside us, Prannan panting at his side. "They're twice as big as this beast. We hunted one once." I didn't know whether to believe him or not; the Stone Peaks were always claiming to hunt dangerous prey. But he was eyeing the rhino calmly, and I was glad to have him there. He certainly had more practice hunting than I did, and that experience could save our lives. I touched my nose to his face in greeting. He gave me a long look, then turned his gaze to the prey.

"They often graze on the plains," RalZun said, "but they'll feed on forest lichen as well. If we can get it to stay in the woods instead of back out onto the grass where it can charge, we have a better chance."

The beast snuffled at the edge of the woods. If we could sneak around it, we could scare it deeper into the trees.

IniMin, his arms folded across his chest and sunlight shining off his hairless scalp, spoke loudly. "We cannot afford to lose more hunters."

The rhino shifted at the sound of his voice, then bent down to pull leaves off a nearby bush.

"That's why I brought the wolves," TaLi said. To the humans she may have appeared calm. But I could hear her rapidly beating heart and smell her anxiety.

A clattering of wood made me jump and startled the rhino from its browsing. It glared in our direction, snorted out a great gust of air, and trotted onto the plain, where it lowered its head and stared at us before disappearing behind tall grasses.

DavRian stood over a pile of sharpsticks that had fallen onto the rock-strewn ground.

"I brought extra spears to help in the hunt." He shrugged.

TaLi eyed him stonily. "You won't stop me, you know."

DavRian just smiled at her. "I brought too many spears and dropped them by mistake," he said. "But if your wolves are really as magnificent as you say they are, it shouldn't matter."

His face was smooth and friendly, but he couldn't keep the sneer from his voice.

TaLi turned from him. "Come on, Kaala."

Stiffening my spine against the trembling in my legs, I walked at her side. Pell strode forward ahead of us. Prannan ran up to my flank and looked up at me with wide eyes.

"Are you sure we can hunt it?" he said.

"A wolf can hunt any prey, if he's smart enough," I heard myself say. It was something Ruuqo had told us long ago, when we were smallpups. I believed it when he'd said it, six moons before, but I didn't now. I didn't believe we could hunt the huge beast. But if Prannan was afraid, he wouldn't hunt as well. His ears twitched uncertainly for a moment and then he dipped his head and fell behind me again. He'd believed me. It made me wonder how often Ruuqo and Rissa had pretended a confidence they didn't have.

The rhino had stomped farther out onto the plain, hiding in the tall grass. At first I couldn't see exactly where it was.

Then the grass wavered where there was no wind. Tlitoo and Jlela flew from the woods to circle above the moving grass. A shaggy hump and the tips of sharp horns poked up beneath them.

"You don't have to do this, girl," an old human said. He spoke kindly and placed his hand on TaLi's shoulder. "A krianan doesn't have to be a great hunter." But he had called her "girl," as if she were a child to be taken care of, not a leader to be followed.

She smiled up at him.

"I'm no great hunter," she said. "But the wolves are. It's just one of the benefits of being one with the world. One of many, and the least of them." She spoke smoothly. She must have practiced that speech, I thought. I wondered if she was as confident as she sounded, or if she was pretending to be, as I did with Prannan. I looked at RalZun, who was smiling at her, and I felt a chill. I liked the old raven man, but he wouldn't be the first to try to use us for his own ends. Was he willing to sacrifice us? To sacrifice TaLi to win his battle in Kaar? I shook myself. We were here, and TaLi was determined to hunt the rhino.

The old human grunted and removed his hand from TaLi's shoulder.

"Let's see what they can do, then."

Ázzuen, Pell, and Prannan were immediately at my side. A moment later, Lallna flopped down next to us. She was still spying on us.

"You'd better not get in our way," Ázzuen said as I lifted my lip at the Sentinel youngwolf.

Lallna's eyes were intent on the waving grasses. "I've always wanted to hunt one of these. Navdru and Yildra won't let us." She panted up at TaLi. "I might learn to like some of these humans."

I couldn't have been more astonished if she'd said she wanted to be friends with a hyena. I looked over at her, taking in her taut muscles, her focused gaze. She could help us kill the rhino. Still, I didn't want her thinking she could take charge.

"It's my hunt," I said. "You follow me."

Her pale eyes rested on my face, a spark of defiance in them. I met her gaze steadily and lifted my lip to show a glimpse of fang. Ázzuen growled, too softly for the humans to hear, and Pell pulled back his lips.

"It's your hunt," Lallna agreed, "as long as you aren't the humans' curl-tails."

I dipped my head to her. Immediately, I began thinking about how she could help us. She was fast, strong, and fearless. As much as I wished she weren't spying on me, I was glad to have her as part of the hunt.

"You'll be with Pell. The two of you can distract it and dodge away." It was the most dangerous task, and Lallna knew it. She grinned at me and tensed her haunches. Pell was watching me carefully. I didn't have to say anything to him. He would make sure Lallna didn't interfere with the hunt.

TaLi was watching me, waiting. She couldn't understand us, but was perceptive enough to know when we were communicating with each other. She looked curiously at Lallna, whom she'd never met. Unlike many humans, she could tell one wolf from another.

"We should come back later," BreLan said to TaLi. "It knows we're here now."

TaLi shook her head. "We'll drive it back to the woods and kill it there," she said.

"ToMin tried that already," DavRian said. "He got a gored leg out of it." ToMin was one of Kaar's best hunters.

"ToMin didn't have the wolves," TaLi said.

She hit the blunt end of her spear on the ground hard, three times, calling the hunters together.

"Like the auroch, Kaala," she said. I licked her hand. We'd hunted the auroch by angering it. When it lost its temper it made fatal mistakes.

TaLi spoke to several hunters, and they trotted into the field. We followed, keeping our eyes, noses, and ears focused on TaLi.

"Now!" TaLi shouted, and several of the humans ran at the waving grasses where the rhino hid.

It actually growled. I'd never heard prey growl before, but it did. Then it bellowed like twenty elkryn, and charged. The humans dodged, agile and quick. They poked at the rhino with their spears, then jumped away. The humans who had not run in surrounded the beast at a distance, holding their spears and spear throwers ready.

"It has the thickest hide of any beast I know," Pell said. "The humans will have to have perfect aim and strong arms."

"Go," TaLi said to us. We ran. Pell loped past the humans and flattened out to run under the low belly of the rhino. Lallna yipped. She charged behind the prey and grabbed its tail in her jaws. She hung on as the rhino kicked and bucked.

When she fell off, she rolled away and tried to grab its tail again.

One of the humans fell on his rump. The rhino turned on him. Other humans standing nearby shouted and pelted the rhino with rocks and spears, trying to distract it, while Tlitoo and Jlela flew at its face. It would not be diverted. It lowered its head and charged the fallen human. TaLi had made a mistake. It wasn't like the auroch, which lost its temper and behaved foolishly. Anger seemed to make this beast even more focused.

Ázzuen realized it, too. "Hurt it," he said. "*Make* it pay attention." Pell, who was close enough to hear, whuffed in agreement.

The human had scrambled to his feet but was still in the path of the rhino. Ázzuen and I leapt on the beast and sank our teeth into it. By the time my fangs made it through the thick fur, they barely cut into its hide. Pell grabbed its belly from beneath, allowing the rhino to drag him. Lallna, watching us, made a flying leap and scrambled onto the creature's back. None of it seemed to do much good.

TaLi saw what we were doing and shouted to the other humans. They dashed in and began slicing at the rhino with their spears. Lallna tumbled from its back but managed to grab hold of its tail again. Pell was still hanging onto its belly, and the humans struck it again and again. Finally the rhino turned from the fallen human, bellowing in pain. It smelled of blood and rage.

Now what? I thought. The beast was distracted, but it was furious—furious with the humans around it, furious with us. But not crazed like an auroch. It was intent on killing someone.

TaLi was shouting something, but I couldn't make out her words.

"Get it to the woods, Kaala!" Pell barked. He had finally released the rhino's belly and lay panting with exhaustion.

I allowed myself to fall off the rhino's broad, shaggy back. I hit the ground rolling and came to my paws. Pell was at my side; Ázzuen stood a wolflength away, while Lallna continued to dart under and around the rhino. Several humans continued to harry the beast. TaLi shouted at them, trying to get them to herd the rhino toward the woods.

"Remember the plains-horse hunt," I said to Ázzuen and Pell. Ázzuen immediately sprinted off while Pell looked at me. "We herded six horses together over the winter. Just follow what we do." He looked annoyed, but whuffed in agreement.

Ázzuen and I darted behind the prey, one on each flank.

"Take Lallna and get its front legs," I said to Pell. He ran past Lallna and spoke to her. Then the two of them were at the beast's forelegs. Ázzuen ran behind it, nipping at its rump. The idea was to trap the prey so it had no choice but to run where we herded it. It had been easy with the horses. They usually went where we wanted them to go. The rhino did not. It kept escaping our trap. It swung its huge head, its horns barely missing Pell and Lallna, then ran off in the wrong direction. It was clever prey.

BreLan was the first human to figure out what we were doing. He gathered others and several of them ran with us. Together we herded the beast to the woods. The rhino lowered its horns and tried to turn. Then the ravens flew at its back and together we drove it deeper into the woods.

It was harder for us to move among the trees than on the

open plain, but not as difficult as it was for the rhino. I expected it to rampage as it had on the plain, but it looked at
me and spoke for the first time. Some prey spoke to us and
some did not. I hadn't known if the rhino could.

"Why do you help them?" His voice was low and grating.
"It is not the way. It is not the way of hunter and of prey."
He swung his head from side to side, snorting gusts of air.
"You should fight them. They will kill you as easily as they
kill me. There used to be many of us. Many, many. Until they
slaughtered us all. That's why I kill them. They will destroy
all of us."

Three humans rushed in. The rhino lowered his horns to
gore them, but he couldn't turn quickly enough. The humans
jabbed their spears into him. He bucked and ran, trying to ma-
neuver among the dense trees. Ázzuen, Pell, and I wove between the trees, appearing wherever he wasn't looking. Lallna
hurled herself at him, biting at his eyes, and barely missed
being gored. A shout sounded from overhead. Several humans
had climbed into the branches to hurl sharpsticks from above.
Three lodged in the rhino's neck and he stumbled and then fell.

"Do not help them," the beast growled to me. "They take
away more than they give." His voice fell to little more than a
grunt.

Wolf and human attacked again, and before long, the
rhino lay dead, his life fleeing his body.

But his warning remained behind.

I shook myself, tossing away the rhino's words. Prey would
say anything to survive, and now that he had stopped mov-

ing, he was nothing more than good meat. And another way to prove our worth to the humans.

I don't know who was panting harder, wolves or humans, as we stood around the dead beast. Lallna was already trying to chew through its thick fur and hide while the rest of us stood staring at the animal.

HesMi watched both me and TaLi. Lallna glanced up briefly from her futile meal to stare at me. She was waiting to see if I would be submissive. I forced my tired legs into action and climbed atop the dead prey, then stood tall, claiming it. I heard a sharp whuff of breath from Ázzuen, but TaLi just smiled up at me. Tlitoo quorked approvingly and flew into the woods with Jlela.

First one and then another human started laughing. When I jumped down from the beast, a large human leaned over me. I expected him to thump me on the ribs the way male humans sometimes did, but instead he picked me up. I panicked for a moment, thinking he might throw me to the ground, but he just turned once with me in his arms and set me down before I could get over my shock.

"I like your wolves!" He grinned at TaLi. Then he picked the girl up and twirled her much the same way. When he set her down, several other humans thumped her on the back. HesMi watched them, smiling. Lallna, who'd finally managed to tear off a piece of meat, grinned at me. Pell dipped his head to me and slipped into the woods and away from the humans.

Unlike the humans in the Wide Valley, the Kaar hunters didn't seem to mind that we claimed our share of prey. They seemed to expect it. In the hours it took the humans to cut through the hide of the beast and begin to strip it of meat, we gorged ourselves, feeling comfortable enough to eat our fill among humans. Every once in a while there would be an altercation over a piece of meat, but it was settled quickly as it would be in any pack. I caught DavRian's aggrieved expression and lifted a lip at him. He watched me for a moment and a sly grin crossed his face. He whispered to IniMin. They were waiting for something, but I didn't know what. I took another bite of rich, fresh meat.

By dusk, the humans had cut away most of the meat and loaded it onto the sleds they used to help transport large loads. Ázzuen had an endless fascination with these sleds, which the humans made by tying, bending, and weaving wood and vines together in intricate ways, and he was chewing experimentally at the place where a taut cluster of vines was tied to what looked like most of the trunk of a young aspen. I was more interested in what remained of the rhino carcass. The humans left good bones behind and some good greslin. We could tell the Sentinels and they could come back for it later.

Prannan trotted to me, his tail waving. Ázzuen, meat-heavy and tired, staggered over to where BreLan was loading meat onto one of the sleds.

DavRian and IniMin stood then, moving quickly enough to make me nervous. They jogged to where HesMi was standing. They each carried one of the lit branches the humans used to light their way at night. I was far away from them, and they didn't seem to realize that our hearing was better than theirs.

DavRian pointed at Ázzuen. "That one was attacking MikLan. Later I saw it standing over him while he was sleeping, waiting to kill him, but it saw me and ran away. The boy left but it stayed behind to try to kill someone else. It's the one we called 'Child Killer' in the Wide Valley. If it bites someone, he'll be as much wolf as human. And the more time they spend together, the more he'll become like a wolf."

It had been Marra who accused before. He couldn't even tell one wolf from another.

"That one's a ghostwolf." HesMi gestured to Lallna, whose silvery fur did glow when she stood in the moonlight. She was so intent on tearing meat off the remaining rhino bones that she didn't look up. "It's a spirit that can suck the life out of a man, withering his crops."

"And then there's Bloody Moon"— DavRian looked at me—"the most dangerous one. They all follow it."

HesMi looked skeptical, but several other humans murmured in concern. I trotted over to Azzuen.

"I heard them," he said. "They've been saying that about me since DavRian saw Marra and MikLan playing." He looked at the humans around us. "A lot of the humans believe him."

Lallna crept up behind us, laughing.

"Ghostwolf?" she gulped. "And you're Bloody Moon?"

"It isn't funny," I said. "It could be dangerous. Marra left."

"You knew he was going to try something, Kaala," she said. "You knew they'd try to stop Tali from succeeding."

"I know," I said, I was tired. "We'll have to be careful, HesMi."

"You will, Kaala," Plannan said, blinking. "we'll help you."

I looked into his trusting eyes. Azzuen, too, waiting to see if I needed him.

"We'll keep listening to what DavRian says," I said. "And we'll keep hunting with the humans." We still had fourteen days until Even Night.

I plodded over to TaLi and, as darkness fell and the humans lit more of their fire branches, I let her lead us back to Kaar.

17

Darkness brought quiet to the village. As soon as they dragged the rhino meat to safety, the villagers of Kaar settled in, making their meals, setting up guards around their homes, and sitting around their fires repairing tools and talking.

I grew more and more anxious. DavRian was making up stories about us, and some of the humans would believe him. The rhino's warning nagged at me, and I still feared that the humans would blame us for bringing him to the village. But most of all, I couldn't stop thinking about the strange little wolves Neesa had shown me. She'd said the humans preferred them to us, that they'd lost the wildness that was wolf, and thus were a threat to wolfkind.

Yet my love for TaLi didn't make me want to be submissive to the humans or give up my will, and the humans of Kaar didn't seem to mind that we weren't their curl-tails. I wanted to know what it was about the streckwolves that made

the humans prefer them to us, and to understand why they were so dangerous. And, I had to admit, they intrigued me. I felt drawn to them as I would to a packmate.

With Even Night only half a moon away, and both Milsindra and DavRian trying to thwart us, I needed to know everything I could about the little wolves.

I smelled Pell and Ázzuen in the woods just beyond the village. Prannan and Amma sat by one of the fire pits next to JaliMin, watching as two humans stretched out a piece of rhino hide and scraped at it with one of their tools. The boy was feeding them small pieces of rhino meat, a look of enchantment on his face. I didn't see or smell Lallna anywhere, but that didn't mean she wasn't skulking somewhere. I needed an excuse in case she came looking for me. I padded over to Prannan and Amma.

"We're going to look for a smallprey copse Neesa told me about," I said loudly.

"We'll stay here," Prannan said. "It's almost time for Jali-Min to sleep." He licked his muzzle. JaliMin gave him another piece of meat. Prannan gulped it. Amma pawed at the boy, who burbled a laugh and held out a piece of cooked rhino. Amma gobbled it from his hand, and licked his face.

I started to say something to them—that their place was with their pack, or that they shouldn't go to sleep just because the humans did. But they seemed so happy to be with the boy, and they could tell Lallna my lie if she came looking for me. I touched my nose to Prannan's face and then to Amma's and trotted out to find the others.

They were sitting by the small stream just beyond the village. Ázzuen was glaring at Lallna. Pell was trying not to laugh.

"Tell her she can't do it, Kaala," Ázzuen said to me.

Lallna crouched down in a patch of moonlight. The moon was almost half full and her fur shone in its light.

"I'm a ghost wolf," she said, her face stern. "I'm going to haunt the humans." Then, unable to hold her serious expression any longer, she slapped both forepaws on the ground twice and ran into the stream and out again, laughing.

"It isn't funny," Ázzuen said, seeing my muzzle twitch. I couldn't help it. DavRian sounded so stupid calling Ázzuen "Child Killer" and me "Bloody Moon." And especially calling Lallna "Ghost Wolf."

"It's important, Kaala," Ázzuen said. "If DavRian keeps provoking their fears, the humans will hate us. Like they started to in the Wide Valley."

A rustling of leaves interrupted him and we turned to see Lallna's tail disappearing into the bushes that bordered the village.

"Stop her, Kaala," Ázzuen said. I hesitated.

"Oh, for the love of the Moon," Pell said. "When's the last time we had some fun?" His tail began to wag.

Ázzuen watched me.

"I can't stop Lallna from doing anything," I said.

"You can if you assert your role as leaderwolf." His eyes were intent on me. "When are you going to, Kaala?"

I blinked at him. I had enough to do without trying to assert authority over Lallna and Pell. But he had made me uneasy. I followed Lallna.

It was dark in the human village, but the moonlight streamed into the clearing, and fire lit uneven patches of ground between their dwellings.

Several humans crouched around the largest fire, talking, eating, working with their tools. A few of their young slept in the arms of adults. It reminded me of the first time I'd seen the humans in their homesite in the Wide Valley. A familiar yearning tugged at my chest, the wish to be with them, to be next to them, inhaling their scent. I looked for TaLi, but couldn't see her.

Lallna had managed to slip unnoticed into a stream of moonlight and stood, eyes slitted, ears tall. The moon gave her coat a strange glow. No one noticed her at first. She looked around impatiently. Then she tipped back her head and gave a long, low howl.

The humans looked up, alarmed. Lallna opened her jaws, showing off sharp teeth.

I'd hoped the humans would think it was funny. I'd hoped they would laugh as they had when we'd chased Jali-Min around, or that Lallna's game would help them bond with us like they did when Ázzuen had played with them on the way to the rhino hunt.

At first they were silent. Then a female clutched the child she held more tightly and turned away, protecting the child with her back. I heard a gasp and then another. Someone threw a piece of wood at Lallna. She howled again. Other humans stared, their faces contorted with fear.

Ázzuen had been right. And there was nothing I could do about it.

"Get back here," I whispered urgently to Lallna. She looked at me out of the corner of her eye and showed more fang. She didn't care that she was scaring them. She wouldn't mind at all if the humans hated us.

Several humans got up the courage to chase her away, and she bolted toward me.

We both ran, pelting as fast as we could into the woods. The humans didn't chase us far, but I could hear their voices rising in anxiety.

We stopped, panting, at the stream where Ázzuen and Pell waited for us. Lallna rolled onto her back, laughing so hard she couldn't speak.

"Did you see their faces?" she finally gasped. "They looked like a cluster of voles that's just realized they're about to be a meal!"

Ázzuen didn't reproach me. He just looked at Lallna in annoyance. Pell seemed as oblivious as Lallna and grinned down at her. She met his gaze and then licked his muzzle. He smiled slowly, then rested his head briefly against her neck.

I wanted to get out of there, and quickly. I knew I should tell Pell where I was going; he was pack. But I found I didn't want him with me. I licked the side of Ázzuen's face and whispered to him.

"Come with me?"

He looked startled, then like he was about to argue, but something in my gaze must have changed his mind. He dipped his head to me and followed me when I slipped away.

"We should find out what the humans are saying," he said.

"We will," I answered, "when we come back. I want to show you something."

He stopped for a moment, then a pleased smile tugged at his muzzle.

"Where?" he asked.

In answer I sprinted away, glad to leave my problems in Kaar behind me, even for a little while. With a happy yip, Ázzuen followed.

We ran full pelt for several minutes, even though I knew we should conserve our energy, for it was hours to the streckwolves' gathering place. It just felt so good to be running side by side with Ázzuen like we used to in the Wide Valley, when we were responsible only for helping with the hunt and winning our places in the pack. I could hear his heart beating in time with mine and felt the warmth of his body as he ran just far enough from me to avoid tripping me up. His paws hit the earth in a solid, steady rhythm and his breath came in easy, even gusts. I could imagine him leading a hunt with me, our pups and packmates following behind. I could imagine coming home to the lush, moonlit copse Neesa had found for us, followed by a contented pack, our bellies full of prey. The thought dizzied me and I almost tripped over my own paws. I tried to focus on the night's task. Before we could even think about pups or territory of our own, we had to survive past Even Night.

I settled into a slower, steady lope, still basking in the sensation of running with Ázzuen through the night.

I took him to the Barrens first, explaining what they were and how they had come to be. He was silent as he took in the desolate lands. The night was nearly half over when we reached the slope downwind of the streckwolves' gathering place. I slowed to a walk, and Ázzuen followed my example. Together, we crept as silently as we could to the crest of the hill.

The moon was bright enough to allow us to see clearly.

Many of the streckwolves were asleep, but several prowled around the edge of the gathering place. Ázzuen watched in fascination while I shared with him what Neesa had told me about the odd little wolves.

The wind shifted and several of the streckwolves lifted their snouts as they caught our scents.

"Let's go, Kaala," Ázzuen whispered.

Instead, I crawled forward on my belly. "I want to talk to them," I told Ázzuen. "Will you wait here? I don't want to challenge them by bringing a second wolf."

I stood, showing myself, and gave a short, welcoming bark. I didn't want them to think I was sneaking up on them. My heart beat faster. Meeting unknown wolves always made me nervous. Even strange little wolves like these.

A lithe, confident-looking streckwolf ran forward to greet me. I had kept my ears politely lowered and tried not to stare at his oddly shaped head and muzzle. It was only slightly different from an ordinary wolf's but enough so to make me uneasy.

"You're Kaala," he said before I could speak. He looked at me with such intensity that I stepped back. "I'm glad you've come. I'm Gaanin."

He knew who I was. And he spoke with confidence. He had the assurance of a leaderwolf, and he looked at me as if I were a long-lost pup. He leaned forward as if to take my muzzle in his jaws. I pulled away. He had no right to assume dominance over me.

He looked startled, then abashed.

"Of course," he said. "They wouldn't have told you about me."

"Neesa told me," I said, trying to figure out why my stomach roiled. "You're the ones the Sentinels say are dangerous." There was something in his scent that was familiar, but I couldn't figure out what. "Your pack's been spying on me."

He didn't deny it. "You're important, Kaala, as are the choices you make. I need to know what you're doing with the humans. I'm sorry that I didn't approach you directly about it, but I have good reason not to do so."

Neesa had told me that the streckwolves were submissive. Gaanin was as assertive as any leaderwolf. His ears, I noticed, looked like those of a normal wolf.

"The Sentinel wolves say that you want to take the humans from us and that the humans will choose you and kill us," I challenged.

Gaanin looked sharply over my head and growled softly to himself just as Ázzuen woofed a warning. I looked over my shoulder to see a wolf pelting across the plain. I swayed, trying to decide whether or not to bolt. When I saw that it was only Neesa running toward us, I relaxed, but Gaanin huffed in impatience.

"Your mother keeps watch over us," he growled. "Probably to make sure I don't talk to you. She still thinks she can keep you safe." He began speaking, much more quickly than before. "They're wrong, Kaala. The Sentinel wolves are wrong about the humans and how we must be with them. They want you to make the humans behave more like wolves, and it won't work. It can't work. The humans fear the wild of the wolf too much, and you can't change that just by hunting with them or playing games with their young."

He narrowed his eyes at me. "I'll bet that since you and

your packmates have been with them, they've been frightened by you at least once." I thought of the humans' reaction
to Marra and MikLan playing together and their fear of Lallna
standing in the moonlight. I said nothing, but something in
my face must have given it away.

"I don't need to spy on you to know that, Kaala, because
it always happens. There is a way to lessen their fear, but you
have to let us help you."

He looked over my shoulder again.

"There's more." He spoke more softly, but his expression
was urgent. "You must come back again, Daughter of the
Moon. Will you do that?"

"How do you know that name?" I demanded. Only my
mother had called me that. It was the meaning of "Kaala."

"Your mother told me," he answered, but his body had
tensed and he didn't quite meet my gaze. He was keeping
something from me.

"What is it that the Sentinels don't want me to know
about you and your pack?" I asked. My mother was almost
upon us. Tlitoo winged above her, easily keeping pace.

Gaanin looked down at his paws for just an instant before
returning his gaze to mine. That's when I knew he was going
to lie to me. My muzzle tightened with the effort not to snarl.

"What I've just told you about the humans. That's why I
need you to come back when Neesa isn't here."

I couldn't hold back a quiet growl. Gaanin was no better
than the Greatwolves, telling me I had to help him and then
trying to manipulate me. He probably was trying to steal the
humans from me, and if he did, the Greatwolves would kill

me. That was the "help" he offered. I thought of the lush territory Neesa had shown me. Gaanin would steal that from me if I let him. He would steal my chance to have a pack of my own.

My mother skidded to a halt next to me, Ázzuen at her side. Tlitoo landed neatly in front of her.

"What did he tell you, Kaala?" my mother demanded. Her face was pinched with anxiety, as much as it had been when Navdru had threatened us.

"That he thinks the Sentinels are wrong about the humans," I said. Ázzuen sidled past Neesa to stand next to me.

"That's all?"

"That's all," Gaanin answered, "but you should tell her more."

"That's not for you to decide!" my mother snapped. She gave Gaanin a long, measuring look, then closed her lips over her teeth.

"You know I wouldn't do anything to hurt you, Neesa," Gaanin said softly. "Or your pup."

"Then let her be, Gaanin," she said, but her voice had softened, too.

He stared at her so long that she turned away from him. He whuffed in frustration and started to speak to her, then scowled at me.

"I will leave you to your mother, Kaala," he said. He licked my shoulder as if I were a packmate, dipped his head to Ázzuen, and bounded away.

Neesa put her muzzle under my chin and lifted my head so that my eyes met hers. "You want to know everything,

Kaala," she said, "but there really are things you need to leave alone." I pulled away from her.

"You've been watching me," I accused.

My mother's voice grew sharp. "Not as much as I should have been! The Greatwolves won't let me interfere with you and the humans, so I've watched this place because I knew you'd try to come here. I am doing the best I can to keep Navdru and Yildra from killing you. If they find out you've spoken to Gaanin, I won't be able to stop them. They'll decide you aren't worth the risk and will abandon the humans and the Promise. I stayed with the Sentinel pack after they killed Hiiln because I swore to him I'd do my best to fulfill the Promise. You have to stop being so reckless."

I could hardly contain a growl.

"Leave it, Kaala," Ázzuen whispered. Neesa must have heard him, but she kept her gaze on me.

I knew I didn't make good decisions when I was upset. And Ázzuen was usually right.

"All right," I said. "We won't come back here."

Neesa sighed. "I wish I believed you. But please, Kaala, stay away from Gaanin and his wolves. Be careful. I will do what I can for you. And get out of here now. Navdru and Yildra are watching both of us." She took my muzzle in her mouth and warmth suffused me. I couldn't help it. I'd dreamed of having my mother beside me for so long. She pulled away from me and loped back toward the woods.

Tlitoo quorked softly. "I do not think she keeps secrets to hurt you, wolf. I think the streckwolf wishes you no harm as well"—he raised his wings halfway and shook them out—"but I do not know for sure. I will ask Jlela to watch them for us."

"Thank you," I said, watching the woods my mother had disappeared into. "What are you doing here in the middle of the night?"

Tlitoo folded his wings against his back. "I would rather be sleeping. But there is something you must see. Come by way of the dead lands, wolves," he ordered, his uncertainty gone as quickly as it had come. I always envied ravens their ability to shake off trouble.

I still looked after Neesa. Tlitoo tweaked my ear. "If you sulk all night, I am going back to roost."

I was tired of being serious. I leapt for him. Ázzuen yipped. Tlitoo gave a great caw and took flight, winging back toward the Barrens. He soared and arced above us, challenging us to keep up with him. Ázzuen and I gave chase. I jumped up, almost snatching Tlitoo out of the air, and he screeched happily and dove for my nose and then my ears. Ázzuen stood on his hind legs and batted at the raven. Tlitoo grabbed his tail and pulled, sending Ázzuen paws over ears. By the time we reached the Barrens, I felt lighter than I had since we'd left the valley.

Tlitoo flew out to where the broken landscape began, and I followed him.

"This is a place of death, wolf," he said to me. "I can easily get to the Inejalun from here."

I glared at Tlitoo and looked uneasily at Ázzuen. I didn't want him to know what I did with Tlitoo.

"He knows, densewolf," Tlitoo quorked.

"I've known for moons, Kaala," Ázzuen said, tilting his head to look sideways at me, watching to see if I was angry. "I figured you'd tell me when you wanted to."

My voice caught. "You don't think I'm aberrant?" I asked. I'd wanted to tell him, but couldn't bear the thought of him hating me for it.

"I think you're Kaala," he said, his face suddenly next to mine and his breath hot on my face. "That's all you need to be."

My heart raced. I could see it. I could see it as easily as if Tlitoo had taken me into the Inejalun. We could have pups together when this was all over. The Stream Lands pack. That could be our name. Ázzuen was my best friend, and if I wanted to I could keep him with me forever. His silvery eyes met mine, and I remembered the first time I noticed their lively glow, when he was no more than a babywolf near death.

"Not *now*, wolflets!" Tlitoo pushed between us. "Why can't wolves find the *right* time to mate?" he grumbled.

Ázzuen turned away, embarrassment flattening his ears.

Before I could snarl at Tlitoo, he plopped onto my back. All scent and sound disappeared, and I had to swallow against nausea as the falling sensation took me too suddenly. Reflexively, I closed my eyes.

When I opened them, I was standing with Tlitoo at the Stone Circle of the Inejalun. Immediately I began to shiver as the Inejalun stole the warmth from my blood.

"We must be quick, wolf," Tlitoo said. "The more you come here, the more dangerous it is for you. But you must see this. I found it when you were eating the rhino. Then when I was trying to sleep, my dreams of this place would not let me be. It was not hard to find you."

He flew out of the clearing and I followed, the pads of my feet tender with cold. Already, I couldn't feel my tail, and my nose was so cold that I couldn't even twitch it. Tlitoo took me to a familiar low hill overlooking the Barrens.

It was not barren now. It was a huge, thriving village, larger and busier even than Kaar. I found myself fascinated by the number of humans striding around it. They were of all sizes and all in excellent health, even though I could tell from the snow on the ground that it was the hungry time of winter.

Tlitoo poked me on the rump. I could barely feel it through the cold.

"There is not time to gawk at humans, wolf. Look at the streckwolves."

I had seen that there were wolves everywhere in the village. Now I looked more carefully. If the streckwolves of Gaanin's pack were strange, these wolves were so odd they could barely be called wolf. Their heads were even more rounded, and many of them had ears that folded all the way down. Their muzzles were too short to hold the proper number of teeth, and they moved with the eagerness to please that one saw in pups and curl-tails. Neesa had said that over time the streckwolves changed even more. This must have been what she meant.

"Look, wolf. See how they are with the humans."

I looked. The humans were as relaxed as I'd ever seen them. They sat side by side with the streckwolves as if they were truly of the same pack. Except for our own humans and the village young, the people of Kaar were never so at ease with us. This village also seemed to be even richer than Kaar. There were stacks of preyskin so tall I would have broken a leg falling off them, and piles and piles of meat drying on fires.

"I saw this and wanted to show you, wolf. The humans do

not have any fear of the streckwolves. They treat them as their own young. Almost all of the humans want to be with wolves, not just a few. It is what is different."

That wasn't the only thing that was different. The streckwolves were behaving like curl-tails, just like Neesa said they would. And suddenly I was overwhelmed with fury. If we let them, streckwolves would slither on their bellies into the village and steal away the humans, as well as our chance to be with them. The humans would choose them over us.

"A lonely creature is a dangerous creature, wolflet," Tlitoo said, echoing the Shadow Wolf's words to Neesa and Hiiln. "These humans are not lonely."

I tried to speak so I could tell Tlitoo that such obsequiousness was the very thing the Sentinels would kill us for, but my muzzle had frozen shut and my chest felt full of ice. All I could do was stare at him and shiver.

"Time to go, wolf," he said, looking at me sharply. He landed on my back and I felt like he lifted me off the ground. It seemed that I fell forever before I landed, and I was so weary I couldn't lift my head to meet Ázzuen's concerned gaze.

"Did you understand, wolf?" Tlitoo quorked.

I understood. I understood why the streckwolves were so dangerous. They really would steal the humans from us. When I was just a moon old and Ruuqo had chased my mother from the pack, I was alone and hungry. I had crawled into Rissa's den, hoping she would allow me to feed at her warm belly. Three of her own pups didn't want me there and tried to push me away, biting me and scraping at me with their sharp claws. Fury had overtaken me then, and I had shoved them away, claiming my place and my chance at life. The same anger overtook me now, but there was nothing I could do, no one I could fight.

I tried to tell Ázzuen what I'd seen, but fatigue forced my head to my paws. Ázzuen lay down next to me. His familiar scent calmed me. Together we could keep the streckwolves from ruining our plans. I tried to tell him so but yawned instead.

"Rest, Kaala," he said. "I'll watch over you." The last thing I remember before slipping into sleep was his muzzle against mine.

18

In my dream, angry humans pelted me with rocks. I ran from them, only to be attacked by a flock of ravens that clouted my head over and over again with their wings. When I escaped the ravens, I ran straight into a hive of bees, who stung me over and over between my ears.

Yelping, I opened my eyes just as RalZun thwacked me over the head again with an empty preyskin pouch.

He stared down at me, as wrathful as a thwarted raven.

I was so hungry my stomach burned and so thirsty my tongue seemed to fill my mouth. Ázzuen sat guard beside me, glaring at RalZun. There was a dried gourd filled with water in front of me. I stood and gulped the water down. RalZun threw pieces of firemeat at my paws and I gobbled them. Only then did I look up at him again.

"If I'd thought you were stupid," he croaked, "I would not have let you near Kaar."

The sun, shining behind him, hurt my eyes. I had no idea

what he was talking about, and I'd had it with everyone, human and wolf alike, ordering me around. I lay back down, my head on my paws.

RalZun hit me on the head again with his pouch. "I don't care how tired you are," he snarled at me. "Get up on your paws and follow me."

"We should go with him," Ázzuen said. He looked at me as if I might bite him.

I was too weary to argue. RalZun stalked away. Tlitoo walked just beside him, mocking the old krianan by bobbing up and down in time with his steps. When Ázzuen nudged me, I struggled back to my feet and followed.

RalZun walked in quick, jerky strides. Still exhausted from my journey to the Inejalun, I couldn't keep up. Ázzuen trotted back to walk beside me. Huffing in annoyance, RalZun slowed down, too.

"What were you thinking?" he demanded.

At first I didn't know what he was talking about. Then I remembered. Lallna had haunted the humans and they'd been frightened. I didn't know how long ago it had been. I often slept for a day or more after going to the Inejalun.

"It was a joke," I said to RalZun.

"It was a stupid one," he hissed. Tlitoo hissed back.

"I know," I said.

RalZun sighed and his expression softened a little. "They're saying you all turn to ghosts at night. They're saying you're not to be trusted. They look upon all of your pack with suspicion."

I remembered the streckwolves Tlitoo had shown me in the Inejalun. Their humans weren't suspicious of them. They wouldn't think they were ghosts or child killers.

"How long was I asleep?" I murmured.

"Almost two days, wolf," Tlitoo quorked. "I am sorry. I did not know you would sleep so long."

Half a moon since we'd left home. Eleven days left before Even Night. And no wonder I was still so thirsty. I stood and began following the faint scent of water until I found a trickle of a stream nearby and lapped from it. Ázzuen drank next to me. I hadn't heard RalZun follow, but when I looked up, he was perched on a rock, watching me.

"The humans are so stupid!" I said. "They believe anything."

"It's not stupid for them," he answered. "The night is dangerous when you have no fangs. The dark is fearsome when your vision fails you."

He sighed again and hopped down from his rock. "You'll have to try that much harder to gain their trust. TaLi has told the elders how you fished for salmon with her. It's one of Hes-Mi's favorite foods. Your girl leads the salmon hunt tomorrow. Be rested by then."

He glowered at me once more and then stalked into the woods.

If he hadn't been so busy scolding me, I would have told him about the streckwolf village. I told Ázzuen. He listened to me quietly, the skin between his eyes wrinkling.

"I don't see what Gaanin and his wolves can do, Kaala. It's only eleven days until Even Night. We just have to keep them away until then." He grinned at me. "And win over the humans. And stop Milsindra from sending more rhinos, and DavRian from making up more stories."

"Oh, is that all," I said, a smile tugging at my muzzle.

He stood on his hind legs and placed his forepaws on my back. "We'll bring them so many fish, they won't have to hunt for a moon," he said. "They'll be as fat as rock bears ready to sleep the winter away."

Grinning, I reared up to knock him off my back. "That is, if you don't eat all the salmon before we get them back to the village."

He nipped me lightly on the nose, barked a challenge, and darted into the woods. I took off after him. We were far from success in Kaar, and there were so many things that could go wrong I couldn't hold them all in my thoughts. But Ázzuen thought we could succeed. I chased after him, leaving, at least for a moment, my fatigue and doubts behind.

▣

At high sun the next day, I stood in a wide stretch of shallow water. Ázzuen and Pell were at my flanks. Prannan sat beside JaliMin on the bank while the boy slipped him bits of food. Lallna watched from the woods, gnawing on a piece of horse bone she'd dug up from a human cache. Six humans, including HesMi, TaLi, and BreLan, watched us from the riverbank.

The humans often hunted the salmon, TaLi had told me. *Fishing* they called it. They had their spears with them, but also large bundles of woven vines. At first I thought the bundles were meant to carry fish, like TaLi's basket, but as the humans unrolled them, it was clear that they were too large and unwieldy for that.

We were upstream from where Ázzuen and I had caught salmon in the fast-running water. The water was calmer here, but I watched TaLi with concern as she waded over to me.

"I told them you'd help us chase the fish into the nets," TaLi said, pointing to the stretches of woven vines. "Usually it takes at least twelve of us to catch an entire run of fish here, but there were four herds of elk nearby and HesMi didn't want to spare so many hunters. Now we can hunt all four herds and the salmon." Her voice rose with excitement. It was a way we could show that we were valuable to them.

She smiled and turned back to the humans. The water came up to just above her knees. "I'll herd the fish to you with the wolves," she called out to the four humans at the net.

She must not have been looking where she was going. She slipped on something, a rock or a slick bit of mud, and fell into the water. It was slower-moving than the place where we'd hunted salmon before, but the current was still strong enough to take her. The other humans might not know that she couldn't swim.

I bounded toward her, Ázzuen splashing behind me. BreLan dropped his end of the net to wade over to her. All three of us got to her at the same time. She had already regained her feet and glared at us.

"I'm fine," she said.

"You have to learn how to swim, TaLi," BreLan said, pulling her into his arms. I pawed her thigh in agreement.

"I have to lead the hunt," she said, gently tugging away from him.

He didn't let her go right away.

He took her chin in his hand and looked down at her. I heard her breathing quicken. BreLan's expression softened.

She smiled. "Later."

He pressed his lips to hers. They stood like that for long

moments. Impatient for the hunt, I shoved in between them, pushing them apart. BreLan glared down at me, then made his way back to the other humans.

Hard bodies hit my legs, making me stumble. I looked down to see the river transformed. So many fish swam by my legs that it looked like a river of salmon rather than of water.

"Now!" TaLi called.

Ázzuen, Pell, and I splashed through the water. Prannan bolted from the riverbank, and Lallna took a running leap to land in the river. I was afraid she would try to steal some of the fish, but she followed my lead as we herded the salmon into the waiting nets of the humans.

The humans worked together as smoothly and elegantly as any pack of wolves. They closed in on the salmon, gathering them up in their nets. Then they dragged the nets onto the shore and into the woods, dumping out the writhing fish.

Lallna stopped next to me, panting.

"Why are you helping?" I demanded, certain she was up to something.

"It's fun!" she said. "You're too serious."

Pell laughed and my ears flattened in embarrassment. He snatched a salmon out of the water and bounded into the woods with it. The humans waded back into the river with their nets, and the hunt began again. Twice more they filled their nets, until the cloud of fish thinned.

We waded out of the water. As we neared the riverbank, I spotted a lone salmon and grabbed it from the river. It writhed and flapped in my mouth. I dropped it when I reached the shore and bit into it.

A human male ran over to me.

"Give it here, wolf," he said.

I looked at him, annoyed. They had netfuls of salmon. They didn't need this one and I was hungry. I was also aware that Lallna would be watching me. Then I caught the scent of bitter spruce. Milsindra was skulking somewhere nearby, too. A smile pulled at my muzzle. I could show both of them I wasn't submissive to the humans.

I didn't growl or even snarl at the male. I just turned away, the salmon in my mouth. He tried to grab it again, and I ducked under his hand. He grabbed at the fish once more, his face dark with exertion and frustration, and I ducked out of his way again and carried the fish into the woods. I turned when I heard a loud thump. The human had picked up a rock and hurled it onto the ground in fury. He looked at the place where I'd entered the forest, anger and shame contorting his face. I didn't worry too much about it. There were always battles over prey.

"He doesn't seem very happy with you," Milsindra said. She yawned as she stepped out from behind a willow. My heart started beating hard as it did whenever I met her. I thought quickly about the rest of the fish hunt. We had not been subservient to the humans in any way.

I set the salmon down. "He'll get over it," I said, grateful that Milsindra was forbidden to show herself to humans other than krianans. If she weren't, she would have waded out into the river itself.

"Perhaps," she said. "But then again, they are not the most reasonable of creatures. They scare easily."

"That's why you herded the rhino to them?" I demanded.

It was stupid to confront her, but I was tired of her bullying. "You can send as many rhinos as you like. We'll still win."

I thought I saw a flicker of fear in her eyes. Then it was gone and I wondered if I'd imagined it. She whuffed a laugh and poked her nose hard enough into my ribs to make me fall. Then she took my salmon in her huge jaws and loped away.

When I got to my feet, I was shaking. When I'd been face-to-face with Milsindra, I'd been able to defy her. Now anxiety made my neck ache and my skin itch so much I wanted to scrape it off. I rubbed against a willow tree, but it didn't help. Then I smelled rotting prey. I followed the scent a few wolf-lengths deeper into the woods, where I found a badger that had been dead at least three days.

I dipped one shoulder into the soft flesh of the dead prey and rolled onto my back, turning back and forth in it until my itching eased and the tension in my neck lessened. I rolled once more in the yielding flesh of the badger. Feeling much better, I set off after the humans.

They had already started back toward Kaar, but it was easy to catch up to them, weighed down as they were by their burden of freshly caught fish. The sun was halfway down the sky and warmed the earth beneath my paws. HesMi, walking at the front of the line of humans, raised her voice in what sounded like a howl moving up and down in pitch. It was just as complex as our howls, with repetitions and rhythms similar to those the humans used when they made what they called *music* by hitting dried gourds or blowing into hollow deer bones. Her voice was beautiful. It sounded like the wind moving through the holes in a cliff. First one human, then another joined her. I stopped where I stood and added my voice to theirs in a song of celebration of a successful hunt. Ázzuen and Prannan joined me, and our voices blended with the humans'. Tlitoo landed next to me and swiveled his head from side to side.

A moment later, I realized that the humans had stopped walking and singing and were staring at us. Our own howls tapered off. HesMi looked perplexed and a bit affronted. Prannan trotted up to her and gave a soft tentative howl, wanting to continue the song. HesMi's face broke out in a grin as if she were JaliMin's age instead of a village leader. She tipped back her head and howled like a wolf would. Prannan's ears folded back in surprise. HesMi's voice wasn't as resonant as a wolf's—it wouldn't have carried across territories and, as far as I could tell, it didn't share a message of any kind, like the location of a group of prey or the status of the pack—but she was obviously trying to communicate with us. She ran out of breath and took another. As soon as her next howl began, I joined in. As I howled, I thought of humans and wolves together, of friendship and of two packs coming together as one.

HesMi's howl harmonized with mine. Wolf packs often synchronize howls to express unity. Ázzuen and Prannan joined in and, after a moment, Lallna's voice lifted, too. TaLi and BreLan howled lustily, and several humans added their voices.

HesMi might just have been howling in camaraderie, to indicate that we might be pack someday, but it could have meant that she was ready to join our packs together.

I ran past Prannan, whose tail was in full wag. Before I could reach HesMi, the human leader collapsed to the ground, choking and gasping. I stopped, concerned that she was hurt, then heard similar noises coming from other humans, and I remembered that this was one kind of their laughter. Several others besides HesMi were laughing so hard they were gasping, and some were just grinning. Even TaLi was giggling. None of them seemed to realize the significance of our joined howls.

Prannan looked at them, wagging his tail. He didn't realize the importance of what had happened, either. Ázzuen did, and looked at me in confusion and then back at the humans.

A human male pointed at me.

"Look at its expression!" he snorted. "It looks like LaMin did when he fell in the pond." He snorted like a forest hog and thumped me on the back. I wasn't ready for the blow and stumbled a little, which made him laugh harder.

Pell walked up to me. He smelled of willow and mud. He'd been watching from the woods.

"I don't understand." My voice shook a little. I was so sure that howling together meant something.

"They think we're a joke, Kaala," he said. "That's all."

"I don't think it's all," Ázzuen said, lifting his nose to the breeze. A light rain had begun to fall, and a scent wafted from the humans' damp skin. It was like the scent that arose from TaLi when we slept side by side, the one that BreLan exuded when he and Ázzuen wrestled. It wasn't as strong, but it was the scent humans gave off when they were one with us. Our howls had changed them in some way.

"It is a step, wolflet," Tlitoo said, striding up to me. "It moves them away from fear. It moves them toward thinking of you as pack."

A step closer to making them like us as much as the humans in the older village had liked their streckwolves. I licked HesMi's hand and she ran her fingers through my fur.

She wrinkled her nose.

"Your wolf stinks," she said to TaLi.

I heard a rumble of displeasure coming from the bushes and saw a flash of gray. Milsindra was still tracking us. She had been afraid of how well we'd hunted with the humans. She knew we were doing well.

"They're old," Ázzuen said thoughtfully. "HesMi and the others. They're older humans."

"So?" Pell said. "What does that have to do with anything?" I was wondering the same thing, but I knew Ázzuen well enough to wait to catch up with what he was thinking.

"So, TaLi and BreLan are young humans," Ázzuen said as if talking to a particularly stupid pup. Pell glowered. "They accept new ideas more quickly. The older humans are slower to see new things. They're set in believing that their way of doing things is the right way." His ears pricked in excitement. "Don't you see, Kaala? We've been expecting them to behave like wolves or like krianans or like human young. We've been expecting them to behave like we do. We have to see them differently. We have to find out what it is that makes them want us."

The streckwolf Gaanin had said we needed to do more than just hunt with the humans. And the wolves Tlitoo had shown me in the Inejalun had made the humans seem relaxed and happy. HesMi and her pack seemed almost as relaxed when we howled with them. The humans were so much like us that I kept expecting them to behave like wolves. But they were not wolves. Ázzuen was right. We had to think more like humans if we were going to overcome their fear.

Lallna bit me hard on the ear. I yelped.

"The other humans are coming," she said. She slipped into the woods. I watched her go, wondering why she'd bothered to warn me. I nosed HesMi and looked in the direction of the approaching humans. A moment later she heard them. She peered down at me, pleased, then ran her fingers gently through my headfur again.

My nose told me that DavRian was among the approaching humans. They were walking from the elk plain back to the village, and their path crossed ours at a large patch of gorse. I sneezed. Gorse always irritated my nose.

DavRian and his group of hunters smelled of frustration and disappointment. There was no smell of dead elk. Hunts fail more often than they succeed, though we seemed to do better when wolf and human hunted together. There was nothing disgraceful about a failed hunt. Yet DavRian also smelled of shame.

We waited for them. TaLi nudged me with her hip and walked to the front of the humans to stand next to HesMi. The girl was carrying a basket of fish that looked much too heavy for her. She wanted DavRian and the others to see how successful we'd been. She couldn't know yet that their hunt had yielded no prey.

DavRian was first into the gorse patch. His eyes darted from TaLi's fish basket to HesMi and back again. Then they rested on me, and a look of defeat flitted across his face. Now the humans could see as well as we could smell that their hunt had failed.

"Did you catch any grass elk?" TaLi asked, her tone friendly. She rested the heavy basket of fish on her hip. I whuffed at her. I knew what she was doing. The first thing the other humans had seen when they walked into the gorse patch was TaLi standing next to HesMi, holding food for the village, with me at her side. The first things our group of humans, including HesMi, saw were empty hands and dejected expressions. The message would be clear. We had succeeded where they had failed. TaLi's eyes held a fierce, triumphant gleam. I whuffed again. If she made DavRian feel more ashamed, he would only hate us more. A strong leaderwolf would sometimes make a point of humiliating a packmate who had challenged her, but only if she was strong enough to win any resulting fight. TaLi was smaller than DavRian and not fully grown. I didn't think it was wise to shame him that way.

DavRian only smiled, but I noticed his trembling hands.

"We didn't succeed this time," he said. "There's always the next hunt. Congratulations on your fishing," he said.

TaLi inclined her head. "I'm glad we can bring the fish to add to the rhino meat. We'll take the wolves to the elk next time. That might help."

DavRian kicked a small, leafy plant that grew among the spiny gorse. He kicked it so hard that some of its leaves flew up into his own face.

"Careful," TaLi said, her voice full of false concern. "That's gallin leaf. It's poisonous. You wouldn't want to swallow any."

DavRian started to snarl something at her, but HesMi suddenly gave a great howl, making DavRian jump back. Several other humans howled, too. Prannan started to join in, but when the rest of us didn't, he stopped. HesMi laughed and clapped DavRian on the back, much the way humans sometimes thumped us in friendship.

"The girl wins this round, DavRian."

DavRian grimaced, then stalked away from HesMi.

One of the younger males came to TaLi and held out his arms. "I'll carry that for you," he said shyly. TaLi blinked at him for a moment. I tugged at her tunic. She needed all the friends she could get.

"Thank you," she said. The young man blushed and took the basket, lifting it on one shoulder and trotting after the others.

I saw the pain on DavRian's face, and found myself wanting to lean against him to offer comfort. Then he saw me watching him. His face darkened and he pulled his lips back in a snarl as fierce as any wolf's. IniMin stepped up beside him and placed his hand upon the younger man's shoulder. He whispered something into DavRian's ear. I tried to hear what he said, but his words were lost in the wind. DavRian smiled grimly at him and nodded, but he looked after TaLi with longing and despair.

19

The humans walked slowly from the gorse patch. The late-afternoon sun and their sluggish pace made me drowsy. I found myself thinking about the best napping spots in Kaar. I didn't realize there was something wrong until I almost ran into TaLi.

All the humans had stopped. We'd reached the stretch of plain just before the woods that sheltered Kaar. The humans watched a figure moving unsteadily on the field. The grass was shorter there than on the rhino's plain, and we could see the figure clearly even though it was at least a hundred wolf-lengths away.

"Crazed," Pell whispered, his voice hoarse with concern. "It's a crazed wolf."

Then I saw that it was indeed a wolf. It was moving so erratically that I hadn't realized it at first. It was running in circles and bucking and rearing like an elk in its death throes.

"That's what happens with wolves when they go mad,"

DavRian said. "It has poison in its mouth and if it touches you, you'll go crazy and die. You'll die in pain as if you've been stabbed by a thousand spears." He looked down at me. "Or if you don't die, you'll turn into a mad wolf yourself."

"Can we kill it?" Prannan asked, his voice shaking only a little.

"Don't try," I ordered. "DavRian's right. If it bites you, it will poison you." Ruuqo had told us about crazed wolves. I'd hoped to go my entire life without meeting one.

"It'll die eventually," Pell said. "But if it bites anyone first . . ."

He didn't have to finish. If it bit another wolf, the disease would spread to that wolf. If it bit a human, it would be disastrous. The crazed wolf caught sight of us then, and charged.

A whirring sound made me cringe. DavRian's arm came down hard at his side and his spear flew through the air. His aim was perfect and he was strong. The spear landed in the crazed wolf's back and it toppled over. It rolled onto its back, kicked its legs several times, and then was still. The humans around us let out great breaths of relief. I looked up to see that most of them had their sharpsticks raised. HesMi gripped DavRian's arm.

"Well thrown," she said. Then she looked down at me, her face puckered in concern, and I realized that the crazed wolf gave credibility to DavRian's stories.

"There's no reason it should have been here," Ázzuen said. "Of all the places it could have been in the territories, there's no reason it would be here right now."

"Milsindra," I said, remembering her words at the river. I should have known she would do more than just watch us.

She'd seen us succeeding with the humans and had driven the mad wolf to us. And, with a dread as heavy as wet fur after a winter rain, I knew she wasn't done with us yet. When a human male gasped and pointed across the plain, my chest grew tight.

Milsindra stood atop a rock, far enough away that she could claim she didn't know she was visible to the humans, but close enough that it was clear that she was no ordinary wolf.

"That thing is bigger than a rock bear," HesMi whispered, fear creeping into her voice. She looked at DavRian. "You were right," she said. "I didn't believe you when you told us about the giant wolves."

"There are huge wolves and there are mad wolves," DavRian said. "And you never know which ones are dangerous."

"I'll get RalZun," Ázzuen said, and darted off to find the old krianan.

The humans were silent the rest of the way back to Kaar, anxiety rising off them like smoke from their fires.

◻

Word of the crazed wolf and of Milsindra reached the village even as we did. As the humans began the long process of preparing fish for their caches and cooking others for their evening meal, HesMi gathered the village elders. I saw Ázzuen at RalZun's side. The old krianan crouched down and, as he listened to Ázzuen, his shoulders stiffened and he clenched his hands into fists. He stood and stalked toward the other elders. They all ducked into the large structure the humans used for gatherings. TaLi, BreLan, and DavRian followed.

Unlike most of the shelters in the village, this one was made entirely of skins, held up by a complex arrangement of branches and the trunks of young birches.

RalZun had told me that this kind of structure was called a *shrin*, and that the word meant both the structure itself and to be movable. When the humans used to roam from place to place like ordinary creatures, he'd told me, they carried a shrin with them so that the elders would always have a place to meet. They still used the shrin as a sign of their commitment to meeting together to make decisions for the village. I wondered whether they would continue to do so if DavRian became krianan and they completely gave up their wandering.

The shrin's soft walls meant that we could easily hear what was being said inside. Ázzuen and I lay down up against one of the sides.

"It's exactly what DavRian warned us about," IniMin was saying. "They seem friendly enough now, but they could turn on us at any moment."

"Other creatures go mad." That was RalZun's rasping voice. "I've seen an auroch run straight into a waiting spear and a brain-sick horse leap off a cliff to its death."

"All the more reason we shouldn't let wild animals into our homes," IniMin said. "That's why we protect ourselves from the beasts of the forest. We're meant to tame the wild, not invite it to sit at our fires."

"Humans run mad, too," TaLi pointed out. "There was a woman back in the Wide Valley who killed three people because she said the Ancients told her to. It has nothing to do with the wolves."

"DavRian said that the mad wolves have poison in their

teeth. And what about the giant wolf?" The voice was familiar, and I thought it might be HesMi's, but the skins distorted the sound, and I couldn't be sure. I whuffed in frustration.

"If that's true, we can't have them around," the female continued. I had to know who was talking. I pushed my nose under the bottom of the shrin. When no one noticed, I pushed the rest of my muzzle under. I waited a few more moments and then shoved the heavy skins up so that I could get my entire head inside.

HesMi sat on a small pile of hides. Most of the humans were sitting around her, but TaLi, BreLan, and DavRian stood. I heard a soft clacking from the folds of the shrin to my left. I dared to push my head in a little farther and saw Tlitoo crouched down, his dark form mostly hidden by the shadows. I couldn't see his eyes, but I imagined he was staring beadily at me.

"It isn't true," RalZun said impatiently. "Those are stories to scare children and those too foolish to know better." His voice carried enough authority to make several of the humans murmur in agreement. "The wolves TaLi has brought to us have done nothing but help us."

"It isn't worth the risk," DavRian said. "We learned that back home. What if just one of them goes mad? It could kill half the village."

"Has it ever happened?" RalZun countered. "I've never heard of it."

"My grandmother said we've lived with wolves before," TaLi said. "None ever went mad. And sometimes wolves grow large, just like people do. I've never known them to be dangerous."

IniMin coughed softly.

"There is something else you should know," he said. "Something DavRian told me. I didn't want to say anything. I didn't want to be unfair to TaLi." He looked at her as if they were friends. "I'm sorry, TaLi, but I must tell them."

TaLi looked back at him, perplexed.

"DavRian told me that this girl, TaLi, herself has run mad. That she bit two of her tribemates and tore off the ear of one of them. That it has happened to those of the Wide Valley who call themselves krianans. And"—he lowered his eyes as if sorry to speak—"to those here in the wilds around Kaar as well. Those who call themselves the old krianans have abandoned the Ancients. They worship the trees and the bushes of the wilds. They speak to the animals of the forests as if they were human." He whispered. "Some can even become animals."

Silence met his speech. TaLi broke it.

"That's the most ridiculous thing I've ever heard." I wanted to whuff in agreement. He may as well have said that a tree could turn into a rhino.

"I know people who've seen it happen," DavRian countered.

"Did DavRian tell you he chewed dream-sage and pretended to talk to the Ancients?" TaLi asked.

The humans began to speak over one another as they had our first day in Kaar. One shouted, then another. I wasn't able to hear what they were saying.

HesMi put two fingers in her mouth and whistled, a sound so high-pitched it felt like someone had thrust a thorn through my head. The humans in the shrin quieted.

"I will not let this village be ruled by rumor and fear," HesMi said. "Nor will I risk the safety of anyone here. We are not in immediate danger, so the wolves may stay. It is clear that some wolves are dangerous, so we will watch them carefully."

RalZun caught sight of me and frowned. I backed out of the shrin before any of the other humans saw me. Ázzuen was watching me, his eyes wide.

"Now what?" I said, leading him a few paces away from the shrin.

"I don't know, Kaala," he answered. "We have to make sure nothing we do scares them."

I sighed. "While not being submissive to them." That made me wonder where Lallna was. If she'd heard what the humans were saying in the shrin, she'd tell the Sentinels. I lifted my nose to the air, searching for her scent. I found her lying next to a group of young humans, two of whom had their long arms slung over her. When she saw me watching her, she rolled to her feet, shook herself, and darted into the woods.

I started back to the shrin, but several humans now stood outside it. I paced instead, waiting for the humans to finish their long discussion, wishing that the babble of their overlapping voices didn't keep me from understanding what they were saying. Ázzuen watched me silently from where he sat next to a small fire pit. Finally, when the pads of my feet were sore, I settled down next to him.

We sat there side by side as the warm sun set behind the trees and the night air began to cool the village. I kept expecting the humans to come out of the shrin and go into their shelters to sleep, but it wasn't until dawn that they emerged, clambering in ones and twos from the preyskin folds of the shrin. Several looked concerned, but it was the look of fear on the faces of many of them that worried me. That fear was dangerous. It meant they didn't trust us.

I folded back my ears and softened my expression. Then I trotted to three of the fearful humans—all young males—and let my tail wag. I couldn't offer them my belly with Lallna so near, but I could try to set them at ease. I remembered Ázzuen playing with the humans on the way to the rhino hunt and picked up a bit of wood that had fallen from a fire.

I brought it over to the humans, lowered to a play crouch, and wagged my tail harder.

"Look at its eyes," one of them said. "It could go crazy any second."

Another one of them picked up a piece of wood—larger than the one I had—and hurled it at me. He missed.

"Stay away from us, wolf," he said. The three of them stalked away.

I felt Lallna's gaze. She was watching me from the edge of the woods. She started toward me. Then she froze and lifted her nose. A snarl pulled her lips away from her teeth. She lowered her head and pointed her muzzle to a thick sage bush. Wolf paws stuck out from beneath it, and a nose twitched, taking in the scents of the village.

"Streckwolf," Lallna growled. "How dare it come here." The wolf in the bushes scuffled a little farther into the village and I saw its rounded head and short muzzle. A streckwolf was spying on us again. It might even have heard what the humans said in the shrin, and had certainly seen the human throwing wood at me. It would tell its packmates that the humans were afraid of us and they would sneak back and take Kaar from us.

Lallna bolted for the woods. The streckwolf yelped, turned itself around, and scrambled away. I chased after Lallna.

I caught up with her as she tried to force her way through a thick tartberry patch. I ran around it, passing her. I quickly found the streckwolf's trail and ran after it, limping a little after a tartberry thorn pierced my forepaw. The scents of sage and gorse and moss blew past me as I ducked under and around bushes and tree roots.

I rounded the huge trunk of an ancient yew to find the streckwolf staring at me, panting. It was a young male. I tackled him, rolled him onto his back, and stood atop him.

"Why were you spying on us?" I demanded.

"I wasn't," he said. "I wanted to see the humans. It's not fair that we can't. They're ours."

Standing over the little wolf, I felt the urge to lick his muzzle as if he were a pup. Something about his soft eyes and open, friendly expression made me want to take care of him rather than rebuke him for trespassing.

"Why are they yours?" I asked.

"Because it's our task to be with them, to give them something to cherish other than themselves. Something they never have to fear."

Lallna slammed into me, knocking me off the streckwolf. Then, in the time it took to pluck a salmon from the river, she ripped his throat out.

"Why did you do that?" I gasped. "Why did you kill him?"

She licked the streckwolf's blood from her muzzle. "It

came to the human gathering place," she said as if it were obvious. "You can't be soft with them, Kaala. I know they seem like pups, but they're not pups. They're an abomination. They're a threat to all of wolfkind. They give up the wildness of wolf for a few scraps of meat. It's our duty to kill them if they come near the humans." She stepped off the streckwolf and, with her back paws, kicked dirt over his body before trotting back toward Kaar.

I stood over the dead streckwolf. He looked so much like a pup. I was angry with him for spying on us, but I didn't want him dead. We killed hyenas who challenged us and even other wolves that tried to take our lands, but killing the little streckwolf seemed wrong. He reminded me of my littermates, slaughtered before they'd had a chance to taste their first meat. I shook myself. I had to remember what was at stake. If the streckwolves took our place among the humans, the Promise would fail. They would help the humans create another Barrens, like the strecks Tlitoo had shown me, and Navdru would kill everyone I loved.

I didn't want the little streckwolf dead, but if I had to choose between him and my pack, between him and TaLi, I would have killed him myself.

20

"I hear something," Ázzuen said.

He sat perfectly still at the edge of the central clearing, staring into the woods. It had been a full day since Lallna had killed the little streckwolf, and I'd done my best to distract myself from my guilt by studying the humans, trying to figure out which ones DavRian had already won over. Now my head felt like it was full of moss. I was ready for a run or a swim in the river to clear my mind. I padded over to Ázzuen. I hadn't told him yet what Lallna had done. What I had helped her do.

"At the edge of the village," he said before I had a chance to say anything.

I listened, but heard only the sounds of the forest.

"Is it a wolf?" I asked. I couldn't bear to see another streckwolf killed.

"I'm not sure."

Then he pricked his ears and pointed his muzzle toward the woods. Then I heard it, too. A soft and urgent mewing.

We loped into the woods. I recognized JaliMin's scent. The other scent was familiar, too: longfang. I could never forget it now.

JaliMin crouched in front of one of the longfang cubs, trying to feed it bits of sourtree fruit. I almost laughed aloud. JaliMin liked to feed us every bit as much as he liked to take food from us. The cub took each piece delicately in its front teeth, then spat it back out. I didn't know if longfangs ate fruit or not, but this cub didn't want it. Each time it spat out the fruit, it mewed again at the boy. It was a sound of desperate, yearning hunger. The cub's ribs poked out sharply through its flat fur.

Neither boy nor cub noticed us at first, so intent were they on each other. The boy held out another piece of fruit. The cub, clearly frustrated, swatted at him. He hadn't extended his claws fully—if he had he could've taken the boy's arms off—but he'd frightened JaliMin, who screeched and ran back to the village. The cub looked at me with hollow, hungry eyes.

Ázzuen took off after JaliMin. I knew I should follow, but I couldn't leave the longfang cub. I knew what it was like to be small and hungry.

"Wait here," I said. I snuck to the humans' cache and took a small piece of dried rhino meat and brought it back to the cub. He bolted it down.

"What's your name?" I asked him.

"Fierce Hunter of the Golden Plains," he said with great dignity. I managed not to laugh. "My sister calls me Gold."

"Are both of you hungry, Gold?" I asked him.

"All of us are," he answered. "There is not as much food and the humans chase us away. My mother and sister and I are hungrier than the others. We are not liked."

He reminded me of Prannan. He reminded me of the streckwolf.

"I'll bring you all some food if you wait here," I said. It was a crazy thing to do. He wasn't wolf. He wasn't pack. I wanted to feed him, though. I couldn't save the streckwolf, but I might be able to help Gold. I dashed back to where I had hidden a salmon. I returned to the cub and set the salmon between my paws.

"Show me where your mother and sister are," I said. He looked so hungrily at the salmon, I thought he might snatch it away.

"I can bring more to you later if I know where to take it," I said. Gold cocked his head, then took off into the woods. I grabbed up the salmon and followed.

"What are you doing, wolf?" Tlitoo asked, flying above me. He always asked me questions when my mouth was too full to answer.

"I'm not sure," I mumbled.

I didn't need Gold to lead me, after all. He took me right back to where I had first seen the longfangs. I wondered why they didn't move from place to place.

Gold tumbled onto the plain toward his anxious mother. I followed, my head and tail high, the salmon in my mouth, trying to ignore the urge to take a bite of the succulent, half-decayed fish. I suddenly realized how foolhardy it had been to come. I was alone but for a raven. The longfang mother could easily take the salmon and kill me. For all I knew she and her cubs were hungry enough to eat another hunter. I'd heard that rock bears would do so.

I thought of turning to run, but the longfang was at least as fast as I was. Although she was watching me hungrily, she made no move to attack. I walked halfway out to her, then set down the salmon.

"I'm sorry I took food from your cubs," I said. "I didn't know they were starving."

She said nothing. She looked behind and around me as if expecting a trap. She probably thought I'd brought other wolves with me again.

"I'm alone," I assured her. It might have been foolish, but I wanted her to take the salmon, to know I'd brought it to her. The other cub darted out from behind her and ran to the fish, tearing into it. Gold bolted over to her, and the two of them tore at the salmon.

Their mother and I stared at each other for long moments. Then I backed away, pawstep by pawstep, toward the shelter of the woods.

"I am Sharp Claw, Slayer of Aurochs," she said. Her voice was a low growl, like the sound of far-off thunder. The ground beneath my paws throbbed. I watched her face closely, looking for signs she might attack. Her eyes were light-colored with dark lashes. Her muzzle was shorter than a wolf's, and the long, curved fangs that protruded from her mouth moved up and down as she spoke. The short, light fur on her body was dense as a wolf's and she had a darker, thicker ridge of fur along her back. She spoke with great dignity, as Gold did, but it didn't seem silly coming from her. I waited for her to say more, but she just stared at me.

"I'm Kaala," I said. Which seemed insufficient. *I'm Kaala*

of the Swift River Pack of the Wide Valley, I almost said. But that's not who I was anymore. "I'm Kaala of the Stream Lands pack."

"And I'm Prannan of the Stream Lands pack," a voice piped up from behind me. Prannan picked up a huge elk rib bone. It still had large chunks of meat on it, and I couldn't believe he'd carried it all the way from Kaar. He dragged it over to us, lowered his tail, and scooted behind me. Sharp Claw watched him, amused.

"I thank you, Kaala and Prannan of the Stream Lands pack." She spoke as she might speak to a cub. Then her tone grew serious. "I did not know wolves brought food to other hunters. Your pack will not mind?" She narrowed her pale eyes. "Your human pack will not mind?"

"Kaala's pack leader," Prannan offered. "She doesn't have to ask anyone."

Sharp Claw regarded him. "Is she, now?" She looked at her cubs, who were tussling over the elk rib. She walked over, pushed them out of the way, and took two huge, hungry bites, devouring half of the meat, then stalked back over to us.

I knew that I should get back to Kaar before anyone noticed we had stolen food, but her amber eyes caught me and I couldn't move. I remembered stories about the longfangs, that they could stare at prey and make it go to sleep with its eyes open, making it easy to kill. Terror began to rise up in me as she took long, stalking steps toward me. I wanted to tell Prannan to run, but I couldn't speak. Sharp Claw stalked two steps closer to me while I stood as still as a fear-struck rabbit.

She bent her head down to me, her elk-scented breath

heavy and warm on my face. I tried to pull my lips back in a snarl, but I was too scared to move even the smallest muscle. She huffed at me and licked her nose with her long tongue.

"You have helped me, young wandering wolf," she said. "I will help you. I will tell you something you must know."

I found my voice. "What's that?" I whispered.

She smiled as if she could sense my fear, which I'm sure she could.

"You can capture the humans," she said. "It can be done. It has been done. But to do so, you must give up something. Something that may be too valuable to surrender."

"How did you know . . ." I began.

"Every creature with a brain sharper than an auroch's knows, young wanderer," she said. "We all know that the wolves wish to make a pact with the humans. That it has been tried before. If you make a pact with the humans, both you and they will grow stronger and many other hunters will die. Maybe all other hunters. There are many who say that I should kill you to stop that. Others say it is the only way to stop the humans from destroying everything that moves. We starve because they take our prey and kill us when they see us. But you have brought my cubs food and I will not kill you for that. I might have, back when I first saw you, had I known you were *that* wolf pup."

I stared at her in shock. Other hunters knew what we were doing. I wondered if she knew our legends.

Sharp Claw drew back her lips. Her fangs were even longer than I'd thought.

"We do not understand the humans the way you do. Their packs are like yours. You have your leaderwolves, your secondwolves, and those among you who prefer to follow. We do not. We fight for dominance as you do, but those who lose do not accept it as easily as your kind does." She looked curiously at Prannan. "Like that one does."

Prannan cocked his head at her. "I'm part of my pack," he said. "I'm not a weak wolf because I'm not a leaderwolf."

"I did not think you were," Sharp Claw rumbled. "But you do not mind that you will always follow?"

"No." Prannan looked from me to the longfang. "I'm pack. I follow my leaderwolves."

It had never occurred to me that a wolf would not want to fight for status, to be a secondwolf if not a leaderwolf. But it made sense. Trevegg had said that Werrna was content being a secondwolf and that that was why Rissa allowed her to stay. Minn hated being the pack's curl-tail but never did anything about it except to harass us when we were pups.

"Your packs work well because there are those among you who wish to be led. None of my kind likes to be told what to do." Sharp Claw whuffed what sounded like a laugh, then grew serious. "I believe that is why we will not survive. There are only a few of us left. A few grass lions, a few rock bears. The large hunters will not do well with the humans. Even your Greatwolves. And wherever the humans go, the largest prey dies, too. It is one of the reasons we are starving. I do not think my cubs will live to have cubs of their own."

"I'll try to bring you more food." I wasn't sure why I said it. I wasn't sure why I cared.

Sharp Claw sniffed the air and growled a warning. She swung her head from side to side and whipped her tail back and forth then bounded to her cubs and snatched up the remaining elk meat. She dragged it away into the woods, her cubs stumbling behind her. Prannan yelped and something hit me hard on the back.

I turned snarling to see DavRian standing above me, fury on his face, the dark, jagged blade he favored in his hand. He raised his arm to strike me again with the flat side of it. His arm was caught mid-swing. RalZun and TaLi held him, TaLi leaning back on her heels to use all of her weight to stop DavRian. HesMi stood next to DavRian. Several other humans ranged behind them. Ázzuen stalked back and forth behind the humans, out of DavRian's sight, but close enough to help me if I needed it.

I flattened my ears. A moon ago, I would have at least snapped my teeth at DavRian to let him know he had no right to hit me, but I controlled my anger and waited, watching the humans. Then I stared into DavRian's eyes. Even though I didn't move toward him, he stumbled back. Tlitoo arced down from above, landing next to me.

"It's unnatural for a wolf and a knife-toothed lion to be together," DavRian said, his voice rising, his jaw tight with anger. "The wolves brought the lion to the village. Just like the rhino and the crazed wolf. They let it hurt the boy."

"JaliMin's injured?" I asked Tlitoo.

"Gold scratched him," Ázzuen said from behind the humans. "Not badly, but he has claw marks on his arm." I should have paid more attention. I'd thought Gold had missed him.

"It isn't natural," DavRian said again. "For all we know, the bears and lions will follow them to the village and kill all of us." He stomped his foot.

"We'll keep a closer watch," HesMi said, speaking slowly. I had noticed how carefully and deliberately she came to her decisions. Her forehead wrinkled when she thought, just like Ázzuen's. "It may be coincidence that she is here and the knife-toothed lion was at Kaar. They have come before and JaliMin has been caught feeding young creatures before." She nodded to the others and turned back toward Kaar. TaLi shot me an anxious glance and ran after her. The other humans followed.

It seemed like each time we had some sort of success with the humans, two more challenges arose. I wished I hadn't taken meat to the longfangs. Every time we gave the humans reason to doubt us, it made our task harder.

Ázzuen trotted over to where Prannan and I stood. Tlitoo stared beadily at me.

"I know I shouldn't have done it," I said, "but they were starving." I explained to them what Sharp Claw had told me.

"Maybe you should not have," Tlitoo answered. "Maybe you should. There is much we don't know."

That was certainly true. Prannan whuffed impatiently.

"I'm hungry again," he said.

"Why weren't you afraid of Sharp Claw?" I asked him.

He looked at me as if the answer was obvious. "Because you were here, Kaala. I'm safe with you."

I sighed. "None of us is safe, Prannan."

He considered that. "No wolf ever is," he agreed, "but I'd rather take my chances with you." He offered me his muzzle and I took it in my jaws. Then he bounded off after the humans. I looked at Ázzuen.

"We'd all rather take our chances with you, Kaala." He grinned. "That's why we're here."

I looked at Ázzuen, a strong youngwolf now, who would be an asset to any pack. He wasn't stupid. Far from it. He was the smartest wolf I'd ever met. Marra was fearless and could lead a pack in her own right, and she had said she'd come back to be with us. I was not their leaderwolf by any means, but if they believed in me, I could at least act as if I deserved their confidence. Although my tail wanted to bend between my legs and my ears started to droop, I raised them both.

"Let's go back to Kaar," I said, in as confident a voice as I could.

Tlitoo grabbed my left ear and pulled hard.

"Don't overdo it, wolflet," he said, and flew off. I laughed, then knocked Ázzuen with my shoulder and raced him back to the village.

21

DavRian stomped around the village the next morning, pushing his way into shelters and interrupting people at their meals, trying to convince each human he saw that we were at fault for JaliMin's wounds. He insisted that we would lead longfangs and rock bears and crazed wolves into the village. Most grew tired of his ranting before the early-morning sun had time to warm the ground. Some humans had certainly believed that the crazed wolf proved that we were dangerous, but most seemed unconcerned, at least in the bright morning light. When TaLi and BreLan announced that they were taking us to hunt smallprey, HesMi picked up her sharpstick and came with us. JaliMin trailed behind her. Other humans, both adults and young, followed. The humans, like wolves, let their young come on safe hunts so that they could learn the way of the hunter. RalZun watched the humans gather and jerked his head to me in approval, grabbing up his own sharpstick and whistling loudly. I yipped happily to him.

Even Night was a quarter moon away, and a few more successful hunts could mean our victory.

"They'll scare away all the smallprey," Lallna grumbled.

"Then we'll hunt something bigger," I answered. "And
you don't have to come with us."

"I'm supposed to keep an eye on you," she said, her snout
in the air. What she didn't say was that two of the humans
who'd been stroking her the night before she killed the streckwolf were with us. I grinned. Lallna was beginning to like the
humans. Tlitoo dove down and yanked her tail. She yelped
and darted away from him.

We found no prey, but the humans led us several hours
from Kaar, to the top of a steep cliff.

They walked to the very edge of it and looked over. The
rich scent of firemeat set my stomach rumbling.

TaLi trotted to my side. She bent down to stroke me, then
stood quickly, coughing. "HesMi's right. You smell awful." She
stood a little farther from me. "IniMin hung food to keep it
safe from the rock bears," she said. "But the rope frayed and
now they can't get it back up."

I didn't know what she meant. The humans used tools in
ways I often didn't understand. Ázzuen peered over the edge
of the cliff, ears twitching. I lay down next to him. There was
a large sack made of the hide of a horse swinging back and
forth at the end of one of the humans' ropes, sixty wolflengths above a lake. Sharp, rocky outcroppings stuck out
from the cliff all the way down to deep water below. Tlitoo
flew down to perch on one of them and peer up at the sack.

A few of the humans were leaning out precariously, trying
to grab the sack. A young female had a long stick to which

she'd tied several other sticks at an angle. She used it to try to snag the sack.

"The sack is tied to that rock," Ázzuen said, glancing at a rock sticking out from the face of the cliff. "The *rope frayed*"—he savored the human words—"and now if they try to grab it, the rope will break and the meat will fall. If it catches on the rocks they'll never get it."

I looked from the sack to the cliff and back again. It didn't make sense to me, but I believed Ázzuen. He whuffed in concern. One of the humans held the young female by the legs as she tried to reach the sack with the stick. The sack swayed back and forth. Suddenly the vine rope unraveled more and the sack slipped farther down the rock face. The humans backed away from the edge.

"We can tie a rope around someone and send them down," IniMin said, eyeing TaLi.

"Or we could drop it to ToMin and LaraMi," RalZun rasped, glaring at IniMin. The old man stood just behind me. "It's safer."

I looked over the cliff to see that two humans had run down to stand at the edge of the lake.

"It'll get caught on the rocks," BreLan said, frowning. He leaned over, bending at the waist to try to swing a looped rope around the sack. He slipped forward. Ázzuen yelped, and TaLi and another human grabbed BreLan by the arms, hauling him back.

"Don't do that again," TaLi ordered.

Several human children had crept to the edge of the cliff. A small male looked at HesMi, whose back was turned. He was not quite old enough to be considered a hunter but old enough to want to prove himself one. He flopped down onto his belly at the very edge of the cliff. Several humans shouted. The child scooted forward, reaching out for the unraveling rope.

RalZun prodded my rump with his foot.

"Why are you still standing here?" he rasped.

I darted forward and grabbed the boy's preyskin leg-covering in my teeth. He yipped and looked over his shoulder at me, his mouth open and eyes wide as I dragged him back from the edge.

The humans' shouts changed to laughter and I turned to see several of them looking at me, smiling. HesMi dipped her head in approval, as Rissa might have done when one of us acted quickly to stop trouble before it started. RalZun grinned smugly.

My tail wagged. More and more, the humans treated us as pack. I looked for TaLi to see if she had noticed and saw her watching BreLan worriedly. He was still grimacing down at the sack.

"I can get it," he said softly.

"You already tried," TaLi snapped. "You almost fell over."

Ázzuen watched his human step purposefully toward the cliff. Then he moved so quickly, I couldn't have stopped him even if I'd figured out what he intended. He took a running leap off the cliff, landed with his forelegs on the sack, and took the rope in his teeth.

I yelped and BreLan shouted. My stomach twisted. Ázzuen swung back and forth, so that the rope arced over the lake. He kept his forelegs on top of the sack and scrabbled his back legs until he had chewed through the frayed part of the rope. I yelped again. The rope gave way and the sack, with Ázzuen still on top of it, fell. I watched in terror, waiting for Ázzuen to crash against the protruding rocks, but he had timed his fall perfectly so that the rope broke just as the sack swung over the water.

Both wolf and sack sank into the lake. Ázzuen surfaced and began to swim to the rocks. The two humans jumped in the lake and hauled the sack ashore. Then, as Ázzuen tried to scramble up the rough rocks, the humans grabbed him by the scruff and pulled him to safety.

BreLan was already picking his way down the long, narrow path to the lake. I nearly tripped him as I sprinted between his legs. The two humans were pulling open the sack, checking its contents, while Ázzuen grinned at them.

"What did you think you were doing?" I demanded when I reached him. "You could have died!"

"I would have fallen into the lake with or without the sack," Ázzuen said. "I could tell by the angle of the jump. I wouldn't have been hurt."

Lallna reached him then and almost knocked him over with her enthusiastic leap.

"That was so smart!" Lallna said. "That was the best hunting trick I've ever seen!" She licked the top of his head.

"You can't have known that you'd fall in the lake!" I said. "You could've slipped, you could have lost your balance and hit the rocks." My throat was so tight the words came out a rasp.

Lallna looked from me to Ázzuen. Her ears twitched. She backed away from us slowly, turning away too late to hide her grin. Tlitoo winged down from above, landing next to her.

"You take risks all the time, Kaala," Ázzuen said. His intelligent eyes looked huge, staring out at me from wet fur.

It's different, I wanted to say. I looked down at my paws. I couldn't win the humans over without his clever ideas and quick mind. I looked up to meet his eyes to tell him so, and what I saw there took my breath away.

Ázzuen had not pursued me as Pell had. He hadn't spoken to me of pups or mating, but in his silvery eyes I saw such a warmth and tenderness that I forgot that I was surrounded by humans, forgot that Lallna was standing next to us smirking.

His voice, when he spoke, was gentle. "You have to know I've always wanted you as my mate. I didn't say anything because I knew you weren't ready, Kaala. I know you need to succeed here first. But I always wanted a pack with you, ever since the first day you helped me get milk in Rissa's den." He lifted his chin. "I've waited for ten moons. I can wait longer. Next year, when we've won, and we're safe, we can have a pack at the Stream Lands Neesa showed us."

I'd always wondered how one wolf knew that another was meant to be her mate. Whenever I saw Ruuqo and Rissa together, I couldn't understand how two such different wolves could build a pack together. I'd thought finding my mate would feel like the thrill of the hunt or the giddy, heart-pounding moments just before I brought down prey. But it wasn't. It was like drinking from a sweet, quick-running river when I was thirsty, or finally sinking down into sun-warmed earth after a long journey.

I placed my head over Ázzuen's neck and pulled him close to me.

Tlitoo burbled a soft warning as the bushes next to us rustled and Pell stepped out onto the path. His eyes narrowed and I could see the disappointment and pain in them. I took a step away from Ázzuen. I didn't want to hurt Pell any more than I had to.

"You've chosen him, haven't you?" Pell said.

Lallna surprised me by looking at the three of us, eyes wide, and then slipping discreetly away. Tlitoo stayed, quorking softly.

I met Pell's gaze. I wouldn't lie to him.

"Yes," and as soon as I said it, I knew it to be so. Ázzuen whuffed in pleasure, but I kept my gaze on Pell. "Are you going to leave?" Pell was a strong wolf. I needed him.

"I stand by my word," he said. "I'll help you like I said I would. But I'm going back to the Wide Valley for a little while. To check on Marra." He scuffed his paw in the dirt. "You're doing fine without me, and I'll come back once I find out what's going on at home. And you can send one of the ravens for me if you need me."

I opened my mouth to protest.

"Let him go, Kaala," Ázzuen murmured. "I'd need to if I were him." He briefly met Pell's gaze. "Tell Ruuqo and Rissa that there are strange little wolves trying to get to the humans. They need to watch for them."

Pell glared at Ázzuen, but said nothing. Then he nipped me lightly on the nose and slipped back into the woods.

As I watched him go, doubt swelled in me. I'd come to depend on Pell's strength and knowledge. Now Ázzuen and I were on our own.

BreLan reached us then and clouted Ázzuen enthusiastically on the ribs. The other humans clustered around, thumping Ázzuen and running their hands through his wet fur. One picked him up and then set him down again. Tlitoo took flight with an annoyed shriek.

TaLi crouched down beside me.

SPIRIT OF THE WOLVES

"They're all saying how much they like you and Ázzuen."

She hugged me close, and I licked her face. "And you still smell awful." She pushed me away. Ázzuen, still surrounded by grateful humans, caught my eye and grinned.

The humans spread out along the shore of the lake, eating and resting in the warmth of the midday sun. Lallna slept half in, half out of the cool lake water. Ázzuen curled up next to BreLan and TaLi.

I lay down, Ázzuen on one side of me, TaLi on the other. Three other humans settled around us. My heartbeat quickened. We were so close to succeeding. In a quarter moon, the humans would have their festival, and it looked more and more like they would choose TaLi. There would still be work to do if we were to teach the humans they were part of the world around them, but the Sentinels would let us live to do so. And Ázzuen loved me and wanted a pack with me. He snored next to me, and I licked his soft fur.

DavRian's voice rose above the quiet conversations of relaxing humans. He crouched next to IniMin and lowered his voice to a whisper. IniMin frowned and looked at me. They would be even more determined to stop us now, and DavRian was ruthless. Milsindra, too, would do everything possible to make me fail. With Pell gone, I had lost a strong ally. So many things could still go wrong.

I stood and began to prowl along the rocky shore, trying to calm down enough to nap.

I caught a distant wolfscent. The aroma was subtly different from ours, more like pup than grown wolf. It was the scent I had come to associate with the streckwolves. That was another problem. Navdru had said I was just as likely to be-

friend streckwolves as to fight against them, and Milsindra
would be doing her best to convince the Sentinels I was more
loyal to humans than to wolves. That alone could make them
decide we were too much of a threat to wolfkind even if we
succeeded with the humans.

I could still lose Ázzuen. I could still lose TaLi. I forced
myself to stand still and think. If I told Navdru I'd found
streckwolves far from their gathering place, it might help convince him I was loyal to wolfkind. It wouldn't solve the problem, but it might help. If he believed me. I needed someone
else to confirm what I'd scented.

I looked back at Ázzuen. He was still sleeping next to the
cluster of humans, and I couldn't wake him without disturb-
ing them. RalZun was stretched out on his back on a flat rock,
snoring in the sun, and his nose was no better than an ordinary human's.

Lallna still napped by the lake. Navdru trusted her, and in
the last few days, she had been more an ally than a rival.

I walked as quietly as I could to her side, and nosed her
awake.

"Streckwolves," I said. "Can you smell them?"

She lifted her nose in the air and sniffed twice. Then she
grinned at me, rolled to her paws, and took off in the direction of the scent.

I stared after her, too startled at first to move, then followed.

I'd planned to talk to Lallna about the streckwolves and,
perhaps, to go with her when she told the Sentinels about
them. I should have known better. Lallna was not a patient
wolf. I loped after her, following the streckwolves' scent. I

grew uneasy as their aroma strengthened. There was something about it that worried me.

"Don't be a coward," I told myself. "A leaderwolf shouldn't be afraid of things."

"You are talking to yourself, wolflet." Tlitoo had followed me from the lake.

I nipped at the air beneath him. That was when I heard Lallna give three quick, sharp barks. She paused, then barked three times again. I ran faster, then stopped short. The wolfscent was mingled with the aroma of unfamiliar humans. The scent of our own humans at the lake had hidden it from me.

I dropped into a stalk, moving slowly until I reached a wood of elm, birch, and sage. Much of the lands beyond the Wide Valley were made up of the trees that lost their leaves each winter. Now they were lush with the onset of spring, reminding me of how soon the humans would make their decision and the Sentinels theirs. When I reached a birch grove, I lowered myself all the way to my belly. Just beyond the grove stretched a grassless plain. The scent came from there.

I found Lallna crouched at the edge of the plain and lay down beside her. Tlitoo hunched down next to me. Lallna took a deep breath, ready to bark again.

"Wait!" I said.

"What for?" She looked down her muzzle at me. "The strecks won't notice a few barks. That's why Navdru told me to bark instead of howling if I found them with humans. It's our signal."

Because the Sentinels will kill them if they find them, I wanted to say. But she knew that. And if I told her I didn't want to see the little wolves die, she would tell Navdru and Yildra.

She barked three more times, then settled on her haunches. I lay next to her, desperately hoping the streckwolves would leave before the Sentinels came.

The streckwolves and humans relaxed together, just as they had in the thriving village Tlitoo had shown me in the Inejalun. There were human young playing like pups with some of the streckwolves, and grown humans stretched out on the warm ground with others. They showed none of the tension or suspicion I was used to seeing from all but the youngest humans in Kaar. Several of the streckwolves sprawled on their backs, their ears folded, allowing the humans to stroke their bellies.

I wanted to be there with the streckwolves, loved by the fearless humans. I couldn't bear the thought of the Sentinels killing them. I crept forward, away from Lallna. If I could catch a streckwolf's eye, I could find a way to make it understand that it had to get its packmates to leave.

Lallna placed her foreleg across my back.

"Where are you going?"

I stared at her stupidly. "To get a closer look," I managed to say after much too long a pause.

Her eyes narrowed. "If they see you, they'll run away." She pressed down on my back with her foreleg. "We have to stay until the others get here."

I could have thrown her off me. I'd beaten her in a fight once before. But then she would know I cared about the streckwolves. She would tell Navdru and Yildra I had chosen them over real wolves.

"You have to stay here, wolf," Tlitoo whispered. "You must."

I didn't want the little wolves dead. But if I warned them I would put everything I cared about at risk. I backed up, and Lallna removed her paw.

"If Navdru and Yildra don't get here in time, we'll tell them what we saw," she said. "That way the strecks won't know we've seen them."

A streckwolf smaller than Prannan crawled on his belly to a human, and a burst of fury took me by surprise. We were working so hard to keep the Promise, and these aberrant wolves threatened our very lives. For the briefest moment, I thought the Sentinels might be right to kill them. Then a human girl threw her arms around a small streckwolf and laughed. She sounded like TaLi. As suddenly as it had come, my anger left me and I was ashamed. The little wolves weren't really doing anything wrong. They were just loving the humans the way I loved TaLi. When I was a smallpup, everyone had told me it was wrong to go to the humans and yet I couldn't stay away. I couldn't blame the little wolves for loving the humans as I did.

The sun began its descent, and the humans picked up their bundles and sharpsticks and walked away. The streckwolves stood and stretched as they watched the humans go. My tense muscles loosened. The little wolves were safe.

That was when the Sentinels attacked. They had been downwind of me and I hadn't smelled them. At least eight of them, including Milsindra, Navdru, and Yildra, pounded out into the grassless plain, pounced on the smaller wolves, and began to rip them apart. The streckwolves were no match for the Sentinels. They died like prey.

Lallna leapt over me to land on the plain. She joined the fight. I watched in horror as Greatwolves tore the little wolves apart.

"I cannot help them, wolf," Tlitoo said. "The Grump-wolves know you and I are pack." He hunched his head down between his wings.

Telling Lallna about the streckwolves had been a terrible mistake. I should not have been so eager to gain the Sentinels' approval.

Two streckwolves ran straight at me. When they saw me, they skidded to a halt, their eyes wide, their ears flat.

"This way," I said. They just stared. I made my voice strong and stern, like a leaderwolf. "Follow me. Now." I turned without waiting for a response and strode away from them. I heard frantic pawsteps behind me. I found a strong-smelling dream-sage bush and crawled into it. The two streck-wolves followed.

I looked them over. They blinked back, waiting for me to tell them what to do.

"Why were you with the humans?" I asked them. The sounds of fighting wolves forced me to raise my voice.

"Because it's where we're supposed to be," one of them answered. "It's our role to be with them." She spoke with dig-nity. "They need us, and they're our pack." There was no doubt in her, no sense of the conflict I often felt. And she didn't seem weak or foolish. She was proud and steadfast.

Like Gaanin, she seemed halfway between an ordinary wolf and the completely deformed wolves Tlitoo had shown me in the Inejalun. I remembered how peaceful that village from the past had been. But it had been destroyed because of the loss of the wild. It had become the Barrens.

"You can't just be with them," I said, swallowing against my horror at the sounds of dying wolves. Both of the streckwolves were trembling. Again, I felt the urge to protect them as I would pups. "You have to keep the wild as well. It's part of the Promise. Otherwise the humans will keep destroying things."

They both looked perplexed. They had no idea what I was talking about.

I heard a wolf slipping toward us and crouched down. Gaanin poked his nose under the bush, then crawled in with us.

"Thank you for sheltering Whitefur and Short Tail, Kaala," he said, touching his nose to my cheek. I wrinkled my muzzle. Those were the sorts of names a pack might call small-pups, and the two streckwolves were at least my age. A wolf's scream tore the air. Gaanin winced.

"They shouldn't be with the humans!" I said. "You should keep them away or the Sentinels will kill your whole pack."

"I can't keep them away, Kaala, any more than your leaderwolves could keep you from your humans in the Wide Valley. We are even more drawn to them than you are."

I didn't see how that could be. "But they don't understand about keeping the wild, or about the Promise."

Gaanin licked his muzzle. He seemed to be deciding whether or not to tell me something. Tlitoo krawked a warning from the other side of the bush. Gaanin lifted his ears.

"They're coming. You should have returned to me, Kaala, as I asked you to. You think you know what you're doing, but there is so much you don't understand." He whuffed in frustration. "And there is no time now."

The heavy pawsteps of Greatwolves approached. The Sentinels wouldn't only kill the streckwolves if they saw them, they'd kill me for helping them. Gaanin listened hard for a moment, then barked an order at the two other streckwolves.

"Attack!" Gaanin shouted. Then all three streckwolves leapt at me. Whitefur bit my shoulder and Short Tail ripped into my haunch. Gaanin scraped his claws along my belly. Then all three pelted from the bushes, bolting past Lallna and Navdru. I crawled out after them.

Lallna looked at my bleeding face and haunch.

"You tried to fight three of them?" she said. "You can't take on three alone. They fight well for all they look like pups."

"Thank you for leading us to them," Navdru said. He looked down at my horrified expression and whuffed kindly. "I know it's hard to see even such wolves as these die, and you're a youngwolf yet, but we have no choice, Kaala. It's us or them." He gave me an approving look and licked the top of my head. Then he and Lallna loped back toward Sentinel lands.

Shaking, I looked out on the plain. Some of the streckwolves had escaped, but most had not, and I counted at least ten bodies lying unmoving in the grass. Prey died so we could live. Weak wolves died so that the strong lived. This should have been no different. But it was. I remembered my brother and sisters, killed by Ruuqo when we were four weeks old. The streckwolves on the plain didn't seem so different from them, and they were dead because of me. Tlitoo bobbed up and down in front of me, waiting for me to say something.

I shook myself. Navdru had said it was us or them. And it couldn't be us.

The sun was more than halfway down the sky when I returned to the lake. I wanted to tell Ázzuen what had happened, but when TaLi called me, I went to her.

"HesMi says that you wolves are the best thing that's ever happened to the village," she whispered. "She said if I can bring more of you, I'm an asset to the village, and she can't imagine why we shouldn't keep to the old ways." She hugged me close and ran back to help the humans gather their packs and sacks together.

I saw RalZun watching me. I knew I should tell him about the streckwolves, but I didn't want him to know what I'd done. I didn't want him to know that I was no better than a Greatwolf, letting wolves die so I could get what I wanted. I looked away from him and ran after TaLi instead.

It was full dark when we returned to the village. The humans clustered around their fires. I'd learned that if I wanted to see well at such times, I had to avoid looking directly into painfully bright flames. HesMi was sitting comfortably, eating cooked rhino meat. RalZun sat next to her, gnawing on a bone. DavRian and IniMin crouched to one side.

"The decision isn't made yet, DavRian," HesMi said, "but the girl is proving herself well. I don't see any cause to change the way we're doing things. We can always change our minds next year."

RalZun smiled at DavRian but kept silent.

"There is cause!" DavRian said. "TaLi's entranced you just like her grandmother entranced some in the Wide Valley before the wolves started killing people. Next year will be too late."

It would be too late for him, at least. Once TaLi was krianan, we would have time to win the humans completely over to our side.

"So you say," HesMi grumbled, "but you haven't shown us any proof."

"What proof do you need?" IniMin asked. "Everyone in the village dead from their treachery?"

"We have six days until the festival," DavRian said, his voice suddenly reasonable. "We can show you why they're dangerous."

My ears twitched. DavRian was usually the one who lost his temper. His self-control worried me. I wondered what he was plotting.

"Do so, then," HesMi said, losing patience. "But stop prattling at me and leave me to my meal."

IniMin frowned and opened his mouth, but DavRian whispered to him and pulled him away, guiding him into the woods. I followed the two males as they stomped into the forest. They stopped at a moss-covered rock and sat on it. I hid behind the nearby yew tree, close enough to hear them but hidden from view.

"They're going to keep the old ways." IniMin's voice shook. "I can tell. Once the girl is krianan, it will be too hard to change things."

"We've been too timid," DavRian said.

He rose to a crouch on his rock and looked over his shoulder. As if his weak human eyes could see anything in the dark. He whispered to IniMin, "First we have to get rid of some of the wolves. I'll tell you how. Then we need to convince HesMi how dangerous they really are. But we'll need help if we're to do so in time."

He grinned at IniMin. "Who do you trust?"

22

Dense clouds hid the half-moon, darkening the night. I had watched DavRian carefully over the two days since I'd seen him plotting with IniMin. Several times I came upon one or the other talking to a cluster of humans, telling them that TaLi and RalZun were under our spell and that they would run mad because of us, that our teeth were poisoned like the crazed wolf's, or that we could drive a person mad with our nighttime gaze. Some humans listened to them, but many laughed at them. If that was DavRian's plan, I thought, I had very little to worry about. Two nights after we had retrieved the sack, I'd relaxed enough to stop watching him so closely.

So had RalZun. The old krianan came to me, a smile on his wrinkled face.

"I had no idea you would do so well so quickly," he said. He cocked his head. "I expected you would need more help."

Pleased at what passed for praise from the old man, I licked his hand.

"I am going to the krianan village," he said. "It is time for us to come out of hiding. We will prepare to come to Kaar after the festival." His smile broadened. "It will please me to be the one to tell IniMin he has lost."

He bent his head in one of his jerky bows, and loped from the village.

We'd both underestimated the power of the humans' fear. The dark night made them wary. I'd noticed that they were more watchful at such times, when their night-weak eyes made them more vulnerable. DavRian and IniMin knew it, too.

All Ázzuen did was to walk into the village looking for me. He caught sight of me lying next to a fire, and ambled over.

DavRian shouted a warning, then stood and hurled his spear at Ázzuen, who just managed to dodge out of the way. DavRian and three other humans ran straight at the two of us, spears raised. We didn't wait to find out what was going on. We pelted into the thickest part of the woods around Kaar. Once we realized that no one was following us, we doubled back and hid in the bushes to watch the village.

DavRian stood with his arms crossed over his chest. Ini-Min, poised next to him, held out his spear as if guarding him.

HesMi stalked over to them, dragging TaLi by the arm. "What was that about?" she demanded, releasing TaLi.

DavRian's voice was low and frightened, but he smelled of excitement and spite.

"It was a yil-wolf," he said in a whisper.

"A what?" HesMi was mystified.

"A yil-wolf. It can change from wolf to human and back again. Like I told you when we saw the mad wolf. BreLan and his wolf have become one creature. Soon they'll become like the mad wolf that almost attacked us."

"That's ridiculous!" TaLi said, lifting her lip in derision. A ripple of laughter ran through the village.

"If it's so ridiculous," IniMin said, "where's BreLan? If he isn't the same as the wolf, where is he?"

"I don't know," TaLi said. "Probably hunting."

"At night?" IniMin challenged.

"It happened once before in the Wide Valley," DavRian added. "If a yil-wolf bites you, one of three things happens: you'll go mad, turn into a yil-wolf, or die."

HesMi shook her head. "I've never heard of such a thing." But her voice was uncertain.

I couldn't believe she'd even consider it true. RalZun had said that the dark was fearsome to the humans who could not see well in it. Perhaps that was all it took to imagine monsters. I looked for the old man, but then remembered that he'd gone to the krianan village. I realized that many of the humans who favored us were also gone. DavRian had picked his time well.

Prannan and Amma chose that moment to dart into the clearing. I tensed my haunches, ready to run to their aid. But JaliMin gave a squeal of pleasure and ran to them. Prannan was carrying some cooked meat in his jaws, and JaliMin took it from him. Several humans had raised their spears when Prannan and Amma ran into the village, but now most of them were smiling.

"The wolves brought me more food," JaliMin said in perfectly clear speech. He smiled and rested his head against Prannan.

HesMi's expression softened. "They have done so much more than improve our hunt," she said. "It's almost as if they are family. I can hardly believe they are truly a threat."

"Our stories tell us the wolves are good for us," TaLi said. "We're better people when they're with us."

"Until they kill us in our sleep," DavRian muttered.

"We will keep it in mind," HesMi said, nodding to DavRian, but she had turned her attention to her grandson. It was clear she had dismissed DavRian.

I thought DavRian would be frustrated or angry, but he just smiled at HesMi and turned away.

I began to crawl out from the bushes.

"Wait, Kaala," Ázzuen said. "Look how uneasy some of the humans are."

I stopped. Small groups of them clustered together. They were whispering to one another, their shoulders tense. I recognized the male who had thrown the chunk of wood at me after we'd seen the crazed wolf. The smell of fear wafted through the village.

"He's going to keep trying to get them to fear us until he succeeds," Ázzuen said grimly.

"He doesn't have enough time," I said. "It's almost Even Night and HesMi doesn't believe his lies."

We waited until the humans had calmed down before walking as quietly as we could into the village. DavRian's friends whispered and pointed at us, but the other humans ignored them. I found TaLi curled up by one of the fires and lay next to her. Ázzuen settled on my other side. DavRian watched me, staring at me in challenge. When no one else was looking, I lifted my lip at him. He turned his eyes away, ceding dominance to me. Satisfied, I curled against TaLi and basked in the warmth of the humans' fire.

My nose twitched, awaking me from a fitful sleep to the morning bustle of humans preparing for their day. There was meat nearby and the scent of it had set my stomach rumbling. I prodded Ázzuen awake, and we followed the scent to the warmest, smallest clearing that lay at the edge of the village. The humans were wasteful, and they often threw away bones that had good meat on them. Still, I didn't expect to see the good-size pile of cooked elk meat at the clearing's edge. This meat smelled old. I remembered then that when prey had been dead for several days, the humans didn't like to eat it unless they had preserved it. They didn't appreciate the strong taste of older meat, which was probably why they'd left it for us.

I ran to the pile of elk, then stopped. Something about it smelled wrong.

"Don't eat it, Kaala," Ázzuen warned.

"I know." I sniffed. The meat reeked of the gallin leaf, a plant so toxic that one bite would make a wolf violently ill. More would be deadly. And there was a lot of it in the elk meat. Another smell was just as strong. DavRian's scent. I remembered what he had told IniMin about trying to get rid of us, and I remembered him kicking the gallin plant at the gorse patch after the salmon hunt.

Ázzuen was growling softly. I thought about leaving dung atop the meat, to let DavRian know exactly what I thought of him and his attempt to kill us, but Trevegg had once told me that gloating over an enemy's failure only strengthened his resolve. Instead, I kicked dirt onto the pile of meat. Any wolf who found it would know from its smell that it was poisoned and would avoid it.

If I'd had any doubts before, I had none now. DavRian had stopped trying to become krianan by fair means. He intended to defeat us. And he would kill us to do so. I snarled in contempt. If he wanted us dead, he was going to have to do better than that.

TaLi and BreLan were waiting for us by the herb den. TaLi had a huge grin on her face. I wondered how she could be so cheerful when DavRian was so intent on making her fail. I sat next to her, watching her carefully.

"Come on, wolves," BreLan said. "We're going to teach TaLi how to swim!"

I stood and knocked my shoulder into Ázzuen's. I'd been trying to find some way to convince TaLi to learn to swim for as long as I'd known her. Somehow, BreLan had gotten her to agree, and I wasn't going to wait for her to change her mind. Prannan, Amma, and Lallna were all sleeping in the morning sun. We left them to their naps.

BreLan led us to a shallow, slow-moving part of the river. TaLi had a small pouch at her waist, and I could smell fire-meat in it, as well as the leaves of the fat-stem plant, which grew profusely along the streambed near Kaar. Its flowers were temptingly fragrant at night, but its leaves were too bitter to eat. TaLi kept giggling and then stopping herself. She'd been so reluctant to learn how to swim, I couldn't figure out why she was enjoying the prospect so much now.

BreLan stood on the shore while TaLi waded into the river until the water was up to her waist. Tlitoo winged down to stand on a rock in the middle of the river. He looked at me and chortled, then flew to the far side of the river.

"Come out here with me, Kaala," TaLi called.

I waded to her. BreLan walked at my side while Ázzuen watched from the riverbank.

As soon as I was chest deep in the river, TaLi lost her footing and fell. I bolted to her, but when I reached her, the water was only up to my neck, which meant TaLi could stand easily. Confused, I looked from her to BreLan. TaLi surged to her feet, and she and BreLan tackled me so that everything but my head was submerged. Then, as BreLan held me, TaLi rubbed the fat-stem leaves all over me, covering me in their scent. She and BreLan dunked me under the water again and again until the foam from the fragrant leaves was washed away.

"*Now* you smell better," TaLi said with a huge grin. BreLan thumped me on the side. Tlitoo flew above us, cackling.

I slogged out of the water, glowering at all of them. I shook as hard as I could, trying to shake off the indignity as much as the water. Ázzuen was laughing at me and trying to hide it. I ignored him and found a sunny spot where I could dry off.

BreLan did try to teach TaLi how to swim, towing her back and forth in the deeper part of the river while Ázzuen and I lay in the sun. But every time BreLan let her go, TaLi sank. She got angrier and angrier. Forgiving her for dunking me, I went back out, Ázzuen beside me. Even with all of us encouraging her, she kept sinking. Frustrated, she tramped to shore. She and BreLan lay down together and fell asleep in the sun. Ázzuen and I settled beside them. Soon his even breathing told me he slept. I closed my eyes, but before I could fall asleep, I smelled sweat and dream-sage. I snapped my eyes open. A shadow crossed over me, and I twisted my neck to see DavRian watching us from the trees. I didn't know how long he'd been there, or how much of TaLi's failed lesson he'd seen. I was uneasy for a moment, but didn't see how TaLi's swimming ability would affect the way HesMi saw her, and DavRian couldn't hurt the girl with both BreLan and me at her side. He slipped back into the woods and I placed my head protectively on TaLi's belly.

"You're wet, Kaala," she complained. Then she smiled. "But at least you don't smell like rancid meat anymore." We lay in the sun, enjoying the warmth of the day. I thought of days to come, when we could relax with our humans without worrying about DavRian or Even Night, or the Sentinel wolves.

At late-sun, TaLi and BreLan rose and started back. When we ran, they followed us, racing us back to the village.

⊡

The wail of grief reached us when we were twenty wolflengths from the village, and it stopped us short. The last time I'd heard a sound like that was when one of Rissa and Ruuqo's pups had been trampled to death and the pack had sung his death song.

We walked forward slowly. Humans were lined up along a path that led to the warm side of the village, where the smallest clearing lay. One by one, humans looked up at us, their faces bleak. Tears dampened the face of a woman, and I put my nose to the back of her hand. She stroked my head.

A smaller group of humans clustered around something. TaLi gasped and my throat constricted with dread. The cry of grief rose again. It was HesMi's voice. I pushed between the legs of two humans.

JaliMin lay perfectly still, his chest not moving, his eyes wide open, his face stiff in death. There were no wounds on his body, and even from where I stood I could smell the elk meat on him and the scent of the poisonous gallin leaf. He lay not five wolflengths from where the poisoned meat had been. I crept toward him, forcing myself to look at his face. He stared at me in reproach.

Ázzuen slunk up next to me, his tail so low it dragged in the dirt.

"We should have buried it, Kaala. We should have marked it better."

We should have. I could imagine what had happened. JaliMin had grown accustomed to our feeding him. He had found food by our paw prints, so he ate it.

None of the humans seemed angry with us. None of them seemed to understand our part in JaliMin's death. But none of them knew that DavRian had poisoned the meat, either. I staggered back to where the tainted meat had lain. It was gone. I paced around the spot several times. There was just damp ground, the scent of gallin, the scent of wolf, and the scent of JaliMin.

The humans would never be able to figure out what had happened. They wouldn't know DavRian had set out tainted meat. I watched them as they grieved. Some were bent over JaliMin. Some were weeping and some were still and silent. All were mourning.

Except for DavRian.

I thought he might look remorseful. I expected, perhaps,

that he would be horrified by how, in his attempt to poison us, he had killed a beloved child instead. But though his expression was sorrowful, his body and his scent belied his show of sadness. He smelled of anticipation and his muscles were taut as if he were ready to run after prey.

The murmuring started with IniMin. "DavRian warned us that all of the wolves have poison in their teeth." His whisper carried on the wind. "JaliMin played with them all the time. It was only a matter of time before their poison killed him."

I slunk to Ázzuen. "He can't have planned it," I said. "There's no way he could've known it would kill JaliMin. He'll have to be more careful now."

"Not if being careless gets him what he wants," Ázzuen answered.

DavRian walked up to a weeping HesMi and spoke to her, head bowed.

HesMi shook her head. "The boy was always getting into things," she said, tears in her voice. But she looked at us long and hard. DavRian gripped her arm and spoke more urgently. HesMi shook him off. "I will make no decisions tonight," she said. "My grandson is dead and I will mourn him."

Prannan slipped up to HesMi and butted the human leader's hand. HesMi stroked his head absently. When she ducked into a shelter, she allowed Prannan to follow.

I felt someone watching me. I lifted my head to see DavRian looking down at us, a smug smile spreading across his face. He turned and walked away with a swagger. When he shoved aside the preyskin opening of the shelter he had been given, he smelled of triumph.

23

hey buried JaliMin, as was their way, in a small field not far from the village. I could smell the bones of other humans under the earth, and I found myself glad that JaliMin would not be alone.

The humans were subdued when they returned home at darkfall, many of them still weeping. HesMi returned to her shelter and stayed there, and no one dared go in after her. The others went about their tasks as they always did, but with such quiet that I wanted to howl. Prannan lay unmoving in the center of the clearing where he and JaliMin played together. When I went to him and tried to take his muzzle in my jaws to comfort him, he turned away from me and lowered his nose to his paws.

I prowled the village with Ázzuen at my side, wanting more than anything to take the humans' sorrow away, but there was nothing I could do. When I could bear their grief no more, I fled to the edge of the village, where I found TaLi and BreLan sitting side by side, their arms wrapped around each other. I sat next to TaLi, leaning up against her. Ázzuen sidled up to BreLan. My eyes grew heavy. I wanted to comfort the humans, but my own sorrow and guilt over JaliMin's death had drained me of all energy, and I closed my eyes, just for a moment. I could figure out what JaliMin's death meant to our plans later. Without meaning to, I fell hard asleep.

A sharp scream awoke me. I jumped up, knocking over TaLi, who was scrambling to her feet. As I blinked against the midday light, Ázzuen rolled to his side and onto his paws in a swift, graceful movement.

I smelled human blood.

A group of humans gathered around the spot where DavRian had left the poisoned meat. Grief and horror weighed down the air like the damp before a storm. DavRian and IniMin stood next to HesMi, supporting her by her elbows. I looked for RalZun. He was still nowhere to be found.

I peered through the legs of the humans who stood in front of me. A woman lay on the ground, her throat torn out. The blood was not yet dry, and warmth still rose from her body.

I knew what DavRian would say before he opened his mouth. I stood frozen, unable to stop it.

"It's the wolves," he said. "Look. Their prints are all around her."

I had paced that spot, trying to make sense of JaliMin's death. My paw prints were everywhere. Ázzuen stumbled up beside me, breathing hard. TaLi stood next to me and gripped my fur. For a horrified moment, I wondered if Milsindra had attacked the woman to make the humans hate us.

Ázzuen shuffled forward just a pawswidth. "It looks like a blade cut, not like teeth, Kaala." Relief tinged his voice.

He pushed through the humans toward the woman's body. "It's obviously a blade," he said to them, forgetting for a moment that they didn't understand us.

Then a young female ran panting up to HesMi. "There are four more people dead. With no wounds or anything. Just like JaliMin." She looked fearfully at me.

I stared at DavRian in horror. JaliMin's death had been an accident. Now he had deliberately killed five people to make us look like a threat. He'd told the humans they should guard against crazed wolves, but he was the one who was mad.

HesMi's composure broke.

"Get it out of here!" she shouted and kicked out at Ázzuen. It sounded like all the grief and sorrow in the world were in her voice. She had lost her grandchild hours before, and now more death haunted the village. She kicked out again, striking Ázzuen in the side. He yelped and rolled away from her as several humans raised their sharpsticks to spear him.

"Run!" I woofed. Ázzuen was already moving. He scrambled between human legs to dash into the woods. I stayed where I was. The humans looked after Ázzuen, fear and anger contorting their faces.

Then BreLan walked into the village looking for us, just to the left of the bushes Ázzuen had used to make his escape.

"The yil-wolf," DavRian bellowed. "He went into the woods and turned human! I told you! A second ago it was a wolf."

Someone laughed at DavRian, but someone else shouted in fear. BreLan stared at DavRian, perplexed. He was completely unprepared when DavRian hurled a spear at him.

BreLan was fast, though, and dodged well enough to avoid being pierced through the chest. The blade sliced through his shoulder, making him stagger back. Ázzuen darted from the woods and pulled BreLan back by his tunic.

"Go, Kaala!" TaLi gasped. I ran for the woods. If the humans were distraught enough to believe that a wolf could turn into a man, they could not be depended on to behave rationally. I was several wolflengths beyond the village when I realized TaLi wasn't beside me.

I went back for her. Humans already guarded the edge of the woods, spears raised, staring out into the trees, their fear and anger turning the air rank. I stayed low, trusting they wouldn't see me in the undergrowth.

"It was *not* the wolves," TaLi shouted. "DavRian did this before, when he killed NiaLi."

HesMi looked down at TaLi, her face rigid. "Or the wolves have done it before and you have been lying to us all along."

TaLi stood face-to-face with HesMi, her hands gripped into fists at her sides. "I'll prove it to you," she said. "The wolves didn't do this."

HesMi's voice hardened. "I knew NiaLi from when I was no more than a girl," she said. "And for her I will spare you. But leave this village now or I cannot assure your safety."

TaLi made her voice soft and reasonable. "I can show you, HesMi," she said. "I can prove it was DavRian and not the wolves."

The tall human shoved TaLi and she fell. I growled and moved forward. Shouts greeted my appearance.

"Kaala," TaLi whispered. She looked from me to HesMi, who had raised her spear. TaLi scrambled to her feet and ran to me. She grabbed a handful of my fur and pulled. I followed her into the woods.

I led her to Ázzuen and BreLan, who stood at a stretch of the stream shaded by willows. TaLi ran to BreLan's side. His shoulder was still bleeding.

"I'm fine," he said, his smile shaky. "DavRian doesn't have very good aim." But he winced when TaLi pressed her hand against the wound.

"It's not deep," she said. She wrapped her arms around him. They stood enfolded in each other's arms for long moments until I grew restless and pawed at them. They stepped apart.

We heard shouts then, and TaLi and BreLan ducked into a thick patch of pines. We followed.

DavRian and three other males stopped, gasping for breath, just a few wolflengths from us. They set down their spears and crouched to drink from the stream.

"The wolves are easy to kill if you sneak up on them," DavRian said to the others, splashing water on his face. "They always sleep after they eat."

"He learned that from watching us," Ázzuen whispered. After a big meal it is almost impossible for us to stay awake. It is the time when we are the most vulnerable.

The humans finished drinking from the stream and gathered up their spears.

"Let's get rid of them for good," DavRian said. The other humans murmured in agreement and they set off in search of us, too nose-blind to know we were within wolflengths of them.

TaLi took BreLan by the hand and led him deeper into the woods. She found dark, bitter-smelling leaves and held them to his wound. Then she returned to the stream for some of the thinnest, most pliant branches of the willow, and used them to bind the leaves to BreLan's shoulder. She had been learning to be a healer back in the Wide Valley. "You're not going anywhere until the bleeding stops," she said. "Then we'll figure out how to convince HesMi that DavRian's lying."

She made him sit against a rock, his arms raised, and sat cross-legged in front of him, his spear on her lap.

"Now what?" Ázzuen said. He had watched silently as TaLi tended to his human. He squeezed in between the two of them so that he could sit next to BreLan, who reached his good arm out to stroke him.

If HesMi believed that we had torn out the throat of one human and killed five others with some sort of venom we were supposed to have in our teeth, we would fail disastrously. DavRian would become krianan and the Greatwolves would kill us.

"We have to help TaLi prove that DavRian killed the humans," I said.

Ázzuen's eyes lit up. "The gallin leaf, Kaala! There's a bush by the gorse patch. If we bring it to your girl, she'll figure out that that's how DavRian killed JaliMin and the others! She knows it's poisonous. Then she can show HesMi."

"You're brilliant," I said, standing and stretching.

I looked for Tlitoo. He could get to the gorse patch and back more quickly than I could, and could take the leaves in his beak by the stem.

"Tlitoo!" I called softly. There was no answer. I didn't dare howl for him lest I alert the Sentinels that something was wrong, but I didn't want to leave the humans where DavRian might find them. I paced the woods, waiting for Tlitoo to find us, as he always did. When the sun was halfway down the sky, I decided I couldn't wait any longer.

"I'm going to get the gallin leaf." It was less than an hour's lope to the gorse patch. "Don't let the humans leave."

Ázzuen dipped his head in acknowledgment. As I started off toward the gorse patch, TaLi struggled to her feet. BreLan reached out an arm to her and pulled her down.

"I'll be back soon," I promised, though I knew she couldn't understand me. She must have recognized something in my expression, for she sat back down and watched me go.

I made it safely to the gorse patch, without anyone, wolf or human, finding me. Gingerly, I took the gallin leaves in my mouth, trying to hold the bitter leaves by their stems. I could only hope it wouldn't hurt me to carry them this way. I had just pulled the leaves from the bush when a shadow darkened the ground in front of me. I looked up to see Lallna standing beside me, scowling. I hadn't been as lucky as I thought.

"You have to come with me, Kaala," she said. "Yildra and Navdru want to see you."

She glowered at me. I was tired of her sneaking and spying. I carefully set down the gallin leaves.

"Get out of my way," I snarled at her.

"Can't do it, Kaala," she said. "Yildra and Navdru said I had to bring you to them."

"Not now," I growled.

"I don't have a choice," she said, lowering her eyes just a little, then raising them again in defiance. "And neither do you."

Three wolves closed in on me, all Sentinel Greatwolves I

didn't know. They pulled their lips back in sharp-toothed snarls.

"You'll come with us if we have to chew you bloody first," one of them said. Another tipped back her head and howled, announcing that they'd found me. There was nothing respectful or kind in their manner, nothing to indicate that I was the potential wolf of legend. One of the wolves pushed in front of me and the two others loped at my sides, forcing me to run in a straight line. Lallna followed behind, nipping at my tail when she thought I wasn't running fast enough.

I thought about asking them what was happening, or if they knew about the deaths in Kaar. Their grim expressions convinced me to wait. To my relief, I saw the shadow of a raven on the ground in front of me. Tlitoo had found me, and he flew overhead, dipping and weaving to keep pace with us.

They took me to a large pine and juniper grove not far from the Hill Rock. Tlitoo cawed in distress. The scent of wolf blood clogged my nose.

Navdru and Yildra stood at the edge of the grove, watching me impassively. Milsindra sat next to them. My mother was there, too, guarded by two Greatwolves. A strong wind blew through the trees, scattering twigs and the smell of death.

The Sentinel leaderwolves prodded me forward, cutting off any opportunity for me to run back the way we'd come. I walked toward the death smell, slowing when the pines began to thin. At the edge of a small clearing I stopped, staring at the bodies of Greatwolves, limp with recent death. Milsindra strode past me to stand in the middle of what was clearly a Sentinel pack gathering place.

"I only walked away for a moment," Milsindra said to the

Sentinel leaderwolves who had followed behind her. "I chased off some longfangs. When I returned, they were all dead."

Milsindra had been the wolf on watch. She had left the others unguarded in their sleep to be slaughtered. On purpose, I was sure.

"You didn't wake another wolf?" The sharp voice was Neesa's.

Lallna growled in agreement. "Traitorwolf," she whispered. No one reprimanded her.

Milsindra snarled down at her, then lifted a lip to Navdru. "You allow smallwolves to speak to you this way?"

Navdru swung his head from Milsindra to Lallna and Neesa, but said nothing. I walked past them and into the center of the clearing, stepping over wolf bodies. All bore the marks of human spears. A few had their throats cut.

It was my fault. I hadn't thought to warn the Sentinels when DavRian said he was planning to kill wolves. Somehow, I'd never thought of them as so vulnerable.

Tlitoo strode over to me. "Do not falter now, wolflet. It is not the time."

I realized I was standing with one forepaw raised. I placed my paw down carefully, as if the ground were full of thorns. I looked at the wolves around me, trying to find something to say.

"No pack leaves itself unguarded." That was Neesa again.

Navdru ignored her to address me. "This is what happens when we get close to the humans, Kaala. This is what we warned you about. This is what we hoped you would be able to keep from happening."

"Now will you kill this drelshik?" Milsindra growled. "Before more wolves die?"

My mother shifted back and forth on her paws, as if readying to fight Milsindra, Yildra, and Navdru all on her own. I gathered my courage.

"You let the humans into the gathering place on purpose," I said to Milsindra. "And you drove a rhino to Kaar and the crazed wolf toward the village, and you let humans see you."

"Drelshik!" Milsindra snarled at me. "No youngwolf behaves in such a way!" She began to stalk toward me, her head lowered between her shoulders and her lips drawn back.

Navdru stopped her with a growl.

"This is my pack, not yours," he reminded her. "And I am not unaware of your attempts to frighten the humans." He looked down at me. "I allowed it, youngwolf, because I wanted the humans afraid. I wanted to see if their fear would make them dangerous, and it has. Did you have any idea they would react in such a way?"

"I didn't," I answered.

"She's lying," Milsindra said. "Just today the human from the Wide Valley killed five other humans and blamed the wolves. She should have come to us then. Her father's blood influences her too much."

My mother slipped past her guards and walked calmly to stand by my side. I should have lowered my tail and ears and asked for forgiveness, but I was too angry.

"Hiiln was a better wolf than you are," I said to Milsindra.

Milsindra laughed and Neesa looked embarrassed.

"Hiiln wasn't your father, Kaala," she said, avoiding my gaze.

I looked at her, confused. Hiiln had to be my father.

"I will tell her if you will not," Milsindra purred. "I would have done so before, Kaala, but I only just found out myself. But it makes perfect sense. Will you tell her, Neesa?"

I watched Milsindra warily. Anything that gave her that much pleasure couldn't be good. She smiled. "I know that you met the streckwolves."

"Yes," I said, wondering at the change of subject.

"Did you meet one named Gaanin?"

I hesitated, not knowing if I should admit that I'd spoken to the streckwolf. I looked at Neesa.

"Gaanin is your father, Kaala," Neesa said. "That's why everyone is so concerned about you. When I dreamed of having pups that would save wolfkind, I went in search of Hiiln. We were mates for only a short time." She whimpered softly, then lifted her chin. "When he was killed, I vowed to honor his memory and to fight for the cause he had died for, even if it killed me, too. I found Gaanin, and thought that if I had pups with him and raised them in the Wide Valley, they might be the ones to succeed where we had failed. You have the wildness of the wolf mixed with the strangeness of the streckwolf and their love of the humans. All of the Wide Valley wolves have some streckwolf in them—which is why we have always been watched so carefully—but you have the most. It is why Ruuqo killed your littermates when he learned I had mated outside the valley, and why the Greatwolves of the Wide Valley saved you. We thought that you might be able to retain your wildness where streckwolves could not."

"It's a mistake we won't repeat," Milsindra growled.

"It wasn't a mistake," my mother growled back. "It was the best way, the only way." She lifted her chin to the Greatwolves. "She found her way to the humans when she was only four moons old. She won their love without submitting to them. All on her own, she almost made it work."

"But blood will tell," Milsindra growled. "She saved streck-wolves when we tried to kill them four days ago. She sheltered them. And, in the end, her wildness made the humans hate her. In the end, her wildness made them kill."

The wind had grown stronger and roared so loudly in my ears that I had trouble hearing what the Greatwolves were saying. I was part streckwolf. That's why I was so different. That's why I was aberrant. I lay down and placed my face in my paws. Neesa had said that their very existence was considered a threat to all wolves. If I was half streckwolf, then maybe I really was the destroyer of wolfkind. It was beginning to look that way.

Tlitoo pecked me hard between my ears. "Enough whining, wolflet."

I got to my paws and shook myself.

"DavRian is just one human," was the first thing I thought of to say. "There are good ones, and we will help the good ones overcome the bad." I lifted my chin, mimicking my mother's boldness. "I have to get back to our humans now." I turned my back on the Sentinels and walked away.

Large paws pushed me to the earth and I rolled over to look up into Navdru's gaze. I heard a yelp and then a scuffle. Two Sentinels hustled Ázzuen into the gathering place.

"This one was hiding in the bushes, watching us," one of them said with a smirk. "Maybe he was planning an attack." Ázzuen glared up at them and trotted over to me. Navdru let me get to my paws.

"Next time, don't challenge them directly," Ázzuen said,

licking the top of my head. "You aren't as big as you think you are."

"You followed me."

"Of course I did," he said as if I were as simple-minded as a grubfinder bird, "when the Greatwolf howled that they'd found you. I heard what Neesa said, Kaala, about Gaanin being your father. It doesn't matter. You've done more than any other wolf to bring wolves and humans together." Then he lowered his head to mine. "It's bad, Kaala. HesMi believes DavRian. She says we're vicious and should all be killed."

My stomach clenched so tightly that I retched, and my tongue was so thick in my mouth that I could hardly breathe. HesMi wanted us dead. We had failed. Because I was the daughter of a streckwolf. An aberrant wolf. The destroyer of wolfkind.

The Greatwolves around us began a low, rhythmic growling like none I'd ever heard. They formed a half circle around us, heads lowered and swaying. My mother rushed back to my side. Tlitoo hovered above the Greatwolves, his beak opening and closing.

Navdru looked at me, compassion in his gaze. "I'm sorry, youngwolf."

My haunches tensed as I prepared to run or to fight. Neesa barked a challenge. Ázzuen rumbled a deep, threatening growl. His face was contorted in a snarl so fierce that I would have been afraid to be on the other side of it. The Greatwolves advanced.

Then Navdru's head snapped up. I heard the heavy footsteps of humans in the forest around us a moment after he did.

We all bolted out of the clearing and hid among the thick junipers.

DavRian's voice flew on the rising wind, as he led a large group of humans into the clearing. They all carried their fire branches and their spears.

"I told you there were giant wolves," he said, pointing to the Greatwolves' bodies. "Just like I told you the wolves would poison us."

Navdru growled beside me. "That's the one who did this," he said. "I can smell his scent all over my pack." He stood then, and strode into the clearing to confront DavRian as he would confront any wolf who had injured a packmate under his protection. He still didn't understand how different the humans were from us, how much more dangerous. Yildra walked at his side. Milsindra, grinning at me, gave a loud bark and followed them.

The humans whirled to see three huge wolves stalking them. One of them screamed, terrified. Another threw his fire branch at Navdru, who knocked it away with a swing of his huge head. The wind took the flame, and the thick juniper bushes surrounding the clearing caught fire.

Then all of the humans were running toward us, their fire branches waving. DavRian raised his high, lighting the pine tree next to him. The flame jumped from one bough to another, carried on the howling wind.

"Burn them," he screeched. He lit another juniper, and the dry bark of the pine next to it caught fire. Then, in a frenzy of fear, the humans began to set fire to everything around them. It made no sense, but their fear-fevered eyes were not the eyes of sane creatures. They were like the crazed wolf, running in circles that would take it nowhere. But they were more dangerous than a hundred maddened wolves.

"They'll burn everything," I gasped. Ázzuen stared, unmoving, at the flames as if he were merely watching the humans make use of one more of their clever tools.

"They couldn't have picked a worse place," he whispered, his eyes wide. "Pine and juniper burn better than anything."

"Run, stupid little wolves," Tlitoo rasped, poking me and then Ázzuen hard on our rumps.

Ázzuen shook himself, still staring, mesmerized by the flames. Neesa slammed into us.

"The wind is blowing the fire toward the village," she said. "The Sentinels will run toward Hidden Grove to escape it. Get away from them while they run. Head back to the Wide Valley. There's no way they'll let you live now." She slammed into me again. "I'll try to lead them away. Go!"

She turned from us and ran toward the Sentinels. There was no need to lead them away. They scattered before the fire like mice fleeing a hawk.

If the flames were moving toward the village, they were moving toward our humans.

Ázzuen still stared at the flames. I bit his shoulder.

"We have to get TaLi and BreLan."

He snapped out of his daze and shook his head, making his ears flap.

"Follow me, wolves," Tlitoo croaked.

We sprinted toward the stream, the flames biting at our tails. Dark smoke blinded me and clogged my nose, and I kept losing sight of Ázzuen. Tlitoo flew just above our heads, which must have been painful in the choking smoke, and he called out to us whenever the thick smoke blocked him from our view.

Just when I thought I couldn't take another breath, I felt cool water on the singed pads of my paws. I stopped as I saw two humans in the stream, running away from us. I recognized TaLi's gangly shape.

They were smart, running in the water where the flames should not have been able to reach them, but they were running the wrong way—right into the fire's path.

I couldn't gather the breath to bark a warning, and I didn't think they'd hear it through the howls of the flames even if I could. Ázzuen and I chased after them, and for the first time, I was glad that the humans moved more slowly than we did. We were nearly upon them when they left the stream and scrambled into the woods that led to Kaar.

"There is more fire that way, wolves," Tlitoo shrilled.

We bolted after the humans.

The wind had carried the flames more quickly than we could run. Bushes surged with fire as if they had been lit from below. We found TaLi and BreLan, clinging together, trapped by a circle of flame.

The heat shoved against me. I forced myself to push back.

"This way, Kaala!" Ázzuen had found a spot where the flames were no higher than our chests. He leapt over it and I followed, feeling the fur of my belly singe.

"Kaala!" TaLi choked, falling to her knees and throwing her arms around me. BreLan hauled her to her feet.

"Can you get us out?" he asked Ázzuen.

Ázzuen found enough air to yip to him. He watched the fire.

"What are you doing?" I gasped. "We have to run."

"We have to wait," he said. "The flames surge and ebb. Follow me when I run." He hadn't been stunned when he watched the flames back at the Greatwolves' killing ground. He'd been figuring them out, as he did with everything he saw.

"Now!" he woofed.

He shoved BreLan's hip and ran. The humans and I followed him, crossing through a break in the flames.

The humans were even slower than usual. "We have to get them somewhere safe," I wheezed to Ázzuen.

"Come with me," Tlitoo rasped.

I didn't see how the raven could lead us to safety. Flames licked the trees all around us. The humans gagged as they stumbled at our sides. We ran until my paws hurt and my tongue hung down so far I tasted dirt. I could barely breathe. I was sure we would be burned like firemeat by the flames that pursued us.

Then, when I thought I could run no longer, the Hill Rock rose in front of me. Tlitoo had known where he was going after all. I scrabbled up it, making sure that the humans were with us. They moved almost as quickly as we did, using their agile hands to pull themselves up above the flames.

Tlitoo disappeared into a hole in the rock. I peered in after him. There was a deep cave I'd never noticed from the ground. The humans crawled into it and we followed.

The damp air soothed my lungs. Ázzuen explored the back of the cave, sniffing in the corners.

"No one's here," he said. "It's safe."

The humans were too tired to check the cave for danger. They sank down on the cool ground. TaLi held her ankle. I dragged myself over to her.

"I sprained it, Kaala," she said.

BreLan bent over her, examining her ankle. I licked it, over and over again, grateful that she wasn't more seriously injured. Ázzuen paced the cave as if he could guard against the smoke and flames. When Tlitoo strode to the mouth of the cave, I went with him.

I stood on a ledge outside the cave and looked down at the woods below us. The flames couldn't reach us, though the smoke still clawed at my throat. For as far as I could see, the woods were burning. Hidden Grove Gathering Place was ablaze. I heard the screams of prey and hunter alike as every creature in the woods sought safety.

I tried to howl for my mother, but my throat was too raw. I shouldn't have lost sight of her. She could be anywhere, burning or choking down below. Prannan and Amma could be dying in the flames, too. Ázzuen was safe, and TaLi, but the rest of my family could be burning to death below me. I was supposed to be a pack leader, but I was as helpless as a new-born pup. For the fire burned so far and fast that it seemed nothing could escape it.

DavRian and his friends must have lit a thousand fires. I couldn't see Kaar from where I stood, but I couldn't believe it would survive the flames. DavRian had been willing to poison humans to get to us. Now it seemed he didn't care if every-thing in the land died. In trying to destroy us, the humans were destroying everything around them. They were uncon-trollable, and my attempts to influence them had led once again to horror. I was no more than a drelshik, causing pain wherever I went.

I could do nothing but stand gasping above the flames, watching as my hopes for fulfilling the Promise burned.

24

H ot stones burned my paws, and sharp bits of wood poked painfully between the pads of my feet as I picked my way down the Hill Rock the next morning. The fire had burned itself out, but the late-morning air was still bitter with recent smoke. Tlitoo hovered above me, scanning the desolate land below us. Ázzuen watched from the mouth of the cave, guarding BreLan and the wounded TaLi as the humans slept, exhausted from escaping the fire. I was tired, too, but I needed to know what had happened in the human village and the Sentinel lands, and if I really had failed as completely as it seemed.

From the time we were smallpups, barely able to scent the difference between the tracks of a rabbit and those of a hare, we were told that if humans and wolves came together, disaster would follow. I hadn't believed it. I had thought it an exaggeration, a way for the Greatwolves to keep things the way they were. I didn't believe that the love I felt for TaLi and the

bond my packmates felt for their humans could be so dangerous. I believed that DavRian was a malicious human and that
his killing of NiaLi and JaliMin were acts of isolated madness.
I could not have been more wrong. I'd thought that if I loved
the humans enough, that if they loved us enough, it would
stop the vicious humans from destroying us. It had not.

I reached what had been the forest floor. Oak trees, willows, and birches remained standing; their moist trunks and
high branches had protected them somewhat from the
flames. The pines and spruce were gone, or so charred as to be
unrecognizable. I made my way carefully through the burned
land.

A dead fox stared up at me, its eyes fixed, its mouth frozen
in a snarl. I kept walking. A family of rabbits lay dead next to
what must have been their den, and I understood that I had
brought death to more than just wolves. The burned place
seemed to go on and on. I came upon the gorse patch and realized I was headed the wrong way. I closed my eyes to better
smell the land around me and picked up the faint scent of
running water. I followed it to the stretch of river where
BreLan had tried to teach TaLi to swim. I lapped at it thirstily.
Tlitoo drank beside me.

"Wolflet," he said. "Someone was just here."

He was peering down at a paw print in the mud. I lowered
my nose to it. My mother's scent rose from it, and it was
fresh, left after the fire had passed through. My legs weakened
under me with relief. My mother was alive, or had been right
after the fire. The knowledge that she lived gave me as much
strength as had the fresh water in my parched throat. I
couldn't bear the thought of losing her again.

"Do you want to follow her, wolf?"

The scent led into the river and then disappeared, which meant she had run in the water, whether to avoid detection or cool her paws I didn't know, but it would take time to track her. I took a deep breath. She was alive. Ázzuen and TaLi were alive. I could handle whatever else came.

"Later," I said. "Let's keep going."

Neither of us spoke as we left the river to make our way to the krianan village.

The fire had burned so hot there that nothing had survived except the oldest, strongest trees. I hoped some of the krianans might still live. They knew the woods as well as any wolf, and they might have sensed the fire coming. They might have had time to get away.

The flames had been too fierce. One by one I found the krianans, their bodies charred almost beyond scent recognition. I didn't understand why the krianan village had burned so terribly. There were rocky fields between the start of the fire and the krianans' home that should have offered them some protection. I remembered that RalZun had returned to their village to talk to them. I prayed that the crafty old man had escaped before the fire came.

"Kaala," Tlitoo said. He had never called me by name before, in all the time I'd known him. His voice was loud in the silence around us. There was no sound of prey or other creatures, just the warm wind lifting and spreading the ash around us. "We must go to the big village."

I didn't want to. I didn't want to find out how badly I had failed. I didn't want to see more humans and wolves dead because of me, or hear living ones say that we'd destroyed their home. But that was a coward's way out. I allowed Tlitoo to lead me toward the village.

I knew we'd reached the edge of Kaar by the stack of rhino bones piled high near the charred remains of the spruce grove. The village was almost completely destroyed, but bits of the larger structures still stood smoldering in the center of the largest clearing. It was abandoned, at least by the living. There were bodies everywhere. There were so many dead that I wondered if any of the people of Kaar had survived. I made my way through the village, sniffing as I went. Jlela winged down from the branches of a singed elm to land beside Tlitoo. It was an old tree, and it had stood alone without bushes or smaller trees around it.

"They wished to burn you from their territory," Jlela croaked. "They said wolves poisoned the land and the land must be cleansed. I hid in the tree and heard them say so. The one called DavRian burned the krianan village on purpose, too. He said the old krianans are as much a threat as the wolves. That was how the fire got away from them. They burned their own home." She warbled and flew back up to an elm branch. "Everything burned. Most of the village died. The ones left are going to Laan village. They have agreed that the old krianans are a danger to them and that they will no longer follow their ways."

I growled to myself. I'd known as soon as HesMi chased us away from the village that we'd lost the humans of Kaar. Now DavRian would turn other humans against us, too. The ravens croaked to each other. I watched as they walked a few paces, took flight to land on a pile of bones or fallen shelter, and then hopped to perch on another pile of death or destruction.

I lifted my muzzle to the air, trying to sniff out who was alive and who was dead, but my nose was clogged with the scent of smoke. I sat and sneezed several times, then picked up the faint scent of wolf and followed it.

That was when I found Prannan and Amma lying dead next to two humans.

"They were sleeping in one of the humans' shelters," Jlela quorked. "They stayed at their slow humans' side and did not escape in time. I tried to lead them away but they had eyes only for their humans."

I felt such a powerful wave of shame that I could hardly stand. The first responsibility of a leaderwolf is to protect the wolves who follow her. Amma and Prannan had trusted me and I had led them to their deaths. I'd done everything I could think of to win the humans over in order to save wolf-kind. Instead I had killed the wolves most deserving of my protection. When I was born, of mixed blood and with the mark of the crescent moon on my chest, Ruuqo had said I was unlucky. Milsindra said I was the destroyer of wolfkind. They were both right.

"Wolf, come here," Tlitoo said. He was standing over something that moved ever so slightly.

I trudged over to him. He bent over a raven, its chest moving up and down with great effort, its beady eyes half open.

"He says that some humans ran away. HesMi did not. She stayed to save the others and died with them," Tlitoo said. "He says we must not give up. He says we are close to what we need. He says not to forget what you have learned as Ne-jakilakin."

The dying bird lifted his head and glared at me, opening and closing his beak. "You do not have time for regret," he croaked. "You do not have time to be foolhardy. You must not make the mistakes those before you have made." There was something so familiar about him.

"She must find a way to talk to the girl," he ordered Tlitoo. "There is a way. Find it."

I realized then what was so familiar about the old raven. His raspy voice and piercing gaze were the same as RalZun's. RalZun, who leapt down from the trees as if he had wings.

I lowered my nose to him. He smelled of coming death. I wanted to comfort him, but the fierceness in his gaze stopped me.

"Are you human or raven?" I asked him.

"I am Nejakilakin," he clacked at me. "Before that I was the raven king. I have stayed alive as long as I could so the new Neja can take over. Do not waste my effort."

"I won't," I said.

He struggled to his feet, panted hard, and flew a few wolf-lengths from us. Then he fell and did not rise again.

"Can you do that?" I whispered to Tlitoo. "Can you become human?"

"I do not know," he said. "I have never heard of any raven who could." He gently prodded the old raven's body. "But he was very old and I am very young. You have met him before, wolf."

"Hzralzu," I said. He was the ancient raven who had hunted with Navdru when he was a youngwolf, and who had stood with Indru when I'd met him in the Inejalun nearly a moon before. I didn't understand how a raven could be human and bird at the same time. I didn't understand how he could have lived since the time of Indru only to die in the flames of DavRian's fire.

His words had shaken me from my self-pity. I looked at Prannan and Amma and buried my nose in their fur one more time. They were not badly burned, but looked as if they had suffocated, as creatures did in a fire. They had died for the Promise. RalZun had died, and HesMi and so many others. If I gave up now, their deaths would have been for nothing. DavRian would win. I got angry, and my head cleared. I would not just roll over like a curl-tail and give up. I would fight DavRian until there was no more breath in me. The humans were slow. Perhaps I could get to Laan village before they did.

"How far is it to Laan?" I asked Tlitoo.

"It is just beyond the field where the Sentinels killed the streckwolves," Tlitoo answered, his eyes agleam.

"Let's go," I said.

An hour's lope later, past charred woods and creatures burned so badly I could not tell what kind of beast they were, we reached the end of the fire's path. I found a stream and drank deeply. Then I sank my head into it, allowing the water to run into my eyes and out of my nose, clearing away the burned scents. My nose began to pick up the scents of life: a family of mice skittering behind me, a grouse picking its way to the water. My mother's scent was there, too, less than an hour old. All around us, the creatures that had not been killed began to stir. I heard the buzzing of insects, then the hesitant steps of the grouse. I snapped up a small fish from the stream, swallowing it whole. My stomach came to life and I began stalking the grouse. It was as fire-weary as I was and didn't smell me coming. I pounced on it, making a clean kill and devouring it so quickly that I had to stand still for a moment to keep it in my belly.

Feeling revived, I set out again. In the woods beyond the grassless field where the streckwolves had died, I found the village of Laan. Nestled in a clearing in an elm wood, it was smaller than Kaar, but still larger than TaLi's village in the Wide Valley. I hid for a moment in the wood surrounding it, watching the village from behind a juniper. A stocky dark-furred male seemed to be their leader. When I saw him standing alone near a shelter, I began to creep toward him.

Then I heard DavRian's voice, and IniMin's. They called out a greeting as they approached Laan. I cringed. I had hoped to get to the villagers of Laan before they did.

IniMin led a tired group of humans into Laan. There were perhaps twenty of them, all that was left of the village of Kaar. From the way the others followed behind him and waited for him to speak first, it was clear they saw him as their leader now that HesMi was gone. DavRian stood just to his right, his head held high.

The humans of Laan came forward, and the stocky male greeted IniMin.

"I'm sorry for the loss of your village," he said. "Is this all of you who survived?"

"As far as we know," IniMin answered.

The stocky male narrowed his eyes. "How did your lands come to burn?" he demanded.

IniMin nodded to DavRian, who stepped forward.

"It was the wolves," he said.

I listened as they told their lies about us, saying that we had poisoned everyone in the village except for the few who had escaped, and that they had set fire to the place we were hiding to keep us from killing them all. DavRian said that he had set only a small fire, but that we had taken their fire branches ourselves and spread the flames throughout the lands in revenge. He also said that TaLi and RalZun had encouraged us to do so, that we weren't smart enough to think of it on our own, and that the krianans who favored wolves were as dangerous as we were. He said that they had tainted us and we had tainted them. The humans of Laan muttered to one another in fear.

"They believe him," I whispered to Tlitoo.

"You should know by now they will believe anything that feeds their fear, wolf," he answered.

Leaves rustled behind me and I smelled the welcome scent of dusk sage.

"Their fear overwhelms their reason every time."

I couldn't hold back a yip of joy as Neesa lay down next to me. Her paw print by the river and her scent at the stream had told me that she'd survived the fire, but that wasn't the same as seeing her safe and alive. I had lost Prannan and Amma, and had failed in Kaar. But I still had my mother. Six moons ago, I would not have believed I would ever lie at her side. I rested against her, smelling smoke and worry. She lay her head down atop my back and then began to wash the fur between my shoulders as if I were a smallpup.

"I found your scent," she said, "but I had to see for myself that you were alive."

"For now," I couldn't help saying. "The Sentinels will kill me if they find me."

"They will. Navdru and Yildra are alive, though Lallna did not survive. Navdru has given the order that you and your packmates are to be killed on sight. He announced it to the entire pack as soon as the fire stopped burning."

"And the humans won't accept TaLi as krianan. DavRian told them she's as dangerous as we are." I forced the image of Lallna's face, and of her courage in the face of rhino and Greatwolf alike, from my mind. I would mourn her later.

"Get your humans, Kaala. I will try to convince the Great-wolves to let you leave these lands. Don't follow me," she ordered. "I will find you once I've spoken to them."

Before I could answer, before I could tell her not to put herself at risk, she stood and bolted into the woods. I couldn't help but fear I wouldn't see her again.

I watched the humans a little longer. DavRian and IniMin squatted next to the leader of Laan, whispering to him while the rest of the survivors from Kaar huddled with other villagers. They would spread their lies and there was nothing I could do about it.

"Come on, wolf," Tlitoo said.

I backed away and into the woods, and started toward the cave.

If the humans of Laan believed DavRian, they would give up the ways of the true krianans. The Greatwolves were looking for us and would kill us when they found us. Neesa might be able to convince them to let us go, and to spare those of my blood back in the Wide Valley. If she couldn't, I had to find a way to keep what was left of my pack safe. Tlitoo flew just above me. "Now what, wolflet," he quorked.

I had no idea, except that I wasn't ready to give up. I tried to think like a leaderwolf. I couldn't change what had already happened, but that didn't mean I had no options. If it wasn't safe for us and our humans in Sentinel lands, we could find a place to hide until we figured out what to do, and we could send word to Rissa and Ruuqo to join us before the Sentinels got to them. Pleased to have at least some sort of plan, I loped toward a small hill on the plain. I began to climb it so I could get a better view of the lands beyond Sentinel territory.

"Be careful, wolf! The rocks are not solid."

At Tlitoo's warning, I looked down to see the loose rocks beneath my paws. I didn't know how I'd made it so far up the hill without noticing.

I tried to step carefully, but when I set my left forepaw down on a rock, it slipped out from under me. I stuck out my right forepaw to try to stop myself from falling, but the rocks beneath me gave way and I tumbled down the hill. I scrabbled, trying to get my paws under me as Tlitoo squawked above my head. I wasn't so far up that the fall would kill me or even injure me badly. I was more concerned about someone's hearing my clumsy descent.

I landed hard at the base of the hill, the force of the fall knocking the air from my lungs. I lay there for a moment, dazed.

"Move, wolf!" Tlitoo screeched. I tried to get to my feet, certain he had seen humans or Greatwolves coming. Then a rock hit me on the side and another on the leg. I looked up to see the hillside coming down on me. Rock after rock pelted down, some hitting me, some barely missing. I tried to dodge out of the way but couldn't escape them. Then, just as the on-slaught slowed, a large boulder right at the base of the hill toppled over, trapping my right hind leg beneath it.

I pulled hard, but my leg didn't budge. I twisted around to shove at the rock with my forelegs and succeeded only in pulling a muscle along my ribs. I dug my forepaws into the soft earth at the base of the hill and tried to drag my leg from beneath the boulder. It settled, pinning me even more se-curely. Tlitoo stood a few rocks away, swiveling his head from side to side. He hopped to peer at the boulder that pinned me and quorked in concern.

"It is too heavy. It would take too many ravens to lift it. I will go back for your humans."

We were still far from the Hill Rock, but I couldn't think of any other way to get free. If DavRian or IniMin or any of the Sentinels found me, they would kill me where I lay.

Then I heard unfamiliar human voices, and they were get-ting closer.

"Stay here!" I ordered Tlitoo. Panic made my voice shake. DavRian had stalked the woods near Kaar looking for wolves to kill. I remembered the torn throats of the Greatwolves and could almost feel DavRian's spear slicing through my haunch. I whimpered.

"I hear them, wolf." He stood protectively above me. I pulled my leg as hard as I could, using every bit of my strength, and I felt the rock move, just a little. Encouraged, I pulled hard again, and then again. The rock shifted and fell back again, sending a new deluge of rocks down on me. I squealed in pain as they crushed the lower part of my body. I tried to be quiet, but I hurt too much and couldn't keep from whining.

The human footsteps drew near. Now I did force myself to be quiet, and tried to press myself into the rocks, hoping they wouldn't see me. Tlitoo hunched in front of me.

"It came from somewhere over here," a male human said. "I heard it whimper."

They rounded the hillside and one of them stared right at me. Three others, two male and one female, stopped and stared, too.

"It's trapped," one of the males said. There was sympathy, not anger or hatred, in his voice. He smelled like curiosity and, just a bit, of yearning. He tentatively came forward and removed a rock from the pile that immobilized me. Tlitoo, seeing what he was doing, hopped aside, quorking curiously.

I lifted my head and the human jumped back, his face rigid, his scent infused with anxiety. I lowered my ears and licked my muzzle. I don't know why I did so. The humans were probably thinking about the best way to kill me once they freed me.

"It wants you to help it," one of them said.

They looked at me silently and I looked back. I expected them to pick up more stones and throw them at me, but they just watched me. They kept their distance, sharpsticks raised.

The male who had removed the first rock took another one off me. Then another. Tlitoo warbled encouragement to him. Each time he moved a rock, he leapt back as if I would pounce on him, even though I couldn't move.

His fear was so real, so intense, that I wished I could talk to him, tell him he was safe. I made my eyes soft and whuffed gently. He cried out and jumped back again. I remembered the stories that DavRian told. That we killed indiscriminately, that we wanted nothing more than human blood. That our mouths were full of poison. I realized how much courage it took the human to try to help me. He wasn't young either, he was a male halfway through his life, the kind that was usually the most distrustful of us, and he wasn't helping me for his own gain. I wasn't bringing him prey or protecting him or any of the other things that the humans valued about us. He wanted to help me. He was behaving as if he couldn't bear to see me in pain. It was almost as if he thought of me as a human pup.

Finally, rock by rock, he had all but freed me. Just the one large rock was left. He started to lift it and I tried to pull my leg out. As soon as I moved, he jumped away, letting the rock fall again. I yelped in pain.

"It's just scared," the female said. "It wants you to help it. It won't hurt you."

The male moved forward again and tried to lift the rock, but several smaller rocks held it down. He could have moved it more easily if he'd leaned close to me, but he was afraid to do so. He bent over at an awkward angle, one foot on each side of the rocks above me. He wedged a thick wooden stick in between the rocks and heaved, to no avail. Then another human, walking a wide circle around me as if I might suddenly leap to my paws, jumped up next to him. Together, they leaned on the stick and the rock lifted.

The instant I pulled my leg out from under the rock, the humans ran. I bolted in the other direction into the sparse woods, dragging my sore leg behind me. I stopped when I reached the cover of the trees and looked back. Tlitoo settled next to me. The humans were watching the bushes that hid me. Their expressive faces showed relief but also happiness, pleasure in what they had done. They smelled of contentment, like TaLi did when I lay next to her in the sun.

I'd always thought that there were just good humans who liked us, and bad ones who feared the world around them. It wasn't true. I had sensed that these humans wanted to help, wanted to like me but were afraid. The frightened male had freed me in spite of his fear.

They walked away, looking over their shoulders at the spot where I had run into the forest. I wanted to go out and thank them but I was worried that their fear of me might turn them vicious. The humans settled beyond the rock fall and built one of their fires. It was still light out, but they settled around their fire and took out food.

I watched them as they sat around their fire, relaxing and eating their meal. For the first time I really wondered what it would be like to be so alone. Even when we killed prey or fought other hunters, we knew we shared the world with them, and that we were part of the Balance. The humans were beginning to forget that.

Except when they were with us. Some, like TaLi or Jali-Min, welcomed us as part of their packs without question. They could accept us as we were. But others, like the human who had freed me, were afraid of us. Yet they still yearned for us, for the connection to us.

I remembered the way the humans had been with the streckwolves, both in the village from the past and on the plain, before the Sentinels killed them. I'd been so envious, and so furious that the streckwolves might take the humans from us, that I hadn't really thought about what it meant. The humans wanted us to be pack, but they feared us too much to keep us near. They didn't fear the streckwolves. They loved them without fear. And if the humans could love them—those little wolves so close to wild and yet not truly so—maybe they could learn to love other, wilder things, to love the wildness all around them.

The Greatwolves said the streckwolves were our death, but they'd been wrong before.

Perhaps Gaanin and his pack were our way in. If the humans trusted the streckwolves and came to love them, perhaps they could one day accept us, too.

Gaanin had twice tried to tell me something, and I'd refused to listen. If he was alive and I could find him before the Sentinel wolves found me, we might still have a chance.

Tlitoo ran his beak through my headfur.

"I am glad you are all right, wolf," he said.

I told him my thoughts about the streckwolves and the humans.

"It might not be too late," I said.

"Of course it isn't, dimwolf," he said.

I waited until dark so that I could leave unseen, then set off for the Hill Rock to get Ázzuen, listening as long as I could to the contented murmuring of the humans.

25

Twice on my way back to the cave, I saw the moonlit shapes of Greatwolves prowling in the distance. Both times, I hid until they were long gone. My mother had said she would try to reason with them, but they were not reasonable creatures. By the time I reached the cave, it was nearly light, and I was as jumpy as an elk among longfangs. I had to get to the streckwolves before the Sentinels found me.

TaLi's ankle had swollen and turned dark. She sat inside the cave, leaning against one of its rocky walls and scowling at BreLan.

"I'm coming, too," she growled.

Ázzuen greeted me with a quick touch of his nose to my muzzle. My skittering heart calmed just a little at his touch.

"BreLan's been to Kaar," he said. "Now he wants to see if anyone survived and went to Laan." Ázzuen sounded worried for his human. "Tlitoo and Jlela are here, too, roosting in the back of the cave."

Tlitoo, impatient as always, had flown on ahead of me. As quickly as I could, I told Ázzuen about DavRian's lies and about the humans who had rescued me. When I told him of my plan, his ears twitched.

"Yes," he said. "It might work. If we can convince both Gaanin and the Sentinels." He didn't sound particularly confident. "We can at least try."

TaLi rubbed her ankle impatiently. "If HesMi's there, I need to talk to her," she insisted, peering out of the cave. She didn't know the human leader was dead, and I couldn't tell her.

I went to the girl and sat beside her. She stroked my fur.

"If she is, I'll come back to get you," BreLan answered, "but we need to know if DavRian's been there and what he's told them. I promise to come back as soon as I know what's happening."

TaLi struggled to her feet. She took a few steps, wincing, then sighed.

"I'll slow you down if I come," she admitted, sitting next to me again. I whuffed a sigh of relief. If she had insisted on going with BreLan, injured as she was, I would have had to go along to guard her, and I needed to get to Gaanin.

"You have to find out if HesMi and RalZun are there, and if DavRian and IniMin survived," TaLi ordered. "If they did, you have to learn what they've said to Laan's elders. If there's a chance Laan will let me be their krianan, we need to go there."

Pride in her determination and courage filled me. She had grown into a true krianan since we had left the valley. It would do her no good to go to Laan now that DavRian had spread his lies. Still, the sooner she knew that, the better. I would need her to follow us wherever we decided to take her, and if she was trying to go to Laan, she would resist us.

I padded to BreLan and licked his hand. He smiled, stroked my head, then rubbed Ázzuen's ears and ducked out of the cave. Ázzuen followed him.

Tlitoo and Jlela stalked from the back of the cave, blinking sleepily.

"We heard your plan, wolf," Tlitoo said. "We will watch the girl until you return."

Two ravens weren't much protection, but TaLi was well hidden, and I needed Ázzuen's clever mind with me when I talked to the streckwolves.

"Thank you," I said, trying not to sound too doubtful.

I licked TaLi from chin to headfur and loped into the early-morning light.

◻

BreLan walked with us as far as the edge of the burned land, then set off for Laan. Ázzuen watched him worriedly.

"You can go with him if you like," I said, not really meaning it. I wanted Ázzuen with me.

"I'll find him after we talk to the streckwolves," Ázzuen said. "I wouldn't let you go alone, Kaala."

I licked his muzzle. I knew how hard it was for him to let his human walk off unprotected. We watched BreLan until he disappeared into the unburned woods, then we set off for the streckwolves' gathering place. We ran full pelt past the Barrens and up the slope above their home, which had been spared the fire's rage. We had just started down the hill when I saw wolf shapes running toward us. Strange wolf shapes with rounded heads.

Gaanin was in the lead. Two streckwolves ran with him.

When they saw us loping toward them, they stopped to watch us approach, sitting straight, with their paws placed neatly before them. When I reached them, I realized that I had no idea what to say.

I looked at Gaanin and he looked back. There was no reproach in his expression, but no welcome either. I remembered the dead streckwolves on the grassless plain and dropped my gaze.

"They burned the woods," I said. Which was stupid. Of course they would know that. The two wolves with Gaanin looked suspiciously at Ázzuen.

"That's Ázzuen," I said. "He's pack."

"Your mate?" one of the streckwolves, a female, asked curiously.

"Not yet," I said, then lowered my ears in embarrassment.

She panted a small smile, then grew serious. "We know they burned the woods, young wild wolf. What are you going to do about it?"

I'd planned to make an impassioned plea to get the streckwolves to do what I asked. I'd tried the whole way from the cave to find the eloquence to sway them. Instead, I blurted it all out. "I want you to come with me back to the humans. They need wolves that they aren't afraid of. They need something to love that they don't fear. I don't know why they fear us so much, but they do. So, if they have wolves with them like you, wolves they aren't afraid of, then maybe they'll stop killing and we can go back to them. You have to get them to accept you and then let us take over."

"It is their own wildness that they fear," Gaanin said. "In you, they see what they once were, one animal among many, a beast rather than a creature separate and greater than all others. In us, they see something they can love that does not challenge their vision of themselves."

"You knew that already," I said.

"It's why we have sacrificed what is most wild in us," Gaanin said. "It's why we are willing to let the humans command us in the hunt, to take our territory, and rule our packs as if they were our leaderwolves."

I couldn't imagine giving up the thrill of the hunt and the exhilaration of biting into thrashing prey when and where I chose, or the joy of running through my territory with my packmates. Ever since I'd met the streckwolves, I'd thought of them as less than wolf. But they were willing to give up even more for the Promise than I was.

"It's what I was trying to tell you before, Kaala," Gaanin said. "But you weren't ready to listen."

My tail lowered at his reprimand. Then, angry at his presumption that he had the right to scold me, I lifted it back up.

"You hid other things from me," I said, jutting my chin at him. "You didn't tell me you were my father."

"It wasn't my secret to tell," Gaanin said. He lowered his own tail in apology. "We tried many places to breed wolves that the humans could accept without demanding obedience. I have more wild wolf in me than others in my pack and have fathered many pups. You, of all of them, have come the closest. But it was a foolish hope. They are still too fearful."

That's all I was to him. One more experiment. I thought that when I finally met my father, I'd have a thousand questions for him, but I was no more to him than a tool was to a human. He looked at me expectantly. I liked Gaanin. He was as brave as any wolf I knew and willing to do anything for the Promise. I didn't want to be nothing more than a tool to him. I shook myself. Trevegg and even Ruuqo had been good fathers to me.

"You aren't a submissive wolf," Ázzuen said to the streck-wolf when I remained silent.

"I am when I'm with the humans," Gaanin answered. "It is a choice I've made. My children's children will be more so. Those who are not will pretend to be. The humans are frightened, lonely creatures and they need us to teach them that the world is not such a terrible place." He smiled a little, as if the humans were smallpups just out of the den.

He cared about the humans as much as I did. It didn't seem to matter to him that he was my father, but the humans and the Promise were as important to him as pack. More, for his packmates had died trying to teach the humans love. As much as I wanted him to care that I was his pup, I needed him to help us win back the humans more.

"Neesa told me that if humans lived with wolves like you," I said, careful not to call them streckwolves, "your children's children would forget they were wolf. They'd forget the Promise. Like Whitefur and Short Tail."

"Yes," Gaanin replied. "They will remember only that they are to be by the humans' side. They will not be conflicted about what is best for wolfkind. They will not even know that part of the Promise."

Which was why we would have to take over from the streckwolves. The wild had to be preserved so that the humans created no more Barrens. I respected Gaanin's willingness to go to the humans, only to step aside for us.

"It is our hope," Gaanin said, watching me carefully, "that

if the humans can love one creature other than themselves, a creature that does not threaten them, they will find a way to love the world around them. We have tried everything else. It's our last chance. And theirs. But we cannot succeed unless you wild wolves leave us be."

"Because the Sentinels keep killing you," I said.

"Not just the Sentinels," the female streckwolf said. "It's happened before with other packs. The wild wolves hate our kind and have killed us again and again. Your kind is sometimes no better than the Greatwolves."

"You saw what happened to my wolves at the grassless plain," Gaanin said. He glowered, and for a sickening moment I wondered if he knew I'd led the Sentinels there. I waited for him to accuse me. Instead, he whuffed anxiously. "Now the humans have burned the woods. It may be time for us to leave this place and hide until things have calmed down, as we have done before. But I fear this may be our last chance. If we wait, the humans may be too far gone."

I swallowed a yelp of panic. It would certainly be too late for us if Gaanin took his pack away.

"We'll find a way to convince the Greatwolves to leave you alone," Ázzuen said. I had no idea how we could do such a thing, but I tried to look as confident as Ázzuen sounded.

"IniMin and DavRian are already at Laan, spreading lies about us," Ázzuen continued. He sounded as calm as if he were discussing an upcoming hunt. "And they said that our krianans convinced us to burn down the woods. What if they are afraid of you, too?"

"The humans there don't think of us as wolves, or as wild," Gaanin said. "Kaala saw that before the Sentinels slaughtered us. IniMin and DavRian pose no threat to us. We can slip past their fear. We will go to Laan and watch the humans there. We will find out if they believe IniMin and DavRian's tales about your krianans, and if it is safe for your humans to stay nearby. But you must make sure Navdru and his pack do not kill us."

"I'll talk to the Sentinels," I said.

"We can wait until moonrise tomorrow." The female streckwolf shook herself. "We'll be in the woods near Laan."

"If you do not get the Greatwolves to agree," Gaanin said, "I will need to take my pack into hiding. Again."

He dipped his head to us and darted into the woods.

I waited until they were out of hearing range to turn to Ázzuen.

"You don't have a plan to convince the Sentinels, do you?" I knew him well enough to know when he was bluffing.

"Not yet," he answered. "But we have to find one, don't we?"

I sighed. "We do."

He nosed my muzzle. "We'll figure something out, Kaala, I promise. Can I go find BreLan now?" I saw that his own muzzle was tight with anxiety. He'd probably been worried about his human the entire time we were talking to Gaanin. I thought of TaLi, alone but for a pair of ravens.

"Yes," I said. "I'll meet you back at the cave."

He nipped me lightly on the nose, turned, and loped toward Laan. I missed him the moment he was gone, but shook myself and began to make my way back to TaLi.

I was halfway back to the Hill Rock when a frantic flapping of wings filled the air above me. Jlela flew straight into me, the full impact of her weight knocking me over. I scrambled to my paws, coughing.

"What are you doing?" I growled.

Jlela only hissed in answer.

I bared my teeth at her, then took in her appearance. Her feathers were mussed and her ruff stood almost straight up. There was a desperate look in her eyes.

"What happened?" I asked, panic tightening my throat.

"They have taken him."

"Who?" I asked. I'd just seen Ázzuen, and I couldn't think of who might take BreLan anywhere.

She glared at me and spat a twig right in my eye.

"Tlitoo! The Grimwolves have taken him! And your girl."

"Why?" I asked, frantic. "Where?" I felt as if Jlela had jabbed her beak into my chest and speared my heart. I could face the Sentinel wolves and DavRian and a hundred burning forests, but I couldn't lose TaLi and Tlitoo.

"At your girl's hiding place!" she rasped. She took flight and winged back toward the burned forest. She flew so quickly that by the time I took my first stumbling step, she was no more than a dark speck in the sky. I followed that speck, terrified that by the time I reached TaLi and Tlitoo, it would be too late to save them.

□

Jlela waited for me at the bottom of the Hill Rock. As I neared her, she flew halfway up the rock. I squinted up at her through the glare of late sun. She clacked her beak impatiently.

"I don't have wings," I muttered to myself. I also didn't want the Greatwolves to know I was coming. Every muscle in my body screamed at me to run straight up to the cave to find TaLi, but if I did so, I would be visible long before I got there. If Ázzuen were with me, he'd tell me to find a quiet way up the rock instead of rushing in. I sat and looked up at the cave. I saw that the outcropping in front of it went halfway around the rock. I could sneak up to the very edge of the cave without being seen, then find a way to get to TaLi and Tlitoo. I ran in back of the rock and scrambled up it onto the ledge, then crept along it as quietly as I could. When I neared the entrance to the cave, I lowered myself to my belly and crawled forward, pawswidth by pawswidth.

I stopped at the mouth of the cave and lay flat. Jlela hung upside down under the ledge, opening and closing her beak silently. I rested my head against the stone and listened. I couldn't hear a thing, and the air still smelled so much of smoke I couldn't pick out any scents. I was just about to ask Jlela if she was sure they were in there when hot breath on the top of my head made me look up into Milsindra's smug gaze.

"What took you so long, Kaala?" She smiled. She grabbed me by my scruff and rolled me head over tail until I landed in the cave, splayed on my stomach. Greatwolves closed in around me.

I smelled TaLi and Tlitoo, then, but couldn't see either of them through the fur of what seemed like a hundred Greatwolves. My throat was so dry with fear that I couldn't speak even if I could think of what to say. I'd been in such a hurry to get to the cave that I hadn't thought about what I'd do once I got there. I had been foolish to come alone, without a plan. Now I was trapped, with no way to stop the Greatwolves from killing all of us.

I needed to calm down and think clearly. I closed my eyes for a moment. Shutting my eyes while surrounded by enemies wasn't a good idea, but I was under no illusions. If the Greatwolves wanted me dead, keeping my eyes open wouldn't help me, either. I took several deep breaths, hoping an idea would come to me. None did. I waited a little longer, then opened my eyes. I would do TaLi and Tlitoo no good lying there like stupefied prey.

I counted eight Greatwolves, not a hundred, including Milsindra and her mate, Kivdru. At first I thought that the other Greatwolves were strangers to me, but then I recognized Galindra and Sundru and several other Wide Valley Greatwolves who supported Milsindra. I still couldn't see TaLi or Tlitoo. I heard a yelp of pain and then another, and a young Greatwolf scooted forward. Tlitoo swayed behind him, his beak full of fur. TaLi sat next to him, curled against the cold wall of the cave.

Tlitoo spat out the fur and what looked like a bit of skin. "You should not have come, wolflet," he said, "but I am glad you did. We will make them sorry now." He crouched down low, holding one of his wings at an awkward angle. Jlela flew into the cave and darted between Greatwolves to get to him. She quorked something to him, and he answered with a soft, urgent croak. Two Greatwolves lunged for Jlela. She dove between them and, as they tried to snatch her from the air, swooped past them and out of the cave. They started to run after her, but her strong wings had already taken her beyond their reach. All they could do was growl after her. I took advantage of their distraction to bolt to TaLi. No one stopped me.

TaLi threw her arms around me. Her skin felt damp and cold, and she was shivering. I pressed as close to her as I could and turned to face the Greatwolves. I expected them to snarl at or threaten me, but they just stood watching me. They knew I had no chance to escape.

"What do you want?" I asked Milsindra, daring to meet her eyes for a moment before looking over her shoulder.

"We want to know what you do with these two," she said. "We know that you enter the realm of the spirits. Neesa said that you can go into the minds of other wolves, and the wolf who can do that can also cross into the spirit world. We have all been told so since we were pups. There are secrets there that belong to us, secrets that can help us stop our kind from dying out, and it has been too long since we have been able to talk to the Ancients. That is what the drelshik does, isn't it?" I couldn't mistake the envy in her voice. "You will take us there or watch your human die."

I didn't know what the Greatwolves really wanted in the Inejalun, but I didn't want to give Milsindra anything that might help her.

My head pounded, and I thought that if I were any more afraid, it would burst apart. I forced myself to think. I couldn't get past them, and I couldn't fight my way out. I had to trick them. Tlitoo clearly had the same thought.

"It is us," he clacked. "We are the Neja. You must have me, the wolf, and the human girl."

I was angry at first that he had included TaLi, but then grateful. If they didn't need her, they might have killed her already. Tlitoo looked at me, blinking rapidly. He was plotting something. "If one of you lies next to us, you will be able to see what we see," he quorked.

I had no idea what Tlitoo had planned, but also had no ideas of my own. I would follow his lead. Milsindra was watching me. I dipped my head in agreement.

TaLi chose that moment to try to escape. She stood and

took a step toward the cave entrance. Terrified that the Great-wolves would hurt her, I knocked her knees out from under her so that she sat again. Several of the Greatwolves snickered. Then Tlitoo stalked over to crouch beside us. The Greatwolves gathered around us, but none of them came too close to me. I wanted to laugh. They pretended to be so fierce and strong, but they were afraid of what Tlitoo and I could do.

"What happened to your wing?" I whispered to Tlitoo.

"It is broken, wolf. I cannot fly," he said loudly, then dropped his voice to what was barely a whisper. "You must let a Grimwolf lie next to your girl. I have led them to believe that the human opens the gate to the Nejakilakin so they would not kill her. Now we can use that. But you must allow it."

I didn't want to let a Greatwolf anywhere near TaLi, but it was our only choice.

"All right," I said.

"Gruntwolves," Tlitoo said arrogantly to the huge wolves around him. "One of you must not be a curl-tail. One of you must sit next to the girl. If you hurt her, you will never get to the Inejalun."

Milsindra stepped forward. She was shaking, and her fear gave me pleasure. TaLi shrank away from her as she drew near. But I nudged her toward the Greatwolf and licked her hand. "You need to sit next to her," I said to TaLi for Milsindra's benefit. "Stay there."

TaLi stayed still, shaking almost as much as Milsindra did.

"She obeys you?" one of the Greatwolves asked.

I didn't answer him. It went against every instinct I had to let Milsindra near TaLi, and even the thought of it made me so sick to my stomach I had to swallow to keep from vomiting in front of the Greatwolves. I dipped my head to Tlitoo. He hopped awkwardly onto my back.

Tlitoo took me straight to the Inejalun. The sensation of falling, the lack of smell and taste, and the shock of the cold hit me so quickly I didn't have time to adjust. My thoughts froze. We landed in the Stone Circle, exactly where we always found ourselves when we first entered the Inejalun. But this time, the Shadow Wolf did not come to greet us. Tlitoo cawed loudly several times, and I tried to put aside my fear that the Greatwolves could hear us and would attack TaLi in revenge. I heard answering raven calls from somewhere beyond the Stone Circle.

"Listen, wolf," Tlitoo said. "We will escape the cave and then you must follow me. You must not be exhausted and frozen, so there is no time to explain. Will you trust me? Will you do whatever I say?"

Out of the corner of my eye, I saw a shadow move.

"Wait," I said, stepping away from Tlitoo.

I followed the shadow behind a large rock. The Shadow Wolf was just about to slip into the woods.

"Is it true?" I asked. "Can we bring others to the Inejalun?"

The Shadow Wolf stopped and looked over his shoulder. "I have heard that it is so," he said, "but I cannot guarantee what will happen if you do. I do not like the solution you have found. I do not like the wolves that are not wolves taking what is ours." He muttered something to himself, then raised his head. "But we forsook the Promise, and our attempts to fix what we have broken have failed. It is no longer for us to say what is the right thing to do."

"I need your help," I said. "You have to tell the Sentinels not to kill the streckwolves." My tongue was thick with cold.

He shifted restlessly. "I can try," he said. "But if I do, you cannot falter. If we let the little not-wolves live, it will mean the end of our kind. The humans will be strong enough to kill us. If I agree to make that sacrifice and let the little wolves live, you must promise me you will do whatever you must to honor that sacrifice."

"I promise," I said.

The Shadow Wolf lowered his great head. "Then I will try. The time of the Greatwolf is past, but yours may not yet be."

"Wolf," Tlitoo rasped, "you cannot stay longer. If you fall asleep we cannot fight."

"I can help with that, this one time," the Shadow Wolf said. "You will be weakened, but will be able to go on." He touched his nose to my chest, and for just a moment I felt warm.

Tlitoo hurled himself against me and I found myself lying on the ground of the cave, which seemed much too warm after the cold of the Inejalun. I was tired, but the Shadow Wolf's touch had made it possible for me to stay awake.

Tlitoo flapped his good wing and looked up at the Great-wolves. "It does not work here, surrounded by rocks," he said. "The Ancients cannot reach us."

The Greatwolves grumbled and some of them moved forward, teeth bared.

"I cannot help it, Grumpwolves," Tlitoo said. "I do not choose when and where the spirits speak to us. There is a place they have always come to us before. I can take you there."

Milsindra growled low in her throat, but Tlitoo just blinked at her. She growled again, more ferociously. Tlitoo clacked his beak and turned his head from side to side. Then he began poking at bits of dirt as if looking for worms. Milsindra whuffed impatiently, then led the way out of the cave. If she weren't a Greatwolf trying to kill me, I might have felt sorry for her. She needed Tlitoo to help her save her own pack, and I'd never met a wolf that could force a raven to do anything it didn't want to do.

Four Greatwolves kept close to us as we made our way down the hill and into the woods. Two more herded TaLi, who was limping badly. Tlitoo rode upon my back, holding out his broken wing.

Then, between one breath and the next, Tlitoo took flight, his supposedly broken wing slicing through the wind. I darted to stand in front of TaLi, trying to protect her from the Great-wolves. She had other ideas. She took several sharp rocks from her clothing and threw them, one by one, at the Greatwolves, striking them with fierce accuracy between their eyes. They snarled and stalked toward her. I had no choice but to fight. I bit down hard on Milsindra's leg and she yowled. I grinned in spite of my terror. I'd always wanted to bite her.

I don't think it had occurred to the Greatwolves that we would attack them. Milsindra and Kivdru growled and snapped, but Galindra and Sundru just blinked stupidly. Tlitoo returned to smack the Greatwolves with his wings and stab at their vul-nerable eyes with his sharp beak. TaLi and I ran.

We made it as far as a small grove of elms before they caught us. Kivdru tackled me there, knocking the air from my lungs. He laughed, then stepped off me. Two Greatwolves trapped TaLi between them. Before I could get up, Kivdru whuffed a command, and Galindra and Sundru sauntered into the grove. Sundru gripped Jlela between his sharp teeth. Galindra held Tlitoo. She dropped him at Sundru's feet. Before the raven could move, Sundru pinned him beneath his great paw. Tlitoo croaked in fury. I scrambled to my paws and darted to stand as close to TaLi as I could get.

"I'll go tell Milsindra you found the stupid pup," Galindra said and trotted away.

Sundru grinned as he tightened his grip on Jlela, his teeth piercing the bird's breast. Jlela kept perfectly still, blood from several puncture wounds—bite marks—dripping from her wings down Sundru's chest and into Tlitoo's feathers.

I was frozen in place, immobilized by horror and helplessness. One bite of the Greatwolf's huge jaws and Jlela would be dead. There was no way I could get to the Greatwolf quickly enough to do anything.

Milsindra loped into the grove. Kivdru whuffed in greeting.

"You will not try to escape us again," Milsindra said. She didn't even bother to look at me. "You will take us where you go with the Neja. If you do not, I will kill that raven"—she pointed her muzzle at Jlela—"and then the Neja."

I looked down at Tlitoo. His body trembled beneath Sundru's paw. At first I thought he was as terrified as I was, but then I saw the look in his eye, and it was a look of rage.

"Let her go," he croaked, staring at Jlela, gripped between Sundru's teeth. "You do not threaten the raven clan."

Sundru laughed, stepping down hard enough to make Tlitoo cry out in pain.

"It is too late, Greatworms," Jlela rasped from between Sundru's teeth. "You can no longer see the memories without the ravens and we will not take you. Wolflet"—her beady eyes met mine—"Gripewolves can come with the Neja and the Moonwolf. That is what they want from us. They can see the spirit world with us and cannot see it without us and they think to find ways to keep their power. But we will never take them again." Sundru closed his jaws more tightly around her, forcing her into silence.

"It is simple, Kaala," Milsindra said. "Make the raven take us with you, or we will kill not only these two but each and every one of your friends. Smallwolves and humans are as easy to kill as ravens. We will not allow ourselves to be supplanted by wolves such as you."

I found myself trembling as much as Tlitoo was, and with just as much fury. Milsindra was not only willing to kill all of us to save her kind, she was willing to shatter the Promise. I opened my mouth, trying to think of something to stall the Greatwolves.

"You must not, wolf," Jlela rasped, trying to flap her wings against Sundru's jaws. "The Nejakilakin must not be compromised."

Kivdru huffed a command to Sundru, who closed his great jaws so quickly, I couldn't even yelp in protest. Jlela's eyes did not leave mine, and I watched as the life faded from them.

Tlitoo hissed in anger and in grief. "You will never walk safely again," he rasped. "Your time is done. Your kind will soon no longer walk these lands." The Greatwolves ignored him. Furious and grieving for Jlela, I hurled myself at Sundru. He stumbled and loosened his hold on Tlitoo, who flew high up into the trees, screeching.

Sundru flung me to the ground and stood on my chest, forcing the air from my lungs, then took my neck in his sharp teeth. TaLi shrieked and tried to run forward, but two Greatwolves blocked her path. I looked high up into the leaves above me. For some reason, the only thought in my head was that there shouldn't be so many leaves on the elms after the fire.

Then the leaves began to shift and seethe as if blowing in the wind. But there was no wind. The rustling was suddenly very near me and a raven landed on a rock just to my left. Another alighted in the dirt beside me, and then another. The trees above me teemed. What I had thought was thick foliage was really the motion of hundreds of wings. That was where Jlela had gone when she flew from the cave: to get the other ravens. A loud, deep-throated croaking filled the woods as more ravens than I could count dropped from the trees to surround us. Others hovered just above the Greatwolves' heads. The Greatwolves snarled, then growled and stepped back. I struggled from beneath Sundru's paws and ran to TaLi. Raven after raven descended, croaking and screeching, flying just above Greatwolf heads and just past Greatwolf tails.

"Better scramble, wolflet," Tlitoo rasped, flying past my ear.

I scrambled, buffeted by wings and scratched by talons as the ravens attacked their prey. TaLi and I stumbled together from the grove. Kivdru and Sundru howled in shock and pain. Milsindra bellowed in fury. As soon as I had TaLi safely out of range, I had to turn back to look. The Greatwolves were so quickly buried under a writhing mass of wings and beaks and talons that it was as if they'd suddenly disappeared and been replaced by a seething river of ravens, their cries drowned out by the shrieks of the furious birds.

I couldn't stop watching. One bird flew past me with a large paw in his beak. Another grasped what looked suspiciously like an ear. A tail, bloody at one end, hung from a low branch. The ravens surrounded what was left of the Greatwolves' bodies and began to hum. At Tlitoo's call, they rose and flew away.

26

M ilsindra was dead. She had stalked me and haunted my dreams. She would have killed me if she could, and all of those I loved. She would not have the chance now. Yet horror was mingled with my relief. I'd known Tlitoo for most of my life and had no idea that ravens could be so deadly. I'd never known that they could kill us anytime they liked.

I hid with TaLi in the bushes and tried to stop trembling. All that was left of the Greatwolves was a scattering of fur, blood, and chunks of flesh.

Tlitoo landed among the remnants of the Greatwolves and stalked over to us. His legs were scraped and bloody, and his chest heaved with the effort of breathing.

"You're hurt," I said.

"I am fine, wolflet. It is the Grumpwolves who are hurt. They should not have angered the raven clan. They should not have murdered Jlela."

TaLi watched him, her eyes wide. Then she reached out and gently stroked his chest feathers with the back of her hand.

"Thank you," she said. "Thank you for saving me. And for saving Kaala."

Tlitoo warbled, pleased. "Your girl has more sense than you do, wolf. Which is not saying much." But he ran his bloodied beak through my headfur. "We do not hurt those who are our friends. You must be strong now, wolflet. We have angered the Grimwolves and there will be war because of it. We will win, and their kind will be no more, but it will be bloody. You must not waste our effort." He gave a mournful croak. "You must not waste Jlela's life." He shook out his wings. "Your friends wait for you at the Hill Rock. It is time to finish what we started."

He spread his wings and cawed loudly, then took flight.

I stood and stretched my fear-stiffened muscles. I looked up at TaLi. I needed to get back to the cave. BreLan and Ázzuen would be waiting for us there.

"We have to go," I said, and tugged at her tunic. She looked down at me and, as she sometimes did, understood what I meant even though we did not speak the same language.

"All right, Kaala," she said wearily. "I'm coming."

▣

Ázzuen and BreLan stood on the ledge outside the cave, two wolves at their side. I halted, unsure whether the wolves were friend or foe. When the wind changed and I caught their scent, I yipped in welcome.

Pell and Marra pelted down the steep face of the rock. Ázzuen and his human made their way down more slowly. Marra and Pell tackled me, dumping me into the dirt. I rolled on top of Marra and nipped her ear, then licked Pell's muzzle. I got to my paws, my tail wagging just a little. So many wolves and humans had died. We all might be dead before darkfall, either at the hands of the humans or by the teeth of the Sentinels, but we had a much better chance of surviving now that my pack was together again.

"We saw the fire and thought you were dead," Marra said. She stood on her hind legs and placed her paws on my back. "We thought you were all dead." She dropped down to all fours.

"Prannan and Amma died," I said, my tail drooping as guilt and sorrow hit me once again. "And Lallna didn't survive." My throat clenched as I realized others might be dead. "Is Swift River all right? Did the Greatwolves kill them?"

"They're fine. At least for now," Pell answered. "But those odd wolves have come to the valley. They were hiding with the Vole Eater pack. Now they're living with the humans at the Lin and Rian villages. The Greatwolf council is waiting to hear about what happened here before they decide what to do about them. That's what we came to tell you. The council is waiting for you and Milsindra to come back."

"Milsindra won't be going back," Tlitoo croaked.

Ázzuen and BreLan reached us then. BreLan held his arms out to TaLi and she limped over to him.

"Did you go to Laan?" she asked him.

He grimaced. "I tried, but two of their hunters chased me away before I got to the village. They don't know me. We'll have to go back and talk to their elders."

I didn't want them to go to Laan. DavRian and IniMin had been there, telling lies. I whuffed in frustration, desperate to be able to talk to our humans.

BreLan held TaLi so tightly that they looked like one creature. That was when I realized that Pell and Marra were standing very close together, too. Like mates did.

Marra saw me staring at her and grinned. Pell averted his eyes. He certainly hadn't waited long to find another wolf once I'd rejected him.

Tlitoo poked me in the rump. "They must know the rest, wolflet."

I told them about how Milsindra and her followers had died at the beaks of the ravens, and about the humans who had saved me. I told them of our plan to get the streckwolves to open the way for us to be with the humans. And, reluctantly, I told them what Tlitoo and I could do together, about the Shadow Wolf and our plan to bring the Sentinels to meet him.

I waited for them to turn from me in revulsion or even in anger. Pell watched me for a long moment, then laughed.

"I should have known there were things you weren't telling me."

Marra's eyes were bright with curiosity. "So you can bring the Sentinel pack with you? You can show them the Shadow Wolf?"

"I think so," I said, relief almost knocking me off my paws. I had been so certain that my packmates would despise me when they found out what Tlitoo and I did together. I'd been afraid that once they knew how abnormal I was, they would shun me and I would be alone. Instead, they treated my journeys to the spirit world as if they were no stranger than Marra's quick legs or Ázzuen's cleverness.

A warning howl echoed through the burned-out lands. It was my mother's voice. I longed to run to her. Now that my pack was together, I felt I should be able to go somewhere safe with them and leave all the trouble and sorrow of Kaar behind. But I could not. Neesa wasn't calling us to a hunt or to explore new territories. It was a howl of warning. The Sentinels had found our trail.

"Run!" she howled. I looked at the determined expressions of my packmates and our humans. I was through with running. It was too late, anyway. The huge shapes of Greatwolves crested a rise on the plain before us. The fire had burned away the trees and bushes that would have hidden us, and they could see us as easily as we saw them in the fading evening light.

Neesa was in the lead, running before them. They overtook her, charging toward us.

"Stand firm, wolf," Tlitoo said, and I looked up to see at least twenty ravens hovering above us. Many had bloodied beaks and talons.

Pell, Ázzuen, and Marra stood at my flanks. The humans stood behind us, their sharpsticks raised. Ravens hummed above us. The Sentinels, led by Navdru and Yildra, ran faster. There were only six of them, and I found myself thinking that we might have a fair fight.

Navdru must have thought so, too, for he skidded to a halt when he reached us. Neesa bolted past him to stand at my side. Navdru looked from the five of us wolves to TaLi and

BreLan with their deadly spears, and then up at the hovering ravens. The fear in his eyes when he saw them told me that he'd heard of the other Greatwolves' deaths.

"The rest of the pack is coming," he said, his voice raspy from smoke. He looked up at the ravens.

"They may not get here in time," a raven warbled.

Navdru inclined his head. "Perhaps not in time to stop you from killing us, though I am not sure you can, but in time to stop this drelshik wolf and her pack from destroying all of wolfkind."

He raised his chin, and in that moment I saw everything it meant to be a leaderwolf. Navdru was willing to die to do what he thought was right and I had to admire that. Even if what he thought was right was killing me.

His gaze met mine.

"Now do you believe us?" he said. "Now do you see what the humans do when they fear us?"

He expected me to apologize. In some ways, I was sorry. I'd made mistakes with the humans, and that was one of the reasons they'd burned the woods. But the time for apologies had passed.

"We have a plan," I said.

My mother interrupted me. "Let her go. Let her take her humans and go. I will make sure they stay away from the humans."

"I'm not leaving," I said, and Yildra snarled.

"It's too late for that, Neesa, you know that," Yildra said. "They have failed in everything they have tried, as has every wolf before them."

A distant Greatwolf howl sounded across the land. The rest of the Sentinel wolves were on their way. We were running out of time.

"Now we know more than we did before," I said, "and you need to know it, too." Neesa whuffed a warning.

"I think they need to meet the Shadow Wolf," I told her.

"But they can't!" she said.

"They can," I said. *At least I hope so*, I added to myself. I didn't know what I'd do if Tlitoo couldn't really take them with us to the Inejalun.

"What is she talking about?" Navdru growled.

"Milsindra was right," I told him. "There is a place between the worlds, and Tlitoo can take me there. He can take other wolves with us, too." I paused, gathering courage for what I said next. "I am the drelwolf." I pointed my muzzle at Tlitoo. "We are the Nejakilakin."

I had never said it aloud before, never even admitted it to myself that I could be a wolf of legend. But whether I wanted it to be true or not, it was clear that my actions might very well determine the fate of wolfkind, and I had to have the courage to acknowledge it.

Tlitoo glided down to land next to me. "One of you at a time may come with us. You cannot stay long. The Inejalun is not a place for living beings. You will grow cold, and if you stay too long, you will die. If the drelwolf stays too long with each of you, she will not survive."

He hopped up on Navdru's back and quorked a challenge. Navdru began to back away, snarling. Before he could give the order to kill me, I jumped, slamming into the Sentinel leader. Tlitoo put one foot on my back and one on Navdru's.

Then we were falling. The last thing I heard was Navdru's gasp of terror before all scent and sound deserted me. A few dizzying moments later, we stood in the Stone Circle.

"It worked!" Tlitoo screeched. "It worked, wolflet!" He ran his beak through my backfur.

"What is this place?" Navdru's voice shook so much I almost didn't recognize it. His eyes were wide in shock. "I know the Stone Circle of the Wide Valley, but this can't really be it." He took a shuddering breath. "I can't feel my paws."

"It's just the cold of the Inejalun," I said. I'd forgotten how terrified I'd been when I first came to this place.

"There is no time to blather, wolves," Tlitoo reminded us. He stalked to the edge of the Stone Circle.

"Take me out of here," Navdru demanded, crouching down as if to avoid an attack from above.

"I will not," retorted Tlitoo. "I will leave you here to freeze and die alone if you do not come with us. You promised to watch over all of wolfkind. Are you too afraid to do so?"

Navdru straightened, and lifted his head. "I will do whatever I must for wolfkind."

We walked through the Inejalun, stopping to show Navdru the village full of streckwolves that had stood in the land that was now the Barrens. We let him see how relaxed and happy the humans were with the little wolves. He growled when he saw them. Then we took him to the Shadow Wolf's cave. Navdru stopped at the entrance, refusing to go in.

"I've been here before," he said, his voice full of dread, "in the real world. The wolf who lives here is said to speak for the Ancients. I came here with my pack when I was no more than a pup."

I wondered how long ago that was. Greatwolves lived a very long time.

The Shadow Wolf loomed over us and Navdru backed away. Tlitoo bit his tail, making him stumble forward.

"The Greatwolves have not fulfilled the Promise of wolf-kind," the Shadow Wolf said, stepping over the wolf bones that littered the bottom of the cave. He was larger than I remembered, and moved with grace and ease. "You left it to this youngwolf." He inclined his head to me, then lifted a shadow lip to Navdru. "Now you must make it up to her. You must take your wolves and leave the humans' new companions be." His muzzle tightened in distaste. "You must let the streckwolves be. You and your pack are not to kill any of them. You are to take yourselves away and give the humans to Gaanin and his children, for the Greatwolves' time is nearly done."

Navdru sneezed and tried to answer through frozen lips. Tlitoo didn't give him the chance. The next thing I knew, we were back by the Hill Rock with the Sentinel wolves staring at us.

Navdru was trembling.

"What did you see?" Yildra demanded. Navdru shook his head. "You won't believe me. You must see for yourself. But I think we have been wrong."

I was so tired I had to swallow a whimper, but if taking Yildra to the Inejalun convinced her to spare our lives and those of the streckwolves, I would make the journey a thousand times over. Yildra stepped forward, quaking just a little.

I staggered to meet her. TaLi blocked my way.

"What's wrong, Kaala?" she asked, looking down at me in

concern. I was so tired I was weaving and stumbling. I licked her hand and shoved her gently aside.

Yildra stayed silent when I took her first to watch the streckwolves and then to the Shadow Wolf. My paws, tail, and nose, already cold from when I had taken Navdru, had not warmed when I returned to the world of life. By the time we reached the Shadow Wolf's cave, my muzzle, legs, and face were frozen, too. When we returned to the Hill Rock, I found that I'd tumbled over onto my side and was gasping for breath.

"That's enough," Neesa said, worry making her voice ragged. But the other Greatwolves were watching us expectantly.

"It is too important a decision to make if we are not sure," a pale-coated female rumbled. "We must be certain."

"We have to keep going," I said to Tlitoo.

"You can't show every Greatwolf in the pack," Ázzuen snarled. He lowered his head as if planning to attack the surrounding Greatwolves.

"It is too much, wolf," Tlitoo quorked. "You have never spent this much time in the cold place." I blinked up at him and he hunched his head down between his wings. "If I take you there again, it must be the last time for many days. It will not be safe to return. Even going once more is very risky. I do not want to lose you, stupid little wolf."

I was the one who had led the Sentinels to the grassless plain. It was my fault Gaanin was ready to leave, and if the Greatwolves didn't agree to let the streckwolves live, we would fail.

"We have to get them to leave the streckwolves alone," I whispered.

"All right, wolf," Tlitoo said. Ázzuen growled softly. Tlitoo spread his wings and rasped at the Sentinel wolves.

"We will show one more of you, and that is all," he said. The female who had spoken stepped forward. I tried to stagger to her, but could not. She came to me, leaning against me almost gently. TaLi came, too, and this time I did not have the strength to shove her away.

Tlitoo moved so quickly from the Stone Circle to the streckwolf village and to the Shadow Wolf's cave that I could barely keep up.

"Slow down!" I gasped, my throat aching.

"There is not time, wolflet. You have been here too long already."

I knew he was right. Already, I could not feel anything but my chest and belly. Everything else was so cold. My heart was beating too slowly, and I couldn't fill my lungs. By the time we had shown the Greatwolf the Shadow Wolf's cave, only my chest remained warm.

Then, just as Tlitoo was about to yank us from the Inejalun, I saw TaLi sitting on one of the rocks in the Stone Circle. She must have leaned up against me, and somehow been dragged into the Inejalun.

"Kaala?" she whispered.

"You can't be here," I said urgently through a muzzle that barely moved.

"Why not?" she asked. "You're here."

In the moment it took me to realize that she had understood me, Tlitoo yanked us from the Inejalun. Then we were all back at the Hill Rock. Tlitoo quorked curiously at TaLi but all I could do was lie on the ground, panting.

I tried to talk to the Sentinels, to explain why they must leave the streckwolves alone, but four journeys to the Inejalun had wearied me too much. I toppled onto my side and into unconsciousness.

◨

It seemed only moments later that Tlitoo poked me awake. I rolled over with a groan. The Sentinels had left. Neesa remained. Ázzuen was lying next to me, his strong, solid body warming me while Pell and Marra stood guard. TaLi and BreLan squatted on their heels, waiting. I was still so tired I couldn't move. I looked up to see the sun high overhead and wondered what day it was, and if we were too late to meet the streckwolves.

Neesa lowered her nose to mine.

"They have agreed, Kaala. We will give the humans to the streckwolves and leave the streckwolves unharmed."

"We woke you in time to get to them, wolf," Tlitoo said. He sounded worried.

"The Sentinels agreed?"

I couldn't believe it. We hadn't failed yet. We might even have won. Only hours ago, I'd thought the Promise broken and everyone I loved at risk. Now we might all live. I might be able to be with TaLi and Ázzuen after all. Stream Lands was lost to me, burned in the humans' fire, but a pack with Ázzuen and TaLi was not. Following the streckwolves to the humans was not. I wanted to leap to my paws to celebrate but was too exhausted to do more than lick Neesa's muzzle in thanks.

"I waited for you to wake up," she said, "but it's time for

me to follow the others. Navdru and Yildra insist that I go with them so I do not breed with a streckwolf again, and create another wolf such as you." She grinned at me. "They find both of us troublesome." She licked my ears. "Will you come with us? Navdru has said that you will have a home with the Sentinel pack, and the others have agreed. I would like to have more time with you."

I'd dreamed of being in a pack with my mother since the day she left me. For just an instant I allowed myself to imagine it: running every hunt with her, sleeping in the warm sun beside her while Ázzuen's and my pups played. But the Sentinels would never allow our humans in their pack.

"I need to stay with TaLi," I mumbled through a stiff muzzle. I'd clenched it so hard against the cold of the Inejalun that the muscles had seized up. I wouldn't give TaLi up, even to go with my mother. Neesa looked disappointed but not surprised. She lay her head over my neck and pulled me close to her.

"Find me again when you can," she said. "I hope that we will be within a few days' run of these lands. I have no intention of losing you again." She licked me between the ears once more, then loped away, following the Sentinels' trail toward the distant hills. I watched her go. I'd thought once I found my mother, I would stay with her forever. Now she was leaving me again. I swallowed my whimper. This time, the choice was mine.

My packmates watched me silently. It was Marra who finally spoke.

"We're leaving, too, Kaala. We're going back to the Wide Valley," she said. "We need to tell the Greatwolf council what the Sentinels have agreed to. And MikLan is there. We'll come back with him if you're going to settle here with your humans."

"We are," I said. Of course we were. "We'll stay near Laan until the streckwolves get the villagers comfortable enough that we can try to get them to accept us. If we can."

"You will, Kaala," Pell said. "Marra and I will be proud to be part of your pack."

Marra and Pell nosed my face and Ázzuen's neck, then galloped back toward the mountains and the Wide Valley.

My eyes drooped, luring me back toward sleep. I forced them open. Gaanin would be waiting for us. I stood and stretched the aches from my stiff muscles.

I tried to move quickly, but Ázzuen, BreLan, and even TaLi with her hurt ankle had to keep waiting for me as I stumbled along. I hadn't slept long enough after my journeys to the Inejalun, and I couldn't force my body to move any faster. Finally, BreLan lifted me in his arms and carried me. The humans kept talking about what they would say when they got to Laan. We would have to find a way to lead them away from it, as we had led them from the valley.

I was grateful to BreLan for carrying me. I licked his face and laid my head against his shoulder.

The streckwolves were waiting for us in front of the woods that led to Laan. Our humans watched the streckwolves curiously, but without fear.

I wriggled in BreLan's arms. He set me down, and I staggered to the streckwolves. Ázzuen walked protectively at my side. The two humans sat back on their haunches, watching the streckwolves curiously.

"The Sentinels have agreed," I said to Gaanin.

"And you believe them?"

"I do," I said.

His muzzle tightened. "That will have to be good enough."

"Let's go to the humans," I said. I was still cold. All I wanted to do was sleep, but the sooner we got the streck-wolves to the humans, the better.

Gaanin looked at me, an apology in his gaze. His voice, however, was firm.

"You can't go near them, Kaala. Neither of you can." He jutted his chin at Ázzuen.

"What do you mean?"

"You have too much of the wild in you, remember?" he said. "That's why they burned the forests. You have to leave with the others. Your kind must stay away from the humans from now on, like the Greatwolves. The task of keeping the humans part of the world around them is ours now."

A growl throbbed in my throat. "You said that you wanted the humans to learn to be with other creatures besides you and your pack. You told me that you hoped that if they were able to love you streckwolves, they would learn to love the world around them."

"I meant what I said. But it cannot be in my lifetime or yours. I'm sorry, Kaala."

He had deliberately misled me. My growl deepened. Tlitoo hissed at the streckwolf.

"What about the Barrens?" Ázzuen demanded. "If the humans have only wolves that aren't wild, they'll create more Barrens."

"They will," Gaanin said. "It's too late, much too late, for us to be able to get the humans to accept wildness in its true form. We must go more gently. In the meantime, they will create more Barrens. They will take over more forest and destroy it. Someday, if the humans can accept the bit of the wild that will remain in our children's children, they might indeed learn to accept the greater wild. We have to hope they do so before the world becomes a Barrens."

I wouldn't do it. There was no way I'd leave, not after everything I'd done. I was the one who had brought the wolves and humans together. I had faced Greatwolves who were ready to kill me and brought them to a world between life and death. I had let packmates die.

I met Gaanin's eyes and saw the challenge in them. He had lost packmates to the Promise, too.

"Tell me, Kaala, will you be like the others?" he asked. "Like the ancient Greatwolves who shirked their responsibility? Like Milsindra, grasping for power and her own gain? Because if so, you are no pup of mine. I will take my pack and leave."

The Greatwolves had failed and failed again because of their pride and selfishness. The streckwolves had come closest to succeeding because they were unselfish and willing to do anything to gain the humans' trust. Whitefur and Short Tail had assumed that their only task in the world was to give humans love, and the humans on the grassless plain had been happier than any I'd ever seen.

I had known. I knew that the streckwolves were better for the humans than we were the first time Tlitoo showed them to me. When I saw them in the Inejalun and on the grassless plain my fury had been born of envy. The streckwolves

seemed to change the humans into a different kind of creature. Less wary and more open to love. I had known that it
had to be them.

Prannan and Amma had died for the Promise. So had
many others. If I refused to let the streckwolves have the humans, knowing they were more likely to succeed than I, then
I was no better than a Greatwolf. And if I had to choose between being like Milsindra or like the little not-wolves, I
would rather be a streckwolf.

I remembered the vow I'd made to the Shadow Wolf. He
had known I would come to such a choice.

"We'll take our humans somewhere far away," I said at
last, my throat tight with regret. At least we could keep our
humans with us.

Ázzuen was watching Gaanin with narrowed eyes.

"You still need us," he said, speaking quickly as he did
when he was figuring something out. "The Sentinels were
right about that. We have to preserve the wild so that when
humans realize they need it, it will be there for them."

Gaanin dipped his head. "Yes. The Greatwolves' time is
done. You and your children must keep the wildness of the
wolf. If after accepting us the humans can stop killing your
kind and other creatures of the wild, there is hope. But there
must be those left who remember the Promise. You must help
with another task, as well." He looked at TaLi where she
squatted next to BreLan. "The other krianans are dead,"
Gaanin said. "As the wolves must keep wildness in trust for
the humans, your girl must keep the knowledge of it for future krianans. She must pass along the understanding of the
importance of the wild to her children, and their children's

children. Wherever you take her, you must make sure she does so."

That made me remember DavRian's lies about TaLi and RalZun.

"Did you go to Laan?" I asked, beginning to shake from fatigue. I had been standing for too long. "Do they believe DavRian about our krianans? Are TaLi and BreLan safe staying nearby?"

"They are not," a female streckwolf said. "I heard the humans of Laan say that the old krianans are as dangerous as wolves. They will kill your girl and her mate if they find them."

We were only hundreds of wolflengths from Laan, and TaLi and BreLan intended to go there.

Tlitoo krawked in alarm. "You should have told us that first, dimwolves!" he screeched to Gaanin. "There are several Laan humans coming our way, wolf," he said to me. "I saw them. They will find your humans."

Which meant I had to get TaLi away quickly. And I had no way to communicate with her, no way to ensure she would not walk into her death. Or did I? She had come, in that one moment, to the Inejalun, and she had spoken to me. She had understood me.

I staggered to TaLi. "Take us!" I gasped to Tlitoo.

He didn't ask me where, just quorked at me in concern. Ázzuen looked back and forth between us.

"I told you it is not safe, wolf. You are still weary. You have been to the Inejalun too many times."

"There's no choice!" I said, beginning to panic. "She has to know before the Laan humans find them." I was disoriented and shaking from exhaustion after taking the Sentinels to the Inejalun, but it was my fault, not TaLi's, that the Sentinels had killed the strecks on the grassless plain and made Gaanin threaten to go into hiding. It wasn't her fault I'd been too long in the Inejalun. I would not fulfill the Promise only to have her die.

"All right, wolf," Tlitoo said. "But we must go quickly."

I sat next to TaLi on the ground and whined to get her attention. She crouched down and put her arms around me.

"What's wrong, Kaala?" she asked.

For just a moment, I allowed myself to sit next to her, letting her scent fill me and the warmth of her skin next to my fur comfort me. She had grown in the last moon, her long limbs and straight angles beginning to soften into the curves of womanhood. She and BreLan could mate soon. They could have pups not long after I would have mine if Ázzuen and I decided to mate this year. The thought of raising our pups together made me happy, though TaLi's young would grow much more slowly than mine. They would still be pups when I was long dead. I shook off my thoughts and looked up to Tlitoo.

"It has to be now," I said. "Are you able?"

He picked up a twig and tossed it in the air.

"I am fine. It is you who must be careful." He hopped down.

"Guard us?" I said to Ázzuen.

"Of course," he said. I touched my nose to his muzzle and settled my aching muscles as the streckwolves watched us curiously. Tlitoo pushed in between me and the girl.

The cold was more intense than it had ever been before.

At first Tlitoo and I were alone in the Inejalun. Tlitoo blinked rapidly at me.

"Wait, wolf," he said. "I am not sure how to bring her here."

He disappeared and I was alone. The cold increased so much I thought I would break into pieces. Then he was back.

I didn't see it happen, but a moment later, TaLi was sitting on one of the rocks.

"Silvermoon," she said. "Kaala."

I walked over to her, and touched my icy nose to her skin.

"TaLi," I said, and she smiled. She looked exactly the same as she did in the world of the living. "You're here."

"I thought I imagined it," she said. Her grin grew. "You sound just like I thought you would. I talked to the wolves before," she said, "when I was small. To Jandru and Frandra."

"I know," I said. "NiaLi told me." I licked her face. Just as the Inejalun had no scent, it also had no flavor. I tried again. I didn't like not being able to taste her. I couldn't wait to get back to the world of life so that I could savor her scent of herbs and smoke, and lick her warm, salty skin.

"The first time you did that," she said, "I thought you were going to eat me."

"You were my pack from that day," I said. "You're always my pack." For some reason it was important for me to tell her that. I couldn't believe I could actually talk to her. I wished I could stay there forever. I wished I could tell her everything I'd never been able to communicate. But there was no time. I couldn't feel my legs at all, and my muzzle was beginning to freeze.

"The little wolves," I said, "the strange ones. They're going to stay with the humans instead of us." As quickly as I could, I told her what we had learned about the streckwolves and the humans, about how the not-quite-wolves would help the humans keep the Balance, and how they would remind them to protect that which was wild.

"That which is loved but not feared," she said. She was just as clever as Ázzuen.

"I can't stay here long in this place," I said. "You can't either." She was already shivering. I wanted to curl up against her, but that would only have made her colder.

"And you can't go to Laan. DavRian is telling everyone that you're the reason Kaar burned. They'll kill you. There are Laan humans coming now. You and BreLan have to come with us to escape them, right now. Then you have to find other krianans, or teach more. You have to tell them to keep the stories of the wild."

"Will you help me?" she asked.

I licked her hand in answer. Of course I would. I started to tell her I loved her and that she was the best thing that had happened to me, but the words didn't seem sufficient. I'd thought that not having words was what kept us from understanding each other. But, now, all I wanted to do was to press up against her as I would in the world of life.

"It is time to go, wolflet," Tlitoo quorked. He hopped over TaLi. A moment later, the girl was gone.

My chest had grown so cold that I couldn't breathe. Panicked, I tried to whimper for Tlitoo to come for me, but nothing came out. For one terrifying moment, I couldn't feel my heart beating, and the pressure behind my eyes was so great I thought my skull would break open. Then the heat of the summer sun flowed through me. My chest warmed. My muzzle thawed and my throat loosened. The Inejalun was flooded with scent. Tlitoo returned. I thought he would take me back to TaLi, but he just blinked at me.

"What are you waiting for?" I asked.

"I am sorry, wolflet," he said, lowering his head between hunched wings.

"It's all right," I said. "Just take me back."

"I cannot, wolf. We waited too long. You spent too much time here before. Look." He peered down.

I followed his gaze. The Stone Circle dropped off abruptly and, below us, TaLi, BreLan, Ázzuen, and all of the streck-wolves surrounded something. It was a dead wolf, a young one, with the mark of the crescent moon on her chest. That was what Tlitoo meant. We had waited too long. I could not go back. I could never go back.

Ázzuen howled, a hollow, dismal sound, and TaLi crouched at the youngwolf's side. I could see, just beyond the trees, the villagers of Laan approaching. DavRian was with them, as was IniMin. I barked a warning.

"They cannot hear you, wolf." He disappeared from my side again. Below me, in the woods, a raven landed on Ázzu-en's back, pulling hard on his fur. Ázzuen looked toward the woods. He tugged on TaLi's tunic. The girl looked up, her face contorted with weeping, and spoke to BreLan, pointing in the direction of Laan.

BreLan bent down and picked up the limp form of the young wolf. I was glad he didn't leave me there. They moved quickly away from Laan as the streckwolves ran to greet the approaching humans. Gaanin looked back at BreLan carrying me in his arms and shook himself once before following the others.

BreLan set me down by a shady stream in a part of the woods the fire had not touched. They stayed with me until the sun set and the moon rose in the night. Then BreLan took TaLi by the arm and led her away. Ázzuen buried his nose deep in my fur, then walked slowly after his human. I yearned to walk beside them. This time, I could not do so.

After the moon set, I left a scent mark on the largest rock in the Inejalun so that Ázzuen might find me when it came time for him to leave the world of life. I wanted to feel his fur against mine and TaLi's warm, damp skin against my nose. I wanted to smell the smoky, rich scent of the humans, and lie with them by their fires. My heart ached. I could not be with TaLi or Ázzuen, but they would live and carry on the Promise, and I would help them do so in any way the land of the spirits would let me. I watched what was left of my pack a little longer: one wolf, a raven, and two humans, making their way to the distant hills.

TaLi would do her part, and the wild wolves theirs. The streckwolves would do their best with the humans.

They might fail just as I had. The streckwolves could not force the humans to accept them, nor compel them to embrace the wildness that was so much more a part of them than their clever tools. All the streckwolves could do was to give the humans a chance. They could give humans the opportunity to love something they did not fear. What happened after that would be up to them.

The humans marched purposefully through the woods. Tails lowered and ears folded over, the little wolves walked beside them.

Epilogue

I t got warm.

It got so warm, the legends say, that the ice at the top and bottom of the world melted, and the great bears that lived upon it swam the endless waters looking for a place to rest, until their strong legs failed them and they sank to the bottom of the sea. The forests turned to desert and the creatures that depended on streams and rivers lapped at the dry ground until they could move no more. The oceans rose, swamping those who lived at the water's edge, and great storms raged across the land.

On a hot summer day, not long after the last of the forests burned, a young boy threw a red rubber ball. He sweated in the heat but did not stop his game. The creature at his feet would not allow him to stop. It panted up at him, tongue lolling, begging for one more throw, one more moment of play.

Off in the distance, a mournful howl arose. Once, the boy's mother had told him, wolves roamed everywhere. Then, like the bison and the tigers, they were hunted nearly to extinction. It was said that only a few were left. The boy threw his ball again and his companion brought it back, tail awag. The boy thought that he did not want to live in a world without howls. He looked toward the barren hills and the howl rose again. The creature at his feet whuffed softly in response.

The boy looked down into brown eyes filled with love and smiled. When the distant wolf howled again, he threw back his head and answered.

ACKNOWLEDGMENTS

The strength of this wolf is most definitely her pack, and this book would not have been written without a packful of remarkable people. I don't have the words to express how grateful I am to my wonderful family and friends. I was lucky enough to hit the family jackpot and to have the infinite support of my father, brother, and sister. Their wisdom and encouragement helped bring *Spirit of the Wolves* into being. My mother was my first writing buddy, and her influence is on every page, including the story of Kaala's involuntary bath. Thank you to Shannon McClenaghan and Carl Shapiro. It's wonderful to have you in my life. A deep and heartfelt thank you to my other family—my dear friends who are as loving and loyal as any wolf pack. I would never have been able to do it without all of you.

My profound thanks to Jennifer Weltz, amazing wolf agent and ally, for her fierce support, invaluable advice, and humor. My editor Emily Graff's sharp eye, editorial prowess, and deep understanding of the wolves and their story made the book much stronger and richer. The fabulous Mollie Glick was the wolves' first champion back when *Promise of the Wolves* was fifty pages and some big ideas, and continues to be an indispensable partner, mentor, and friend. Kerri Kolen masterfully shaped the first two books of The Wolf Chronicles and shared them with the world. Thanks to Amanda Ferber for great ideas on marketing and writing and to the publicity and marketing team at Simon & Schuster for sending TWC out into the world. Many thanks to Heather Florence for sound advice and guidance, and production editor Stephen Llano and copyeditor Anne Cherry. Thank you, Murray Dropkin, Rick Hanson, Frances Hesselbein, Cheryl Jones, and Tzipora Krupnik for your wisdom. Thanks to Lori Cheung and Melissa K. Smith for great wolf photos and to Sam Blake and the wolves and wolfdogs of Never Cry Wolf Rescue for the photo ops.

Everlasting gratitude to and admiration for my writing buddies Pamela Berkman, Mary Mackey, Harriet Rohmer, Elizabeth Stark, and writing buddy/on-call anthropology consultant Jaida Samudra, as well as to life consultants Bonnie Akimoto, Cheryl Greenway, Laura Mazzola, and Johanna Vondeling. The exchange of ideas, creative energy, and guidance has been precious, delightful, and challenging. Thank you to the women of WOM-BA for the inspiration and support, especially in helping me find my way back to writing after my mother's death.

My martial arts practice is central to my writing and my life, and I am grateful to the wonderful White Crane Silat community. Special thanks to Peter Ajemian and everyone at Soja Martial Arts for creating such a warm and special place to call home. Thanks to Mark Davey for the story about the bear and the sack of food hanging off the cliff.

Always and forever, I am so grateful to those who have been there to talk to about life and publishing, and who were there for tea, a phone call, or a chat when I crawled out of the writing cave: Bridget Ahern, Diane Bodiford, Allison Brunner, Paul Foster Rafael Frongillo, Lesley Iura, Pam MacLean, Karen Murphy, Tom Murphy, Debbie Notkin, Jennifer Obrochta, Donna Ryan, Dave Shirley, Jin Tsubota, Kari Tsubota.

I read countless books and articles about wolves, ravens, evolution, and nature (see my website for a list!) and am deeply indebted to the authors of these works for their wisdom. Thanks to Amy Kay Kerber for being on call for wolf info, and to Susan Holt, Julia Charles, and Marc Lenburg for the articles and scientific insights. All mistakes are, of course, mine. Thank you to all the wolf conservation and environmental organizations that fight for wolves and the lands they need.

Many thanks to the librarians and to the bookstore owners and staff for helping to get The Wolf Chronicles to readers, and to the Squaw Valley Community of Writers, where I worked on the first chapters of the trilogy. Humble thanks to the science fiction and fantasy community for welcoming the wolves to your world, and to the libraries everywhere for the free access to all the knowledge on the planet.

Thank you, thank you, thank you to the readers of *Promise of the Wolves* and *Secrets of the Wolves* who have shared Kaala's journey so far, and to those who have written to me expressing your enthusiasm for her story. Your notes and emails got me through many a long writing day.

I love to write in cafés and am grateful to the café owners who let me camp out in their lovely spaces. A special thanks to Espresso Roma and Philz and all the great people who work there.

Many howls and treats to my research assistants, including Burrito, Inna, Akela, Milo, Moose, Nike, Talisman, Lucy, Rollo, Shelby, and Flower, and those beautiful beasties who have gone to doggy heaven, Happy, Jude, Noni, Ice, and Kuma. Rufus, Sasha, and my beautiful, beautiful Emmi, who died shortly after this book was completed and who taught me every way in which dogs make us better people. And to their cousins in the wild. May we someday be wise enough creatures to deserve you.